THE PLUTONIUM MURDERS

An Alex Seacourt Thriller

A Novel by
Robert Charles Davis

THE PLUTONIUM MURDERS
An Alex Seacourt Thriller

A Novel by Robert Charles Davis

c/o: Horizon Press
32436 Old Franklin Drive
Farmington Hills, Michigan 48334
(810) 539-2979 (phone)
(810) 539-2980 (fax)
Seacourt@Concentric.net (e-mail)

PUBLISHER'S NOTE
This is a work of fiction. Names, characters, places and incidents either are the product of the author's imagination or are used fictitiously, and any resemblance to actual persons, living or dead, events or locales is entirely coincidental.

If you purchased this book without a cover, you should be aware that this book is stolen property. It was reported as "unsold and destroyed" to the publisher and neither the author nor the publisher have received any payment for this "stripped book."

And then there was Alex Seacourt. Thirty million people were going to die if he didn't act now. But what was it? What did he have to do?

His head...was going to explode, and time was desperately running out. Thirty million souls and he was the only one who could save them.

BOOKS BY ROBERT CHARLES DAVIS

Plutonium Murders
Doomsday Kiss
A Time to Die
      (January '98 release)
Ghosts of the Dead
      (Summer '98 release)

Robert Charles Davis has been a practicing physician for fifteen years. Most recently he has completed four novels, with three others in progress.

I

Present Time

Alex Seacourt was hallucinating. He felt as if he was dying. He tried to remember... He was in a make-believe world listening to Santana's "Black Magic Woman" through headphones that melted into his cranium. The bass was ca-booming in his ears.

Gotta get the devil out. Gotta stop the pain. Gotta stop it!

Was it a delusion, a nightmare playing out before his bloodshot eyes? Was it the poison, the snake venom? Or was it the plutonium?

He wanted to scream, to purge the pernicious leech.

Good night. Good death. Au revoir. And then the voice said, *"Ticktock you're dead."*

Alex stopped mumbling to himself. He tried to focus, tried to push into the light his lingering sanity. He tried to think of what he had to do. Something important. He had to stop someone? And if he didn't...*everyone would die!* Time was desperately running out.

President Hoover? President...Hoover?

"Ticktock, the bomb blew her up." He was losing it again. "Stop! Gotta get control. Gotta...what?"

Alex struggled to stand, to stop his brain from spinning. Where was he? A hotel room? And the bigger question...why?"

He managed to look to the left. The room was cloudy. He saw the king-size bed, the green and beryl pastel as if suspended in an unearthly fog.

"Twelve o'clock or everyone's *nuked*."

His head was pounding.

"The funeral, the *President*. Ticktock — high noon or else!"

He looked into a mirror mounted in front of him, the edges framed with ersatz mahogany and oakboard. He had been sitting at a desk in a hotel room. "Where was he?" Alex gazed into the looking glass. The silver base reflected a gruesome picture — a face swollen, eyes blackened, nose bruised, maybe broken. His cheek bones pounded with each throb of his heart.

President Hoover...what? Twelve noon...where?

Black dominoes bouncing against one another on a green felt blanket. Surrealistic black dominoes, with lily-white spots. Larger-than-life. Monster size.

Alex leaned forward. His hands were distended and his left elbow sore. He balanced his head on his shoulders and forced his eyes wide open. Pain flashed up the back of his neck and exploded into his skull. He stumbled.

Alex closed his eyes, leaned on the desk and tried to remember. Out of the corner of his vision he could feel the heavy drapes concealing the light of day, with splotches of sunlight leaking precariously into the room.

"The dominoes, what about the dominoes." In his mind's-eye he saw black ivory rectangles with rounded edges snap together as they mixed on a green field.

What time was it? His watch was gone. Psychedelic thick colors: reds, coppers and pale oranges faded in and out of his wrist. They bled in turbulent spirals.

Then it stopped. Consciousness flooded his mind like a dam exploding in a torrent. Alex knew he had to *stop someone* or everyone was going to die.

President Hoover and the Southwest United States. He needed to act before it was too late. There was something he had to do, something that would save the lives of millions.

And then...he remembered. *The lives of thirty million people depended on what he was going to do next.*

2

Thirty-two years earlier
May 8, 1967

The last fat raindrops ricocheted off the Miami runway. The summer rain subsided, and steam rose from the crushed stone and tar in delicate layers, like tiramisu cake. Sun blasted heat through a scant veil of billowy clouds.

The Boeing B707, with Pratt and Whitney engines and long range fuel tanks, normally would seat one hundred and seven. But refurbished with a stateroom, full bathroom and shower, and two conference rooms, its passenger space was much diminished. Large oval windows, tinted charcoal gray bathed thick burbur carpet and wall panels were lined with fine art, including an Escher, a Picasso and a Monet.

The jet, Man's Excess, was owned by the Robbins conglomerate.

Billy Robbins, the family patriarch, was the only son of a poor Irish farming family. During the famine of 1902, Billy's parents died in a cholera epidemic, and young Robbins fled to America at sixteen. He stowed away on a tramp steamer. Once he arrived he worked three jobs, for a total of not less than twenty hours a day. At twenty-one, he bought a neighborhood butcher shop. He cut shank, sirloin and brisket, but he had vision.

Within three years, young Billy had four stores; within five years he had 80. By World War II, he sat atop the first nationwide grocery store chain, Robbins — 247 supermarkets expanding at a rate of eight units every other month.

As the war wound down, Billy, who had been an inveterate bachelor, met Claire Smith. Claire was a 17-year-old orphan, who was honest and enthusiastic, and worked at Robbins' Rochester grocery store as a check-out clerk. Claire was very much like Billy. She was hard working, diligent and virtuous. At first sight they fell in love. They married within a year.

In the mid-1950s Billy purchased a pharmaceutical company. Robbins found Kodmore, a fledging drug company on the verge of bankruptcy. The business which he eventually bought for $150,000 and the assumption of more than $3 million in debt, became the backbone of the Robbins family fortune. Within three years, Kodmore Pharmaceuticals, which had plunged into a financial abyss, grew into America's second largest pharmaceuticals manufacturer. In 1959, Robbins' holding company purchased American General Can and renamed it Robbins Can, and in 1960 Robbins acquired the American First Insurance Company, the 6th largest insurance concern in the United States. By 1962 Robbins' estimated fortune was in excess of a billion dollars.

Billy and Claire Robbins were very much in love. They were cut out of the same gingerbreadman molds, and both were intensely private and religious Catholics. The Robbinses sired eight children. By May 1964, their ages were two through sixteen; a symmetrical four boys and four girls.

Each Sunday, no matter where in the world the Robbins family was, they went to church and thanked God for the blessings they had been given. As much as possible, Billy Robbins made sure he and his close-knit clan traveled together.

Not unlike many other pre-eminent men of his day, Billy Robbins had made enemies along the way. First, his pharmaceutical company was under attack. Kodmore Pharmaceuticals had the number one selling drug in the world, Relaxol, a valium-like tranquilizer that had no hangover side effects. Relaxol accounted for over $80 million in worldwide sales. By the summer of 1964 Kodmore was on the verge of delivering to the marketplace, what many believed would be the next universal best-seller, Pepsafe.

Pepsafe, an anti-ulcer drug that reduced stomach acid, would be the first of its kind released on the market. Estimated global distribution projections put sales figures at roughly $2 billion. But, Hartax Pharmaceutical Company, which had developed a similar drug, Duomet, was approximately one year away from the release of their drug. Only final FDA approval of Hartax's clinical trials stood in the way of the drug's release. Hartax would give anything to stop Kodmore from introducing its new gastric medication.

Also, Robbins had big-time problems with Robbins' Can, which now produced 70 percent of all tin cans in the United States and 30 percent worldwide. In Brazil, where Robbins mined much of its tin, environmentalists and primitive tribal chieftains had threatened to stop the company from coming into the Amazon jungle estuaries and strip mining their land. Already an engineer and a project foreman were murdered while mapping out one of the company's newest excavation sights, 180 kilometers northwest of Brasilia, deep in the Amazon jungle.

Trials and tribulation came along with any successful venture. Billy Robbins understood that, and as always he was prepared for just about any eventuality. He had hired three full-time bodyguards, each of whom stood no less than 6'4" tall and weighed at least 280 pounds. One bodyguard was always at his or his family's side.

At 3:20 p.m. the black, glazed Goodyear tires skidded onto the runway leaving a trail of smoked rubber. The Robbinses had arrived home from London.

After 4,680 feet of runway 27 Right was used up, the four engine Boeing rolled quietly to a stop. Billy, Claire and eight children, including thirteen year old Bart Robbins, unbuckled their seat belts, a mandatory rule on any Robbins flight; as "Man's Excess" taxied to just outside the Delta terminal where it was met by the Robbins' stretch limousine. The windows, doors, roof and floorboards were all bulletproof.

The family disembarked, traveling briskly down the portable stairs, placed in position by a Delta ramp truck.

Within five minutes the clan was on their way to their Coral Gables home — a 14,000 square foot mansion with Olympic lap pool, two tennis courts (one clay and the other asphalt) exercise and ballet rooms and an ocean view. In the rear the Robbinses docked their 125 foot Chris Craft yacht.

The limousine ride from the airport was the "same-old, same-old," a blasé trip they'd done so many times before. Palmetto trees, photinia bushes and oleanders lined the tollway, as the limo glided down the concrete freeway at 55 miles an hour.

Inside, the children were playing. They were restless and excited to get home after spending a boring week in balmy London. Shopping in Picadilly Square, touring Buckingham Palace, the Tower of London, and Westminster Abbey, while patriarch Billy was meeting with government officials — was not the stuff that made young children happy.

Ahead of the Lincoln was the tollgate. The sleek limousine slowed to a crawl, as two other cars lumbered before them. The bomb was mounted between the floorboards and gas tank. It was activated by the vehicle's decelerating to less than 45 miles an hour. It was designed to detonate just prior to the toll booths.

At 3:36 p.m., fifteen feet from the toll station, the Lincoln burst into a cannon of flames leaving a ten foot crater underneath its vaporized steel frame, destroying all of the southern toll booths within a 75 foot radius of the blast.

Miraculously, Bart Robbins was thrown from the vehicle, along with his four year old sister Helen. They both survived.

Bart was hurled into a large photinia bush, his body on fire. Helen was flung into an opposite traveling El Camino pickup truck, bouncing off the windshield. She landed headfirst onto a concrete abutment.

Initially, young Bart with his body ablaze, attempted to free himself from the perennial's clutches. Stuck in the photinia bush, he was unable to escape his agony; he was incapable of rolling to the ground and putting out his own flames.

Eventually, fortunately or unfortunately for Bart, his life was spared by an off-duty paramedic who was driving in the opposite direction heading toward Hialeah. The savior smothered Bart's blistering body with his fireman's jacket, and performed CPR until an ambulance arrived.

3

CARACAS, VENEZUELA
Monday, May 16, 1999

The International Hotel was built upon a rocky grass knoll that overlooked exotic Caracas. The city itself was a cosmopolitan metropolis of three million people set in a lush jungle 3,025 feet above sea-level, in a high rift valley surrounded by two mountain groups, the Cordillera del Littoral and the Serrania del Interior. Caracas lay 11 kilometers south of the Caribbean Sea and just north of the equator.

The International Airport, located oceanside, was one of the busiest in South America. And because of terrorists, security leaving the airport was tight. Militia armed with shoulder-slung Uzi machine guns dotted the highway.

Bart Robbins, who turned forty-five in March, ran the Robbins empire. Since Bart's ascension to the business throne, as decreed by the family will, Robbins International had grown to the fourth largest United States corporation, behind only General Motors, Ford and Exxon. The Robbins empire had expanded to include oil exploration and refining, textiles, satellites, computers, electronics, tobacco and worldwide fishing. There seemed to be no business either directly or indirectly, that the Robbins tentacles did not touch.

However, despite all of Bart's massive fortune, he was unable to ameliorate his appearance. The burns and horrific disfigurement that nearly consumed his body and still engulfed his thoughts, were incurable. When he was thrown into the photinia bushes, his body a ball of human burning flesh, his lungs scorched by the inhalation of one-thousand degree gases — his odyssey of dread had just begun.

Sometimes Bart hated the paramedic for saving him. His humanity, his mercy, had been burned away with his flesh.

Broiled and sweltered in the conflagration, the paramedic smothered the flames with his fireman's jacket. Almost an irony in its golden color, it matched Robbins' bacon crisp skin that had melted to a shallow flaxen.

No one at Jackson Memorial Hospital thought Bart would survive. He had lost most of his body fluids. The proteins in his brain, heart, and lungs had been denatured. His burns were deep and were considered massive. Over 70 percent of his body surface area was affected.

In addition to the anathema of the burns, Bart suffered from other compounding horrors: phenols and phosphorus residues released with the bomb caused a type of exotic blood poisoning. Thirty-two of his two hundred and twelve bones were either broken, crushed or disintegrated. Bart was beyond pain, unconscious and mercifully expected to die. His red blood cells had burst and much of what remained of his muscle tissues had sloughed-off as a result of lack of circulation. Twice, he went into cardiac arrest, and twice he was resuscitated from death.

Miraculously, and in perverse retribution for a sin that he did not commit, Bart Robbins survived the first week, then the second and third. By week number four, excision and removal of the burn slough became a full-time job. Robbins had twenty-seven operations to create clean fresh wounds that would heal properly. Highly experimental grafts were placed on his back, chest and abdomen and then his hands, upper extremities, feet and lower extremities in that order. Bart's face was a visage from a bad Twilight Zone dream. He was a Halloween fright. Since 70 percent of his body was disintegrated, the use of grafts from his own tissue was impossible. Instead viable skin from cadaver donors and skin from porcine sources were used. Grafts were meshwork horrors and eventually healed in uneven grids.

During the fifth week Bart awoke to begin his lifelong nightmare. The hospital room became his tomb. For nearly two and one-half years he lived in his dimly lit, IV tube- infested sarcophagus.

Broken bones had not mended properly. In some cases, Frankenstein-like bolts and screws in erector-set fashion were jerry-rigged along with Victorian metal and alloy devices to hold his bones in place.

As a result of broken bones growing together in jagged edges instead of smooth ribbons of calcium and cartilage, Bart's appearance was exaggerated. He had become a human caricature.

Because physical therapy relentlessly persisted from the onset of Bart's consciousness, Bart grew to know pain as a taunting older brother who never ceased his mean-spirited tease. Positioning, exercising and splinting to prevent contractures; Robbins' joints were put through white-hot exercises twice daily, every day, no matter what.

When the hour finally came for him to leave the hospital , one which by now he rued; a new doleful personage sprouted its wings. A fifteen-year old, not emotionally mature, was transformed into a living sideshow freak who could no longer function or be seen in public. No Sunday afternoon movies, nor picnics and sunning at the beach. His life had been forever changed.

At forty-five years old Robbins sat at the large conference table in his penthouse suite of the International Hotel. He waited impatiently for his guest. "What would it have been like to have grown up normal...without the scars?" Not to be a checkerboardman...a monster?" The introspection was painful.

Bart Robbins only wore one outfit, his uniform — the same Italian tailored black slacks, the Swiss black socks, shoes, and sports jacket. His hand-sewn raven silk shirt buttoned to its last eyelet, and then underneath, an onyx turtleneck.

In public, the rare times that he went out, he wore a swarthy fedora, dark Ray-Bans, a midnight silk scarf over his face, and the softest crush black-leather gloves weaved from the skins of fetal calves. Only the smallest amount of alien flesh was exposed to the world.

Bart drummed his gloved fingers onto the rose marble table. There were ten chairs, two at each end and four on both sides. The chairs were red Moroccan leather and thickly cushioned. Behind him stood two aides. Like his father, he had behemoth bodyguards.

They were vicious and loyal. One, a Sicilian, Michael Palmeritti had served him over the years and had also become more than a protector, almost a confidant — someone Bart ranted to, and also someone who didn't talk back.

Bart stared at a painting, an oil rendering of a Scottish castle sitting above a small expanse of brush and wild bluegrass, meadow fescue and flowering perennials. There was a short-coated dog lapping water from a brier pond in the foreground. In his mind, Bart entered the painting. He walked amongst the verdure and petted the dog.

Then he stopped and thought about Helen. What he was about to do was for her; for Helen and for *his unborn child*.

There was a knock at the door, in the outer foyer. A third guard, who was posted in the anteroom, let the man in. He showed him to the conference room, after first patting him down, checking for weapons or a wire. There were none. As the olive-skinned Colombian walked into the conference room, he observed Robbins whose gaze was still fixed on the painting. In the background the opera singer Luciano Pavarotti was singing Rossini's *Il barbiere di Siviglia*.

Without flinching Robbins said, "How appropriate. What a fitting libretto." In an instant of ironic realization he conceived that he was the wicked Barber of Seville.

The Colombian extended his hand to Robbins. Bart did not reciprocate.

"Sit," he ordered unemotionally in a low voice.

The Colombian followed his directions. He had been trained at Harvard where he received a BS in political science and an MBA in international finance. He spoke with only the slightest hint of an accent.

Bart said nothing, but pierced the Colombian with his severe eyes, the only normal part of Bart's face. He tested the foreigner's mettle.

The Colombian, a professional, did not flinch. He had seen worse, but not much; and he had done worse while working for the Santos-Castillo cartel. He pulled up a chair closest to Robbins, on Robbins' left. He leaned forward onto the conference table. His one thousand dollar suit jacket brushed onto the marble.

"How much can you get me?" Robbins asked, his haunted reflection scrutinizing the Colombian's character on the polished surface.

"To make a bomb?"

Bart sat in silence. After a thoughtful moment he said, "I need much more than to make a bomb."

"To make a bomb?"

Again, there was a pause. Bart glared at the Colombian. His eyes were razor blades. "I need as much as you can get."

The Colombian carefully measured his response before replying. "It depends on how much you want. It takes approximately 8 1/2 kilos to make a device. 8 1/2 kilos will cost..."

"How much can you get?"

"8 1/2 kilos will cost you plenty as it is. I'm sure..."

Robbins motioned over his shoulders, looking scantily behind him. Shannon his other bodyguard lifted a black leather briefcase that sat on the floor next to Robbins. He laid it on the table. The bodyguard opened the briefcase revealing its contents. He slid it to the Colombian.

Wide-eyed, the Harvard-trained MBA looked down at the 1,000 dollars bills. He did not bother to count them.

"Two million dollars," Bart said in monotone.

Harvard looked up at Bart, regaining his composure, and continued, "It takes 18 pounds of 94 percent plutonium 239 to make a Hiroshima-strength bomb."

Bart stared back emotionless.

"It's not as easy as you think to make a device." Bart said nothing. "You know, the basic principles of bomb technology are available to anyone who knows where to look up the information." Harvard looked down at the money again. "You'll need the resources of a friendly country to help you." He slid the briefcase back to Robbins, who was impassively studying the MBA.

"It comes in two-pound gray-metal bars. You can't bleach the shit," his Latin American accent slipped through. "It's extremely toxic. One grain can cause lung cancer. So you need to have real pros work on your team."

Bart's eyes lit up. A smile began to appear at the corner of his disfigured baboon lips, but just barely. "How so?"

"Alpha radiation."

"Alpha radiation?"

"Plutonium has a half-life of 24,400 years. The alpha particles are released as the plutonium decays. They cause chromosomal abnormalities. They're extremely deadly at short range. Also, plutonium, if absorbed into the body, binds with iron-transporting proteins in the blood and is conveyed to iron-storage cells in the liver and bone marrow. It causes liver and bone cancer, and leukemia. In addition, it's concentrated in the testicles and ovaries where it can cause genetic mutation to be passed on to future generations, and in some cases, cancer of the testicles."

"That's a fact?"

"I make it my business to know my product."

"Go on."

"Plutonium 239 also has another deadly characteristic: it produces americium, a by-product with a half-life of 460 years. It's real bad stuff."

"Good." Bart said. "What's the most you can get?"

The Colombian weighed his response, "The absolute most?" Pavarotti struck a high C and held it in dramatic dénouement. "Two hundred pounds."

"I need more... much more."

The Colombian wanted to ask why, but didn't. He, who was an expert of espionage, for the first time in his life felt fear. Not since he was ten and he had witnessed his best friend Rafael mangled by a drunk driver while playing in the streets of their Bogota neighborhood, had he similar feelings. "Three hundred pounds?"

"I need more." Robbins removed a small note pad from inside his jacket, and with a black-felt pen scribbled down a number. He ripped off the sheet and slid it to the Colombian.

The Colombian looked at the number. His eyes grew big.

Robbins continued, "Two million now and eight million upon delivery, in any currency or way you want."

"The best I can do, the absolute best is 400 pounds," Harvard said with a tremor in his voice. "And that'll take me a month, maybe more."

"The amount I need, or else. Thirty days, that's all you've got." The rich operatic andante filled the air.

"Ninety days. I can do it in ninety days, possibly."

"Where?"

"I'll contact you through my messenger. We'll deliver somewhere in the Caribbean."

"Done," Robbins said. He then stood up abruptly, and gestured the Colombian back to the anteroom.

The Colombian cautiously closed the money-laden briefcase and extended his hand to conclude the meeting. Robbins rebuffed his exchange.

"Ninety days and I'll have your money. I expect the plutonium and nothing less than what I need."

"You'll have it." the Colombian said, "Just one thing. What do you plan..."

"Good-bye."

Without a word the bodyguards escorted the Colombian out of the conference room. Bart looked again at the wall painting and daydreamed about splashing his webbed feet into the Scottish bog. He felt it mush between his toes.

4

New York City

It was early fall and the air was biting. A brisk wind swirled down the avenues of the Big Apple. The New York that Alex had envisioned was one of a financial giant bristling with skyscrapers, the dream-city of immigrants. It was all that and more.

He had come from Salt Lake City, his home for the last ten years. He had traveled nonstop on the redeye to Manhattan for a seminar on "New Approaches in the Treatment of Zollinger-Ellison Syndrome Patients" at the Columbia School of Medicine.

Alex hadn't been to New York since he was thirteen, and that was on a loop that he and his family drove in their over-crowded station wagon. His father took a week off work in August. The weather was gloomy. They rattled from Detroit to Windsor, Ontario; and then to Toronto where they toured the Old Parliament Buildings and the Canadian National Exhibition. They drove east to Niagara Falls and then they twisted down the worn interstate through Buffalo to New York City. He barely remembered seeing the Rockefeller Center, Radio City Music Hall and the Statute of Liberty.

He remembered the trash that had piled high on the streets due to a Teamster's strike, and the stench that filled the air, and the squalid turnpike ride home over the George Washington Toll Bridge, through New Jersey and Pennsylvania on I-80.

He remembered the arguments that he had with his father during *most* of the trip. Those were not good days. In fact, most of his life with his father was filled with unpleasant memories. Alex felt guilty about that, much of which later he realized was his fault.

In recent years, he tried to patch things up. He did the best that he could. It was hard for him. It was difficult for him to express his emotions, to be in touch with his "inner child" as the therapists said. Whatever his problem was, and he knew that he had one, he had tried to work through it. It was a painful process.

Today Alex was going to treat himself and window-shop the city. He had his itinerary in order. He was going to start at the World Trade Center, walk to the Empire State Building, then down Fifth Avenue to St. Patrick's Cathedral. From there he'd weave his way to the Museum of Modern Art, to Bergdorf Goodman, north to Bloomingdales, past 79th Street to the Metropolitan Museum of Art, tour Central Park including the Delacourte Theater, Shakespeare Garden, Tavern on the Green and finally the American Museum of Natural History on Central Park West. All this before he arrived at Columbia.

New York was a city of life. He wanted to experience it and purge himself of anguished memories.

Alex heard that the people who lived there would say that "New York was where they had to be." It was a place of vast industrial resources, of an extensive cultural life and a vigor that was matched only by its aesthetic and culinary awareness.

He had his choice of over 10,000 restaurants, from Greek coffee shops to bijou bistros, to worthwhile soul food at Sylvia's in Harlem.

There was a mixture of freedom and foreignness in New York City they said, which was unsurpassed anywhere in the world. New York City had energy and animosity, clutter and great charm. FAO Schwarz on Fifth Avenue, the world's greatest toy store; Maxilla & Mandible, on Columbus between 81st and 82nd Street, was a shop specializing in skeletons, except for endangered species. There were Art Deco cufflinks; horse tack from an 1875 riding boutique; or any one of the savory old-world high-cholesterol goodies at Zabar's, the deli located on Broadway at 22nd.

On sultry summer nights there were free operas and concerts held on the Great Lawn in Central Park, and Shakespeare in the outdoors, or even the Philharmonic Orchestra. He could visit botanic gardens and historic buildings; the Lincoln Center or the New York Stock Exchange.

Alex was on Fifth Avenue at the Trump tower near the corner of 57th when his SkyTel pager buzzed. He was riding up the four-story escalator in the ostentatiously plush atrium that was inundated with a riot of greenery. He had planned on window-shopping the twenty-five stores and then browsing the crystal and jewels next door at Tiffany & Co., the perfect old-money foil to Trump's flashy excesses.

He was listening to a courtside pianist passionately play her rendition of Tchaikovysky's "Pathetigue." The nimble *Julliard School* fingers breezed effortlessly over the keyboard.

Alex found the nearest pay phone and placed an 800-number call to his answering service. He entered his security code. There was one message on his voice mail. It was scratchy. He played back the recording again and again.

"Alex," his mother was crying profusely, barely able to get the words out, "It's ... It's your father. He's dying. He's had a heart attack." Her sobbing dominated the words, making her plea difficult to understand. "Come quickly...before it's too late. The doctors ...don't think he has much time." Alex was devastated.

He ran with abandonment through the crowd. He pushed his way past a blur of bodies and slid down the brass and silver-plated escalator, and then charged through the atrium and entranceway until he reached 57th Street. It was lunchtime and there was a crush of people on 57th. Alex shoved his way through them all — pushing secretaries and white-shirt, power-red-tied business executives out of his way. Yellow cabs, some dinosaur old and rust undercoated, inched along. He needed to catch a taxi back to the Waldorf-Astoria, pack his bags and then make a beeline to the airport and the first flight to Detroit.

The cabs were all full. Only a few travelers were exiting while many more wanted in. Alex blindly shoved past those waiting, and into the street. He found a cab in the middle of 57th that appeared to be letting its fare out.

"Excuse me," he said in a huff as he Roller Derby jammed past two Wall Street types who were also waiting for the same cab.

Alex slammed into the taxi's rear door just as the fare was leaving. "Bam!" he rammed the man over and spilled his black-leather briefcase onto the pavement. Legal documents and architectural drawings scattered into the puddle-strewn street. The renderings fell into a rut with exhaust-brown water right next to Alex.

"Idiot!" the man screamed. "Idiot!" In lightening speed he bent down to collect his documents.

"I'm sorry. Here, please let me help." Alex quickly said. Alex crouched down to help him with his plans. Water was beading up into the vellum paper.

"Idiot! Get your hands off those!"

"Sorry, all I wanted to do was..."

The man who wore black slacks, a brown sports jacket covering a dark shirt, and alligator cowboy boots, pushed Alex out of the way and into the cab. "Imbecile! You don't know what you've just ..."

"Sorry," Alex said.

"Idiot!"

Alex realized he could be of no further help so he slammed shut the cab door and hurried to his hotel.

Once at the Waldorf-Astoria, he found a message waiting for him at the front desk. It read: "Come quickly. Your father's at the University of Michigan Medical Center in Ann Arbor in the Intensive Care Unit. Love, Mother."

Frantically, after making numerous phone calls Alex found a Northwest Airlines flight that left in two hours. He had to do some quick talking, but with the assistance of an understanding ticket counter supervisor he boarded the overbooked plane.

5

Bart Robbins lay in wait in his secluded Belizean mansion. Adjacent to the villa was a 15,000 square foot clinic with the most modern equipment. Built fifteen months earlier, it was nearly empty now. The ultrasound, the Magnetic Resonance Imager and CT-Scanner were installed in a separate third facility behind the clinic. They were used only once. A staff of the best OB-GYN's, nurses, and radiologists that money could buy were gone. His laboratory rivaled any facility that any professional could find at any university medical center. Even the pathologist that he employed was first in his class at Cornell.

And all of this was for just one patient. Actually two. His sister and his unborn male child.

Now the clinic lay nearly vacant. The staff, except for one nurse and one doctor that Robbins had hired for his own needs, were gone.

Bart scrutinized his bedroom. One of five, though his was really the chamber room from where he could rule his empire. In one corner, next to a Renoir, was a computer terminal with five monitors. They were hidden behind a mahogany wall, which moved at the touch of his remote control. With his command, the Robbins' "satellite" center would spring to life. And through this nerve plexus, though only an appendage of the electronics command nucleus nestled in a concrete bunker below the house, in a second subbasement, Robbins had access to every aspect of his business.

Robbins had eventually settled in Belize for two reasons. First, to avoid United States income taxes by expatriating himself and becoming a nationalized citizen, Robbins could save a billion dollars a year in potential IRS obligations. All this, his property and bribes, only cost him two million dollars — a million for the property and a million for the enticement. The second, was because of the country's tropical beauty.

Through his command appendage, Bart controlled 175 acres that his computer screens compound sat on, and indirectly another 2,500 more. In a country not much bigger than Connecticut, 2,700 acres was considered a substantial amount of land.

Bart pushed the remote. The walls separated and the computer screens came to life. One flashed intermittent views of his estate, from one of 20 strategic video camera locations. A new picture flicked on every three seconds. Another displayed a video ticker-tape, reeling off the prices of various stocks that Robbins controlled. Another was a direct link to any of his major offices: New York, Los Angeles, Dallas, London, Paris, Rome, Sydney, Sau Paulo, Mexico City, Miami.

"It was too bad about Miami. At least his best people wouldn't be there when..." he mused.

Robbins drifted almost trance-like. He looked at his burnt hands, at the flesh on them that had melted into snake skin. He was no longer human, had not been since he was thirteen. He was an abomination.

Despite being a monster he had more control than anyone he ever knew. In this way Bart Robbins was a paradox. Maybe he was like Hitler, or Cypselus at Cornith, or Stalin. Bart surmised in his perverted way, that he was tragically defiled as a result of his "trial by fire." He was godlike, in a gargoyle's body. And there was only one thing he was predestined to do—procreate with his own. It was the kraken's fate.

Bart remembered when he was thirteen, in the Burn Unit at Jackson Memorial Hospital. He was outside the plastic bubble where he lived, in the world busy all around him. The tissue, his skin, smelled like death. He could taste the proteins and cells and the plasma greasy fry. He was transformed in an instant into something so hideous that only his mother could bear to see him. And she was dead.

He could feel the seat blow out from under him and the limousine burst into flames around him. He could envision his mother's face melting into an organic chemical soup. He thought about his sister, pretty Helen who could have looked like him, had he grown up to be normal. She was now dumb from the head injury. Brain damage had ruined her forever. From the outside she appeared normal. Brown hair that was soft and long like summer streamers, thick yet smooth as silk. But she could just as well have died, since she was cursed to live in the body of an adult with a five-year old's mind...or was it a blessing in disguise?

Then one day it came to him. His destiny was to continue the lineage, pure like an Aryan race. Unfettered. His bodily humiliation and nearly total tattoo was really a benediction. With his heavenly mandate he followed his kismet to its conclusion.

So Bart had the clinic built. The complex installed its own generator, laboratory and radiology department. All for just one patient and one project — the artificial insemination of Helen.

The money was copious. The doctors took every precaution to ensure that the delivery of the *boy* that they had genetically engineered would be perfect. The process was complicated, but certain. Separate the male from the female chromosomal carrying sperm, and then only the healthiest ones would be used. The sperm with the greatest chance of success would be injected into Helen twelve hours after ovulation. The ejaculate was fresh, pristine. Every safeguard was taken.

Once impregnated, Helen was carefully attended to. At least one nurse was always at her side. Daily she was monitored. Optimal weight gain was planned at 25 to 30 pounds. The pregnancy went perfectly. The child, half Bart's, half Helen's was flawless.

The fetus developed routinely up until the 6th month. That was when Helen developed her first signs of preeclampsia.

Initially there was an increase in blood pressure. Then two weeks later she developed swelling of her arms and legs. These symptoms were managed with medication. But, after a while, the medicine stopped working. Helen slipped into a state of eclampsia. By the seventh month the team of highly trained professionals could no longer attend to Helen at the Robbins compound. She was flown to Miami and Jackson Memorial Hospital.

It was there she developed disseminated intrascular coagulation, where she started having protein deposition in her blood vessels, and her red blood cells burst as they were pumped through her body. She and the unborn baby bleed into their skin, brains, stomach and intestines.

A heroic attempt was made to save the unborn fetus, but to no avail. At 12:10 p.m. on February 3, 1997 they both died.

That was Bart's *sign from God*, but not the God that he had previously known or revered, but from Beelzebub himself.

Outside the cotton clouds turned gray as a late Caribbean summer storm was imminent. A palm and two guanacastes trees wailed in the downdrafts. An armadillo scurried across the Bermuda grass in front of the complex just beyond Robbins' second story room.

In the distance Bart could hear the cry of a toucan, with its multicolored beak, yellow headdress and black eyes and body. Bart was the avian, the toucan. A freak. His family was no more. There were no relatives, no cousins, aunts nor uncles. No mother nor father. No siblings. He was alone. Revenge was to be his. Retaliation, the requital of society's sins was Bart's plan. Robbins would settle the score for his sister, dead family and his unborn male child. Bart's tragedy needed to end with a carnage that would dispose of all the guilty.

His motive was pure.

6

Somewhere in the Caribbean

The Paradise Grand Hotel was still a world class resort, the only difference was that the two penthouse floors were closed to the public. The hotel itself was fourteen stories, and with the Robbins' acquisition of the property and segregation of the upper two levels, the resort still seemed full when it was at twelve story capacity.

Three men arrived by a limousine. One was unwilling. The reluctant captive was awkward, drugged. He looked like an old country bumpkin farmer, but with an academician's clothes. He had dark hair and horn rimmed glasses. His eyes were red, and his face at one time had been full of arrogant scowls.

The 6'6" flanking man was unmistakable. He was intimidating and all sinew. His head was bald, shaved mean. He was Sino-Eurasian. His father was Chinese and his mother a Muscovite. He was intelligent and trained in weaponry, assassination, poison, pyrotechnics, and electronics. He could fire a Makarov 9mm automatic from 100 yards with pinpoint accuracy. His vision was better than 20/20 at 20/15. He was a 6th degree black belt and his knuckles were pure callus.

The other man was equally foreboding. He had recently lost vision in his right eye, the one used for sighting. Nevertheless, he could fire a pistol as good or better than any. To date he had logged 97 kills, though there were many more that were not confirmed. He was a professional's professional. Though Russian, he was originally from Czechoslovakia.

He was tall. His hair was dark and cinnamon colored, and his cheek bones high and aristocratic. He was built in an ominously robust manner, but with the svelte of a cross-country runner.

They entered the hotel and took an express elevator up to the 14th floor. From there they were escorted to the alcove. The floor was bamboo and expensive terra cotta. Cyprus marble tables lined the walls. The wallpaper, sofas and chairs were brightly keyed in exotic hues with paletted flowers, birds and undersea life. The drapes were permanently closed, and the lights were dimmed low.

"My reality," the morose Bart Robbins said, uncomfortable with any scent of the room's viability. He preferred the shadows away from the drapes. "Do you collect things?" he asked as the men were escorted to a table and sat down in front of him. He was holding *his* court.

"I collect souls," Andrei replied with earnest.

Robbins turned around. He pivoted military style on his heels and walked to the far side of the room, away from his guest. "And how so do you do that, sir?"

"By selling death...as I'm selling it to you."

The drugged man was haunted by the answer. Yet, his force of will would not allow him to protest. The barbiturates that he was given to "subdue him" were overpowering, especially for someone of his age and condition.

"Souls. Did you know that the Egyptians called them *ka*, or breath?'"

"No."

"And that they thought it survived death, that the soul remained near the body, while the spiritual *ba* proceeded to the region of the dead?"

"No," Andrei replied, "But I do collect *breaths*."

"How so?"

"That's not relevant."

Robbins continued slowly pacing, his black fedora covering his head. He was a movie parody. His inky scarf wrapped his neck, revealing a small portion of his burnt face. "I thought there were going to be two of you?" he asked.

"There are. He's my insurance policy," Andrei said gesturing to the worn professor.

"Insurance? For what?'

"From you."

Robbins howled, his pain echoing like a rabid jackal. "From me? That's a joke. No one can buy insurance to protect themselves from me."

"I think not."

"Ta..." Robbins pivoted then asked. "Do you play pool?"

"Yes."

"Eightball?"

"Yes."

The two men left the Sino-Eurasian and the professor and walked into an adjacent billiards room. Inside was an antique English pool table that had been used in the London 1919 championship game at the English Billiards Association and Control Council. The one that was won after a 27-hour marathon round by Sir Jeffery Herramin.

Robbins racked the balls. His hands appeared to be covered with black tissue paper. Andrei broke. Robbins noticed that Andrei's eyes were fixed onto his hands.

"Two thousand dollars a pair. I have them specially made."

"I would imagine."

"And they're not calf skin either."

Andrei knew what Robbins had inferred, but he wasn't going to delve any deeper. He just smiled and said, "Yes. They're *like real skin* aren't they?"

"They are."

With the break, the ivory cueball careened off the stripped balls, sending the solid blue two into the right side pocket.

"Good shot."

"Thank you. So..." Andrei said while lining his sights up on the maroon seven, as he would a victim with his 9mm. "what do you plan on doing with all the plutonium. Blow-up the fucking world?"

"Maybe. Would it make any difference?" Robbins said, more curious as to whether his question would disrupt Andrei's game, than the truthfulness of his response.

"Yes it would. That is...if it's my world you're going to nuke."

"Well, that just depends on what your world is, doesn't it?"

Both men studied each other. Andrei pocketed the seven, and then set his sights on the next ball.

Robbins walked to a briefcase that was sitting on top of an

antique chestnut end table. The drop-leaf table was dark brown and had the same Victorian legs as the billiards table. He unsnapped the locks and flipped open the large case. "Two million dollars," he said walking away from the money, back towards the game.

Andrei glanced over nonchalantly. He pressed on with his game. "Good," he said. He took aim on the three, and in combination using the twelve ball, he banked the red target into the corner pocket.

"You're a decent player."

"I know," Andrei replied, as he walked to the end table and gave the briefcase the once over. He ran his fingers through a bundle of thousand dollar bills, and then set the stack back into the brief-case and closed the lid.

"The rest of the money is on delivery. Where's the plutonium?"

"In the 'Painted Lady,' a tramp streamer of Panamanian registry, 50 miles off shore."

"You have the amount that I need? All of it?"

"It's all there. High grade, reactor, nuclear-warhead ready. 100 percent of it."

"Any problem getting it?"

"Some, but I called in some old comrade chips."

"KGB?"

"Whatever."

"That's your business."

"Is that it?" Andrei asked.

"No. I need you to do another job?"

"And that is?"

"It's complicated, but I'll pay you an extra two million up front, and then another two upon completion."

"Two million dollars up front. That's an awful lot of money."

"And twenty million isn't?"

"It depends on what services you're buying. You know I've got costs."

"And how much could that be?"

"Substantial."

"It's all relative isn't it?" Robbins asked.

Andrei closed the briefcase and set it next to the pool table. He picked up his stick, which was leaning against the end table, and proceeded in a businesslike fashion to run the table. Within two minutes he had won the first game without Robbins shooting one shot.

"Play again?"

"So you like games?" Robbins undauntedly asked.

"I do. How 'bout a thousand dollars a point. I've just come into some money."

"Done," Bart replied, his adrenaline pumping — finally a challenge; someone to match his skill.

By day's end, arrangements had been made for "The Painted Lady" to sail into the Port of Miami, and for her to clear customs. The plutonium which was originally in gray bars, had been milled into a fine grain. It was in lead-lined containers six inches thick, which in turn were packed in wooden crates. Yellow letters were stenciled on the outside of each crate that read "Baby Formula." The amount of plutonium that was being smuggled into Miami was mind-boggling.

Nevertheless, Bart Robbins had a plan that he had carefully thought through. Just as he had built his father's business into the leviathan that it was, so too would he revenge his sister, his unborn boy child, and himself. He would settle the score for the lifelong suffering that he had endured.

"A destroyer will come against Babylon; her warriors will be captured, and their bows will be broken. For the Lord is a God of retribution; he will repay in full"

Bart Robbins was the Lord.

7

September 7, 1999

How could Alex explain his feelings? He was overwhelmed. His father dying of a heart attack.

The father with whom until recently he had not been able to show his love. "Why?"

Alex had distanced himself for most of his life from his father. Perhaps it was the competitive spirit that they both had, or his inability to accept and understand his father for what he was, a fallible human being. During most of college, he rarely spoke to him. And even in high school, when the bonds of the father-child relationship should have been their strongest, they were in decay. The generation gap they developed was more than the adolescent schizophrenia of "finding one's self." The rift was a deeper-rooted sense of abandonment. A sense of longing and yearning for emotional support, that Alex never received.

Benjamin was a workaholic. And maybe that's what Alex also saw in himself. The unquenchable drive to push harder, to succeed — to be his best. Yet, at the same time Alex left behind him the essence of a loving relationship. As he matured, went to medical school, he eventually found himself. But that process was slow and painful. It took time, and Alex needed to do some healing. The problem was his, not his father's. Eventually, Alex began to mend the attachments that slipped away years earlier, gradually weaving one strand at a time. He loved his father, but had a hard time expressing it, at least until now.

The drive from Detroit Metropolitan Airport was monotonous. Alex never liked Michigan, and thus his reason for moving south and then west. Seventy percent of the year the sky was gray and overcast as a result of the Great Lakes effect. The fog-like billow depressed him. Today was no different.

After undergraduate school at the University of Michigan, he had his choice of several medical schools. He was accepted at eight. He eventually settled on the University of Miami and lived on the ocean on Brickel Avenue for three of his four years of study.

After Medical school he traveled west to the University of Nevada and residency training in Internal Medicine in Las Vegas, of all god-forsaken places. But that was the "luck" of the National Intern and Residents Medical Matching Program draw. And as it turned out, the three years in Vegas were some of the best times of his life.

Finally, after residency training, he a born-again skier, moved to Salt Lake City, Utah to surf the deep powder slopes of Snowbird, Alta and Solitude.

I-94 heading west towards Chicago and Lake Michigan was bumpy, and the concrete inimically pitted by the spring thaws. It had been a while since Alex had been in Ann Arbor, a place that he had rather not return to. This was one of those times.

Memories at the University of Michigan were charged with mixed emotion, and represented both the best and worst of times. Those were the days of his struggle to get into medical school, his passionate personality in overdrive, and his need to get all A's, which became an obsession.

People say that things are never the same when one returns. This was certainly the case in Ann Arbor. The roads as he had remembered were wider. The streets longer. The students looked younger, or was it that he was getting old.

He drove in through Ypsilanti, down to Geddes Avenue, past Stockwell, Mosher-Jordon and Alice Lloyd dormitories; beyond the observatory, the Kresge Research Building, around the medical school and finally to the hospital. The University of Michigan Medical

School sat adjacent to the hospital and was one of those self-described hyperbole places — exceptional facilities, one of "America's best," etc. It was as terrible and intimidating as he remembered.

The outside of the building was early Midwest 1930's brick and mortar facade, and then portions later refurbished in 60's concrete and dolomite.

The September air took its first bites into his skin. Though Alex was fond of most of Ann Arbor, he never liked the University Hospital. Maybe it was the pseudo-professionalism, or perhaps his competitive spirit to be "the best," and the feeling that he couldn't compete with some of the egghead physicians who thought they were better than him, smarter than him. Many of them were.

Alex's father was in the Coronary Care Unit. He was unconscious and tethered to a telemetry monitor. IVs ran into each arm and a ventilator was attached by an endotracheal tube that slipped into his mouth. Air was regularly pumped into his lungs. He wore two white-and-blue hospital gowns, one tied frontwards from underneath, and the other tied from the rear. His hair was thick, black and graying. Benjamin Seacourt did not look 70 years of age.

When Alex walked in, Mary, his mother, was sitting at her husband's side holding his hand. A nurse was just leaving.

"Mom."

"Son." She reached out and hugged him.

"Mom, is dad going to be alright?" Alex asked.

"He's real sick?"

"How bad?"

"He has fluid in his lung?" she said.

"What are the doctors doing?"

"They're giving him a medicine to take fluids out of his lungs, and then something to make his heart pump stronger."

"Who's dad's doctor," Alex felt nearly impotent, knowing that he could take care of his father, fix him, but *he shouldn't.*

"Dr. Lasky, he's the cardiologist, Dr. Brown the internist, and I think, but I'm not sure, Dr. Stewart or Stevens...something, is his lung doctor."

"A pulmonologist? Is it that bad?"

"I don't know. You'll need to speak to them."

"My God." Alex was nearly in tears. He looked down at his father. He felt guilty. Alex placed his father's hand in his own. "I'm sorry I wasn't a better son," he said. "I love you dad." Alex waited for a response from his father, for him to open his eyes and acknowledge his existence, but he didn't. Alex knew instinctively that his father had heard him; or so he hoped.

"Mom," he said, "I need to find one of the doctors." He grasped her hand momentarily. "I need to talk to them. I'll be back in a few minutes."

Mary did not want to release her grip. Her face was worn, her cheeks dispirited, her eyes red-rimmed.

"I'll be right back mom. I promise." Alex slid his hand away from hers and left Room 8, closing the door behind him. He walked to the Coronary Care Unit desk, around the corner and identified himself as "Dr. Seacourt." He read his father's chart. Alex did not need to speak to any specialist. He could figure it out for himself. Out loud, in a low voice, he read the bad news. "Right anterior cardiac infarction, pulmonary edema secondary to acute onset congestive heart failure, ventricular atopic arrhythmia's secondary to myocardial infarction…"

And the cornucopia of drugs that he was on was a grocery shopping list, "Verapamil, Digoxin, Lasix, Mevacor, Streptokinease, Compazine, Potassium Chloride 2m eq/ml in 250ml. etc." It wasn't a pretty picture.

The pulmonologist's report was worse. This is what Alex was afraid of. "Possible pulmonary embolism and/or pneumohemothorax secondary to streptokinase therapy."

Alex's father had been treated with a heart saving medication that had side effects, potentially worse than the cure. It looked like he might have had those. Benjamin was bleeding into his lungs. In addition, the doctors believed that he had thrown blood clots off into his lungs.

Alex sat heavily in his chair. He closed the metal chart. He was sick to his stomach. His father probably would not make it. From his experience, he would guess maybe a 30 percent chance to survive. Hoping that possibly he misread the data, Alex popped back the plastic clip that held the chart shut, springing it open. The EKGs, the rhythm strips, the lab work, were unmistakable.

"Doctor, can I help you?" a nurse asked him as he studied the rhythm strips.

"Thank you, but no. It's my father."

"Not too good?"

"No."

She shook her head, affirming Alex's statement. "Thanks," he replied. Alex returned to the Coronary Care room and sat with his mother. He was dumbstruck in a chair next to her. Both of them watched the ventilator force air into Benjamin's lungs and then back out They were quiet for nearly an hour.

"He's not going to make it, is he?" Mary painfully asked. In her voice Alex could tell that she was imploring him to tell the truth, but hoping for a lie.

"Mom ... Dad'll be just fine. Be patient." He comforted her.

After a while, close to two hours, Dr. Lasky the cardiologist came in.

"Dr. Seacourt." Alex stood up and shook hands.

"Tell me, I noticed in the chart that my father had several episodes of severe bradycardia?"

"That's correct."

"What's that?" Mary asked.

Dr. Lasky replied. "Your husband's heart is damaged, sick. Part of the normal tissue has died as a result of the heart attack. The atrial-ventricular node, or tissue that's used to spark the heart to make it beat, is not working properly."

"Uh, huh."

"As a result of the damage to your husband's heart, it has sometimes been beating slower than it should. We think that we're going to need to put in a pacemaker. Pacemakers are used to jump start the heart if the beats drop too low."

"I see," she acknowledged calmly. "Is it a difficult surgery?"

"Usually, no. But because of your husband's condition there are more risks than normal. I think that we should watch him carefully. If there are anymore episodes of bradycardia, or slow heart rates, then we should insert a pacemaker."

"Whatever you think," she said looking at Alex for affirmation.

"Thank you Dr. Lasky," Alex said, "Whatever you feel is the most appropriate. I just want to make sure my father gets the best care."

"Of course."

Dr. Lasky left, and eventually several of the other specialists came in. They had similar conversations with Alex and his mother. Soon, near 6 p.m. they were gone, and Alex and Mary were left alone.

"How are you doing?" Mary asked.

"Fine...I think."

"Alex, are you all right?"

"Yes, mom."

"You don't look all right."

"I don't? How am I supposed to look?"

"How are you feeling?" Mary probed deep into his eyes.

"I feel guilty about not being a better son. I am afraid dad'll die."

"Me, too."

"Yeah."

"You did the best you could. We all did."

"I suppose."

Alex sat for several hours, thinking, his mind churning. His father was soon possibly gone. It was too much.

8

Miami

The warehouse next to where "The Painted Lady" eventually moored was on a sleazy sliver of the Miami River, underneath a concrete and steel freeway that ran nearly one hundred and fifty feet overhead. The backwaters were stale. The stemless biscayne palms with their wilted fan-shaped leaves and silvery undercoating stood along the inlet, surrounding the warehouse on three sides. On top, their pleated tufts had began to yellow with age and fungus. The decrepit pier and the dock frontage in nearly a half-mile in both directions was owned by Beck-Quail Shippers, one of Robbins' many subsidiary companies. Except for the fact that there was activity about the ship and at the canal's edge, the warehouse appeared abandoned.

The walls and frame were tin, and many of the windows had the appearance that they had not been washed in nearly a quarter of a century. Peculiarly, however, none of the windows have been broken. Upon closer inspection it was obvious that many of them had been recently replaced. They were made *to look old and dingy.*

The building's facade was sun-faded and painted a slate green that was deliberately chipped and aged after two coats were applied. No cars were parked in front. The lot was empty and scattered with yellowed newspapers and debris. Anyone who came or left from the structure was bussed in and out by van. And except for the smoke that drifted out of an inconspicuous brick stack, there were no signs of life.

There was a security panel that allowed admission with input of an I.D. card and a six-digit code. The panel was hidden behind a weather-worn wooden trim piece at the door's edge.

Inside the warehouse, the building was anything but a warehouse. The facility looked like it might have been a high-tech semiconductor factory. To enter, there were two sets of double doors. Then there was a changing room where each technician undressed and slipped into their dust and static resistant outfits with masks, head covers and latex-like gloves. Their faces were canopied with hoods and goggles. Each worker communicated through voice activated headsets. Robbins had spent more than $25 million to equip his "repository."

Each of the wooden crates that contained the lead-lined "baby formula" were removed carefully by a rusty, wheeled crane, that sat high upon a girder landing tower. The crane slunk along a steel-and-concrete track from stern to bow as its operator cautiously unloaded the vessel's lading.

When "The Painted Lady" was unloaded its crew slid it out into the Miami River, and from there toward the Atlantic and back to it's Albanian port of origin.

In a concrete-and-lead chamber, robots unloaded the plutonium powder from their crate lead-lined vaults. Then, there were a series of sophisticated reaction flasks, funnels, condensers and an elaborate electronic Rube Goldberg-type apparatus that desolidified and condensed the plutonium, while cooling it and absorbing the deadly alpha particles with liquid sodium. Great care was taken since the liquid sodium was highly reactive to oxygen and explosive if exposed to air.

Once the plutonium was turned into a confluent mush it was combined in a series of complex reactions with several catalytic agents, including phosphorus trichloride, acetic anhydride, cholorobenzene, anthranalyic acid, sodium hydroxide, hydrochloride acid. Then, in two final steps, using a platinum catalytic conversion process the plutonium in its naked, anhydrous form, was individually, atom-by-atom, combined with a plastic polymer.

At 12:30 p.m., Bart Robbins and two of his thugs along with Andrei and Boriskov, arrived in a Mercedes 600 limousine to inspect the facility.

By 1:30 Robbins was well into his tour, showing-off his state-of-the-art facility He boasted like a child bragging to his friends about his Christmas-new Gilbert Chemistry Set. He was ready to get down to business.

Robbins stopped walking. "About four years ago one of my chemists in Switzerland was working on a plastic-polymer for hospital mask application. Something that was porous enough to allow single atoms of oxygen through, but that would not allow molecules of carbon dioxide through. He stumbled onto something that...well let me say this. At first he thought that he had the *absolute filter.* A one-way system. A material that would prevent viral penetration — AIDS, etc., and at the same time be extremely safe.

"However, what my Swiss scientist stumbled upon was something that would also prevent *radiation emission.* Kind of like a super lightweight lead."

"So," Andrei acknowledged, uncomfortable in his radiation outfit.

"Well, the problem was that the polymer tended to be water soluble. It did a great job stopping radiation, but get it wet and it broke down. So, practically speaking the applications were limited. That is until now. You see," Robbins paused with a nefarious gleam, "it blocks *alpha wave emission.*"

"And."

"Let me explain. Alpha waves, or alpha particles, are a positively charged particle indistinguishable from a helium atom nucleus, having two protons and two neutrons. What makes *alpha particles or alpha emissions* so dangerous is that, though they aren't very penetrating, they are emitted, or ejected from plutonium as it decays at 1/10 the speed of light. In air, they have a range of about four inches, and they have a corresponding energy burst of about four million electron volts."

"What does that mean?" Andrei asked, beginning to see the possibilities. He liked Robbins' way of thinking.

"What that means is this: First, plutonium when it is *not* used in a bomb can be *manipulated* into other more applications. It can be real nasty, since it's half-life is roughly 25,000 years. Second, when within range, and I mean close range, and you bombard a human being with alpha particles, then well... after a relatively short while, you can kiss that person good-bye." Robbins made a smacking motion with his grotesque baboon lips. He put his index finger and thumb together and pressed them against his lead-lined glass shield. Then he blew an imaginary kiss into the air.

"Good. Very good." Andrei said.

"So... I have this plastic polymer that I can coat every individual atom of plutonium with. The polymer, as long as it's not exposed to water is invincible. The plutonium is 100% safe to handle, and *undetectable*," he paused waiting for Andrei's response.

Andrei gazed at Robbins. He did not respond.

"It can be stored and placed anywhere safely, until I'm ready to use it...then...when the moment's ripe..."

Robbins again began to walk. Andrei, Boriskov and the bodyguards followed. Complex glass and Pyrex tubing ran from a liquid sodium condenser. The plutonium was fluxed, then shot through a number of catalytic steps where the atoms were ultimately combined with the complex plastic polymer. Individually, each new polymer-coated atom of plutonium was tested for alpha wave emission in an intricate mechanism, and then processed in a vacuum. There, the plutonium-plastic polymer composite was stripped of all but one molecular polymer layer. This left the plutonium protected by only the thinnest shield.

Finally, the composite was collected as a powdered resin and shifted through a series of microscopic filters to ensure uniformity of size. The powder was hermetically sealed in thick plastic bags. Each package had a predetermined amount of plutonium.

"I need your help with some devices," Robbins requested, but was in actuality ordering.

"Devices...plural?" Andrei asked, his eyes lighting up, realizing a bigger profit in this than he initially anticipated.

"Devices."

"Possibly. But first a question. What do your men think they're doing?"

"Working for peace...of course," Robbins grinned as he continued walking.

Boriskov snickered.

"You find that funny?" Robbins asked, looking at Boriskov who had a roguish smile on his face.

Boriskov was close-lipped. He quickly regained his trained composure. Then, before he could answer, Robbins continued, "I do.... In fact, I find it real funny. I have the best people in the world working for me, for almost peanuts. And they're doing it for the love of their work. They *think* that they're working on a safe way to store and dispose of nuclear waste. Making the world a better place to live in."

They came to the end of their tour, having walked through much of the nuclear complex.

"No more dumping sites in the middle of the Utah desert or Washington State, or New Mexico. But drilling ultra-deep wells, 25 to 50 miles below the earth's surface, and then burying the nuclear waste there...in its air-tight packages of plastic polymers? Actually an excellent idea. Too bad it won't be implemented."

They returned to the decompression chamber between the set of double doors. They entered the room. Once inside, the air possibly contaminated with plutonium dust was filtered out. Outside ambient air was piped in. They carefully climbed out of their spaceman suits and placed them in special baskets. They walked into Robbins' office.

"You want me to place it...in critical locations that you can't get to yourself."

"Something like that."

"I see."

"Two million dollars now and two million upon completion."

"Okay. So where do you want me to put the devices?"

"I have the perfect spot for the first one." Robbins sat down and placed his feet up on his desk. He looked at Andrei and Boriskov. He hit a remote, and from behind him two half wall-size walnut panels retracted. A giant twelve-foot wide by six-foot high map of the United States appeared. To it were pinned tiny light bulbs. Lots of them. Robbins hit another button and a number of lights lit up on the map.

"See," he spun around and pointed to the high altitude view that was shot by a number of his telecommunication satellites, and then combined into one large high resolution color photograph of the United States.

"There," he pointed with his finger and hit the remote again. A green and white light turned red. "Or should I say here."

"Tell me about the device." Andrei's interest mushroomed.

"Ahhhh. You'll love this one. I would imagine it's right up your alley. Actually, it's pure genius if I must say so myself."

9

At 7:00 p.m. Benjamin Seacourt's condition worsened. His heart slowed to nearly 20 beats a minute, the normal being 60. The doctors declared an emergency and rushed him into surgery. By 8:20 p.m., after a complicated carotid artery entry, an atrial-ventricular pacemaker was implanted and Benjamin's heart once again began beating at a normal place. At 9:54 p.m. he was back in his Coronary Care Unit bed.

Dr. Lasky approached with a glum face.

"What's wrong?" Alex asked sensing a problem.

Lasky answered uncomfortably. "I've good news and bad...."

"Go on," Alex said, his nerves frayed. Alex's mother reached over to hold his hand.

Lasky was looking at his shoes. "The surgery was a success. From the point of view of treating the heart attack and the arrhythmia, we're on our way home..."

"But?"

"I think that your father might have thrown off a clot during the procedure. I have him on anticoagulants. We might have a stroke situation. I've got the neurologist coming in, and a brain scan ordered. We'll do everything in our power."

Alex didn't challenge the cardiologist. He knew that this was the risk of streptokinase, the clotbuster used for his father's heart attack, and then the pacemaker surgery. Streptokinase could have easily caused the bleeding, and even possibly the breaking loose of a plaque in the carotid artery, or something thrown off during the pacemaker emplacement. Alex knew that it could happen. He had to accept it.

Over the next hour and a half, a team of doctors buzzed in and out of Benjamin Seacourt's room, doing everything humanly possible to save his life. By nearly 11:00 p.m. they were finished. The rest was up to God.

When everyone had left, except for Alex and Mary, they sat there quietly, praying and hoping that Benjamin would survive the night. It was nearly midnight when Mary insisted that Alex leave, and get a hotel room. She could spend the night with her husband. Alex didn't need to stay any longer. Despite his protests, he knew what his mother was really telling him—was that she wanted to be alone with Benjamin. Alex, weary, fatigued and confused, left.

His walk to the elevators was a dirge. Everyone in the hospital seemed surreal. Make-believe.

"Why my father? Tears of anguish and depression welled in his eyes.

He pushed the down button. Alex was the only one on his way out. He waited nearly a minute until the elevator, which had been idle at the first floor, rose to the third. Slowly the doors opened and he stepped in. As he did, a man from behind him rushed to the doors. Alex held the doors open for him.

The man was dressed in a dark trench coat. His topcoat collar was raised, and he wore a sailor's Popeye or "watch cap."

Just as the doors were about to slide shut, a nurse ran down the hall from out of nowhere. Alex hit the push-bar to stop the doors from closing. "Could you hold the doors!" she yelled, but not too loud, as her pudgy feet scampered. The elevator reopened and the nurse, frazzled around the edges after just finishing her second shift, got on.

"Thanks," she said, huffing for breath as she reached into her purse, searching for cigarettes. Her nicotine fit was overwhelming.

"Anytime," Alex replied. He looked at her face.

She shared a smile. "You okay?" she asked.

"Me?"

"Yes, you." she replied, ignoring the man who melted into the wall.

"It's...just my father."

The nurse nodded, and despite the rules, pulled out her Kent's to light up. "I'm sorry. Mind if I smoke?" She looked at both of them this time.

"No, not at all," Alex replied.

The elevator settled on the main floor, and her question asked out of courtesy became moot. They left the elevator. The nurse lit up as Alex walked toward the main doors. She was parallel to him. The man, who had remained quiet in the elevator, was annoyed. He had other plans, and at least momentarily he faded into the shadows.

"Are they treating him well?"

"Yes, thank you."

Without further conversation, she peeled off as fast as she had arrived, heading toward a side door. A lone security guard sat at the front desk and watched Alex leave. The man behind Alex, who was veiled in darkness, gave him a head start.

Alex's hotel was two blocks up the street. Instead of getting his car, he decided to walk. The night air would do him some good. The first half of the block was on a slight knoll that rose 60 feet from where he started. Then, afterwards, there was a fairly level walk to the Bell Tower. On his left he could see the lights of Ann Arbor, the Student Union and Rackham Auditorium where once he saw Bette Midler in concert. That was when he was twenty, and she on the first of her many twenty threes. The campus lights illuminated the night and stirred Alex's memory. Recollections poured in: studying for final exams, trying his first marijuana cigarette, his sophomore organic chemistry lab that he hated.

On the right were thick bushes and barely any street light. Far off he could hear voices of coeds giggling after drinking one too many beers, trying to park their brown Nova with a scuzzy top, and running over an empty aluminum trash can. Otherwise, there were no cars. Then...in the distance, he could hear footsteps behind him. Suddenly they came faster. Alex began quickening his pace.

Spit. He felt air whiz by his ear. He spun around. In the shadows of night he saw the man with the watch cap. A street light briefly brought a pistol with a silencer into view.

Alex ran hard, just making it over the knoll, when again, came "spit...spit." He had made it over the rise in time. He cut right and ran through the bushes out of sight, charging into the deep foliage at full-speed ahead. The man followed, running up the rise and toward the hotel, where he momentarily stopped. He looked for his prey. Then, in an instant, he caught his target: the shadows of movement running through the underbrush, down a hill, past the parking structure and toward the hospital's emergency room on the opposite end of the complex. The man gave chase.

Alex ran through a thicket and deep untamed brush. He glanced only momentarily over his shoulder. He passed two parched evergreens, the pine needles pricking his face.

Another "spit" pierced the air. The bark of a birch in front of him exploded in flying splinters. Alex dodged right, then zigzagged. Thundering behind him came the lunging steps of the trained killer.

Alex ran nearly one hundred yards, then hopped over a small brambling creek. Ahead of him, his sanctuary. An open field where hospital staffers played Frisbee with their dogs on Saturdays or Sundays, and then a short retaining wall. On the other side was the driveway entrance to the University Hospital rear and the Emergency Room. Seventy-five yards farther was the hospital's north entrance.

The problem was, that Alex would be exposed. He would be easy to kill on the wide-open field.

Nearly out of breath he stopped. He had to think fast. Then he got it. He doubled back to just before the stream and found a clump of thorn bushes. He threw his body into the brambles.

Moments later an inky silhouette ran by. The man jumped over the brook and into the field. He ran through the field up to the retaining wall. Alex had fooled him.

As the man was about to hop the wall, Alex got up. Alex cocked his legs, ready to spring across the stream. However, in his attempt to jump the brook he misstepped the bank's edge and slipped on the muddy soil. He fell into the water. The man spun around, saw Alex, and wildly fired. Branches and wood chips exploded in every direction.

Alex ran back through the trees the way they came. The chase was on again. This time, Alex had a substantial lead as he ran back up to the road toward the hospital's front entrance.

Within two minutes Alex made it to the deserted drive. He turned back to the hospital. Not far, but far enough behind him was the killer, his trench coat flapping in the wind as he sprinted with the demon's dispatch.

Suddenly an ambulance screeched. An inexperienced driver who should have taken his patient to the emergency room, barreled down the wrong road. He was headed straight toward the killer and Alex. The killer had reached the street as the ambulance with its bubble-gum red and white lights and horn blaring sped passed him en route to Alex and the hospital's front entrance. He angrily slowed and slid his weapon inside his trench coat.

With the killer temporarily inoperative and the noise of the ambulance covering Alex's flight, Alex slipped to his left down a small nook immediately next to the hospital's front. He ran through a park and around the hospital's side retaining wall toward the rear emergency room entrance. By the time the killer realized what had happened, Alex had made his escape.

"I need the police," he panted. "Get me the police!"

The emergency room admissions clerk paged overhead. Within five minutes, an officer who was assigned to a substation at the teaching hospital arrived.

"I've been shot at!"

"What?" The cop was a rookie who barely looked like he had graduated from high school. He was surprised that anyone would shoot at anyone in Ann Arbor.

Alex machine-gunned his story to the cop. He explained how the killer had followed him into the elevator from the 3rd floor and his chase through the park. The rookie called his station commander and shortly thereafter several other cops arrived. Alex was given hot coffee and a wool blanket to wrap around his wet, shivering body.

"We'll need to have you speak with homicide in the morning," the police sergeant said. He was smarter than he looked.

"That's fine, I just don't want my mother to know what's going on. My dad's sick enough. She doesn't need anymore worries."

"I don't know."

"Please promise me, at least for now."

"All right."

Within an hour, Alex had given the best description he could of the man who had followed him. The characterization was basically useless since Alex never really took a good hard look at him. His mind was elsewhere when they were in the elevator.

By 2:00 a.m. the authorities were done. Alex decided not to get a hotel room. Instead, he spent the night in the doctor's lounge. He fell asleep in an old recliner; one with a handle that opened up the chair. At five in the morning a surgeon came in and woke him up.

Alex showered and returned to his father's room. His mother was asleep in the chair at Benjamin's side. This time, however, a police officer was conspicuously posted outside the Coronary Care Unit.

10

J ack Tandy was the president of the powerful pharmaceutical arm of the Robbins family fortune. Kodmore Pharmaceuticals was based in Atlanta, Georgia. Jack had been a loyal ally and best friend of Billy Robbins, the family patriarch. Jack had helped build the Robbins conglomerate into the giant that it was.

Back in the early 50's, when the Robbins empire was expanding into frontiers other than the grocery business, Jack a magnum cum laude fresh out of Harvard's MBA program, was hand-picked by Billy Robbins. Jack's forte was finding undervalued companies and building them into giants. He was invaluable in that respect.

Kodmore was one such company that Robbins found. Kodmore was a budding pharmaceutical concern based in Athens Georgia. Kodmore's niche had been a non-narcotic cough suppressant. However, due to poor market research Kodmore had introduced their flagship product when their was a glut of narcotic cough suppressants available to the consumer. The narcotics were far more popular, and easily obtainable through a physician's prescription.

The company scraped by for the next five years. In 1956 they unveiled an over-the-counter steroid skin preparation. Once again, their product was released at the wrong time — when numerous more effective prescription medications were easily obtainable from physicians. The second preparation, though perhaps before its time, was about to bring Kodmore into a state of nonexistence.

Kodmore was on the verge of bankruptcy. With a profit-to-equity ratio that was pathetic at best, and creditors that were nipping at the company's heels, Kodmore was only weeks away from closing.

Jack Tandy had heard about Kodmore through the grapevine. It was well run, well managed and just needed an infusion of cash combined with better luck and clearer market vision.

When Jack investigated the company further, he found *the goose that could lay the golden egg*. What he discovered, eventually turned into Relaxol and Pep-Safe, the number one and number two best-selling drugs in the world.

It's rare to find a company with one solid drug on the "back burner," but two is next to impossible. And that's what Tandy was good at, the next-to-impossible.

One year after the acquisition of Kodmore, Tandy had moved the company to Atlanta and had received an accelerated FDA approval of Relaxol. It was significantly less addicting than valium and in short-term usage, for about two weeks, it also had an antidepressive action.

But the real *mother lode* was Pep-Safe — the anti-ulcer medication, the first one on the market; an H-2 receptor blocker that replaced Maalox and Mylanta (antacids) which were at the time the only known treatment for ulcers. Within six months of Pep-Safe's release, worldwide sales topped $1 billion.

Timing was everything for Pep-Safe, which by nine months preceded rival Hartax Corporation's Duomet. Duomet, also an H-2 receptor blocker, never caught on like Pep-Safe.

Unfortunately for patriarch Billy Robbins, he wasn't around to see the job that Jack Tandy had done for him with Pep-Safe and the Kodmore Pharmaceutical Company.

After the Robbins' family murders, Jack was at Bart's side daily for the next two years, until Bart left the hospital. Tandy had set up a satellite office in Miami, where he worked while watching over Bart.

Initially, by a majority vote of the board of director's, Jack Tandy became the CEO and president of the Robbins conglomerate, though ownership was 70 percent held by the two remaining Robbins heirs, Bart and his sister Helen.

In the mid-seventies, Bart Robbins took over the company's reins. He had his father's mind and star-pupil intellect. Robbins had been home schooled by some of the world's best Ph.D.s. All he did was read, absorb and learn. He was a gifted monster.

Jack Tandy was a large man. During his undergraduate days, before Harvard Business School, he attended the University of Georgia where he played defensive tackle for three of his four college years. His face was stern and he had wrinkle lines that suggested that he frowned too often.

His pensive eyes were framed with bifocals. His hair was mostly white-gray with sparse streaks of black, and he had liver spots on his hands and some on his forehead. His mouth was too small for his face.

He was very deliberate and walked with a cane, due to hip replacement surgery in 1981, the result of an old football injury.

Today, Jack was on the telephone from the top floor of the twenty-eight story Kodmore Building on Peachtree Street.

"So," the mysterious voice said on the other end, a voice that was powerful enough to get Tandy's direct private line, "I understand there is some unfinished business?"

"What?" Tandy asked quizzically, "Who's this?"

"That doesn't matter. What matters is May 19th, 1964, thirty-two years ago." Jack did not respond. He was silent. Memories returned in a barrage. They flooded his brain.

"Still there?" the voice from the past asked. The timbre was vaguely familiar.

"Yes.... Who is this?"

"You know that there is still unfinished business?" Then there was a long pause before the connection continued. "It's time we come full-circle."

"Who is this?" Tandy demanded.

"I'll meet you in Miami tomorrow at noon. Be at the..."

"Who is this?"

"...Coconut Grove Grand Bay Hotel, registered under the name William J. Smith. Someone will contact you." Then there was a click.

It had been more than thirty years since the Robbins car bombing. The FBI, CIA, ATF, Miami Police and Sheriff's Department investigated. All leads led to dead ends. The suspects were the environmentalists and native tribal leaders in Brazil where the Robbins corporation had its tin strip mining concern. The other likely suspects were the powers at the Hartax Corporation. The death of Billy Robbins, theoretically could have put a halt to the release of Pep-Safe, and thus Hartax's Duomet would have gotten a jump into the marketplace, and worldwide dominance.

Then again, anyone could have been a suspect. Robbins was a vicious businessman who did whatever it took to make a deal work. During his career he trampled on many people's toes. More than even he realized.

11

One week later

The plutonium processing was complete. Inside the clandestine warehouse, the fifteen scientists were huddled in the large conference room. On one side, pushed up against the wall, was a banquet table with a white tablecloth. On top was bean-ground coffee, fresh-squeezed navel orange juice, Danish, fresh kiwis, bananas, papayas, mangos and melons.

Bart Robbins, Andrei and Boriskov sat at the head of the table. Robbins, the recluse, made an unprecedented appearance before his staff. Standing slightly behind them, were Robbins' two aides and plant manager.

"Gentlemen, first I want to thank you. The project has been concluded substantially ahead of schedule. I'm very pleased and amazed at your productivity."

There was a round of applause.

"The Robbins Corporation has been working in a hand-in-glove manner with the National Security Commission. As you know, before any of us were brought on board to this project, each one of you went though a vigorous security clearance process. I need to,

however, once again remind you of the importance of absolute secrecy with our project. Because of foreign terrorist concerns, it is
entirely imperative that our operation be continued in absolute secrecy."

The plant manager bent forward toward Bart and said, "I can
assure you Mr. Robbins, that every possible precaution has been
taken to ensure complete secrecy."

"Excellent," Robbins replied addressing his engineers.

Each scientist was hired from outside the Southeast United States.
Prior to bringing them to Miami, they were placed incommunicado
and told that they would be going to the Orient for two months to
work on a top secret industrial chemistry project in a joint effort
with the Japanese.

Upon their arrival in Miami, they were then told their true
agenda. Each scientist was housed in the Robbins estate in Coral
Gables on the ocean. Each was given his own room, a personal valet
and access to a computer that only accessed the warehouse/factory.

Every morning, seven days a week, they were bused in two vans
to the plant. The bus's windows were blackened so that the scientists could not see where they were going.

"Gentlemen, over the next several weeks we'll be dismantling
the plant."

"Dismantling?" an eager nuclear engineer stood and asked.

"Yes. We'll be moving to a larger facility, outside of Myrtle Beach,
South Carolina."

The crew chief who was responsible for handling the liquid sodium spoke up.

"Mr. Robbins, sir. I don't mean to be disrespectful, but we may
have quite a problem with disassembly."

"What's that?" Robbins asked.

"Many of the assembly components have been, or currently are
contaminated with radioactive plutonium. In addition, we have an
extremely dangerous situation with the liquid sodium which is being used in the plutonium distillation and cooling process. It's very
unstable."

"I'm well aware of your concerns and I want you to know that
I have already addressed them. I'm bringing in a special team to
assist in the dismantlement process."

"Mr. Robbins, sir, I don't know if you really understand. If the
liquid sodium is exposed to air or more specifically oxygen, it'll explode and could level an entire city block...or more. It's extremely
dangerous."

"I'm well aware of that, and that's why as part of the dismantlement team, I have also included a group of technical advisors from the NSC that will be consulting in our endeavor."

The Berkeley-trained scientist had his worries allayed. He sat back down.

"Now gentlemen, I want you to enjoy yourselves. This evening we'll be having a party at my estate. And...I have to say that I've been saving this surprise for last. I've made special arrangements to fly each of you to Nassau once the dismantlement is complete. Your families will be flown in to meet you. You'll each have a two-week paid vacation at the Paradise Grand Hotel."

There was a second round of applause.

"Finally, " Robbins concluded, "over the next several days you'll take orders from General Andrei Tokarev, who is our Moscow liaison. General Tokarev has been assigned to our project by the National Security Commission." Andrei nodded his head in acknowledgment.

Robbins left. As he did a porter brought in additional food: Beluga Caviar, Oysters Rockefeller, Dom-Perignon, smoked salmon, sauted frog legs and escargot.

By Wednesday the teams had shipped the majority of the equipment, including all essential records. The last that was scheduled to be transported was the polymer-coated plutonium, the liquid sodium and the contaminated robotics hardware.

By 11:20 a.m. Andrei arrived with a 26-foot white Mercedes van. The plutonium polymer complex packed in lead-lined, airtight containers was cautiously loaded on board. Twenty minutes later the plant manager and Boriskov, who was designated second in command as Andrei's assistant, had one final meeting in the conference room with the staff. Boriskov's job was to assure Mr. Robbins that there had been absolutely no breaches in security. The scientists adequately reassured Boriskov of the project's utter secrecy.

With that business concluded, Boriskov opened a small satchel that he had set on the conference table. He withdrew an Israeli Uzi submachine gun, chambered in 9mm parabellum. He lightheartedly smiled at the 17 scientists and seven technical advisors. Mechanically he pumped out 192 rounds, expending six magazines, into the white lab-coated men. Empty cartridges flew everywhere. The brass shell casings bounced off the floor in ballet slow motion. By the time he was through, none of the scientists were recognizable. The room was splattered with blood. Boriskov thought that he had done a good job.

By 1:20 p.m. Boriskov had single handedly loaded each of the bodies into one of the two converted Ford Aerostar vans that were used to transport the men to and from the Robbins estate and the warehouse.

He then planted the C4 plastique charge next to the concrete bunker and the liquid sodium. With his remote, Boriskov had a detonating range of five miles.

The sky was fortuneteller clear. A solitary hoary seagull flew overhead. It circled the van as Boriskov pulled out, and followed the truck as it made its way down the coral gravel road. The warehouse once again looked like it had been deserted for 20 years.

Boriskov slowed his van on top of the I-95 and 836 cloverleaf, en route to Miami Harbor. From a distance of more than two miles he could see the disheveled warehouse sitting on river's edge. Looking downward while driving cautiously he activated the transmitter. He then flipped a toggle switch closing the circuit.

The first explosion was a small fireball. It blew the roof off the building. The second almost simultaneous detonation rocked the freeway and Miami in a 30-mile radius. When the five hundred pounds of liquid sodium was exposed to oxygen, the building and everything within a four block radius vaporized.

The pilings on which the cloverleaf stood rocked Boriskov's van. Then an air/sound shock wave slammed into the freeway and all the vehicles on top. Traffic ground to a halt. Within a few minutes cars slowly began their movement, but only slightly faster than a turtle walk as drivers gawked out of their windows at the massive blaze. Flames and clouds of noxious fumes filled the sky, lighting up the horizon in an ungodly hue.

By early evening, Boriskov and the van were on a 100-ton trash barge heading deep into the Atlantic towards the Grand Bahamas Bank. By 10:45 p.m., the barge's contents, including the van, were dumped into the ocean. Boriskov, a seaman capable of navigating the vessel on his own, emptied two shells each into the captain's and first mate's brains. He then tied them to an anchor chain and dropped them overboard. Then with the skill of an old salt, Boriskov motored the refuse barge to his rendezvous.

Boriskov slowly turned the vessel south and east, in part using the warehouse blaze as a navigation aid. Seventymiles off the coast, he could faintly smell the repugnant fumes coming for the vaporized warehouse. The fire was still raging. Liquid sodium infernos as he knew, were nearly impossible to put out. They pretty much had a life of their own. Just like Robbins' plan.

12

In the morning Alex watched the CNN newscast in his father's critical care room. Overhead the television softly buzzed. Alex was in fresh clothes. He had gotten them with the assistance of a police escort, who walked him to his car and suitcase. He was unnerved from last night.

"Why?"

His mother had her hair pressed to the side from sleeping in her chair. She was still sleeping when the first surgeon came in.

"We'll need to take your father for a CT Scan," the neurosurgeon said, as he and Alex stepped out of the room. "If the test comes back positive, if there's a subdural hematoma, which we suspect, we'll need to drill a burr hole to release the pressure."

"A mannitol drip?"

"We started that last night to bring down the pressure."

"When are you going to do the Cat Scan."

"Right now."

"Try not to wake up my mother. She's been up most of the night." Alex rubbed his tired eyes.

Despite his plea, Mary had heard him come into the room at five-thirty, but kept her head dropped in the semblance of sleep. She just didn't acknowledge her son. She didn't want him to worry about her.

When the gurney arrived to take Benjamin downstairs, Mary and Alex followed him to the CT-Scanner. The machine looked like a giant donut with Frankenstein gizmos attached to its sides. The hole was where Benjamin's head fit. A series of X-rays were taken. The pictures were what Alex and the neurosurgeon had anticipated.

A little after 7:30 a.m. Benjamin was rushed to emergency surgery. This time Alex was at his father's side. His head was shaved. Using stainless steel drills, a burr hole was punched into his skull with fluoroscopic guidance. The entire procedure took a little over an hour. By 12:45 p.m. Benjamin was back in his room, along with Alex and Mary. His odds had changed from 30 percent survival to 10.

"Do you think he'll make it?' Mary asked her son, hoping for a miracle.

"Dad'll be just fine. Everything went well."

"Are you sure?"

"I promise mom. Don't worry."

"Are you positive?" she asked no longer willing to hold back her tears. She was spent. The tangled complex of wires and tubes, monitors and IV bags gloomily hung from various shiny poles. They were akin to her frazzled feelings, sullen and morose.

"Mom, dad... 'll be just fine." Alex tried to be convincing, but before he could finish a nurse interrupted him.

"Dr. Seacourt, there are two men to see you."

"Tell them I'll be just a second."

"What's that about?" Mary asked.

"Oh, probably nothing. Maybe one of the other doctors. I don't know. I'll be right back."

"Okay."

But it wasn't. The men were suits. They didn't look like physicians.

Alex walked out of Room 8 and introduced himself.

"Detective Hirsh, Detective Smith, Homicide," Hirsh said making his introduction as he extended his hand. "Can we speak with you in private?"

"Sure. Whatever." The three of them left the Critical Care Unit and walked to one of the doctor's conference rooms.

Alex was tired. He stopped at a drinking fountain and had a sip of water. "*Funny*," he thought. "Tastes like almonds."

The cops sat down in two of the three generic hospital chairs.

"What can I do for you?" Alex asked as he closed the door behind him and sat down. Detectives Hirsh and Smith wore nearly identical hundred and fifty-dollar suits. They were a dull gray/brown. Detective Hirsh wore a white shirt with a maroon and gray-stripped tie. Detective Smith, a washed-out yellow button-down shirt with a burgundy, white and green tie. Their ties were clip-ons.

"Tell us about last night," Detective Hirsh asked, his notepad propped on his crossed right knee.

Alex told them how he was followed from the Critical Care Unit, and then outside on his way to the hotel. How he was shot at and chased through the park. He explained how he dodged the bullets, and then only in the nick of time was saved by an ambulance heading the wrong way toward the hospital's front entrance.

"Can you recognize your assailant if you saw him again?"

"I don't think so. I wasn't really paying attention to him when he got on the elevator."

"How tall was he?"

"Maybe 6 feet, maybe more. I'm not sure. I was tired. I've had a lot on my mind."

"What's that?"

"My father's heart attack and emergency surgery for a subdural hematoma. I presume you know that."

"Yes about the heart attack, but not the surgery."

"Were there any identifying marks?" the other detective asked.

"Nothing that I can remember."

"Are you sure?"

"Positive."

"If we show you some photos do you think you might recognize him?"

"Listen, I gave a whole report last night. You should have all that information in your files."

"We do," Hirsh replied, "I've read the report." Hirsh paused briefly to pull out a second small note pad that he had used last night. He scanned through his scribblings. "Could the man who tried to shoot you ever have been a patient?"

"I don't think so.... I have no idea. Why?"

Detective Hirsh ignored Alex's question. "Is there any reason to suspect why anyone would want to kill you?"

"No, not that I know of."

"Dr. Seacourt we understand your frustration, but the fact of the matter is that someone shot at you last night, and that's just not the kind of thing we're used to seeing in Ann Arbor."

"Look, why would I pull your chain. Someone just tried to kill me."

"People get shot at all the time in Detroit, but when someone follows you out of the hospital and tries to kill you; then there's got to be a motive and we want to know what it is"

"Yeah...you're right. I'm sorry. I know you're just trying to do your job."

"Do you have any idea who might be doing this and why?" Alex asked.

"We're still investigating." Detective Hirsh answered, flipping through his second pad. "I suggest that we find you a secure hotel tonight. We're going to assign you police protection, at least for the next couple of days. Do you have any objection to that Dr. Seacourt?"

"No, none." Alex replied, licking his lips slightly. They felt sticky, a little numb from the water. "I forgot how bad the drinking water tastes around here."

The agents and Alex met for two hours. They reviewed again in great detail the events of the previous night. They asked questions about Alex's past and about any enemies he might have had. They didn't show him any photos.

13

Miami

At 11:10 a.m. Jack Tandy had checked into the Coconut Grove Hotel under the name William J. Smith. He paid ninety-five dollars cash for the room. By 11:35 a.m. he was sitting on the bed beside the telephone. At precisely 12:00 noon the phone rang. The orders were inflexible. Tandy was to be at the bayside jogging park, directly across from the hotel, in exactly ten minutes. He was to walk to Station 19 of the Fit-Trail. Next to the oak "hamstring pull" workout station were two green park benches that faced the exercise platform. Tandy was to be there at exactly 12:20 p.m.

Tandy set the receiver back on its cradle. He was furious. It had been 32 years since Billy Robbins' death. The bomber was never apprehended. Now a ghost had come out of the machine to haunt him.

Tandy arrived two minutes before the preappointed time. He sat down on the bench, facing the exercise station. The Coconut Grove Marina was nestled behind the park, and Tandy could see a two-masted 50-foot schooner, with its mainsail and jib rolled in, motor slowly into the marina's cove. The breeze was faint and he could taste the ocean salt.

On the bench next to him was a young Cuban couple, with a small wicker picnic basket. They were on their lunch. He was a shoe store manager at Kinney's and she a nurse at Mercy Hospital. They had laid out their bologna, Swiss cheese and mustard sandwiches, and four slices of ripe honeydew melon on a red and white checkered cloth napkin. Next to them they had a Panasonic boom box stereo/CD player, with attachable speakers. They were listening to a jazz station, WTMI 93.1 FM. A Louie Armstrong classic saturated the air. In the background Jack could hear a faint scratch on the '32 vinyl recording .

Two joggers puffing, sweat beading down their foreheads into terry cloth sock bands, and their tee-shirts soaked, began their Station 19 exercises. 20 hamstring and 30 sit and pull stretches later, the two generation Xers continued their fitness run.

After they left, Louie Armstrong finished. The 12:30 p.m. news report prattled on. Tandy could faintly hear, "The pierside warehouse explosion that rocked downtown Miami has been attributed to improper storage of more than 10,000 gallons of turpentine. Authorities have not ruled out arson... Police Commissioner Laird stated that the abandoned warehouse may have been the target of vandals who have been terrorizing downtown Miami and Little Havana over the last several months....The fumes from the fire, paralyzed traffic in Downtown Miami for nearly four hours until firefighters were able to contain the blaze..."

And then from behind Jack came a voice. "Don't turn around." Tandy wanted to jump, but instead he was paralyzed. An ominous breeze picked-up. It blew through Jack's hair.

"We need to handle this problem," the man said.

"What problem?"

"Now, now Jack. We know what problem."

"How much?"

"Oh...we're a little more eager to do some housekeeping now that our memory is jogged. Take care of old business, huh?"

"How much, goddamn you?"

"To finish business..." the man responded. Tandy began to turn around, but the man firmly grasped him, clasping both of his hands onto Tandy's earlobes and tugged down on them painfully. Jack was unable to move.

"$250,000? Is that what you want? That was the price last time.... Wasn't it?"

"Hmmm."

"Goddammit, this is no fucking game. How much?"

The man continued to tightly hold Tandy locked in a throbbing vice-grip.

"I'll get back with you in a couple of days." The man let go of Tandy's earlobes. They stung.

"Wait a second," Tandy said. There was no answer. "Wait a second!" Slowly, Tandy turned his head around. The man was gone. Tandy heard a car door slam. A dark, late-model vehicle that been parked just behind the bench squealed off.

"You son-of-a-bitch!" Tandy yelled rising to his feet and clenching his fist, "You motherfucking son-of-a-bitch!"

The man knew exactly what he was doing. He stirred up old wounds. He poked a red-hot stick into the scar. He was making Tandy pay for his sins, as deeply and darkly as he could.

In the background the radio continued to drone. "Investigators have focused renewed attention to earlier, unsolved cases of arson in Little Havana and Hialeah. This includes a renewed investigation into a fire at the Havana Palace, a Cuban-American restaurant that killed seven people..."

"The fucker is going to want a million bucks." Tandy said. "The motherfucker — thirty goddamn years later; and now the motherfucker is going to want a million bucks. I know it!"

The worst part was the anticipation. Not knowing when he would be contacted next. Making him think about it. Think about the unsolved murders, the bombing that killed two bodyguards, Billy Robbins, his wife and six of his eight children. The car bombing that left Bart Robbins a burn victim monster, and his sister a brain damaged imbecile. The bombing that still had suspects and had gone unsolved for all these years. The assassination that had *no statute of limitations*.

Jack was going to stew. And Jack full well knew he had to pay up, no matter what the cost.

14

Jackson Memorial Hospital, 7:16 a.m., Tuesday, September 21, 1999 Miami, Florida

Anna Lopez came to the hospital early to see her mother Guadeloupe who had come in overnight with a gallbladder attack. She had been warned about eating too many potato chips and fatty foods, but the night before she gobbled down two helpings of seafood paella, an avocado and some chicaron. By 10:30 p.m. her stomach was killing her. She was writhing in pain, bending over nearly touching her toes and then curled up into a ball as the waves of agony struck.

Guadeloupe was admitted to the surgical floor to have her gallbladder removed. She was sedated, given Demerol injections for the pain and scheduled to have surgery at 10:20 a.m. Dr. Vanguard was her surgeon.

In error, Anna parked at the N.W. 12th Avenue parking structure. She should have parked off Bob Hope Road, which would have been a shorter walk. Due to this mistake Anna had to enter the main hospital through the Mental Health Building. This made her uncomfortable, walking through the "psyche" hospital. Actually, it gave her a headache.

In route, Anna decided she needed to take two aspirins. She had the start of a throbbing migraine. She stopped at one of the "psycho ward's" drinking fountains and in one big gulp swallowed the pills. Going down it tasted funny, almost metallic, like bad nuts.

Bob Carr, a thirty three year old janitor, was just getting off his shift. He had worked all night waxing and then buffing the West Wing floors. His shoulders and back were sore. He knew that when he got home he would just miss his two kids who would have left for school, peddling off on their ten-speed bicycles. Bob was divorced, but had custody of his children. He loved and adored them. If it was not for the help of his sister, Susanne who lived with him, he would have never been able to make it.

Bob changed his clothes. He dumped his dirty uniform into a canvas employee laundry basket, and put on a gray pair of sweat bottoms and a Miami Dolphins sweatshirt top. He slipped into a pair of Avia Crosstrainers that had fresh-cut grass stuck in their tread. He figured that he would drive down to Key Biscayne and jog ten miles while it was still relatively cool.

Just the thought of getting going, running the jogging track, parched his mouth. Normally he would grab a soda before he left work, but the employee vending machine was broken. So, Bob had a drink of water from the drinking fountain. He thought that it tasted funny.

Dr. Harold Kreisler was a Jewish doctor who had moved to Miami with his Israeli born wife and their three year old daughter. Harold was from the Bronx and met Rachel at synagogue when she first immigrated to New York to study International Affairs at Columbia. She was working on her masters. He was completing residency in Internal Medicine.

Harold liked Miami, the sunshine and his staff position at Jackson Memorial Hospital. He was teaching part-time at the University of Miami Medical School, which was a boost to his sometimes fragile ego.

Last night, Harold was on call. This was a once-every-five-day ordeal with his medical group. Harold was up most of the night with his seven admissions, as he supervised his two first and one second year residents. Now, however, it was time to go home, hit the sack for a couple of hours until he had to come back to the office and see patients from noon until 5:30, but more than likely 7 or even 8. He never turned anyone away.

On his way to the employee parking lot, just in front of the Royce Building School of Nursing, Harold stopped for a drink of water. Today the water tasted extraordinarily bad. Of course, the water at Jackson Memorial Hospital was always a little foul.

Slowly, nefariously, molecule by molecule, a cleverly hidden device was releasing the plastic polymer coated plutonium into the hospital's water supply. Immediately, as the single layer granules came into contact with the water, the plastic polymer dissolved. Then, the plutonium instantly combined with the water molecules to form plutonium dioxide.

The plutonium dioxide pulsated through the hospital's water like a cobra slinking through deep Indonesian river grass. Molecule by molecule, the alpha emitter coerced its way through the plumbing, circulating throughout the hospital, and more.

Plutonium named after Pluto, the God of the Underworld, would soon be everywhere. Less than one-millionth of a gram, an invisible particle, was a carcinogenic dose. That's all that was needed. With just one pound, there was enough poison to induce lung cancer in every person on earth.

The attack had started.

7:56 a.m.

The first person got sick. A nurse in pediatrics, and then another. Nausea quickly ran rampant throughout the pediatric ward. Two nurses, who had just finished their morning coffee, ran to the bathroom to vomit.

Jenny Dupre, the change nurse, couldn't quite figure out what she and her LPN assistant Karen Ludow got sick on. Maybe it was the left over pastries they ate?

8:12 a.m.

Mary Bryum was five months pregnant. She had come for her appointment with her OB-GYN at 8:30. She was early. She liked her tacky blue-and-red plaid maternity smock and was reading Better Homes and Gardens when she first felt dizzy and noticed blood ooze out of her nose in a small trickle. She thought that the nosebleed was probably a normal part of her pregnancy. She already had two kids and she had nosebleeds with her first child. She did have a slight cold and was blowing her nose a little more than usual.

Suddenly, Mary felt faint. While reading her magazine, she keeled over onto the floor.

8:19 a.m.

Dr. Eddy, an ophthalmologist, was in the middle of cataract surgery at the Bascom Palmer Eye Institute when he first felt ill. Maybe he had been standing too long. This was his fourth surgery of the morning that began at 5:00 a.m. His assistant, Dr. Woods, finished the procedure on Mrs. Hudson while Dr. Eddy went to the bathroom and threw up. Eddy's skin had turned a pale white. After he stopped vomiting, he noticed a tinge of blood in the toilet. He had begun to bleed from the gums and nose.

By 9:30 a.m. so many people had suddenly taken ill at Jackson Memorial Hospital that the hospital administrator, who himself was also feeling queasy, needed help. Nurses, patients, visitors were falling to the floor like flies to flypaper. And worst of all, there was no apparent explanation.

George Reeve, the hospital administrator did what he had trained for, but never anticipated or expected: he declared an emergency and called the the Centers for Disease Control in Atlanta, and requested their assistance.

By 10:15 a.m. one third of the Jackson Memorial Hospital staff was sick. Reeve knew he had a major crisis on his hands. He called an emergency meeting of his administrative staff, the heads of each medical department including all three pathologists on duty and their four residents. The conference room, which normally held eighteen was packed to its gills with thirty-two professionals, nearly half of them ill.

"Doctors, gentlemen, ladies," Reeves said raising his initial-embroidered handkerchief to his nose to catch the blood droplets, "We have a crisis on our hands. I need to be frank. Within the last two hours a significant number of our staff have gotten sick with a flu-like disease. I'm not quite sure what's going on, or what you suggest we do. But whatever we do we need to do it immediately."

Dr. Golding, the Director of Pathology with an M.D. from John Hopkins and a Ph.D. from Baylor in Epidemiology, spoke. "I believe that what we may be seeing is an atypical form of Legionnaire's Disease. Legionnaire's Disease, for those of you who don't know, is an acute febrile respiratory illness caused by a Legionella pneumophila, a bacterium, and accounts for 1 to 8 percent of all pneumonia's and about 4 percent of fatal hospital pneumonia's. The natural habitat of Legionella is water: lakes, creeks and rivers. Major outbreaks in hospitals have been associated with aerosolized organisms from evaporative condensers in improperly cleaned air conditioning systems.

"Though I do have to say, that a strain of Vitro Cholera, or cholera, can also cause the symptoms that we are seeing, and did so in Zaire in 1992 with the El Tor biotype."

"To recap," Dr. Whitaker, a Pathologist and Golding's associate stated, "I think that it's safe to say that the symptomatology that we are seeing — the diffuse abdominal pain, nose bleeds, bleeding gums, double vision, joint pain, fainting episodes, nausea, ringing in the ears, and diarrhea may very well be due to Legionella. So far, in the last hour, we've had over forty calls from various departments, nursing stations, etc. asking for help."

"I would agree with your provisional diagnosis," Dr. Webster an Internist interjected.

"How many people do you estimate have been affected?" the administrator asked. "And what immediate steps do we need to take? It seems that from my reports the epidemic has already affected one third of our staff, not to mention patients and visitors...and who knows how many more."

"I think," Dr. Hoskins, an irreverent longed-haired forty-two year old who was Chief of Infectious Diseases said, "that we need to consider transporting all of our patients out of the hospital and declaring an emergency."

"I've already been on the phone with the CDC. They're sending a team down from Atlanta. In addition, I've placed a call to the mayor and the governor. Right now I'm waiting to hear back from the governor, to see what the political implications are and what he wants us..."

"The governor. Screw the governor! We have an epidemic on our hands, with either legionella or cholera, and we damn well better do something right now before a whole bunch more people get sick!" Hoskins demanded.

"Look," Dr. Gaddis, the Chief of Cardiology said intending to throw around his self-important weight, "I don't know about most of you, but I have some pretty ill patients here that are in no shape to be moved."

"I have a question," the Director of Nursing Rene Lapont asked. She was a powder keg with her staff, and would butt heads with any doctor or administrator; but she was intimidated when she spoke in front of a large group, "Let's presume..." she cleared her voice nervously, "the worst scenario. Let's suppose that we need to evacuate the hospital. I mean, worst scenario logistically how do you propose that we do this? How do we evacuate the hospital without panicking the patients?"

"I don't know," administrator Reeve answered with a concerned voice, "That's really the purpose of this meeting. To decide a course of action, and if we need to evacuate the hospital to decide how we go about doing it."

The debate was lively and hotheaded. The staff was split 50/50—to sit and wait until the CDC arrives and they make a recommendation, or to start moving patients out immediately. Everyone was in agreement to *not* notify the press.

Finally, after half an hour of arguing and disagreement on even how to go about *deciding what to do,* Malcom Kingston, a first year pathology resident raised his hand and said what turned out to be the fatal question. Malcom, was half-British and half-Japanese. His parents had immigrated to the United States before he was born. Malcom's grandparents lived in Hiroshima during World War II and died when the atomic bomb was dropped.

As a result of this, Malcom had a morbid fascination with World War II and the bombing of Hiroshima and Nagasaki. He had studied the annihilation of the atomic bombings and the murder of 140,000 people in Hiroshima and 70,000 in Nagasaki. He had learned about the effects of radiation poisoning on the survivors and their offspring. He had vicariously lived his grandparents' and their families' and relatives' misery.

"I don't mean to be disrespectful," Malcom said, timid and even more shy than the Director of Nursing, Rene Lapont, "but this might sound real stupid..." He hesitated not wanting to sound stupid, "But this..."

"Speak up, don't be shy," the associate administrator coached.

"...I think that what we're seeing is radiation poisoning."

"Radiation poisoning?" Chief of Staff Dr. Wright said incredulously, "How would anyone get radiation poisoning at Jackson Memorial Hospital. That's ridiculous!"

"Um...you can get it if someone puts it here. My grandparents were killed in Hiroshima in 1945. I've extensively studied the effects of radiation and radiation poisoning. I mean...I don't want to sound stupid, but this is one possibility we should consider."

"Jesus Christ. What if?" Dr. Hoskins replied, a little freaked-out.

As insane as Malcom's notion was, he had an idea that needed to be followed up while at the same time the source for the Legionella infection and/or cholera needed to be ferreted out.

The first obstacle in investigating Malcom's hypothesis was obtaining a Geiger counter. However, once that problem was solved using a little ingenuity, and borrowing a device that a genetic engineering professor had cubbyholed as memorabilia from a long gone era; *the hospital realized that they were in for the worst possible news!*

15

The Ann Arbor, Michigan police officer outside the Coronary Care Unit was in his mid-twenties, had a chiseled jaw in need of a shave, and had beady eyes.

He paced back and forth in front of the double-door entrance to the Coronary Care Unit. And though there were two entrances that needed to be patrolled, Officer Watson just marched in front of the east set. As a precaution and in violation of fire code he locked the west doors. No one was going to get in or out without him seeing them.

Inside, Alex had kept vigil all day. It was night. He was sick to his stomach about his father's condition. The overhead television set flickered. Mary left the TV on with chatter coming out of the speaker. Her philosophy was that even though her husband was unresponsive, at least he should be able to hear what the world was about.

Mary was his spouse of nearly forty-five years. She was all that was good in motherhood and marriage. She was loyal, and had never strayed. And despite hard times that they may have had for five or six years, while Alex was first in college, Mary stuck to her guns and was a devoted wife.

Maybe it was the seven year itch that happened at seventeen years. Maybe it was just that Mary needed to "find herself." This is what she eventually did.

When she and Benjamin were first married, she was a school teacher. Alex wasn't born until Mary and Benjamin were in their sixth year of wedlock. And despite their attempts to have other children Alex remained an only child.

Eventually, Mary went back to school. She got her master's degree and almost her Ph.D., but never wrote a dissertation. She was not quite sure why she didn't do that, except that it was really a meaningless endeavor. By the time Mary would have needed to write her dissertation, she was already nestled into a comfortable job of teaching children with learning disabilities.

Maybe it was the frustration of not being more, or maybe of not having additional children and providing Alex with more companions, or her "paternal" instinct that was put on hold.

Nonetheless, trouble brewed when Alex went off to college, and didn't quiet down until he finished medical school. But those days were years ago, and Mary wasn't quite sure about the whys and hows. Maybe it was she, or perhaps Benjamin; but in any event they had fixed their chasm without walking or running away from their commitment.

"Alex," she nudged.

"Yes, mom," he replied as he opened tired eyes. Alex had fallen asleep. It was nearly 11:00 p.m. It had been 24 hours since the operation, and Benjamin had still not wakened. His condition was unchanged and critical. However, the longer he went without dying, the better his chance of living. Alex knew that, and in that thought there was hope.

In the background CNN droned. "A Legionnaire's epidemic has stuck downtown Miami, emanating from Jackson Memorial Hospital. Authorities from the Centers for Disease Control have been called in...speculation as to the source of the Legionnaire's Disease is still uncertain. Some experts believe that this airborne organism may have been introduced into the hospital through the air conditioning system or contaminated employee shower heads."

"Alex don't you think that maybe you should go back to your hotel room? There's nothing more you can do here."

"Mom, do you really want me to leave?"

"Please. I think it would be best."

"Are you sure?"

"Yes. Please go. I'll be fine."

"Maybe so," Alex had made arrangements with the hospital to have a cot brought into his father's room, where Mary would sleep at night. Since Benjamin's hospitalization Mary had not left her husband's side. In fact, she was not even aware of the fact that a police officer was posted outside of the Coronary Care Unit. Alex made it a point that none of the nurses would mention a word to her about it.

Alex left. There was nothing more that he could do. The Ann Arbor Police had gotten him a room at another hotel. They had changed his rental car and registered both the car and his hotel room under a pseudonym. Alex left the hospital with an officer. He exited out of the far end of the hospital, at the HVAC building.

Despite his companion, his walk to his rental car was lonely. Alex wasn't sure how he was supposed to cope with his father's possible death. As he walked through the HVAC building he began to cry.

"Why him God?" But there was no answer. Charlton Heston did not come down from the heavens as a gray-bearded, robed Moses, parting the Red Sea. He did not faith heal the dead and fix the injured. This was real life, with real pain and genuine anguish. There was nothing that Alex could do about anything. *At least not yet....*

16

3:45 p.m.
Jackson Memorial Hospital

The governor had declared a national emergency. The National Guard, Miami Police, Dade County Sheriff's Office, State Police, FBI, ATF and Army were called in.

Wearing gas masks and chemical warfare suits, the National Guard and Army had evacuated the hospital except for a few extremely ill patients in the Critical Care Unit and Intensive Care Unit.

The first officials from the Centers for Disease Control were on the scene almost immediately. Investigators from the Nuclear Regulatory Commission were due to arrive within the hour.

Obsolete and seldom-used Geiger counters were gathered from eclectic sources: old civil defense bomb shelters, the University of Miami Florida, International University, Florida State and the University of Florida research facilities. Even the National Guard had a few 30-year-old relics.

Within a one mile radius of the hospital, extending in a line ten blocks in all directions from a square made up of N.W. 14th Street, N.W. 8th Avenue, N.W. 19th Street and N.W. 12th Avenue, the streets were cordoned off.

Special agents from the Nuclear Regulatory Commission arrived with forty men from Washington, D.C., with exotic equipment and state-of-the-art scintillation detectors, which were significantly more accurate than Geiger counters. The "space suits" they wore looked like they were from NASA or a 1960s science fiction film.

The FBI arrived in high-profile strength and enlarged the corridor to a two mile radius. The press went berserk with reporters flooding into Miami from across the country — Europe, Asia, Australia, Indonesia, New Zealand, Central and South America. The radiation closing of Jackson Memorial Hospital turned into a media circus. As of yet, no one realized the gravity of the situation.

Regional Director Bob Hunt, the commander for the joint NRC, ATF and FBI twenty-man purge team planned their assault into the hospital.

"We'll divide into four teams of five," Commander Hunt the seasoned veteran ordered from the team's base of operation in The South Florida Blood Service, immediately east of the hospital. "We'll have a team enter from the Fred Cowell Mall." He pointed to the map of the University/Jackson Memorial Medical Center. The twenty-man sortie squad gathered around a conference table. They had practiced for this eventuality for years. "An insertion team will enter through the North Wing of the hospital, one coming in from the Rehabilitation Center and one from the South Wing."

"Any idea what the source is?" Ron Dupard an NRC Special Projects agent asked.

"Negative. All I can say is that we have a motherfucking hot situation."

The insertion groups disbursed from their football huddle ready for their big third down play. Hunt led his group, Alpha Team, in through the south entrance double sliding doors. Radiation levels were low but significant.

"We've got alpha radiation," Murphy the burly assistant said, reading his scintillation detector. "Plutonium!"

"This is Alpha team to Bravo, Charlie, Delta, over." Hunt transmitted as their group slowly pierced deeper into the hospital's bowels.

"Bravo reads you."

"Charlie here."

"Affirmative for Delta," the three answered in turn from their different locations within the hospital.

"We've got alpha radiation," Donaldson, Bravo team leader from the west radioed.

"Roger, so do we," Charlie team responded, scanning the north lobby entrance.

"We, also," transmitted agent Higgens for Delta team.

"It's all over this goddamn place!" Bravo said. "We're reading ninety-plus normal levels."

"What do you think?" Hunt asked Murphy as they penetrated deeper into hospital's guts, their detectors going crazy as they scanned the lobby.

"I think that it's in either the air ducts or..."

"The plutonium can't be in the ventilation system. Not with these kinds of readings," Hunt interrupted.

They walked past the lobby down a double-wide hallway toward the hospital's center. Murphy flashed the detector in all directions. He looked confused. They walked farther. The levels were dangerously high. "How much time do you think we have? Safetywise?"

Murphy looked down at the meter reading on his elaborate device. "Maybe 15 minutes. No more, unless you don't want to have any more kids."

Hunt looked back. The glare of the overhead fluorescent light shined down and reflected off Murphy's face plate. "Make it 20."

"You're the boss."

"Think it's in the air?"

"No. The readings aren't consistent with that. They'd be more uniform. But damn, I'm confused. The counts are inconsistently high and all over the fucking place." Murphy answered waving his detector wand in all directions throughout the corridor.

They continued their probe, fruitlessly. They came upon the hospital laboratory and entered. Still the readings were diffuse. Next, they scanned the ten operating rooms. Similar readings were found, but not quite as high. They entered several patient rooms, two doctor-patient conference rooms, the hospital administration offices and a record room filled to capacity with charts.

"This is Charlie to Alpha, over."

"Alpha."

"Checking in commander."

"What do ya got?"

"Nada."

"Where have ya been?"

"Everything north of center on the main and second floors. We're hitting the third floor now."

"Nothing?"

"Nada.... Chief we're going to have to bail soon. We have 90 plus normal readings going intermittently as high as 120."

"Affirmative"

"Commander, I've got no idea where this shit is."

"Anyone else?" Hunt asked, frustrated.

"That's affirmative," Bravo replied. Delta confirmed the same.

"Gentlemen, you can withdraw at your own discretion. I want everyone safe. Don't make it any more than 20 minutes, total," Hunt ordered, looking at his extra-large digital watch that he had strapped to outside of his space suit. Hunt needed to be sure that he could gauge his insertion and egress time. They needed to leave soon.

"Boss I think I've got something," Murphy said as he motioned Hunt in his direction. Hunt and his team followed Murphy's lead, as Murphy honed in on an increase in activity. The meter reading grew fast, "110+, 120+, 130+...170+ They swung around a corridor, and toward a patient's room. They could hear a faint sound through their external auditory devices "210+, 220...300+."

Faintly, there was a trickling quaver.

They entered the room, and Murphy's counter went nuts. He followed the trail of radioactivity to its source: a sink in the bathroom where the faucet was dripping ever so slightly.

"Jesus Christ! It's in the water!"

By 6:30 p.m. the president of the United States had declared a national emergency. President Bill Climan's concern was not so much the University of Miami/Jackson Memorial Medical Center, nor the possible destruction of a $400 million medical complex as a result of the radiation sabotage. He was concerned about the water that had left the hospital through the drainage system and where it went from there.

How many people would have, could have been affected? Where and how would the plutonium enter the food chain? He had been briefed. Plutonium had a *half life of more than 24,000 years*. And its breakdown product, americium, was even more potent. How many people may have drunk the tainted water?

And then...the food chain. The contaminated water being ingested by fish, birds, plants and mammals, later to find its way back into eggs, meat, vegetables and milk.

President Climan had a major crisis on his hands, probably much worse than Malcolm's Hiroshima. And...*what about copycats?*

Immediately the hospital's water was turned off. The exit flow was stopped. But where had the toxic water gone? To the Miami Waste Water Treatment Plant, and then to the Miami River and into the Atlantic?

Eventually the poison's wellspring was traced, but only after using three teams of twenty men, working in 20-minute intervals. It took them a day and a half. The source was discovered with a MX-2908 B-1 Mitsubishi robot. In the damp and gloom of the basement of the hospital's physical plant, welded onto a cold-water ingress pipe, hidden in a web of piping and fiberglass insulation was the doomsday machine.

The mechanism was the size of a small television set. It was controlled remotely by a radio transmitter. The device had a large feeder tank, capable of holding a significant amount of plutonium. The feeder tank was empty except for a glistening plastic-like substance that only faintly coated its inner lining. There was no sign, or evidence of radioactivity in the doomsday machine. Approximately two to three feet from the mechanism as water flowed into the hospital, however, were the first signs of radioactivity. This was where, in the chemical reaction, the plastic polymer had dissolved and the plutonium converted to plutonium dioxide. The levels were beyond the meter's highest reading, 300-plus.

The White House, Washington, D.C.

"Mr. President," said Secretary of State Richard Hackwell a robust man in his late 50s. "We have a grave problem that we'll need to jump on immediately."

President Climan listened intently, more aware than any of his cabinet appointees of the possible ramifications of the Miami disaster. The President and his cabinet were meeting in the Oval Office.

"Mr. President," Secretary of Defense James R. Walsh spoke. He had hurriedly assembled a presentation. Walsh signaled to his aide to dim the lights.

"Mr. President, this is the situation as we see it." Walsh used a pen that beamed a "pointer" light onto the projection screen which was set up to the left of their conference table. There was an aerial satellite view of Miami, the Atlantic and its environs. "We believe that, taking into account the amount of plutonium found in the granular substance lining the walls of the device, and we are making a presumption based on the volume of the device's container," another photograph was projected. This one was an image of the doomsday machine. "We estimate that fifty pounds of plutonium, plus or minus two ounces, has been released into Jackson Memorial's water supply." Walsh flipped to a third slide. This was a map of the city of Miami. In the center was Fort Lauderdale, north was Palm Beach and Key West was south and west. A thick black circle surrounded downtown Miami.

"How bad is it?"

"That depends on your point of view. From a public relations perspective, its a nightmare," Walsh replied.

"What about containment?" the President asked.

"Already in progress," the Secretary of Defense responded with certainty. "We're in the process of evacuating the City of Miami and its environs within a 25-mile radius of the hospital. Apparently Jackson Memorial's septic system drains relatively directly, with some minor exceptions, into the City's Recycling Plant. And we already have that under wraps."

"How much of the plutonium could have gotten into the environment outside of normal drainage sources?"

"Well, working on the presumption that the device was full, and that a total of fifty pounds of plutonium was released into the hospital's water supply; I think that we can contain and recover about forty pounds."

"80 percent. What about the other 20?"

Walsh was quiet for a moment. The cabinet members knew that there were no certainties, and if there was one, Walsh would give the President and his cabinet the exact odds of there being one. 80 percent wasn't the answer they wanted to hear.

"Where'd the water go?"

"Most of it to the Waste Water Treatment Plant in downtown Miami. We can pretty much cut off water going in and out of the city. With the exception of the Miami River and the Intercoastal we should have the situation under control within 48 hours."

"What about the unaccounted ten pounds?" President Climan asked.

"Human consumption, environmental liberation: leakage into the soil, into the water tables, the air."

"Long-term prognosis?"

Walsh moved onto the next slide and looked at Secretary of State Hackwell. They knew the answer that was about to be pro-

jected. Walsh read the slide, "We anticipate, *best scenario*:
"Deaths to date - 5
Anticipated deaths within the next 48 hours - **249**
Anticipated deaths within one week - **9,547**
Anticipated deaths within one month - **18,998**
Potential contaminated individuals -
Symptomatic (sick or ill) - **28,981**
Asymptomatic (no signs of illness, but victims may have
    plutonium atoms within their bodies; most likely
    bone marrow and liver disease in later life, or risk
    of passing on genetically damaged chromosomes)
    -**139,800.**

"Excuse me," President Climan said calmly, "Is that last number correct, **139,800?**"

"Mr. President, I'm sorry to say, but we believe it is."

President Climan leaned back in his leather chair, sighed, and then drew in a deep breath of polluted Washington, D.C. air. "That's a **total of 190,000** people affected in one way or another? Is that correct?"

"That's correct Mr. President, and those numbers are conservative. Especially the **139,800.** The problem that we have, is not with the 80 percent containment, but where the other 20 percent goes. We just don't know how, where, and when it might came back into the food chain."

"Is there any cure?"

Walsh was definitive in his answer, *"I'm sorry to say, No."*

President Climan looked back at Secretary of State, Hackwell, "Richard, who's responsible?"

"Mr. President, we don't know. No one's taken responsibility."

"Mr. President, if I may," Walsh said respectfully. He projected a fifth slide, "These are a list of organizations that might be responsible."

Again Walsh read down the list, first explaining with his caveat, "We need to consider not only who would have motive, but also who would have access to this large amount of plutonium. Clearly plutonium is available on the black market. The source of the plutonium could have been anyone: China, France, North Korea, Iraq, Iran, Israel, India, Libya, Pakistan or Russia. More than likely, however, the plutonium came out of Russia.

"As far as who was responsible, that's a good question. The extreme leftist terrorist groups have almost died out as we have known them in the past. Gone are Carlos and his Soviet, Marxist and leftist Palestinian allies who would and could have done something like this.

"The inheritors today are, unfortunately, the Islamic extremists such as the Hizaballah and Hamas and their sponsors, including Iran and Libya. Of course, there is also the possibility that a radical nation like Iran, Libya or Iraq could produce the plutonium and hand it over to a terrorist organization. We'll need to take a look at a number of cult groups similar to the Japanese Aum Shinri Kyo (Supreme Truth) cult that was responsible for the nerve gas subway attack that killed eight and injured 4,700 in early 1995." Walsh then recited a number of other fringe terrorist elements that he thought capable.

"Anyone in the United States."

"Lots of possibilities, including the Coeur d' Alene Idaho Neo-Nazi White Supremacists to mention just one of many."

"Could Castro be behind this?"

"No way. Fidel has too much to lose with the unbridling of his previously closed borders..."

"That's enough," President Climan cut Walsh off. "Any ransom demands?"

"None, Mr. President," Chief of Staff Colin Brown replied. "Specifically, we haven't heard from any group yet who has requested money in lieu of avoiding another Miami situation."

"So, Brown," President Climan looked perturbed at Chief of Staff Brown for not giving him some suspects that he could sink his teeth into. "When do you anticipate a demand?"

"Anytime. And we're ready."

17

The Kremlin, Moscow

Russian President Nikolay I. Cheka was livid when he heard the news from the United States. This could not have come at a worse time. Russia was cash starved. It desperately needed an infusion of foreign currency. And of all the times for some crackpot, fringe group to screw around with plutonium, this was the worst possible time. This whole situation could really put a monkey wrench into President Cheka's plans.

The United States and Russia had just ratified the Russian-American Free Trade Treaty Act. The two countries had agreed as one of the Act's provisions to, over the next five years, build 35 breeder reactors in Russia.

Nuclear technologists had come to look at plutonium as substitute for uranium in nuclear reactor energy production. To eliminate the need for uranium, the "fast breeder reactor" or breeder reactor was developed. The average doubling rate, that is, of producing from uranium twice the amount of plutonium that the reactor started out with, is thirty to fifty years.

In 1979, France's breeder reactor, the Super-Phoenix, was expected to take sixty years to duplicate its plutonium load.

However, in June 1992, the French government indefinitely postponed operations of the Super-Phoenix because they were worried about a nuclear meltdown and/or explosion, and the lack of adequate means to handle a liquid sodium fire.

Furthermore, Germany closed its fast breeder reactor in 1991, and abandoned its reprocessing plant. Britain was planning on closing its fast breeder prototype immediately.

The politics of breeder reactors had been hard and fast. In 1977, President Jimmy Carter declared a moratorium on the operation of commercial reprocessing plants and breeder reactors.

It was first through Bush and now President Climan that Russian President Cheka was able to convince the United States Department of Energy to assist with the construction of a new generation of breeder reactors in Russia — this despite a public outcry by a number of American and world environmental and anti-nuclear groups.

The plutonium to fuel the breeder reactors and also more than likely the same plutonium that was used in Miami, could have come from any of thousands of spent uranium fuel rods stockpiled in storage pools throughout the world, or less likely, from the stockpiles of decommissioned Russian nuclear warheads.

President Cheka knew that the operation of breeder reactors was much more hazardous than that of ordinary commercial reactors. The cores are made of plutonium 239, surrounded by a blanket of uranium 238 which captures neutrons and is converted to more plutonium. Once out of control, a fission reaction in a breeder could cause not only a melt-down, but also a full-fledged nuclear explosion, which the nuclear industry called a "rapid disassembly accident." In addition, the breeders are cooled with liquid sodium, rather than heavy water, a substance that ignites spontaneously when exposed to air and therefore is highly dangerous in its own right.

It had taken President Cheka forever to forge a workable deal with President Climan.

It was a good deal for both sides. The United States saw an opportunity to Americanize Russia, thus extending its economic sphere of influence; while Russia would enjoy the economic benefits.

The democratization process was difficult. Russia was failing and inflation was spiraling. If this failure was complete, it could mean the communists regain power.

Recent Russian history had been one of turmoil, upheaval and change; and that was what Cheka wanted to stop.

The Soviet Union had mutated into the Commonwealth of Independent States. And now President Cheka was in power. The world could be either his oyster or onion.

"Who's responsible?" President Cheka sternly asked Larrenty P. Yezhov, the veteran KGB director. Yezhov had survived Krushev, Brezhnev, Andrepov, Gorbachev, Yelstin and now Cheka. He leafed through a pile of reports that he had spread out on the conference table where he and the cabinet ministers sat. Cheka was directly across from him and just within arm's reach.

"I'm not sure, but..." he said as he flipped through reconnaissance reports in a legal-size file folder, "the Americans think that the plutonium came from us."

Cheka was outraged. He made no attempt to conceal his anger, "Who did it?"

Yezhov scanned through another thick file until he came to a subsection report. He pulled the report out of the dossier and flipped through a few pages. He gazed through his bifocals. He closed the folder and pushed it away. Deliberately Yezhov removed his glasses and set them on the table. The twelve other ministers were looking intently at him, "KGB...ex KGB," Yezhov said with authority.

Cheka did not get to be President of Russia by being stupid. "Who specifically did this, and are there going to be more... can we stop them?"

"My guess Mr. President... is that there will be more. As far as who, I'm not sure. And can we stop him... them? My answer is simple. We damn well better, before the Americans do, otherwise I would anticipate the worst."

Cheka knew what the worst was: Loss of the breeder reactor program and a tumbling down of the political alliance that took his country and predecessors years to mold. It would be a reason for the American conservative right to cut-off the free trade pipeline secured by GATT, and the 1995 Russian-American Free Trade Treaty Act.

"How many dead?"

"As of now 1,840."

"How many anticipated?"

"With morbidity figures included, which are important because anyone who has ingested plutonium can have genetically malformed children as an end result...dead maybe ten to twenty thousand; adversely affected maybe 100,000."

"Mother Russia." Cheka stood and looked out his office window and down onto a small courtyard. Twelve strutting gray and white pouter pigeons had landed. They were pecking at seedlings that had fallen off a nearby bush. "It's my understanding that there was 50 lbs of plutonium in the device."

"That's correct."

"How much total plutonium do you think is out there?"

"That's also hard to tell, but worst scenario..."

Yezhov stood and carried the report around the conference table and personally handed the numbers to President Cheka. Cheka's gut wrenched and he lost all color in his face.

18

Ann Arbor, Michigan

D r. Alex Seacourt went back to his eighth floor Campus Inn hotel room. The room had twin queen beds. He used one to lay
his clothes on. The other bed he slept in. The carpet was gray-beige
and between the beds was an end table and a lamp with a push-
button telephone. The weight of the world had been resting on his
shoulders, and he felt as if it would never let up.

Alex pulled out the upper of the two end table drawers looking for a Yellow Pages so that he could order a pizza. He hadn't
really eaten anything all day. He was famished, yet at the same time
not hungry. His stomach felt empty. There was a searing knot in it.

Instead of the phone book was Giddon's Bible. He removed it
from the nightstand, and ran his fingers through the pages. Then he
stopped. Ominously a Psalm caught his eye, almost like a name had
been spelled out by a Ouija board:

*"Even though I walk through the valley of the
shadow of death, I will fear no evil."*

Alex closed the bible. His eyes drooped. He replaced it into the top drawer, and then found the Yellow Pages in the lower. He withdrew it and skimmed through the worn sheets. His choices: Domino's, Godfather's, Little Caesar's, Pizza Hut and Mystic Pizza. He selected Mystic because it was "non-franchise," probably owned by college business school graduates who were dropouts of the 60's generation. Even the logo, "Mystic Pizza" reminded Alex of a Peter Max painting or an 80's counterculture movie.

He placed his order for a large pizza with extra cheese, onion, green pepper and pineapple. He knew that he wouldn't eat it all, but thought that maybe he'd have some cold for the morning.

The guy on the other end said, "Why don't you just order a 'veggie', it's cheaper," but Alex wanted his concoction.

He undressed. He looked at his naked body in the dresser mirror. He examined his mature stomach. It was larger than he would have liked, but he was at the age. His chest hairs were thick. They were at least one-third gray. He kicked off his boxers and took a warm shower. The water pounded his back and was almost too hot to tolerate. He wondered why all this was happening. He had to just take it as it came, one day at a time. One moment then another.

After he was done showering he towel-dried his hair and brushed back his slick thatch. Alex pulled back the dust cover, the wool blanket and sheet, and laid his naked body down. He did not bother to cover himself.

He took the television remote from on top the nightstand and flicked on the tube. The TV popped onto CMT, where the previous guest had watched country western music and it's MTV-like videos. Alex thought that the songs were always the same —a man lost his wife, who slept with his best friend, but at least he still had his guitar and his loyal hunting dog.

By 10:45 p.m. the pizza boy arrived. He was nineteen and looked like he was burned out on pot. He had long golden curly hair and a ruddy complexion, and scattered acne scars cratered into his face.

"You hear the news?"

"What news?" Alex asked. He had been mindlessly watching the collage of cowgirl/cowboy, "I've got a broken heart" vignettes.

"Something about Miami. A cholera epidemic. Everyone's talking 'bout it dude."

"That's nice." Alex wasn't concerned about any epidemic. It was too bad, but it wasn't his problem. He had enough worries of his own.

Alex paid for the pizza, gave the "kid" a decent tip, and paternally told him to do well in school.

The pizza was transcendental. It was just what he expected from "Mystic Pizza." After three pieces, and a couple of sips of his large Diet Coke, he fell fast to sleep. He didn't dream.

4:00 a.m.

Alex was awakened by screams in the hallway. Simultaneously his telephone rang. The female voice was frantic, "You need to leave your room now! Everyone's going to die!" Then she hung up.

Alex was half asleep. He sat up. He wasn't sure if he dreamt the bizarre telephone call. He dialed the front desk. The line was busy. He tried several times more with no luck. Sleepy-eyed, Alex walked to the hotel window. He pushed back the drapes and looked outside.

The street was lit up like just before midnight on New Year's Eve. Alex stared in bewilderment.

One thing was obvious: all the cars were leaving Ann Arbor, not coming in. They were running away in a river. The road to the hospital was blocked off, and police cars were directing traffic out of the city. Cops were running from house to house, pounding on front doors.

"What the...?"

Alex let the drapes fall shut. He threw his blanket around his waist and left his room. Everyone was running out of their hotel rooms. Many were still in their nightclothes. Women had curlers in their hair, and unshaved travelers hastily crammed their clothes into their suitcases. Shirttails and pant legs were sticking out of their bags.

"What's going on?" Alex yelled to a galloping man. He answered without turning his head. "You need to leave..." his voice trailed off as he hit the stairwell flying, slamming the exit door open.

Alex backtracked down the hallway past his room toward the elevator. He came upon another man, in his early 60s who was a little less frazzled, but nonetheless scared. "What's happening?" Alex asked.

"Someone," he answered, his voice quivering, "sabotaged the hospital. Like in Miami. It's in the water."

"Cholera?" Alex asked, thinking that it was bad, but *not that big a deal.*

"Cholera? Are you crazy?"

Alex wanted to reply, but the man put his hand on his shoulder. His face expressed his dread, "Radiation poisoning. We're all going to die!"

"Radiation? What are you talking about?"

"Plutonium!" But before Alex could ask more, the man saw the elevator doors open, and fled toward the exit. "You better leave," he said running down the hallway.

Alex ran back to his room, dragging his blanket behind him, and again he tried to call the front desk. The line was still busy. He turned on the TV. The country western station came back on the air. A Dwight Yocum video was playing. Alex hit the remote and found CNN. What he saw shocked him.

The journalist, a seasoned African-American, reported the news, "The President of the United States has declared a national emergency. Both Miami, its environs and Ann Arbor, Michigan are currently being evacuated..."

"Jesus Christ!"

"The evacuation plans...unheralded urgency...thousands already dead...the water supply, within Jackson Memorial Hospital, and now the University of Michigan Hospital...the patients are in the process of being evacuated...nothing like this since Hiroshima...the death toll could potentially be in the hundreds of thousands..."

Alex couldn't believe what he was hearing. He was only blocks away from the hospital. Cars, trucks, vans and anything on wheels that could move were streaming out of Ann Arbor.

Alex stopped paying attention to the television. Once again he pulled back his drapes.

Vans, buses and trucks of all sorts pulled up to the hospital. Men in lead-lined radiation suits were ferrying out patients in gurneys, wheelchairs and hospital beds. Black and gold police cars blockaded the road.

The University of Michigan Hospital was a silent killer that beamed deadly alpha radiation. No one was safe.

Alex threw on his clothes. He needed to get his parents out. But what could he do, his father was still in a coma. His mother, he could help.

He ran down the eight flights of stairs and exploded into the hotel lobby. There the last of the travelers were fleeing for their lives.

After traversing the hallway, Alex found a second set of stairs that took him to the underground garage. The environment was a mass of migrating vehicles, all in fluid outward motion.

Alex bobbed and weaved to his rental Buick Skylark. He fumbled for his keys and started the vehicle. Slowly, the cars inched through the garage. A midnight-shift Good Samaritan security guard risked life and limb to direct traffic. One-by-one the cars emerged from the garage's mouth.

Instead of going west as everyone did, Alex broke from the pack and zigzagged east back to the hospital.

And then he thought, "The man who was chasing me, shooting at me. Why? Why these people? Why do this, just to get me? This doesn't make any sense. Why? It had to be related, it had to be one in the same as Miami."

Alex headed toward the police line, where he was stopped by two officers wearing gas masks. The cop drew his sidearm. "You'll need to leave. The city is being evacuated."

"I'm a doctor. I need to get into the hospital. One of my patients!" Alex lied.

"Do you have I.D.?"

"Yes," Alex pulled out his wallet. He showed his doctor's business card and driver's license.

An authoritative lieutenant walked over. He looked at Alex and then the I.D. "Okay, let him through." And then speaking to Alex, "If I was you I'd make it quick. You don't have much time."

"Thanks." Alex drove past the blockade, then another half-mile to the hospital's front entrance where other men stopped him. This time the authorities were in radiation suits. A man in a silver spaceman suit, with an amber faceplate stood in front of Alex's car. He extended his hand in a "halt."

Alex stopped and got out of his car. "I'm a physician and I need to get in, for one of my patients."

"Doctor, no one is allowed past this point. You'll need to turn back."

"But my parents!"

"I'm sorry, no admission. Besides, all the patients have pretty much been evacuated."

"What? Where to?"

"That's classified."

"Classified? My parents were in there."

"I thought that you said you were a doctor?"

"I did. It's just, that my parents were...are inside."

"They've been taken to Henry Ford Hospital. Do you know where that is?"

"In downtown Detroit. Of course, but isn't that too small for all..."

"Henry Ford is where they've gone."

"Why there? Aren't there any closer hospitals?"

"That's where they were taken. That's all I know."

"How many patients were evacuated?"

"That's classified. You'll need to call Henry Ford if you want any more answers."

Alex backed up. He made a U-turn and left.

All this occurred in just a few hours, or did this happen earlier. Alex pointed his car east, toward Detroit. In the extreme early morning, he and thousands of others were headed out of the city. On the radio, that's all that was playing. Disc jockeys and news broadcasters told the public to stay calm. Unlike Miami, the situation in Ann Arbor had been contained in time, and the plutonium poisoned hospital water had been insulated.

The spread of the radiation had not gone beyond a 10-mile radius from the hospital. Everyone within 20 miles in all directions from the University Hospital had been evacuated. But 20 miles was a huge radius within a major metropolitan center. This meant that the entire city of Ann Arbor would be deserted.

By 5:20 a.m. Alex was at Henry Ford Hospital. There were hundreds of emergency vehicles. The radiation victims from the University of Michigan Hospital had been moved to Henry Ford. At the same time, nearly all the regular Henry Ford patients, or at least those not in immediate peril of dying, had been moved to other hospitals in the vicinity.

The hospital itself was old and in a rundown section of downtown Detroit, west of the Lodge freeway. It had 903 beds and was a teaching facility for the University of Michigan. There was a line of cars three blocks long. Everyone had the same idea as Alex. They all wanted to find family and friends, find out what happened to their loved ones. Alex got as close to the hospital as he could and parked his car. The scene was concentration camp grim.

Alex walked through a sea of despondent humanity. At a makeshift reception tent *armed* National Guardsmen stood with their locked and loaded M-16's slung over their shoulders.

"I need to see my parents. I believe they're here. Their names are Benjamin and Mary Seacourt," Alex said. He was apprehensive.

"I'm sorry, but we can't help you until this afternoon," a volunteer R.N. in her rumpled nurse's uniform said. She had just finished her second straight eight hour shift and was now on her third.

"We've more than 500 patients coming in. Everyone is being quarantined."

"But...I need to see my parents."

"I'm sorry, but no one is seeing anyone; at least not until tomorrow, and then maybe not at all."

"But I'm a doctor."

"I don't care if you're God," she huffed, "Unless you're on staff you're not going to see anyone."

"Look, can you at least check and see if my parents are here?"

"I'm sorry but we have an emergency and there is just nothing that we can do right now."

"But..."

The nurse had a national guardsman move Alex aside while she helped the next person. She was prepared to give the same answer all day long.

Alex knew, by just looking at the mob of cars and people, that he wasn't getting in by normal channels. Though he was not familiar with Henry Ford Hospital, he knew that every hospital had a "doctor's" entrance. Armed with his business card, and his doctor I.D., he was prepared to break into the hospital if he had to.

Alex walked around the intimidating facade. Perversely the atmosphere was a carnival-like. The disaster tents and makeshift portable prefab buildings had sprouted on the asphalt parking lots and worn concrete service roads. Hundreds of people were feverishly working, shipping patients out in all different transportation while others come in, under tight National Guard armed watch.

Alex found an entrance where a stream of workers were mechanically entering and exiting the hospital. He melted unnoticed into the crush.

Once inside, he made his way to a second floor nursing station. The place was in a frenetic state. Nurses, those who where lucky enough, had protective outfits on. Others wore OR scrubs with masks, eye-protection and paper hair-covers. Alex found a changing room and slid into a surgical gown. The scrubs were obviously used to just "superficially" protect the workers from the radiation. That was the best Alex could do.

By 6:50 a.m., Alex had found the Intensive Care Unit where his father was. The suite was blocked off by men in radiation suits and side arms. He could not go in unless he had a radiation suit on.

He finally found a young nurse, who's eager beaverness was the hump that he needed.

"Nurse. I'm Dr. Seacourt." He flipped the young girl his business card, that he had stuffed in an outer pocket in the scrub.

"How can I help you doctor?"

"My father Benjamin Seacourt, could you pull his chart please. He's in ICU. Also my mother Mary, I need to know where she is."

"Yes doctor." She found one of her nurse friends who was working the ICU. Within 15 minutes she had returned.

"I'm sorry, I can't help you."

Alex was disappointed.

"You'll need to leave, they're checking I.D., and if you don't belong, they're throwing everyone in jail."

"Who are they?" Alex asked.

"I don't know. The police? You need to go."

Alex slung his head. He headed to the exit.

"Wait," the nurse said running after him. She grabbed his hand, "I did find out that he regained consciousness after his operation."

"He did?" Alex gained hope.

"That's all I know."

"My mother?"

"I don't know anymore. You need to go before you get in trouble. Please."

"Thanks." Alex pulled down his protective face mask and kissed the young nurse on her forehead.

Alex had no place to go. He couldn't return to Ann Arbor and he needed to stay by his parents' side. So he went to their house, the one he grew up in as a child. He had a few medical books at their Farmington Hills home. He needed to look up plutonium poisoning.

By 8:10 a.m. he was in the middle-class suburb of Detroit, fifteen miles northwest of the hospital. It was smaller then he remembered.

The living room, kitchen, entryway, basement and his bedroom were frozen in time — unchanged. He sat at his old bedroom desk. It seemed lower.

Alex had sent his mother some used, slightly dated textbooks: The Merck Manual and Taylor's Family Medicine Textbook amongst others. They were good reference books, that his parents could use to look up medical problems, answer some of their questions, if they needed. The news was worse than he anticipated. In a nutshell Alex reconfirmed what he already believed to be so:

The normal person, through typical cosmic sources, could get anywhere from seven to fourteen rems of radiation a year without any problems. With a dose of five to seventy-five rems from a single exposure, side effects were observable. With a dose of seventy-five to two hundred rems, a person would develop symptoms of vomiting, fatigue and loss of appetite. With more than three hundred rems there were severe changes of blood cells. Hemorrhage occurred. With a dose of six hundred or more rems there was hair loss and the body loses its ability to fight off infection. With eight hundred or more rems death is certain.

The only thing that a physician can do for a patient with radiation poisoning is treat the symptoms. Blood transfusion and antibiotics to fight off the infection are occasionally used. There were also other side effects that occurred later in life: shortened life span, increased chance of developing cancer and cataracts, damage to the genes, and passing that damage on to offspring.

And if all this wasn't bad enough, then came the worse news. Plutonium is one of the most carcinogenic substances known to man. It is so toxic that just one atom is a carcinogenic dose.

"So here was the kicker," Alex spoke to himself. "Forget about everyone that was going to die right away. Say those were only a couple of hundred, maybe a thousand; it was everyone else that even absorbed as little as one atom of plutonium. They eventually would be toast."

He went on to read.

"Found in nature only in a remote region of Africa, and in minute amounts.... Plutonium may be more dangerous than originally thought. Irradiation of mouse and hamster cells by plutonium alpha particles creates chromosomal abnormalities that appear only after several generations of cell divisions.

"Plutonium is a chemically reactive metal, which, if exposed to the air, ignites spontaneously to produce respirationable-size particles of plutonium dioxide....

"Chlorinated water enhances the absorption of plutonium through the gastrointestinal tract....

"Plutonium does not simply vanish at the death of a contaminated organism. If, for example, someone were to die of lung cancer induced by plutonium, and were then cremated, contaminated smoke might carry plutonium particles into someone else's lungs....

"Because plutonium has properties similar to those of iron, it is combined with the iron-transporting proteins in the blood and conveyed to iron-storage cells in the liver and bone marrow. Here, too, it irradiates nearby cells, inducing liver, bone cancer, and leukemia."

Alex knew that if his parents were exposed, they would more than likely die. He was not willing to accept that anyone had to die. He slapped the book shut and replaced it on the shelf. He headed downtown to the Wayne State University School of Medicine Library. *He was not, would not be defeated. There had to be a solution. And if there was, if anyone could find it...he would!*

19

The living room in the Robbins Belizean complex was palatial. It was a hybrid between a dining room, a parlor and an entertainment center.

The dining room had a large antique oak table that sat fourteen and dated back to the early 1800's. Each chair was hand carved, and the wood was darkly stained hickory. At the end of the table was a hearth. The floor was carpeted in a deep silk and cotton Brussels chenille. The colors were a coalescence of maroons, violet and magenta.

This portion of the "chamber" was an anachronism to the rest of the living room. The parlor-entertainment half of the room had a bamboo floor and was laid out in a mosaic puzzle. It was malleable and highly hand-polished. There were three oversized floral couches arranged in a "C" pattern, focusing in on the immense electronics display. There was a satellite digital communication panel, a 120" Mitsubishi projection-screen television, with eleven monitors surrounding it, three on top, three on each side and two on the kitty-corner; and a stereo the size of Cuba. The Mitsubishi could be electronically divided into split screen, quarters or eighths.

Andrei was sitting in one of the sofas reading *The Financial Times*, a pink oversized newspaper that was the English version of the Wall Street Journal. He was facing the panel. The electronics gizmos were off, except for a 400-watt Phillips stereo. Playing in the background was a soothing rendition of Johannes Brahma's second completed symphony, No. 2 in D Major. The violins were trilling in staccato when Robbins stormed into the room.

"What is the *goddamn* meaning of this!" he roared, his scarred face changing chameleon color from sheet-white to cherry red.

"A bonus," Andrei replied. He was concealing his true agenda. He continued to flip through the pages of the *Times,* pausing when he came upon an article on the devaluation of the pound.

"A fucking bonus, you moron! I have a plan that needs to be followed to the 'T'!" Robbins irately grasped the remote, lifting it off the coffee table, as he spit out his words. He flicked on all the television monitors to the same CNN broadcast. He snapped off the stereo, and as fast as the television came to life, he piped the commentary through the speakers.

Boriskov was sitting to Andrei's right. He idly scanned through a copy of *Architecture Digest*. He was drinking Stolichnaya vodka, iced in a short crystal glass, while eating squid which he dipped into a white wine and red marinara sauce. Boriskov set his magazine down.

"You fucking moron! Goddamn you. This was not my plan!" Robbins screamed, circling Andrei, who was unresponsive. Andrei finished reading the sentence and then he slowly set down the paper. He folded the page over to the article to save his place.

"I've done you a favor," Andrei said. He was careful in his gestures not to reveal his charade. He knew that Robbins was a genius. He had done his research. There was no discounting the man, or his capabilities. He had built the Robbins Company into the multi-billion dollar conglomerate on his intelligence and guile. He could be a formidable adversary.

"A fucking favor, I have a *specific design...*"

In the background the reporter uttered her words in disbelief, "This is the second hospital in as many days...thousands of people have been killed, and potentially tens of thousands will likely die..."

"Do you realize what you've done?"

"Instilled more fear. Made everyone in the United States afraid to get sick and go to the hospital. Scared the hell out of every person who even dares drink tap water."

Robbins pattered rabidly around the couches. "This is *my* goddamn plutonium, and *my* plan has to be developed and executed exactly as *I* have designed it! No other way!"

Andrei knew that he could make Robbins' insanity to "revenge his family" work to his advantage. And Bart Robbins wouldn't even have a clue. Not an inkling of what Andrei was up to until it was too late.

Robbins had hired Andrei to do a job: to cause nuclear insanity. It was an interesting problem. Initially, Andrei thought that Robbins was going to use the plutonium to manufacture nuclear warheads, and then sell them to the highest bidder. But that really didn't make any sense since Robbins had as much money as he ever needed. Though sometimes people can always use more.

Then, after Robbins hired Andrei and Boriskov to implement Robbins' revenge scenario, Andrei had a moral imperative. Either stop him, or make the plan work to his advantage. He decided to make the plan work to his advantage.

Andrei was going to ride Robbins' coattails and scare-the-hell out of everyone; and when the time was ripe — he was going to *make more money than God.*

"Look," Andrei calmly said as he prepared for Robbins' next outburst, "I had a problem on the way to the Mayo Clinic."

"A problem?"

"Everything else will go as planned."

"You know," Robbins said storming around the couches while in the background the TVs loudly droned, "Bottled water sales have gone through the roof...the authorities suspect the Ali Ahmen, a fundamentalist Moslem paramilitary group... Those idiots!" Then Robbins very closely approached Andrei stopping with his grotesque trembling face only two inches from Andrei's, "If I wanted to, I can kill you anytime."

Unflappable, Andrei responded, "And if I wanted to, I could do the *same! Kapeash!*?" He paused, contemptuously, then said, "And if I thought you would...I would have eliminated you from the get go."

There was thick silence. Andrei was prepared with his explanation, one that Robbins would buy and still keep Robbins in his trust. But first he needed to let Bart blow-off steam.

"The device self-activated," Andrei said standing up, and walking quarterway across the room to the bar next to the electronics panel. The bar overlooked the pier and an oceanside Ramada. "Something to drink?" Boriskov nodded no. Robbins was too angry to answer.

Andrei walked around the counter and opened a small freezer. He removed several ice cubes and dropped them into a crystal tumbler. The cubes bounced aimlessly against the curved bottom. He withdrew a bottle of Stoli and poured the thick vodka, 1/2 way up the tumbler. He took a sip. He then placed the bottle back into the freezer and gently finessed the door shut.

"My operative got into trouble."

"How?" Robbins demanded, storming toward Andrei, fists tightly clenched.

"The device self-activated."

"It couldn't have."

"It did," Andrei lied. "Look, what would you have wanted me to do — nuke Detroit, or improvise and follow our plan indirectly." Andrei let the response waft, ready for the anticipated answer he knew Robbins had to give.

Bart Robbins did not. Enraged, he paced back-and-forth, pounding his feet on the bamboo. He was mute. Maybe he was too smart to fall into his trap?

Andrei took another sip. He felt the vodka sizzle as it slid down his throat. Then after a minute of stalemate, he continued his ploy. He knew that he had to set his hook or lose his fish. "En route to Rochester my operative encountered a problem. The device must have been jarred. It went into a 24 hour countdown mode. My agent didn't have enough time to make it to Minnesota, so I told him to find the nearest University Medical Center with access.

"Though it would have taken eight hours, maybe ten to get to Rochester, it didn't give him enough cushion to plant the device safely and get the hell out. So I made a decision."

Robbins did not respond, but continued to trudge. He intermittently looked up at Andrei as he slowed his strides. "My operative is invaluable. I needed to ensure the success of our mission. *We* needed to improvise, and that was that."

Robbins slowed. He looked at Andrei in disgust, as Andrei took another sip of his drink.

"No other deviation! It's my show and we stick with the plan, otherwise..."

"Otherwise?" Andrei fenced, "you would what?"

Robbins stopped. He planted his lizard hands on his hips and the flush left his face. "It has to go as planned and only as planned.

If there are any future problems I need to know about them first."
Then as suddenly as Robbins appeared, he left the room.

In the background the journalist reported, "As of yet no group has taken responsibility for the plutonium poisoning. The FBI is offering a $4 million reward leading to the apprehension of..." and eventually, "Some experts suggest that the acts of plutonium sabotage in Miami and Ann Arbor are really the beginnings of a yet to be declared Holy War, possibly by the Ali Ahmen. Abdel Kghalifaa Fhimah and Lamen Besset Ali, thought to be in Libya under government protection, are prime suspects. Radical cleric Megrahi Omar Abdel, who may have orchestrated the 1993 World Trade Center Bombing..." Andrei muted the monitors and clicked the stereo back to the Brahms symphony.

"Did he buy it?" Boriskov asked in obscure Russian slang in case the room was bugged.

"No, but he had no choice. He's as dependent on us as we on him." Andrei replied in dialect.

"Should we be concerned?"

"We should always be concerned my friend."

Andrei took another sip of his drink. He returned to his seat. He glanced at the myriad pictures of morbidity: victims being wheeled out of the University of Michigan Hospital by attendants wearing radiation suits. Some of the victims faces were distorted. They were burnt. Their skin was in a state of grotesque flux.

20

Alex had done research before. In general, the process was tedious. Though computers were available and were the preliminary mode of his attack, he would start with Medline. The Center for Disease Control in Atlanta would not be reluctant to try even an untested antidote considering the magnitude of the disaster. Normal risks would be set aside despite the fact that an untried drug might be dangerous or still in the research stages.

Alex knew, he prayed, the solution to his Gordian knot lie somewhere in the stacks of texts. But the news reports and even the doctors at the hospital all gave the same answer: there was no cure.

He arrived at 9:40 am and spent the entire day plodding through the computer, preparing lists and researching innumerable leads.

Though he in his own way was inventive, his process of derivation was unconventional — he did it through pictures. He drew diagrams on lots of sheets of paper.

It seemed simple enough. Plutonium binds with iron in the body, permanently. And then, from there it's deposited into the body's architecture; especially the bones, heart muscle, intestines and liver.

"What if," Alex thought, "there was some way to reverse the process. To bind the iron bound plutonium, or chelate it in an aggregate where the plutonium complexes in a new chemical compound? Bind it with some type of substrate and excrete it out of the body."

Alex scoured the computer to no avail. When the computer research dead-ended, he began investigating obscure medical journals, nuclear physics publications, engineering journals, old newspaper articles — anything. He cross-referenced the *New England Journal of Medicine*, the *International Journal of Radiation Biology*, the *American Journal of Neuroradiology*, the *British Journal of Cancer*, the *Baillieres Clinical Hematology* and more.

By 4:00 p.m. his head was pounding and his thoughts clouded with stress. His wire framed glasses slid onto his sweat-covered nose.

After reproducing a batch of prospective articles and abstracts from microfiche, Alex returned to his cube. He sat behind a wall in a nook next to a stack of thousands of microfiche cylinders, stored in small cardboard boxes.

His brain had Indian tom-toms beating inside. His forehead pulsated. The vein in the center of his brow throbbed. His hair, like the copy paper, was greasy from rubbing his scalp and running his fingers through it. Alex couldn't think anymore. He needed a break.

He got up and left the Medical School Library. He walked several blocks toward Woodward and Vern's Coffee Shop. On Tuesday, traffic would normally have been heavier. Hordes, however, had left Detroit. They were afraid of the plutonium and of the possible contamination from Ann Arbor, which was only 45 minutes away. Others hibernated out of fear and stayed home instead of going to work. They glued their faces to their television screens or their radios, not missing a beat of news:

"Thousand to die. What hospital next?"

"The nuclear industry: a catastrophe waiting to happen."

Apocalypse deluged the talk shows. They predicted the second coming. Doomsayers pointed their proverbial finger espousing "I told you so" rhetoric.

Alex wanted none of it. All he wanted was to find something, anything that might work.

He briskly walked across the eight lane highway, four in each direction. Only a few cars buzzed past him.

He pushed the 1940's art deco door open. The restaurant was right out of a Mickey Spillane novel. He sat at the counter on a torn stool that was mended with black electrical tape. He ordered a cup of black coffee. His waitress was buxom and had a wry face. She was friendly. She slid a cup of coffee down the countertop. Steam rose from it in a swirling fog.

He ordered a cheeseburger and fries, and a cherry pie. He had extra onions with his burger, poured plenty of salt onto his fries and gushed ketchup onto a corner of his plate. He ate the cherry pie with his French fries first. He finished off the pie before the fries. His plate was clear of the fries before he had his second bite of his burger.

By 5:15 p.m., he was on his way back to the Medical School Library. As Alex crossed Woodward he tasted the tainted Detroit air. He could sense the sulfur which caused his nostrils to cringe. He wondered if his lungs had been contaminated. His head beat. It hammered out of the need to find an answer, desperately.

Alex sat at his small table, 32 photocopied articles before him. He was searching for a needle in a haystack. If all the experts couldn't come up with anything, all the Harvard and Stanford, Yale and Mayo Clinic authorities, couldn't find an antidote, then what made him think he could? "Nothing" was the answer, except for persistence and hope, and the fire that burned deep inside of him.

The world had gone mad, tens of thousands of people were going to die, maybe more. Probably lots more. More than Alex could ever dream of. And what about the babies? And what kind of depraved, truly evil person could have done something like this? What misanthrope, and why?

He was dog tired. He had to press on.

This time Alex sat at his desk for only an hour. Then he tried Henry Ford Hospital on the pay phone, near the sixth floor elevators. He was told only that his mother was stable, but very sick with radiation poisoning. His father was in critical condition and dying. Because of the vast emergency and "their" calls, this was the only information the hospital could give out. No visitors were allowed.

Normally the courtesy extended to Alex as a physician was not returned this time by the attending. Dr. Kress, his father's doctor, who had worked himself ragged. He was taking calls from no one. The charge nurse, an effeminate male with an exaggerated lisp, was kind enough to give Alex the report.

The mood in the hospital was cautious. Each doctor and nurse were scared wary, not knowing if they too would become a victim of radiation poisoning.

Alex returned to his cubicle. He removed his Timex Ironman

digital watch, and placed it with the integer facade facing him. It read:

TU   9.22
6:16.21

"The University of Michigan Medical Center, 558 beds. Boom! How many of those people were going to die?" Alex thought. "Diabetic, did you need your insulin dosage tuned-up today? Come on in and get your fix of plutonium! Transplant patient? Is your body rejecting your new heart, need to change or modify your rejection medication, alter your steroid? How about a fix of the 'Big P'!

"Hey, I got one. Life Flight patient? right this way. Step right up. On special. Today only. Buy one. Buy now. Screw yourself forever.

"Substance abuse? No problem. We'll end your pain. No pain no gain. No pain no fame!" Alex needed to focus. He was tired and felt like he was losing his mind. The library was open until ten. He had three more hours to work. He was taxed to his limit.

Alex pulled 33 more articles and 41 abstracts from the microfiche and photocopied them. It took him until nearly 7:30 to make his copies. He had entered the world of the esoteric; *Oncogene, Journal of Laryngology Oncology, Journal of Clinical Endocrinology Metabolism, Chinese Medical Journal, Indian Journal of Experimental Biology, Mutant Resistance,* etc.

At ten after nine, after reading nearly the entire day, he closed his eyes for a fifteen minute rest. He had plenty of articles to read tonight. He would go home to his parents' house and study. He leaned back, kicked his feet up on top of his desk and made a 45 degree angle between his cubical and the side wall. He balanced the chair on its two rear legs and tilted his head against the double-paned window. He fell immediately asleep.

21

Everyone in Michigan, Miami and pretty much throughout the country was afraid to leave their houses; and especially to go to the hospital, anywhere. The newspaper headlines told the frantic story.

The New York Times:
"Motives Murky in Fatal Hospital Attacks.
Investigators Lack Suspects, No Previous Threats to Foreshadow Tragedy."

The L.A. Times:
"Holy War on Hospitals. Is This the New Terrorism?"

USA Today:
"Hospitals Nationwide on Alert. Officials Urge Use of Bottled Water."

San Francisco Chronicle:
"Poison Water in Hospitals. FBI Seeks Broader Powers. Offers

record $4 Million Reward"

The cover of **Time Magazine:** Upping The Terrorism Ante. Is Plutonium Holding the U.S. Hostage?"

The crisis was the number one topic of every major government's agenda. Could it happen to them? Were they too vulnerable? What was most disconcerting was that no credible group had yet come forth to take responsibility for the debacle.

Britain, France, Israel, Russia, Germany, Italy, Australia, China, Malaysia, Pakistan and India all offered assistance to President Climan. They sent their best nuclear physicists, criminologists, and nuclear plant personnel to assist in the investigation and clean-up.

The FBI, CIA, KGB, MI-6 from the United Kingdom, DGSE (Direction Generale de la Securite Exterieure) from France, Mussad and Shin Bet from Israel, and the Foreign Intelligence Department in the Ministry of Foreign Affairs from China worked hand-in-glove to uncover the forces behind the plutonium attacks.

By 7:00 p.m. eastern time President Climan spoke on national television:

"My fellow Americans," Climan said, stealing from a John F. Kennedy speech, wishing that he had Kennedy's charisma. "I have sadly come to you today with a heavy heart. These are grave times. Our nation, our people are somberly disheartened over the recent incidents of plutonium sabotage at Jackson Memorial Hospital in Miami and at the University of Michigan Hospital in Ann Arbor.

"Tonight, as I speak, there is a fear that permeates every fiber of American consciousness, a terror that any American can become the victim of a silent attack. Let me assure you, this will not happen.

"It has been rumored that other hospitals have also been attacked and that some of our nation's reservoirs have been contaminated. Let me lay those fears to rest. There are no other hospitals within the United States that have been the subject of any plutonium attack, nor are there any other hospitals, nor public nor private water supplies, nor reservoirs that have been contaminated.

"As chief executive of our great nation during this time of crisis, I have developed a twelve-point plan to ensure that all Americans will be safe from any further sabotage.

"First, with the assistance of the Joint Chiefs of Staff, I am instituting a curfew in both Miami and Ann Arbor, and communities within a fifty-mile radius of these cities. I have declared a limited marshal law effective immediately. A 9:00 p.m. curfew will be in

effect for the next seven days. The purpose of this curfew is to ensure the safe and orderly control of the clean-up efforts and to mini-
mize any additional contamination.

"Second, I have empowered a special prosecutor, former U.S.
Attorney Dean Humphrey, to work in concert with the state and
federal authorities. The special prosecutor's role will be to investigate all persons who may have been responsible for the attacks, and
to bring to justice those terrorists to the full extent of the law.

"Third, I have made available $30 million in emergency fund-
ing to both state and local governments in Florida and Michigan for
their emergency cleanup efforts in Miami and Ann Arbor, and their
environs.

"Fourth,..."

The President droned on with his twelve-point plan. He attempted to give the nation a sense of security and to assure the
American people that the plutonium disseminated into the environment and the communities would be cleaned up in a safe, responsible and predictable manner, without any further illness or loss of
life.

The American people, however, were not convinced and did not
have a sense of well-being and renewed security that President Climan
had hoped for. If anything, they were outraged at his **limited marshal law** mandate, seeing it as a reversion to Hitlerist politics and
the days of the Reichstag fire of 1933.

Everyone was pointing fingers. Radical splinter groups, mostly
of Islamic origin, were the focus, especially any organization that
had any affiliation with Libyan leader Maummar Quaddifi, or Iraq's
Saddam Hussein.

Within two days, in the morning's session, Republican congress-
men led by Senate Majority Leader Steve Vole were prepared to pass
emergency legislation to overturn the President's limited martial law.
They saw the mandate as a thinly cloaked grab for political power.

After three days many of the elements of the limited martial law
were rescinded by congress after vigorous infighting. Nevertheless,
Southeastern Michigan and Southern and South-Central Florida remained under heavy police and military control.

A psychology of gloom became infectious. Everyone was afraid,
nervous that they'd wake up with hideous radiation lesions on their
faces or not wake up at all.

22

When Alex rubbed his eyes open he felt that only minutes had passed. He was refreshed, though depressed. The melancholy had weighed heavy. He sat up, his neck was stiff and he placed his pen upright in his hand. He gazed down at his photocopies and writing tab. The library's lighting was dimmer, at least 70 percent so. Alex looked at his watch. It read:

WE 9.23
1:11.43

He had slept through closing. His first instinct was to find someone to let him out. But with the state of crisis, he felt it was his duty to stay and work. Illegally, if he had too. Besides, what was the worst thing that would happen: He'd get arrested for trespassing, for falling asleep and waking up in a locked medical library. Alex returned to work.

At 4:15 a.m. he stumbled across an article in an obscure Japanese publication, *Gan-To-Kogaku-Ryoho* that referenced an article published by Dr. Yevgine Siderenko, a Russian physician and physicist. The referenced publication, *Arkh-Patologic* was not available in the Medical School Library, and Alex doubted anywhere in Michigan. However, the abstract was.

The abstract read:

"Radiation with dose > 7.5 Gy of uranium damages the canine intestinal mucosa. Post-treatment with K-1A2 reduces the damage and causes excretion through chelation of the radioactive material.

"However, the effect of radiation and of K-1A2 on *in vivo* (live) intestinal transport and tissue absorption is unclear. Especially vague is the intramuscular, liver and bone marrow excretion process. Therefore, we determined canine survival, intestinal transport, and tissue mucosal histology of skeletal muscle, liver and bone marrow following uranium ingestion.

"Animals were orally given 10 Gy uranium-238. This was followed by administration of placebo or K-1A2..."

The abstract was extensive.

Siderenko had been commissioned to study the effects of radiation poisoning in dog models. His experiments were performed on German shepherds. German shepherds were used because they were thought to be the hardiest. By accident Siderenko had discovered a possible antidote to uranium poisoning, which he called "K-1A2." Though uranium and plutonium are different, they are similar enough if they are absorbed into a human body.

The catch, however, "K-1A2" was *only effective if given to the canines within 6 days.* It had been nearly 24 hours, 36 hours worst scenario, since Alex's parents had been poisoned. Alex had 4 days

And then...in the dog models, *3 out of 4 of the canines that took the experimental drug, died from its side effects.* In the experiments, excretion of the uranium from the dog models was accomplished though an extreme urination and diarrhea. Apparently the "K-1A2" binds with the uranium and is eliminated from the dog's systems.

Alex went to the pay phone. He called the airlines. The next flight to Moscow was at 9:00 a.m. It was out of New York with a brief layover in Paris. The soonest flight from Detroit to New York was 6:15 a.m.

"Four-and-a-half days. I've got four-and-a-half days." Alex packed his briefcase, filling it to the brim with the most relevant

articles that he could find, tossed on his jacket and ran down six flights of stairs to the main floor. He had renewed hope.

The jog downstairs woke him. At the main floor entrance was a double set of plate glass doors. They were locked. In reverse, the white stenciled-on lettering announced the library's opening at 8:30 a.m. There was no time.

Alex explored the first floor, past rows of tables, through shelves of publications, between the Anatomy and Behavior Science sections, and then Microbiology and Neuroanatomy.

He found a rear fire exit. He pushed the metal crossbar with the fire sign affixed to it. It was illegally locked.

He had no choice, time was running out. He didn't really want to break the front glass door, and wasn't sure if he could. Besides there was a foyer and two sets of plate glass doors. So he returned to the main library area where there were wood desks and study chairs. He removed one of the heavy metal and foam chairs and walked past the librarian's desk. He went down a short hallway and entered the first office he saw with a street view.

The assistant librarian's door was unlocked. "Great security," he thought. Once in the room, Alex decided to abandon the chair. He found a better weapon — a large wooden, four-legged coat-rack. At the top it had a barber's head with a ball. Great for ramming.

Alex removed the three coats, two long and wintry, and one a raincoat. Then he apologized to the assistant librarian who wasn't there.

"Sorry Ms. Uris," looking at her name plate on the desk, "Next time you shouldn't lock your fire doors."

Turning his head to the side, he rammed the double-paned window with his weapon. On his first attempt, the glass gave way with a crash, yielding in tusky jagged fragments. Alex used the coat-rack to clear away the remaining glass. He set the weapon down, replaced the coats, and then climbed out onto a ledge. He was barely six feet above the ground. He walked down a coarse concrete ledge three-to-four feet, to avoid the glass below, and then jumped onto the frozen dawn lawn.

His landing was hard. No alarm sounded. He stood erect, reached upward and grabbed his briefcase from the ledge.

He needed to act quickly!

23

96 Hours Left

Alex sped to the airport. He was determined. By 6:17 a.m., Northwest flight 346 departed Detroit Metropolitan airport. At 7:58 a.m. he landed at JFK.

At a drug store/convenience/magazine rack concession, after clearing security-tightened customs, Alex found two booklets. They were information guides, both on Moscow.

"Can I help you?" the clerk asked, as Alex stood trance-like before her counter.

"Yes." He slid the books across the counter. The cashier had nails that were painted Fourth-of-July red. Her hair was page-boy short and rose sharply above her neck with the back cut in a wedge.

"Anything else?"

"No."

"That'll be ten ninety-five"

Alex reached into his wallet. He removed a twenty. The bill was soiled. He paid for his books. The cashier dropped the travel guides into a clear red sack and handed him that plus his change.

Robotically he took his purchase. He stared blankly at the connected seats and large windows in the waiting area and watched the hub-bub of people shuffle back and forth. "Come again," he thought, echoing the cashier's subtle command to him. "Come again... Mom, dad, I'll do the best I can. I promise. I'll be back. I'll come again."

He walked over to the waiting area and sat down. "They have to have every expert in the world working on this," Alex thought as he regained his composure. "What makes me think that I can make a difference. Someone probably already has contracted Dr. Siderenko and followed-up on this lead. Why am I wasting my time?"

Alex was sleep deprived. With great effort he opened his brief-case and took out his pad of white paper. He sketched ideas: arrows, lines, little boxes, names, clauses.

"Plutonium binds with iron in the body. K-1A2 chelates and binds to the plutonium. And out the body it goes.

"But why did three out of four canines die? In the animal models it was uranium. But K-1A2 should work with the plutonium, shouldn't it?

"K-1A2 has a *cyanide bond* in it. Is that what killed the dogs? Saved from one poison, and killed by another? Uranium and plutonium; similar or dissimilar?

"K-1A2, K-1A2.

"There's never been any real need for a cure for uranium or for that matter plutonium poisoning. Precautions are so omnipresent in the nuclear industry. They never have 'incidents anymore.' Not since Three-Mile Island; mistakes just don't happen. There are back-ups and back-ups to the back-ups to prevent mishaps.

"K-1A2, K-1A2.

"Who is Siderenko? Time is short. The hourglass is running out. "Ticktock, ticktock."

Alex gazed down at his notes, "K-1A2. Why A2? Is there an A3? A4? What does 'K' stand for? Is there a '1' in the series, and then an 'A1?'"

It was time to board the Air France flight 301. The plane was at near capacity for the twice-daily trip to Moscow. Commerce was booming between Russia and the United States. Once the "Evil Empire" was now the bastion of American capitalism.

Alex sat in an aisle seat. It gave him room to spread-out, to work.

"K-1A2, what did it mean? How did it work? Why were the dogs killed?"

The flight to Moscow, via Paris was eleven hours and would

arrive at Sheremetgovo Airport at 8:05 a.m. Moscow time. He would have jet lag after flying nearly halfway around the world on a moment's notice.

Alex read through the thirty-three articles he had copied during the first four hours of his flight, just before he landed in Paris.

By 4:13 a.m. Moscow time his flight landed at Charles de Gaulle airport. Several passengers disembarked at de Gaulle and a few more boarded until the plane was full. At 5:43 a.m. he was airborne. Midway to Moscow, over Frankfort, Germany, Alex began feeling nauseous. At first he attributed this to his lack of food and sleep. Once the jet leveled off, he was served a gourmet meal. He picked at his poached salmon and skipped the creamed potatoes, shchi (cabbage soup) and dessert.

He had another wave of nausea. This one was stronger than the first. At nearly the same time, his vision became blurred, almost double.

Alex got up and walked briskly to the rear of the plane and into one of the unoccupied rest rooms. He splashed cold water onto his face.

He looked into the mirror—his face appear cherubic and noticeably distorted. Bigger? *He saw blood*, tiny trickles that ran down his nose from his nostrils to the vermilion border of his lip. Then, he noticed his knees, they had an unusual sensation. He could feel his kneecaps creak with each bend of his legs. They felt swollen.

And then he thought about The University of Michigan Hospital. Why did someone try to kill him?

Was this who sabotaged the hospital at U of M? Was he too poisoned? Was he really the target and the hospital just incidental? That idea was ridiculous...

Alex wiped his nose and mouth with a tissue. He looked into the mirror and tilted back his head. He examined the membranes inside his nose. He then looked into the whites of his eyes. He pulled down his lower eyelids. He did the same with the uppers. The pallid sclera were abnormally reddened. The vessels were angry.

Had he been exposed?

Feeling no further waves of nausea, he returned to his seat. He laid his briefcase on the floor, instead of on his seat tray-top, removed his shoes, and rested his feet on top of his briefcase.

He closed his eyes. He could feel a trickle of blood begin to run downward from his right nostril. Before he could move his hand to dab away the crimson, he fell asleep.

Seventy-five to two hundred rem exposure caused vomiting, fatigue, loss of appetite. More than three hundred rems resulted in severe damage to red blood cells; *and hemorrhage occurs.* Six hundred rems and hair loss begins. The body loses its ability to fight off infections and then...*death.*"

Where were the plutonium atoms living in him? His bone, his liver, his muscle? There, emitting alpha radiation, causing his slow death? *Was the water he drank at the hospital tainted?*

Thirty minutes before landing, Alex awoke. The stream of blood that began to flow from his right nostril had coagulated. He wiped his nostril and upper lip clean. He ran his fingers through his hair, and gently scratched. His scalp felt like there were ants under his skin. It itched. He dumped the Kleenex that he used to wipe his face and took another tissue out of his pocket. He sucked on the tip and noticed slight streaks of new blood, but this time from his gums. He blotted the tissue under his nose.

He cleaned the rest of the caked blood off his face and then examined his fingers, which he used to run through his hair and scratch his scalp. Under his nails, on the right third and fourth digits were remnants of hair. He checked his left hand, the verdict was identical.

Alex took his right index finger and rubbed his upper gums in an experiment. No blood oozed out. Then he did it to the bottom. He did not need to remove his finger and see the results, he could taste the copper.

"Ticktock the doc is done." He was sick to his stomach.

Alex needed to take his mind off of things. He flipped through the tour books, first a book on Russia, and then the one by Hans Höfer entitled Insight Guides Moscow. He would study their contents carefully.

"Moscow, one of the world's greatest cities.... Moscow played a vital role in Russian history..... For more than six hundred years Moscow had been the spiritual center of the Orthodox Church of Russia."

"There, on the map," he thought, "was Moscow State University, across from Luzniki Park and Central Lenin stadium."

"Moscow University," he read, "now Moscow M.V. Lomonosov State University the first University in Russia. It was founded as a medical and surgical college in 1786.

"In 1812 Napoleon invaded Russia; after a bitter fifteen-hour battle in September at Borodiro on the approaches to Moscow, the

French set fire and eventually destroyed more than two-thirds of all the buildings. Looting was rife....

"The late 19th century was a period of ostentatious building...."

"Thirty-three thousand students, of whom approximately a tenth are from foreign countries."

A chime tolled. First in French, then English, then Russian, "Please fasten your seat belts and prepare for landing." Alex snapped together his latches. The man next to him was nudged awake by his wife and he did the same.

Alex continued to read, "Intricate transportation: Compared with other large cities in most developed countries, Moscow has very few privately owned cars, though their number is steadily rising... Moscow still relies heavily on street cars (trains) and trolley buses...."

And then, "Also important are the Moscow D.I. Mondeleyou Institute of Chemical Technology.... In addition to the large volume of research undertaken in the university and in other teaching establishments, there is a formidable array of scientific research institutions."

"Bingo," he had found what he was looking for.

That's where he was going to start, at the Presidium. At the Academy of Science of Russia, right in front of Gorky Central Park.

24

Moscow

Dr. Alex Seacourt cleared customs at Sheremetgovo Airport in a curious manner. It made him suspect. He had no clothes and only his briefcase; and fortunately for him he had his passport which he kept in his briefcase for "just in case he went somewhere," which he never did. That is...until now.

Alex was beginning to smell like he had not taken a shower in days, and his face showed the stubble of growth beyond the boundaries of his shortly-trimmed beard. He was surprised that he passed through customs so quickly. Why?

He exchanged dollars into rubbles and only lost 3 percent on the transaction. The money was bulkier and wider than U.S. bills and didn't fit well into his wallet. By 9:19 a.m. he stood in line for one of the thirty cloned taxis. The airport was weather-worn, a cross between a '50s Grand Central Station and a modern megatransportation center.

"To the university, please?" Alex asked the cab driver.

"Which one?" The driver replied in crisp English. He was dressed in a smart shirt, fur gloves and an Astrakhan (a hat made of the fleece of the Karakul lamb).

"You speak English?"

"Of course. These are the days of détente. Doesn't everyone?"

"I don't know."

"You need to go where?"

Alex could feel the blood again begin to drip out of his right nostril. He knew now for sure that he had been poisoned by plutonium. "I, uh... need to go to the Academy of Science, at..." He fumbled through his Moscow book.

"Lenin Avenue."

"That's it."

The driver reached over his seat and opened the rear door of the funny looking car. Alex got in. The bench seat was broad, flat and lampblack; and needed more cushion.

"You have any luggage?"

"No."

"Are you here overnight? Business?"

"Yes. Why?"

The driver pulled out of the airport and headed toward Gorky Park and the University. His vehicle was noisy and had a repeating metallic clang that echoed from under the transmission.

"Just wondering. The Tchaikovsky Competition is this week. I thought you might have come for it."

"No."

"You really should go. The American pianist Van Cliburn won first prize in 1958."

Alex removed a tissue from his pocket and wiped his nose. "Yes, maybe." How much time did he have left, how much time? Was he really poisoned?

"And the Russian Realist Theater. Maybe see the Gorky Moscow Art Theater."

"How far?"

"I talk too much?"

"No. How long?"

The taxi driver looked in his rearview mirror at Alex. Alex's brow was sweatborne.

"Soon...You don't feel well? You look, how do you....white. No...pale?"

"How long?"

"Twenty minutes."

When Ilya arrived at the Academy, he parked behind a line of waiting taxies.

"Do you want me to wait?"

"No."

"No problem, really.... I won't charge you."

Alex got out, his briefcase taut in his hand. He pulled his coat down and turned up his collar. The Arctic air which had drifted down from the White and Baltic Seas was biting.

The former eighteenth-century palace was formidable. Now it housed the intellectuals. There were four-foot wide columns rising out of the Slavic marble steps, like monolithic symbols of the great Russian people. The Academy was a monument to Mother Russia and her Presidium to the Academy of Science.

Halfway up the row of thirty steps, each three feet in length, Alex stopped. He bowed his head. A wave of nausea overwhelmed him. He stood momentarily, and slowly attempted to regain his composure. He felt dizzy.

"You need any help? An interpreter?" His taxi driver said out of nowhere.

"I suppose." Alex turned around in surprise. Ilya was standing behind him.

"Are you sick?"

"I think so."

"You want me to take you to a doctor?"

"No. I need to find Dr. Yevgine Siderenko."

"The physicist?"

"You know him?" Alex asked curiously

"He's famous. I know of him."

"How?" Alex was about to ask, but another wave of nausea struck him hard. He could feel Ilya's arm reach around his waist helping him stand. Ilya bolstered him up the remaining long marble steps. A third wave of nausea pounded through his gut.

"Do you need something?"

"Something?"

"A tablet?"

"A pill for nausea?"

"Yes."

"Yes, I do."

"I can get you one from my brother. He's a pharmacist."

Alex did not reply.

They entered the immense Academy of Science through ornate rotating brass doors. Inside the entranceway was an expansive Sergey Knoenkov mural. There was a large reception desk. Past the foyer were additional marble stairs, and then two halls which led to six elevators each.

In Russian Ilya asked for directions to Siderenko's office. The receptionist replied, in what appeared to be a longer than necessary conversation. Alex leaned against the counter. He turned his face away from Ilya. Only recently did the Ministry of Internal Affairs (Vsesoyvznoye Dubrovolnoye Obschestro Sodeystuiya Armii, Aviatssiii Floto S.S.R.) and the Politburo allow Westerners inside.

Great revolutionary period art works hung on the walls. They included oils by Isaak Brodsky, Valentin Serovc, genre paintings of Nikology Kastlein and Yury Pimerou. There were also portraits by Mikhail Nesterou and Aleksondr Geasimov amongst others.

"Come, follow me." Alex turned around, and obeyed Ilya's lead. "Coffee?" he asked.

"Yes."

"It might help settle your stomach."

Alex followed Ilya past the two halls of elevators, through a labyrinth of mosaic tiled floors and then up a back elevator. But before they got on, Ilya stopped at a secretary's office, the office of Experimental Research Institute of Metal Cutting Machine Tools. He filled two ceramic cups two-thirds full with Cuban coffee. He dropped two cubes of brown sugar into each.

"Is sugar all right?" he asked after depositing them.

"It's okay." Alex nodded.

Alex sipped from his mug. They took the elevator up to the fourth floor, and then walked through another maze of halls to the Office of Physics and Scientific Nuclear Investigations.

They walked into a farther set of offices, and eventually came to a far corner lab. The glazed-windowed wooden door had the name Yevgine Siderenko printed in Glasnost script.

Ilya knocked on the door. There was no answer. He knocked again, and then a third time. He tried the door handle. It was locked.

"Can I help you?" A Moscow State University graduate student approached them from the rear. He took off his glasses and swung them in half circles in his hand.

"Dr. Siderenko?" Alex asked.

The graduate student nodded and put his hands up in the air, about to say "No English," when Ilya spoke. Ilya drilled the student about Siderenko's whereabouts.

Again, the conversation took much longer than Alex would have anticipated. Alex attempted to glean some meaning from the Russian discussion, but was unable to find any similarity between English and Russian words. Finally, Ilya finished and took Alex to a nearby cedar bench.

"Why are you looking for Dr. Siderenko?"

"Why? It's personal."

"I need to know."

"Where is he? I need to speak to him," Alex asked somewhat aggravated.

"He's not here."

"Is he home?" Alex asked annoyed

"He's not here."

"Where is he. Can you ask the man where he is?"

"The man is Dr. Siderenko's graduate student," Ilya replied sternly, "One of twenty in Radiation Physics. Do you want to see Dr. Siderenko or not?"

"Of course I want to see him."

"Then you need to tell me why you need to see him, if you want my help."

"I need to meet with him. It's important. I'm an American doctor. My name is Dr. Alex Seacourt. People back home, in the United States, have been poisoned by radiation. Plutonium."

"I don't live in a cave, Mr. Doctor, I know about that." Ilya said sardonically.

"My parents have been poisoned. I've done research in the medical library at Wayne State University School of Medicine in Detroit, Michigan. I came across an article in Arkh-Patologic. I believe Dr. Siderenko may have a cure for radiation poisoning."

Ilya studied Alex before answering. Then, without emotion he said *"He's been missing for two weeks."*

"Two weeks?"

"Yes. And you are not the only one looking for Siderenko."

"Who else?"

"I don't know. And if I did, I do not know if I would tell you."

Alex grabbed Ilya by the lapels. Alex's muscles flexed in fatigued pain.

"Tens of thousands of people are going to die, because of some maniac. I..." Alex hesitated, "My parents may have been poisoned. Maybe Dr. Siderenko knows nothing. Maybe he can't help me at all. But I need to speak with him."

Ilya, bigger than Alex, scrutinized him. He did not bother to remove Alex's hands. "Maybe his apartment."

"Where?" Alex asked as he released Ilya, sorry for his outburst.

"In the inner city. On Kalinin Ave, not far from the Ukraine Hotel."

"Could you take me there."

Siderenko's twenty-story apartment building was close. It was reserved for the privileged. Those few, the vested — the favored novelist, playwrights, high-ranking party, police executives and military officers; those in power who enjoyed access to the best vacations, medical facilities, foreign travel, good incomes and living facilities.

Kalimin Avenue was indispensable European. It had modern apartment buildings and administrative offices. It was within the Garden Ring. Other of the buildings in the inner city where from the 15th, 16th and 17th centuries. It was where the Kremlin, Red Square, Bolshoi Theater, Tchaikovksy Concert Hall, Tolstoy Museum and Marx-Engels Museum lay.

Alex noticed that despite the time of day, the streets were not as pressed as their American counterparts. Mercedes and Volvos were sparse. There were a few Fords and Chevrolets that were sprinkled in between the all white or all black Moskvichs.

Ilya parked next to a street lamp in front of the Vostock Apartment Building. What was peculiar to Alex was that despite the city's amazing growth and rich culture, it was anachronistic. The street lights were not fluorescent, but high energy incandescent. The apartment windows were dingy, and there was a noticeable absence of TV antennas and satellite dishes on top of the high-rise buildings.

"It's on the fourth floor. Apartment 414," Ilya said.

"Let's go up," Alex impatiently said as he propped opened the rear door before Ilya could come to a complete stop.

"You go. I'm going to go to my brother's pharmacy. I'll get you something for your nausea."

"All right."

Alex jumped out, stumbled to catch his balance, and then landed on the concrete with both feet parallel. At the same time he swung the cab door shut. Ilya sped off.

The aroma of the Moskva River drifted in on a breeze. Side-by-side, the new and old buildings endured. The old, looked modern in a functional style of the 30's, in its ponderous form of the late Stalinistic period. Next to them stood the high-rise concrete and glass edifices.

Kalinin Avenue was new. It was built in the 1960s, driven through an area of poorer housing. It was westernized from the Kremlin to the Moskva River. The showpiece of the modern city, it was lined by high-rise offices and apartments buildings, linked at street and second-floor levels by a shopping mall. At its outer boundary the three-winged Council for Mutual Economic Assistance structure overlooked the river.

Alex entered the building and took the elevator up to the fourth floor. He got on with a scholarly couple. She was wearing a bright red scarf, and karakul coat (the black fur of young broadtailed sheep) that covered her to her knees. He, an '80s necktie with paisleys and a silver tie bar propping up his cravat. They spoke gently to one another more like colleagues than husband and wife.

At the fourth floor, Alex exited the elevator. The Moscovites continued upward. The corridor to 414 was aseptic. Its flooring was linoleum tinged with speckled-gray brown and slate chips. The walls were concrete painted dull white. 414 was the sixth apartment on the left. Alex was on a stopwatch. Every second was important. He looked at his Timex. He had reset it to Moscow time. It was difficult to read. His vision phased in and out of double focus. It was 11:45 a.m.

Alex pushed the buzzer. He could hear the doorbell ring in a gritty "brazzzz." No answer. Again he buzzed. Nothing. He waited patiently. Through the presswood door he could faintly hear a telephone ring.

The phone, whose chime was "East-Berlinish," rang seven times. There was no eighth ring. Alex put his ear to the wood. He couldn't hear anyone answer. He waited and then knocked loudly. Again he knocked. No reply.

He felt a sense of desperation. The sand in his life's hourglass was running low. If he was going to do anything, he needed to do it now. Apprehensively he tried the doorhandle. He looked both ways. No one was in the hallway. He forced the handle, but it would not budge. He felt the door pushing against the wood. "It might be flimsy enough." He tried the doorhandle, screwing it with both hands to the right. It wouldn't give.

He checked the corridors. Nobody was around. Alex walked back to the wall opposite the door. Then, with full-speed he charged the door. He could feel his shoulder bone smash into the wood. The pain shot from his shoulder to his neck. Barely, he could tell it gave way. Again he charged the door, but this time more forcefully. The door moved farther. A crack developed behind the doorhandle. A bolt of agony rifled through his upper arm, into his collar bone.

Alex battered the door again. This time the skin beneath his jacket began to bruise. On the seventh charge the door jamb splintered open.

Dr. Siderenko's apartment was bizarre. Yet, expectantly it looked like an academician s home. There was a long corridor with bare walls. The hallway opened into the living room. Books were stacked upon books which were stacked upon other books. There were shelves and shelves of periodicals, many in English. There was an IBM computer, and above were four shelves of textbooks. Physics, nuclear chemistry, nuclear medicine, neuroradiology, oncology, chemistry; textbooks in French, English, German, Japanese and Russian were piled in disarray.

To the right of the desk, the computer and the jumbled library, was a study. Apparently the professor had used his dinning room/ kitchen combination as one large work area, for that matter the entire apartment was a disorganized library.

Alex walked to the study which preceded a hallway which lead to the professor's bedroom. The room was designed as a second bedroom, but was used as an extension of the professor's library. There was a crude blackboard with dark-green slate and chalk sticks that sat in an ashen tray. The chalkboard was two-sided, and spun in $180°$ around a horizontal axis. The writing on the back was up-side down, unless Alex flipped the board, then it was right-side up. He walked around the blackboard. It had been wiped clear, but faint remnants were apparent. In the tray, Alex saw two frayed erasers.

He returned to the board's front. There were notes and chemical formulas in Russian with arrows lengthwise that split in divergent directions. None of the formulas, though some in primitive form, were identifiable.

Alex stood back from the chalkboard and looked at the complex formulas. He tried to understand it. He didn't. He scanned the room. Volumes upon volumes were stacked on the floor, as high as four feet. Many of those were in front of bookshelves that lined all four of the room's walls, and extended to just below the ceiling.

Alex left the study and walked down the hall and into the professor's bedroom. Siderenko's bedroom and bathroom were a calamity. Clothes were sprawled onto the bed and floor. Dirty underwear, sleeveless V-necked T-shirts, workshirts and ties were everywhere. In one corner next to the bed, there was a reading light. In the other was a potted plant that had long since died and served as an astray.

Alex expected to find art work hanging from the walls: paintings or posters of Russian ballet stars, or of the Bolshoi Theater. There was none of that; but off-color facades faded near amber.

Alex was used to the egghead types who were occasionally off-the-wall. Siderenko's apartment personified this and more.

"Ktote?" a voice said from behind startled him. Alex spun around to face the barrel of a World War II German Luger. It was pointed into his belly. He slowly raised his hands. He was in control despite his body being numb with fatigue.

"Do you speak English?" he asked enunciating clearly.

"Who are you?" the girl repeated in perfect English, but with a British accent. Her face was round, and her eyes doe-innocent. Her lips fine at the edges and plump in the center. She was tall and had high cheek bones. "What are you doing here?"

"I knocked. No one answered. The door was open, so I came in."

"It was not."

"I thought..."

"What are you doing here? You SID?"

"No."

"Did the KGB send you?"

"No."

"I locked the door. You broke in."

"Easy," Alex said. He looked nervously down at her gun.

"Are you alone?"

"Yes."

"Why are you here?" Her British accent was peculiar.

"My name is Dr. Alex Seacourt."

"Why are you here?" she demanded. She walked around Alex and sized him up. He did not move. She fanned her gun from his head to his toes.

"I'm looking for Dr. Siderenko. He may have a cure for radiation poisoning."

"Are you with the government?"

"No, but I'm from the United States. Why?"

"Dr. Siderenko disappeared two weeks ago."

"I know."

"He's my father. Did you know that as well?"

"No I didn't. I'm sorry, but do you mind putting that gun down?"

Alex gingerly walked toward the living room. The girl slightly relaxed her trigger finger. He could feel the salt of his perspiration stick to his shirt.

"My parents have been poisoned. They're going to die, thousands are going to die. I thought... I hoped that Dr. Siderenko might have some answers."

Alex walked into the living room and studied the books and Siderenko's desk. He ignored the girl. Then he slowly walked into the study and looked at the dusty chalkboard. "What does this say?" he asked pointing.

"Why?"

"I thought your father might have found a cure, or at least, I read a paper in the *Arkh-Patologic* journal where he was experimenting with German Shepherds. He found a possible antidote for uranium poisoning."

"He has."

"Do you know anything about it?"

"A little."

"What?"

"I know that my father," the girl said as she relaxed the Luger, pointing the barrel toward the floor, "had worked on several experiments with dogs and some with primates."

"Primates?"

"Yes."

"What about the primates?"

"I don't know. I'm aware of the article you mentioned though."

"Yes, and..."

"I know my father had moved past the point of dog experiments and was working with a new formula, something to stop the blood damage."

"The hematological effects of radiation?"

"Yes, something like that, or something else. I'm not sure."

"Do you know where your father is?"

"No."

"Have the police investigated?"

"Yes. The Moscow police, and the KGB because of the nature of my father's security status with the Academy of Science."

"Do they have any idea what happened to him?"

"No. No idea."

"What about his security status?"

"I'm not sure, but even if I knew I wouldn't tell you."

"Does the blackboard mean anything?" Alex asked looking at the formulas.

"I don't know. Most of what's on it I don't understand. But the police, the KGB and scientists took pictures. They went through his computer, his journal, his notes...everything."

"Did they find anything?"

"Nothing. They don't know what happened to him."

"Or...at least if they do know, they're not telling."

"Maybe."

"Your father had a journal?"

"Yes."

"Is it here?"

"No, the police took it."

Alex walked back into the living room. He thought. "Is there anywhere you think your father might be?"

"Not that I know of."

"Anything unusual?"

"No. Not really."

"The bedroom, is it always that messy?"

"Yes."

"Does it look like he might have been kidnapped?"

"No. If you mean is there anything unusual about his apartment, then no."

"The books, his computer and the blackboard, are they always like this?"

"Yes, usually. My father is eccentric."

"Anything at all that you can think of?" Alex scanned through the piles of cluttered volumes, and then looked at the desk, "Anything on his computer, your father's workpapers or on his desk to give you an idea of where he might have gone?"

"No. The police asked me the same questions."

Alex walked into the kitchenette. A small table, with only enough room for four, had more books and writing tablets on it. The countertop had a Mr. Coffee maker, and dirty plates with remnants of herring, stroganoff and borscht. Two forks, a knife and spoon were in a coffee cup still partially filled with mud. It sat on Siderenko's counter.

"Is there any reason anyone would want to harm him?"

"No."

"In the United States two hospitals, Jackson Memorial in Miami and the University Medical Center in Ann Arbor, Michigan have been nuked. A device was used to release plutonium into the hospitals' water supply. Thousands of people have taken ill, and most will die. My parents are two of them. Do you think that your father might have discovered a cure for the poisoning? Could he have been involved?"

"Involved?" The girl was angered. She raised the Luger and

pointed it back into Alex's stomach.

"I mean indirectly...maybe known something he shouldn't have?"

She began to relax. "I don't think so. No, one day he just didn't come to work."

"Let's walk through the apartment slowly, one step at a time, and look and see if there's something we can find."

"All right," she returned her gun to her purse.

Meticulously they started from the kitchen. They went through stacks of books, papers, the professor's computer printouts and a plastic file of computer discs.

"Have you reviewed any of these?" he asked referring to the discs.

"No, I don't have my father's security code. I can't access them."

"Have the police, or KGB?"

"I think so."

"Did they find anything?"

"No. I think the police would have said so if they did."

They searched the blackboard room. Alex pulled books from the vertical stacks off the shelves. Most were in Russian. The girl studied the bookshelves, the stacks and the blackboard. She sat in the room's one chair, an uncomfortable relic, in front of the blackboard.

After several minutes they left the room. The girl hesitated momentarily as she walked out of the study. Alex noticed her falter.

"Is there something?"

"No...not really," she replied as they moved to the bedroom. She hunted through her father's closet. Again, she vacillated midstride. She stopped moving through his wrinkled clothes, hung on ropy wooden hangers, and walked back to the blackboard room.

Four stories below, behind shrubs and out of eyesight from the apartment window, sat a nondescript vehicle. Two men, both in identical trench coats and closely cropped hair listened to the conversation between Alex and the girl.

"Do we arrest Seacourt now?"

"No."

"Are we going to need to take *exceptional measures*?"

"These are exceptional times...aren't they?"

The driver pulled out his gun and checked the Makarov 9mm's action. His eyes seared through the afternoon's daylight, up toward the apartment window.

25

" *Pan,*" the girl said from the other room. Alex had finished rummaging through the bedroom and had worked his way into the bathroom when she again said "*Pan.*"

"What?" Alex asked as he quickly made his way to the study.

"It's not his writing." The girl pointed to the bottom right-hand corner of the blackboard. "I don't know why, but I didn't see it earlier," her Russian accent surfaced in her excitement. "It's definitely not my father's writing."

Written in deeper, broader strokes than the other writing was the word "*Pan.*"

"What does it mean?"

"*Pan*...um; holiday; no, paradise. It means paradise."

"Paradise. Are you sure?"

"Positive."

"Does it have any significance?"

"I don't know."

Alex began to talk and the girl put her finger to her closed lips. "Shuuu..."

"What is...," but before he could finish, she pressed her fingers against his lips. The girl raised her Luger and slipped out of the room.

"Where are you...?" Alex whispered as he quietly followed her.

Then in Russian he could hear the professor's daughter yelling at an intruder, someone else who skulked into the apartment. The man returned her screams, but more calmly, despite the fact that a gun was pointing into his face.

"Ilya," Alex said. His cab driver was hiding next to the wall in the long corridor that lead to the living room. Ilya had entered unnoticed.

"You know this person?"

"Yes, he's my driver. He went to get me some medicine for nausea."

"Why of course," Ilya fumbled. "Here...see, some medicine." Ilya carefully pulled out a pill bottle from his pocket. He cautiously made his way to Alex, handing Alex the vial. The girl kept the automatic trained on him. "Take two now and one every six hours."

"Thanks."

"Your friend has lurked here for the last ten minutes."

"I haven't!"

"Why have you been hiding?" She pointed the gun at Ilya, safety off.

"I haven't been hiding"

"You've been here all along. The door was closed. I heard it open at least ten minutes ago."

"You didn't say anything to me," Alex said to the girl.

"I wasn't sure I heard anything at first. I closed the door behind me. You've been listing to us," she raised the gun to Ilya's jaw, "for ten minutes. Why were you hiding?"

Ilya bungled for an answer. "Yes, you're right," he said. "I didn't want to disturb you."

"Then, why were you hiding?"

"Look guys," Alex said, as he took two pills out of the bottle and placed them into his hand. He tossed the tablets into his mouth and then walked to the kitchen. He ran the cold water and opened several cupboard doors in search of a glass. Eventually he found a clean one, filled it, and drank most of the fluid. He washed down the pills that had gotten stuck in his throat. "I don't give a damn if Ilya was standing in the hallway for an hour or not. We have a problem, or more correctly, I've got a problem. I need to find your father and you," pointing to the girl with his palm outstretched,

"What's your name?"

"Viktoria."

"Viktoria, found some writing on a blackboard that definitely is not Dr. Siderenko's. By the way, Viktoria, this is Ilya, Ilya, Viktoria," Alex said sarcastically. "Please, put that silly gun away and let's figure out a way to find your father."

"Are you sick?" Viktoria asked.

"Why?"

"Are you sick with radiation poisoning?"

Alex demurred. He knew in his own mind he probably was. The abdominal pains, the bloody noses, the nausea, the hair loss. "I think so...or maybe it's jet lag."

"The pills?" Viktoria asked Ilya.

"For the vomits," Ilya answered.

"Look, did anyone aside from your father have access to his apartment or the blackboard. Was he married? A wife or girlfriend, a colleague?"

"No. Since my mother died seven years ago my father has lived a reclusive life. He has no friends, only his work."

"Are you positive?"

"Yes."

"Then why would someone else's writing be on the chalkboard? Could it be the police or the KGB?"

"No, they wouldn't disturb anything."

"Well, then who?"

"I don't know."

"Then we need to find out."

For the next three hours, Viktoria, Ilya and Alex scoured the apartment for clues. Though Viktoria did not trust Ilya, she insisted on his assistance. After meticulous rummaging, including what little Viktoria was able to come up with on her father's computer, Viktoria terminated the exploration.

She spoke to Alex frustratingly. "I have an idea, but it may be illegal. You're interested in a solution aren't you? If you're sick with radiation poisoning my father may be able to help you. Yes?"

Alex looked at his watch. The pills were helpful. The crawling demons in his stomach had gone away. "Yes."

"I can help," Ilya volunteered.

Viktoria pulled Alex aside in the living room. Ilya stood at the other end. "I don't trust him," Viktoria insisted in a low voice. "If you want to find my father it has to be just you and I and no one else." Alex looked at Ilya.

"I can help," Ilya said, "I have friends."

"No!" Viktoria insisted.

"I can...if you give me a chance."

"Thank you, but no," Alex insisted. He looked at his watch. "Let me pay you. How much do I owe you?"

"Forty American dollars."

"Is that all?"

"Yes."

"Do you want rubbles?"

"No. American dollars."

Alex paid Ilya, and then asked, "Do you have a telephone number, if I need to use you again?"

"Yes," Ilya removed a worn-leather wallet from beneath his coat and handed Alex a card. In English it read: "Moscow Taxi and Tourist service, Ilya Frolov," and then a six digit telephone number.

"Thank you. What do I owe you for the pills?"

"No. They are, how do you say, 'on the roof'?"

"On the house." Alex smiled.

Ilya smiled and corrected himself. "On the house." He then courteously left and closed the door behind him.

"So, why don't you trust him?"

"I don't have a good feeling."

"And you trust me?" Alex asked, sitting down at the dinning room table, on the flimsy stainless chair, "You don't even know me."

"You have motive. I believe that you're sick and you need my father's help. I need to find my father."

"How do you know about motive?"

"I'm an attorney."

"A lawyer?"

"Yes. Don't I look professional?" Viktoria asked as she stood erect and straightened her suit jacket. She spoke in her best British English. Alex hadn't noticed what she was wearing until just then. She did look adept.

"You look... just like an attorney. I just didn't take you for one."

"I'm not female enough?"

"No, you're very female."

In fact Viktoria was. She was 27 and trained at Moscow State University. She was in the top third of her class at law school, graduating when she was 24. She was 5'7" tall, thin and sinewy. She was resolute in spirit and mind.

"I've worked at the Politburo for the Central Committee for the last three years as an interpretive assistant."

"What's an interpretive assistant?"

"I help mold policy in the New Russia."

"It sounds like an important position."

"It is. But it isn't. I make suggestions. I try to modernize Mother Russia, but the old politicians don't always appreciate change. They're generally immovable."

"Intractable?"

"Yes." She stopped talking and walked back into the blackboard room. Alex did not follow. "I have access to the computers. The government computers," she said out of sight.

"We should take your father's discs."

"Okay," she said as she returned to the living room.

"Let me ask you a question. Why would the police and KGB come looking for your father, search his apartment and not take his computer discs or hard drive?"

"I thought the same thing," she replied, "I don't know the answer. Maybe they copied them. Maybe there's nothing on them. Maybe my father is coming back. I took it as a sign."

"I see. You know in one vein it makes sense, but then again I don't buy it."

"Buy it?"

"Believe it so. If I was investigating your father's disappearance, and it appears that your father was a very important man, then I would've taken his computer and discs."

"I believe you're correct."

"Let's just find out what's on your father's discs for starters, don't you think?"

Twenty minutes later Alex and Viktoria arrived at the Politburo. It was just after 5 p.m. and most of the bureaucrats had gone home. Viktoria arranged for a special pass for Alex, and by a quarter of six they were in Danlov Misha's office. Danlov was another up-and-coming bureaucrat. He had more seniority than Viktoria, and had access to the powerful Politburo computers, which in a limited way, tapped into the same database the KGB used.

"You know," Danlov, a stocky man, spoke in Russian "We can go to jail for this."

Then he sat down at a computer terminal and faced the screen. Viktoria replied in Russian. As she did, she tenderly placed her hands on Danlov's shoulders and started to massage him. She gently ran her fingers through his curly brown hair, that had just the slightest traces of gray.

"It's for my father. It's our secret."

"All right," Danlov dropped in the first of eight discs into his A drive. Initially he had trouble breaking the code, but eventually he accessed the disc. He began reading. He became very disturbed. "Where did you get these?" he demanded bombastically.

"From my father's apartment. Why?"

"These are top secret documents," he said, scanning another disc. "They involved experiments on *human subjects.*"

"Human subjects?"

"Prisoners in Siberia with life sentences: murderers and habitual felons who volunteered to take toxic doses of uranium and plutonium..."

"Plutonium?" she stopped him dead in his tracks.

Alex recognized the word. "What's going on?"

"One second," Viktoria said in proper English, and then in Russian to Danlov "What about the experiments?"

Danlov was upset, but nevertheless rapidly scanned deeper into the second disc. "Several of the volunteers died."

"Are you sure?"

"Look, I don't want to have anything to do with these classified discs. I don't want to be shot." Danlov turned off his computer screen and faced Viktoria.

"Please, go through all of them," she implored seductively. "Please for my father and me," she said, softly kissing Danlov on the forehead.

"I..."

"Please."

Forty minutes later Danlov had finished reviewing the eight discs. As he proceeded to each subsequent disc he became more agitated. And with each disc Viktoria became more affectionate.

"You need to destroy these. This information can get you in a world of hurt. Damn, what am I saying, these discs can get us killed!"

"Tell me about them," she asked in Russian.

Danlov explained the information and its meaning on each of the discs. Most of the data was beyond his scientific understanding, way out of his league. But some of the important stuff wasn't.

"Is there a cure? Did my father find an antidote to plutonium poisoning?"

"I don't know. It's hard to tell. *From the information it looks like he did not.* However, eighty-nine prisoners died in the experiments. Only three lived after taking the antidote."

"My God."

"You believe in God now? Are you becoming Americanized?" Danlov asked sarcastically looking at Alex, snubbing his nose at the Yankee.

"No. Please continue."

"Good! The problem with the antidote is not the antidote itself. It seems to work fine. It eliminates the bodily plutonium. The problem is something else."

"What?"

"I don't know. I don't understand."

"You need to promise me...to hide the discs. Lock them up somewhere safe, where no one will find them."

"For you, I'll do that." Danlov said hesitatingly. He nobly kissed Viktoria's hand that again had been resting on his shoulders. What was he getting himself into?

"Pan. Does that mean anything to you?" she asked.

"No."

"Will you run it through the computer?"

"All right."

There was a pause while Danlov fed the data into his processor.

"What now?" Alex asked "What about the discs?"

"I'll tell you in a few minutes," she replied in English, "We need to find out about paradise. My father. Why would he do this?"

"Do what?" Alex asked.

"Nothing," Danlov responded in Russian.

"Paradise means nothing?"

"It means nothing. Milton, Paradise Lost. Nothing."

"Are you sure?" Viktoria insisted. "Check again."

"The only thing that comes to mind, really, and I'm not even sure if it's in the computer... but before the end of the Cold War and the normalization of U.S. and Soviet relations there was..."

"There was what?"

"Paradise Island in the Bahamas," Danlov pulled it up on the computer screen. "Years ago it was a base of KGB overseas operations."

"Alex," Viktoria asked in English, "does Paradise Island mean anything to you?"

"No. Why?"

Viktoria read the computer screen and then asked Danlov for a printout. He gave her one.

"Alex, you and I are in grave danger. We need to leave Moscow tonight, for the Bahamas."

"The Bahamas, why the Bahamas and why grave danger?"

"Alex, how many people were killed in the United States?"

"Thousands will die. Hundreds already and many more will have long term DNA chromosomal damage."

"Why would someone do this?"

"I don't know. You tell me."

"We need to fly to the Bahamas tonight, or if there're no flights, then first thing tomorrow. We'll go back to my apartment, I'll pack and we'll leave immediately."

"We?"

"Don't you want to find my father?"

"Of course."

"Then you'll need me."

"Does that mean I have no choice?"

"You have no choice."

"In the article I read, your father experimented with German Shepherds. He discovered an antidote, that is, only one out of four canines that took the antitoxin lived. By my calculations, I have seventy-six hours left to take the drug. That is, if I have plutonium poisoning which I believe I do. Otherwise, I'll die"

"Alex, its worse than that. Eighty-nine Siberian prisoners took the antidote."

"Prisoners?"

"Yes... and only three of them lived."

"Great. How do you know that?"

"On the discs, and there's a lot worse than that."

"Oh, Jesus."

In Russian, "Thank you Danlov. Please hide the discs. We need to go." Viktoria lightly kissed him—this time on the lips—and she and Alex left.

26

Alex and Viktoria escaped the Politburo through a seldom-used rear door, an exit that was used by Viktoria's bosses when they wanted to escort diplomats in or out, unseen.

"I'm scared," she said leading the way.

"You are?"

"Why would my father do this? I don't understand? Why experiment on prisoners? It's not like him. He's a kind man. He wouldn't hurt a fly. I just don't see it."

"Maybe he was trying to help humanity. Maybe he was honestly trying to help."

"Alex, people died from the experiments. Eighty-nine men are dead because of my father."

"Maybe they volunteered?"

"Volunteered? Would you?"

"No. I don't know. There's always two sides to every story."

"I think he was coerced. Forced to do the experiments."

"Your father?"

"Yes."

"Why?"

"I don't know."

Alex followed Viktoria deep into the catacombs beneath the Politburo, and through an underground maze and then into a tunnel. The exit door was unlocked. It sat next to three massive 19th century coal boilers. Next to them, and above and branching around the door were cumbersome piping for hot and cold water.

"Not such a secret door, it doesn't even have a lock," Alex said.

"No one comes through the basement except for dignitaries. And then of course these doors are one-way and locked from the outside. On the other end, the exit, or entrance as it may be, is a voice box and card code device."

"Oh."

"You have to be on line in order to enter."

"Good. I'm glad you have some kind of security."

"Don't worry. We never have a problem with crime."

"Really?"

"Well at least not until recently. Once the Soviet states broke up. Now with inflation, the Mafia as you Americans call them, have become an annoying pestilence."

"Like from home?"

"No. Really street hoodlums capitalizing on black market opportunities."

They surfaced after they climbed two flights of modern stairs, with metal grilled steps wide enough to accommodate four abreast.

The vestibule required a keycard, which Viktoria slid in, and then an overhead voice asked for her identification. She responded "Siderenko, V."

"Not so secret," Alex mumbled, looking above at the video monitor aimed at the two of them.

"What's that?"

"I said, not so secret."

"It is. Trust me."

They exited onto Leninstrassa in the rear of the Politburo into an alley between a bookstore and a warehouse. "Government owned," Viktoria answered Alex's thoughts. She noticed Alex studying his new environment. They traversed the alley and through shrubs that obscured the entrance and out onto the street.

"We'll walk around and get my car."

"Sounds good to me, but..."

"But?" Viktoria asked over her shoulder and not turning around. She began her march.

"I didn't want to say anything, but aren't you a little surprised that someone would leave your father's computer discs in his apartment, with those so called-top secret experiments? For us to find..."

"Yes..."

Alex cut her off before she could continue, "...where people died from radiation poisoning, eighty-nine of them?"

Viktoria stopped dead in her tracks.

"Almost as if," Alex continued, "someone wanted us to find the discs and read them."

"But the KGB and Moscow Police searched my father's apartment."

"Just my point. Why would these two, probably very professional and thorough agencies leave computer discs behind for anyone to find? You tell me?"

Viktoria stood motionless. She put her left thumb and index finger to her mouth. "You're right. It was too easy."

"Good job woman Politburo lawyer. So, the next question is — were the discs always there? When you first went to your father's apartment, when you realized that he was missing, did you notice the discs? Does he normally have them where we found them?"

"I...don't know."

"When did you first realize your father was missing?"

"Two weeks ago."

"How did you find out? The police?"

"No. I stopped by my father's lab. One of his graduate students told me that no one had seen him in three days. That's not like my father."

"Why did you stop by his lab?"

"Because, normally I speak to him, call him once a day. When after a couple of days I didn't hear from him I went to the Academy of Science to find him."

"Did you call the police?"

"No. I went to his apartment next. I have a key. Sometimes I come over and make him dinner."

"Is it normal to have your father's key?"

"What do you mean?"

"I mean doesn't he have...lady friends, someone who you might have walked in on? Someone who we *might* contact?"

"What are you inferring?"

"I'm inferring nothing, except to ask you if your father has any lady friends he might be with."

"No. I told you already, since my mother died several years ago, my father had become a recluse. He doesn't see anyone."

"All right I'm sorry. I just thought that maybe there might have been..."

"That's alright."

They began walking slowly, cautiously down the dimly lit sidewalk, around the back of the Politburo.

"I didn't call the police..." Viktoria hesitated in her cadence, "They were just there...two officers."

"Just there?"

"Waiting for me when I arrived at his apartment."

"Waiting for you?"

"Maybe. I remember a black Lada police car outside my father's building."

"Didn't you think that it was *kinda funny* that two cops would be waiting for your father? How would they know that he had disappeared if no one called the police?"

"I don't...no...I mean, yes you're right!"

"Were they Moscow Police?"

Viktoria thought, "No they weren't. In fact, I'm not sure who they were."

"KGB?"

"I don't know," her British English accent began to revert to Muscovite.

"Did they walk you upstairs, come in the apartment or were the cops waiting for you outside your father's building?"

"I don't remember."

"Think."

"I was in the apartment and they walked in."

"Good. What did they say?"

"They just said they were looking for my father."

"Strange?"

"Yes. Yes, I didn't think about it then, but yes."

"And when you went into the apartment the first time, did you notice anything unusual?"

"I wasn't really looking..." Viktoria stopped walking. They had begun to turn the corner, almost in front of the Politburo. Just beyond eyeshot was her car. And behind it, parked several spaces back, was the same black Lada she had seen outside her father's apartment. Inside the car were the same two ominous characters.

"...the discs weren't there! The computer wasn't there!"

"Are you sure?"

"Positive. I knew when I first walked into my father's apartment something was wrong, something missing, but I couldn't put my finger on it.

"You're positive?"

"Positive. It wasn't that something was missing, but *something new was added.*"

"We need to get a hotel room now. Somewhere where nobody knows us. And in the morning, take the first flight to the Bahamas."

"We've been had!"

"No Viktoria, you weren't had. *You were meant to find those discs and to read them!* The question is by whom and why? Moscow's not safe. These are big stakes. But why the discs? Why the game?" Alex turned the corner first.

The driver sitting in the Lada did not spot him though Alex was visible in his rearview mirror.

"Leave your car," Alex ordered, grabbing Viktoria by the wrist.

"What?"

"We've been set up. We were meant to find those discs, to come here. You said yourself that only a very few people would have been able to key up the discs and access the information."

"Yes, but..."

"The experiments your father performed were barbaric. *Eighty-nine* people, prisoners died."

Viktoria became defensive, "Maybe they volunteered like you said. They might have known the risks."

"Nevertheless, thousands are dead in America and eighty-nine here...that we know of. We need to stop playing by the *game player's* rules and start making up our own." Alex tugged. He pulled her back the way they came. "We need to find a safe place...to think. And then in the morning we go to Nassau. First thing!"

"Maybe you're right."

"Are there any flights to London tonight, or Paris; and from there to the Bahamas?" he hoped.

"No. Nothing out of Moscow after 9:00 p.m. I'm positive. I've traveled extensively with my work, for my politicians, to both places—London and Paris. Nothing after nine."

"Where is the closest hotel?"

Viktoria was upset. This was happening too fast. "The Oktiabrskaya. It's a block away."

"Anything a little farther?"

"The Metropol is near. It's maybe five or six blocks. We can walk."

"Are you sure."

"No, it's eight or nine blocks. That's all."

Behind them, what had crept out of a corner, was a figure in silhouette. The man was a shadow. He began to follow them. His right hand was buried deep in his coat pocket. He wore a dark-leather jacket, charcoal pants and coat; and his head was covered by a knit sailor's watch cap.

Alex and Viktoria walked down Ryad Street heading to the Metropol. It was almost ten and the avenues were nearly empty. Only a few cars traversed their concrete paths.

"Why a set-up?" Alex asked.

"I'm thinking the same thing."

"To get us killed?"

"Nobody knew about me, that I was looking for my father, except for the police."

"Not true. Our meeting was not by coincidence. This whole thing has been staged."

"Maybe." They walked faster.

Closing-in, in arrow's shot was the man. He was briskly catching his prey. And as he did his gloved hand probed deep into his pocket.

"I wonder..." Alex asked.

The assassin withdrew his silenced 9mm automatic. Only three people, 30 feet separated the vulture from his carrion.

"...if my poisoning in Ann Arbor and Jackson Memorial Hospital in Miami were *unrelated*."

"What? What do you mean? Two plutonium poisonings *unrelated*? Impossible!"

The assassin matched paces with his victims, but in larger strides. He cleverly concealed his heavy steps and the sounds of his shoes tanging against the sidewalk.

Alex and Viktoria turned right onto Okhotny Ryad Street. They entered an avenue full of taverns. Just after they turned, immediately behind them, four young couples walked out of a beer bar. One bumped into the man.

"Excuse me," the drunkard apologized.

"Fool!" the man said, his finger on the trigger ready to shoot. "Fool!"

"Hey," another said. He was a Romanian tourist and spoke in angry school-learned Russian, "My friend said he was sorry."

The assassin pushed his way through the drinkers. The tourist, who was insulted by the lack of respect, grabbed the man from behind. The assassin's nerves were on fire. He spun to face the interceder who by now had grabbed onto him and held on tight to his right shoulder.

"Apologize to my friend."

The assassin looked over his shoulder. He did not want to lose his prey. He cautiously watched as more people poured out of another tavern, obfuscating his view. He attempted to push himself free from the man. The assassin was brutally strong. Robust. But so was the boozer.

Turning back to the man, the assassin forced himself free. The interceder grabbed the assassin, but now with both hands.

"Apologize!"

The assassin was forced to stop his progress, and watch as more people spilled out of the tavern. A party had let out and thirty imbibers poured onto the road.

"Hey man!" a second person said, who accompanied the drinkers and also grabbed onto the assassin, "Don't mess with my friend!"

The assassin kicked out the second man's hold with his right leg. On contact he shattered the man's knee cap. At the same time, he maneuvered underneath and around his accuser in a figure eight, braking his grip. But only soon enough to have the third and fourth friend jump onto him. Within seconds, a full-fledged fight broke out. The assassin was tackled from behind, his legs taken from under him by the second man, whose knee cap he broke.

There was no time for this. The assassin fought his way onto his feet. As the first man hurled onto him the assassin spit two shots out of his 9mm Makarov into the man's abdomen. Blood poured onto the assassin's jacket. The assassin pushed the bleeding man off him as a second came at him. Likewise, he delivered a volley of two more shots. "Puff, Puff."

He then easily handled the third man, who realized his friends had been shot. The assassin jolted the third in the jaw with a powerful sidekick. The fourth man ran off.

Once on his feet, the assassin ran down the street, pushing aside everyone as he scurried toward his targets. His gun was drawn.

He had momentarily lost his victims.

27

" There is more to this than meets the eye." Alex said as they approached the hotel, only four-and-a-half blocks away.

"You think the two plutonium hospital sabotages are unrelated! That's nonsense."

"No. Not really. I mean...in one sense, of course they're related. People just don't get plutonium off the street at a five and dime store..."

"Good deduction Mr. Brilliant."

Viktoria accidentally bumped into Alex as a young couple walking in the opposite direction on the sidewalk squeezed her toward him. She could feel his body chemistry.

"I don't mean to interrupt," she said. "And I don't mean to be inappropriate, but can I get infected by standing next to you, walking with you. I don't want to hurt your feelings, but I have to ask?"

Alex nervously grimaced. "No, Viktoria. I'm safe. The damage is already done. Any plutonium that's in my body isn't coming out."

"Are you radioactive?"

"I don't know."

Not far behind, the assassin closed in quickly. The blood on his jacket had darkened and became nearly invisible.

Even closer. The assassin ran in full gallop. Alex and Viktoria were preparing to make their last turn, and then a straight shot to the hotel. Shoving, forcing his way, the assassin could see them now. As he ran he hid his gun in his jacket pocket. There was a special pouch cut into the leather, to securely hold his automatic. He could see them. Closer.

Sixty meters more and he could get off a clean shot. As he closed-in on his targets he inconspicuously slowed his jog to a fast walk. Forty meters, and now closer. Twenty meters. That was it. The silenced automatic came out...when suddenly in front of him two uniformed Moscow Policemen appeared. They headed straight toward him.

Like a sly fox, the assassin slid the Makarov back into his right pocket. He then slowed from a long stride to a normal-speed walk. "Dammit!" he thought. The police officer headed deliberately toward him. "Dammit. They'll get away."

"Your identification," the taller of the two officers said. Both policemen were over six feet tall and two hundred pounds. The assassin knew he could overpower them if he had too, but this could be more than he bargained for.

The assassin reached into his leather jacket. Inside, in the upper left pocket resting on his chest was his identification. He withdrew his billfold. The documents would be sufficient to cause the officers to release him immediately...so that he could finish his hunt.

"More than coincidence?" Viktoria asked as they veered around one final corner.

"When I left the hospital, before the plutonium, a man followed me. I was on foot, walking back to the hotel. He chased me and shot at me. He tried to kill me."

"Really?"

"Yes...But why poison the entire hospital, to get just me?"

"I don't know Alex, you tell me? Don't you think that's a little grandiose?"

"The plutonium was meant for me. I'm sure of it. My gut tells me." Alex said as they passed several haberdasheries en route.

"Let's suppose Alex, you're not delusional. Then why would someone want to kill you? And let's say the hospital in Ann Arbor was *not*, at least, directly related to the sabotage in Miami. Then why all this trouble?"

"That's a good question. I've got my ideas."

The Moscow Police officers detained the assassin. The bigger one reviewed his impressive documents, and then showed them to the other policeman.

"I need to go now!" The assassin insisted reaching for his identification.

The larger Muscovite officer looked at the other one. They shared a clandestine knowledge. "We'll need to call it in."

"Call it in! Do you know who I am?"

"I'm sorry colonel, but we'll only inconvenience you for a few minutes. There's been a rash of identification forgeries by the Mafia. We just need to verify that you are who your ID says you are."

"I cannot afford to wait!"

"I'm sorry. You must," The larger officer ordered as he removed his mobile radio from his holster. He called in the identification. "Come with us, please." The other officer politely asked as he escorted the assassin by his left upper arm to the police car. The Colonel shrugged off the cop's assistance. Regrettably the Colonel knew that he might lose his prey, but only momentarily.

"You have blood on your jacket."

Unconcerned the Colonel answered matter-of-factly, "Cut myself shaving."

"It's not often that we come across a man of your caliber," said the larger officer as they walked to the black Lada whose engine was still purring. "I apologize for the momentary delay."

Alex and Viktoria arrived at the hotel. Alex walked into the hotel bar, while Viktoria registered under a pseudonym. She paid 1,500 rubles and used the name Raisa Kokanin. Then she walked through the westernized lobby, past four capacious red sofas, several high-necked chairs and two ottomans. Steps led down to a conversation pit where a gas fireplace and its ersatz logs radiated warmth.

Past the lobby, directly opposite was The Russian House, a bar that gingerly played off the name of John Le Carr's novel. Inside, the atmosphere was plenteous. American disco thumped in the background. There was an empty parquet dance floor. There were eight crescent burgundy red leather booths. Between the carrels in the center of four three-quarter circles, were smaller four-place cocktail tables. Each had mahogany split-bottom chairs.

"We're in."

"What name did you register us under," Alex asked as he sipped a vodka soda. He was shaking.

"You're sick. How could you drink?"

"Look at my hands, my friend," he replied sarcastically. He stuck out both his hands. He had developed a coarse tremor, similar to an eighty-year-old man.

"My word."

"My word? I can control it, if I want. It just started."

"I guess you do deserve a drink."

"Yeah," he said. Alex took another sip.

"I'll call and find out the earliest flights out of Moscow. Maybe we'll get lucky and there's a late flight I didn't know about."

"Yeah. Sure, lucky."

It was nearly 10:00 p.m. Viktoria left. She returned twenty minutes later. Her face was full of disappointment.

"Nothing until 5:45 in the morning."

"All right."

"We're booked, diplomatic privilege."

"What's that mean?"

"We don't need to clear customs, and we fly first class." Viktoria thought Alex would be happy, perhaps even elated. He was far from anything. He licked the cocktail glass's rim. He looked around the club which was not much different than one in L.A. or Salt Lake, Chicago or New York. "The world," he thought, "is becoming one big city, and I might not be here to see it evolve."

He could feel the effects of the booze. It was muffled, however, not strong nor sharp, just there. He finished his drink in a slug.

"Your parents?" Viktoria asked.

"Good people."

"Are you close to them."

"Sort of. Not really with my father."

"I'm sorry. Alex, I'll do everything in my power to help you, I promise."

"Thanks. I need to go upstairs, to our room and lie down. Do you mind? I'm tired."

"No."

Their room was near the end of the seventh floor hall. They had a view of Moscow at night, the Kremlin, St. Basil's Cathedral, and the Lenin Mausoleum. Alex wondered if this would be the last time he would see a big city's lights. If he would die in his sleep.

In slow motion he undressed in the bathroom. He took a steaming shower. Normally, the water which struck his back would tingle.

Instead—he felt almost nothing. His skin blanched. Steam turned into fog and filled the bathroom, some sweeping under the door and escaping in a mist. After thirty minutes of standing motionless in the bathtub, he emerged from the bathroom.

He wore his underwear and a towel around his waist. He was barefoot. He had neatly folded his clothes in a heap, leaving them resting on top of a knit-wood hamper.

Alex trudged to a sofa in the one bedroom suite and lay down. He nestled his head on a cushion. He always knew he was going to die, just not this soon. He looked at the ceiling. He closed his eyes and listened to the clatter of heat blow through the ceiling vents. It sounded like the hum of distant automobiles.

In his left ear was a voice. "Come to bed, you can't sleep on the couch. You're sick." He did not argue.

The bed gave way to his weight. He took the side closest to the bathroom. Viktoria turned off the lights. He was not sure if she was even next to him. He was underneath two wool blankets and a sheet. He left his boxers on. He fell fast asleep.

Viktoria, on the other hand, could not sleep. She sat dressed in only the slip she had on underneath her proletarian business suit. She leaned back against the headboard and thought about her father, his work and the disc. "What did Alex mean by 'not connected,' 'separate.'" At 1:00 a.m. she fell asleep, only to wake at three. This time she rolled over. She gently kissed Alex's neck. He did not respond. She then kissed him a second time on the lips and then rested her head on his shoulder. She placed his arm around her.

Downstairs sitting inconspicuously in a Muscovite cab, watching the Metropol's front entrance, was Ilya. Ilya, the taxi driver that picked Alex up at the airport and took him to the Institute of Science to find Dr. Siderenko. Ilya, who took Alex to Viktoria's apartment and then snuck in, and listened to their conversation.

28

As a matter of geography, New Orleans is really an island, with the Mississippi River curving around one side and Lake Pontchartrain and its marshes on another.

In some ways New Orleans might even be considered to be the northern-most isle of the Caribbean. Like the Caribbean it had its native form of music, a traditional Carnival celebration, poverty, yet wealthy social class, voodoo, and a form of cooking that is as hot and spicy as the passions of its people.

When Jack Tandy arrived in the City that Care Forgot he could smell alligator sausage and the jambalaya in the air. He was to meet the blackmailer at Galaroie's on Bourbon Street, in between the music and the bars. Inside the French Creole restaurant, that had been around since the turn of the century, he waited. Someone would find him. The well-dressed patrons meandered in around noon for lunch, one hour after Tandy arrived. He was impatient as hell and smoked his tenth cigarette.

Jack had some "Louisiana food." He impatiently ate the cray-fish peppered in roux sauce. The restaurant's smoke was cheesecloth thick by the time an impish twelve-year old in tattered short shorts, a green T-shirt and thongs approached him with a note.

The boy looked through his dirty brown mulatto locks and said, "Are you Mr. Tandy?"

"Yes, boy."

"Have you waited an hour?"

Tandy knew the joke. The guy was screwing with him. Deliberately making him wait. He looked at his watch and tauntingly said, "No, you have another four minutes."

"Yes, boss." And as fast as the boy came in, he ran out. Tandy, not expecting the elf's response, threw his napkin onto the table, slung ten bucks out of his billfold and chased the man-child. The street was full with tourists and Quarterites. "Where the...did he?" He mumbled to himself.

Next to a lamppost was an old black man with some teeth missing and the rest yellow and Tabasco stained. The Cajun finished smoking his bummed butt, threw it onto the sidewalk and snuffed it out with his hole-worn shoe.

"You looking for a boy?" the trickster asked.

"Yes."

"He left me somethin' for you."

"What?"

"Directions."

"Directions?"

"That's right. Ya got a sawbuck?"

Not wanting to argue, and wanting this charade to get over already, Tandy pulled his wallet out of his back pocket and reached into a wad of money. He removed a ten. Seeing the pile of cash he had on him, the old bum said, "Make that three."

Tandy gave him three, and then the vagrant uttered two words in trade, "Jelly Roll's."

"What?" Jack asked pulling out a pen and a small notepad from inside his coat pocket.

But too late, the old man hightailed it into the river of people and disappeared just as the child did.

"Shit. What's a Jelly Roll's?"

Jack hailed a cab. The driver knew what a "Jelly Roll's" was. He took the long way to the 500 block with the smart green awnings of the royal Sonesta, tucked in among the girlie shows and gay revues with signs like "Big Daddy's Bottomless Topless." Jelly Roll's was where the jazz trumpet great Al Hirt held court.

The cabby dropped exasperated Tandy off in front of the cabaret. Then he said with a wry smile and his window rolled down, "The far table in the back corner, next to the john. You can't miss it."

This game had gone on long enough. It served its point. Tandy did not want to admit it, but it scared the hell out of him. It showed him that the stranger could do whatever he wanted.

Tandy found the back table in the dimly lit room. A poster of Fat Tuesday was over the booth and Carnival music pulsated out of seedy old speakers. Tandy recognized the man. He was no stranger after all.

"You have to play motherfucking games?"

The man smirked. "Don't you like histrionics? Just like in the movies?" He didn't care if Tandy liked them or not. He was having fun with Jack, playing him like a cat would taunt its prey. One that he 'd eventually devour.

"Quit the *fucking games*. How much do you want?"

The man sipped his chicken gumbo. It was rich with okra, shell-fish and sausage. "You like some?" He raised his spoon, gesturing to the admixture.

"No!" Tandy pounded on the table, impatient with the charade.

The man, not willing to take anyone's shit and especially Tandy's, grabbed him by the tie. The man brutally pulled the unexpecting supplicant into his face. "I," he said, in his thick foreign accent, "don't like to be fucked with. The deal is," he tightened his grip and watched Tandy squirm, Tandy's face turned red. "...one million dollars in cash."

"What?" Tandy stuttered.

The man released his stranglehold and returned to his gumbo, first blowing off the steam. "The okra. That's my favorite part."

"I can't get a hold of that kind of cash. Not now."

The man ingested another morsel, and then paused in rejoinder. "You know what happened to Robbins?"

"Look. With everything that's going on.... If I withdraw a million bucks, every governmental agency in the goddamn United States is going to be breathing down my neck."

"You have until tomorrow at noon. Be in Tampa at the International Airport. Wait at the Delta ticket counter. You'll be contacted."

"I can't..."

Again, but this time much more forcefully the man ripped Tandy's tie, pulling Tandy violently towards him, nearly across the table. "Noon, tomorrow. Now get out of my face!"

Tandy straightened himself up, as others at tables near them gazed over reluctantly. He regained his composure and stood up. With the certitude of a company president he walked out.

29

Danlov's apartment was a hovel approximately the size of a post World War II tract-house two-car garage. He had a small bathroom and a Murphy bed that pulled out of his dusky wall. This was his second apartment. He had a first which was much larger and had two bedrooms, one for him and his wife and the other for his two girls.

But he had since divorced, and now at thirty-six was starting his life over. He had known Viktoria for several years, she a young lawyer protégé at the Politburo. He had been interested in her, yet, he had shown restraint and kept his feelings private. It was just within the last ten months when Danlov became officially separated from Lesya and then six months ago divorced; that he thought that it was permissible to think about Viktoria.

Danlov had come directly home after his illegal file search. He was scared witless, not only because he could lose his job, but with what Viktoria had found, the radiation antidote experiments, seriously frightened him. What if someone found out *he* had accessed

Professor Siderenko's discs? Somebody was always watching. Could the KGB know? And now... he possessed them.

"Maybe he should destroy them and not hide 'em," as Viktoria persuaded. "However, if he was to do that—destroy them, possibly he could be in worse trouble."

All Danlov knew was that he should have never gotten into this mess and that he was in way over his head. He was knee deep in Russian borscht red shit.

Danlov sat at his desk, a small table with several books on its solitary shelf: the Russian poet Piot Vjazemsky and the "desk top " writers V. Dudintsev, F. Iskander and V. Rasputin. Danlov read the best books, poetry and the classics. He was a closet poet. In his left hand he held the eight computer discs. Tomorrow he'd take them to his sister Ulga's apartment and hide them. Put them in hermetic plastic and bury them in the germanium flower box on the apartment's southern porch, the one that faced the afternoon sun.

Danlov fingered the discs, sliding the metal covers back and forth. Underneath he exposed the magnetic 3.5 inch floppies. He was apprehensive. He was shaking.

"Tonight," he thought, "he would hide them between his bed's mattress and box spring. He would sleep on them with trepidation, and early in the morning he would go to Ulga's. Simple."

Danlov set the discs on his desk. He pulled the bed from behind a cabinet of false drawers, and lifted the drab bedcover. He hid the discs under the door facing side of his queen mattress.

He walked to the kitchenette. He poured himself a double Cognac. He swirled the heavy liquor in his tall tumbler and watched the legs run down the snifter's sides. Danlov drank the double shot. He could feel the hot brandy disappear into his stomach.

"What had Viktoria gotten herself into?"

There was a knock at the door. Danlov didn't have many friends, especially the type that would drop by without first calling. He was sure nobody had followed him, he thought. It had been over forty-five minutes since he arrived at his apartment. He walked from his kitchenette across his grimy carpet. He answered the door.

"Who is it?"

"Moscow Police."

"Moscow Police?"

My god, he thought, how? Danlov turned and looked at his mattress. In indecision he wondered if he should give up the discs and tell the authorities everything. He had never been in trouble. He had never committed any crimes against the state or society. He had been a perfect citizen.

Why should he be worried now? He had an excellent work record. He had a good civil service rating; and though he was young he was regarded politically. Besides, it would have been impossible for anyone to have known about the discs except for Viktoria and Dr. Seacourt. He was being paranoid about "people" watching and the KGB. He slid the hinged metal coverlet and peered out the peep hole and asked. "Can I see some identification?"

The husky man in a trench coat was distorted by the glass. He withdrew his wallet and showed credentials, official identification. "I need to speak with you at once regarding a matter of Politburo security," he said in an accent more Siberian than Russian.

Oh my God. They know, Danlov thought and then said..."Yes. Yes come in."

Danlov opened the door. He did his best to hide his fear and his burning feeling of guilt. He showed the burly cop into the apartment, and to the seat next to his Murphy bed.

"Danlov Voznesensky, did you have a meeting with Viktoria Siderenko and an American, Dr. Alex Seacourt, this evening at the Politburo?"

How did he know? Danlov tentatively answered, "Yes, I had a meeting with counselor Siderenko. She's a colleague of mine." He buffered-up his confidence, "In fact, I wouldn't characterize that we had a meeting at all. She just stopped by as I was preparing to leave work. We spoke for a while."

"And the American, Dr. Seacourt?"

"Viktoria introduced me to her friend, but he didn't speak Russian, and my English is nearly nonexistent. That might've been his name. Why?"

The policeman did not answer. "What did you and comrade Siderenko talk about?" he asked as he stood pensively and began pacing. Danlov tapped his left index finger on his thigh. He was past dread, and yet at the same time he concealed his fright. Then it began to dawn on him, why was there only one policeman and not two? They always come in pairs, don't they? He knew something about police procedure.

Though somewhat timid and with the reassurance of his conviction of suspicion, Danlov stood to ask. "May I see your identification again, please."

The officer's patience was wearing thin. He repeated his question, "What did you and comrade Siderenko talk about?"

"Excuse me officer, but before we go any farther I really need to see..."

The Moscow policeman cut Danlov's speech short as he reached inside his black trench coat and withdrew his 9mm Makarov automatic with silencer. Enraged because he had been challenged, he walked over to Danlov and pressed the barrel into Danlov's left eye, squeezing the globe into its socket, and forced Danlov back into his chair. Then, with his free left hand pulled tightly on Danlov's curly hair, and whispered, "What did you and the girl speak about?"

Danlov began to shake, "Nothing. She... just brought her American friend to introduce me..."

"For an hour and a half?"

"Yes. That's all. Small talk. Nothing."

With his enormous strength the cop clenched a fist full of Danlov's hair and propelled him across the room. Danlov slammed against the entrance door. Then, the Siberian walked over to the crumpled man and again picked him up by the hair. Using his massive free hand, he pistol-whipped Danlov's face. He opened a jagged laceration below Danlov's eye. A second time, without giving Danlov a respite to reconsider whether or not he should answer his question, the cop threw him to the opposite end of the room. Danlov hit the window ledge with the small of his back, and fell onto the wooden section of the floor just past the carpet's edge. He landed in a heap. Blood streamed from beneath his eye.

The "Moscow policeman" walked over to Danlov and kicked Danlov in the gut. Danlov screamed. He spit and coughed up red chunks of blood. He had a difficult time catching his breath.

The Siberian knelt and gently caressed Danlov's boyish hair, then alternatively stroked his left shoulder and the nap of his neck.

"I'll ask you one time and one time only. What did you and comrade Siderenko talk about for an hour and one half. You know...I'm really having fun beating the hell out of you. Maybe it's best you just don't answer me. At least not yet. What do you think?"

Spitting blood and barely catching his breath, Danlov fearfully replied; yet at the same time he was determined to be true to his oath.

"Nothing...really.... She came over to introduce me to her American friend. We...talked about work. That's all..."

"The policeman" pounded his pistol into Danlov's face. Two teeth and blood jetted out of his mouth. Crimson sprayed the "cop.".

"I...I swear."

"You swear. What to God?" the Siberian howled.

"Yes, I swear. That was all. That was it. We didn't..."

Again, before Danlov could finish, another blow crashed onto his cheek. His remaining teeth quickly coated with blood as profuse new streams emanated from two tears inside his mouth. Danlov coughed and choked.

"I swear..."

"You lie my friend. Do you know what happens to liars?" This time lifting Danlov by his scruff, the Siberian delivered an uppercut that broke Danlov's jaw and sent him sailing into the kitchenette table. Danlov fell to the ground wretching.

The Siberian sighed, lifted his left eyebrow and walked to the kitchenette. He opened the tattered refrigerator and looked inside. He closed the door, walked to the sink and noticed a fruit basket. He picked up an apple and bit into it.

The shiny apple was crisp. It's unanticipated juices wet the outside of his mouth. The cop chewed the fruit, swallowed his piece and then wiped dry his lips before taking another bite. He paid attention to the chewing sounds as he moved his jaws back and forth, grinding the apple. He then walked over to Danlov, who was slumped onto the ground.

He knelt down horizontally and side-by-side to him. Danlov struggled to slowly force his back to the wall. The Siberian did the same. Then, the cop put his immense arm around Danlov.

"Is today a good day to die?"

Danlov coughed, spit and wheezed. He thought of his children and slowly said, "No."

"Good my friend. So...tell me everything. What did you talk about?"

"Really...nothing. Her friend was..."

The policeman, an expert at intimidation, reached behind Danlov's neck. He grabbed Danlov's earlobe and ripped it toward him. Danlov's earroot gave way as a portion of the cartilage tore from it's anchoring.

Danlov barked in pain, trying to push his body away from his tormentor. He was unable.

"Now. One last time. I'm losing my patience," the Siberian said gently, almost sexually as he played with Danlov's earlobe. Danlov reached up with his left hand. He tried to force the "cop" off.

"Discs," he moaned.

"Ah.... That's better."

"She had me read her father's computer discs."

Danlov was no longer able to fight his foe. "Computer discs,

Dr. Siderenko's experiments on uranium poisoning." Danlov explained everything. He had no other choice. He was sorry for Viktoria. He felt bad about his betrayal. It took Danlov fifteen minutes to splutter his story. He told everything. Except...that he brought the discs home to hide for his friend.

"Where are they now?"

"I don't know. In the office...I think."

"How could you not know?" the cop asked and then began to roughly tug at Danlov's ear, ripping farther the splayed tissue. Danlov squirmed.

"She...she made me destroy them."

The cop stood up abruptly. He deliberately walked in front of the groveling Danlov and said, "I don't think so."

Danlov's eyes watered. He cried. He begged for mercy. The rivers of red that had flowered from his mouth began to recede. But, where they had dried up in one place they found new estuaries in his ear root.

"She was afraid. She...thought that the best place for them was to...destroy them. She...she had me...in the furnace. At the office...I didn't want to, but...she said if I didn't she would tell the KGB that I knew...that I was involved."

"The KGB?"

"Yes."

Danlov looked at the "cop" with eyes that begged for leniency and prayed for mercy.

The Siberian slowly continued his pacing in front of his serf. He assessed Danlov's veracity.

"I promise. It's the truth."

The "cop" made his final determination. "All right."

"Thank you." Danlov cringed. The Siberian continued to walk. Danlov slowly attempted to right himself. His legs and body were weak. "I need to see a doctor."

The "cop" stopped walking and said "No, you don't." As he finished his sentence he spit off a shot from his 9mm automatic. He hit Danlov in the temple. The bullet exploded on impact. Danlov slumped to the floor.

The Siberian was convinced that Danlov told him the truth.

He began walking out. Just before he opened the door, however, he noticed something peculiar. "Why in the early evening would Danlov's Murphy bed be pulled down?" The bed was made up and there was no sign that Danlov had either laid down on it, or was preparing to go to sleep. Danlov was still in his work clothes.

The "cop" walked into the bathroom. There were no tooth-brushes on the counter, no shower had been run, no sink full of toiletries in preparation for bedtime. The Siberian studied his reflection in the mirror. The stout face hid the true evil that lay beneath the ex-KGB agent's facade. Just over his left eyebrow was a flick of Danlov's blood. The Siberian licked his finger and wiped off the crimson.

He flicked off the bathroom light and returned to the living room. As he reached the door to leave the pathetic apartment, he studied his victim. A pool of blood had surrounded Danlov in a large donut.

Then he looked at the bed. Something was wrong. The center of the bed, nearest him was just ever so slightly unmade, ruffled, as if...

He thought. Why would comrade Siderenko order the discs de-stroyed? She was a lawyer, a government expert. This would certainly not be her style. The "cop" looked back at his victim. The blood congealed to solid. Then he glanced to the pull-down bed. He walked to its side, eyeing the imperfections, the irregularity that made up the corner between the mattress and box spring.

30

60 Hours Left

It took Aerofloat 221 three hours and ten minutes to fly from Moscow nonstop to Shannon, Ireland. At Shannon International Airport, Alex and Viktoria changed planes and within an hour and thirty-five minutes they were en route to Nassau on British Airways flight 629.

Alex slept halfway to the island. At 33,000 feet over the Atlantic and two hours from the archipelago nation he awoke.

"Why did you kiss me last night?" he asked with curiosity.

Viktoria was protectively holding his hand. Her eyes were partially closed. She heard his question and turned her head and looked softly into his eyes.

"Because you have courage."

"Are you saying that because I'm going to die?"

"No. You have courage to come all this way, to come to Moscow, and now to the Bahamas. You did it on a hunch to help others."

"No. I did it because I'm dying."

"Don't sell yourself short. You didn't know you'd been poisoned when you found out about my father and came to Moscow."

"Are you sure it wasn't to help myself?" Alex asked cynically.

"One thing is for sure, and that's that I'm a good judge of character. In a sense, that's been my job at the Politburo, judging character. You're a brave man."

"No I'm not," he looked at her with dispirited eyes, "I've never felt so vulnerable in my whole life. I feel like I'm kicking a brick wall.. I just want to throw my hands in the air and say Uncle."

"Don't. Don't stop believing in yourself."

Alex turned to the window. Through his bloodshot eyes, he could see the azure water below. The abundant coral reefs were swathed with fish swimming just beneath the surface. The schools swam in billowing ribbons.

At 8:00 a.m. Nassau time their British Air jumbo jet touched down at Nassau International Airport, at the northwest end of New Providence Island, just fifteen minutes from downtown Nassau.

Because of Viktoria's diplomatic passport and her now "favored nation" status, VISA-less entry was quick and painless.

Neither of them had luggage. They both looked like a pair of vagabonds in expensive clothes, than an attorney and a doctor.

Alex's endocrine system was beginning to malfunction — a byproduct of which was his stale sweat. His perspiration was thick with salts. Also he had developed an insatiable thirst, but he lacked the ordinary parched mouth. Peculiarly, he was unable to drink large amounts of water. His brain was tricking him into believing that he was thirsty when his body really wasn't.

New Providence was like any of the other chain of Caribbean islands. It was quiet, sleepy with white sand, short saw grass, palm trees, ubiquitous conch shells, blue lagoons and hidden caves and coves.

There was no organized bus system from the airport, but rather a fleet of cabs, driving old Mokis and Fords. Each cabby was a hustler, who if given the chance would take their fare the long way around the island.

There were two groupings of hotels: those on Paradise Island and those on the north shore of New Providence Island in Nassau. Between the two land masses was the large arched two lane Paradise Bridge, which rose 100 feet above the waterline, high enough to allow most ocean going vessels passage. It crossed from Potters Cay to Hurricane Hole.

Alex only had 60 hours left. The principal hotels on Paradise Island were the Club Mediterrance, Paradise Hotel, Club Land d'or, Pirate's Cove Inn, Paradise Grand Hotel and the Paradise Island Resort and Casino. Alex decided to try the latter first.

They took a cab to the Paradise Island Resort and Casino. If they struck out on Paradise Island they would rent a Moki, a small hybrid between a jeep and motor scooter, and from there hit Nassau. The hotels on Paradise Island were all within walking distance.

Viktoria had brought a fairly recent picture of her father. His hair was brown-white and grizzled. He had a rangy white beard, and his pale face showed the wrinkle lines of age.

The first thing they did at the Paradise Island Hotel, was check into a room and buy clothes. Alex had no intention of staying overnight. His fuse was too short. Nevertheless, he needed to shower and change.

He bought two pairs of slacks, one of which was stupid tourist white. He also bought two sunshirts that were Perry Como fifties. The clothes were deliberately tacky because he wanted to fit in with the tourists. Viktoria bought sandal shoes and a culotte summer dress.

They showered and changed separately. Alex carefully brushed his teeth. With even the simplest nudge of the toothbrush his gums bled.

"Where to?" Viktoria asked, studying Alex with concern. He seemed less wily to her than last night. He appeared depleted.

"We'll start with the desk clerks, then bellboys."

Viktoria wanted to split up. She felt that independently they would be able to cover more ground. However, there was only one photo of Yevgine. Also, they might be suspect hunting for her father individually. Maybe a bellboy, or desk clerk might have seen Siderenko, but they might play dumb, thinking that Alex or Viktoria were with the police or Interpol."

They agreed to work together and tell the story that they were husband and wife and were looking for Viktoria's father who "had Alzheimer's and was lost." This would be bitten into hook, line and sinker. Not only was their ruse "legitimate," but it elicited sympathy from the people they approached. Even two different hotel front desk clerks had become detectives on their behalf.

Moscow

"Got him," a voice said at 5:36 a.m. Greenwich Mean Time in

guttural Russian as he passed the message from his computer terminal to his immediate superior. "Comrade Siderenko used her diplomatic passport in Shannon, en route West."

"Don't let the cracks drain water again," the superior barked.

"It's done. We'll have five teams on them yesterday," another
said.

"Good. Good.... Good to make the machine oil and purr like
we use to in the Kruschev days," the Directorate Chief replied.

"We've always been the best and the brightest."

And in another corner of Moskva, in an equally secret unrelated location, came the following:

**Satellite transmission from outpost Kropotkinskaya metro
station via communication satellite Kalina 5 to WestStar 7.**

**Flight left Vnakovo, Airport, destination tracked with target.
En route. Network alerted. Termination inevitable.**

**Western Hemisphere Relay Response
(11:39 a.m. Eastern Standard Time).**

**Plans amended.
Additional instruction to follow at MIA,
A. and V criteria unchanged.**

Paradise Island

"Pay dirt!" Within three hours, using a network of newly re-
cruited enlistees Alex found his most promising lead.

A valet at the Paradise Grand Hotel, Manfred Stykes remembered one of his co-workers, Ahmed, a Palestine/English immigrant
talking about a senile old man who possibly matched Siderenko's
description. A geezer was escorted from a limousine into the hotel.
He appeared to be an *unwilling* guest.

The reason that Manfred remembered Ahmed mentioning this,
was that Ahmed said, "It was kinda bizarre, for *'that'* limo to come
to his hotel *'this* time of year." Manfred couldn't remember who
"that" limo belonged to, but the limo never showed up in the late
summer/fall season. It belonged to some major corporation. That's
all Manfred knew. The best he could do was have Alex meet Ahmed
at 3:00 p.m. at the Paradise Grand.

"I think we might...have found your father," Alex said.

Tears welled in Viktoria's eyes, "Do you think he's all right?"

"I don't know. Manfred thinks he, or at least he described your father, was an unwilling guest."

Viktoria hoped for the best, but anticipated the worst.

"Let's just pray it's the right guy," Alex said.

They were standing outside in the parching sun, near the hotel entrance and the valet. In the distance they could hear the cruise ships signal their arrivals. "Let's go in and sit down. I need to rest. Get my wits," he said.

Viktoria was sympathetic. Though she did not particularly agree with Alex's decision to momentarily retreat from their pursuit, she acquiesced. What if it was not her father that Ahmed saw. They should be more diligent in their investigation. They shouldn't leave even one stone unturned.

Alex led Viktoria through the hotel foyer as gamblers, sunbathers and shoppers bustled past them. Behind them were two men. They wore khaki island knickers and green, yellow and topaz short-sleeve shirts. They drove up in a mustard-yellow Land Rover, with rusted metal joints. They both carried 9mm automatics tucked into their shorts. They were concealed on the outside by their shirt tails that hung loosely over their Bermudas.

"Let me get some coffee," Alex huffed as he looked at his watch and walked through the casino.

"Is there anything — medicine, I can get for you? Should I call a doctor?"

"No. I'll be fine."

They walked past the tempting slot machines that welcomed every gambler into the casino. Women who were deserted by their husbands sat hypnotized on cushy leather half-chair stools. "Brrrrring" a baby jackpot of $497.25 rang. Quarters spluttered out in rapid-fire onto the metal catcher tray.

To the left was a boundless marble black and burgundy bar, with similar stools, but in burgundy. A bartender was minding the shop. He was wiping clean his drink guns.

Behind Alex and Viktoria the two men closed in fast.

"Coffee please, black," Alex ordered as he climbed onto a stool, when a huge hand swooped down onto his shoulder. Alex turned his head, but not his body, with forward momentum. He was too radiation numb to respond in panic. Viktoria, however, was shaken, especially when the man following the first lifted up his shirt tail to reveal his automatic.

"Come with us," the man who was holding Alex ordered with an obvious Russian accent.

There was an additional tug, but Alex resisted.

Viktoria tapped Alex's shoulder. "We better go with them," she said, frightened.

Alex was determined. He was not afraid. He slowly rose out of his seat. The bartender returned with his coffee and asked, "Is there anything else? And you gentlemen?" he inquired in a picturesque West Indian accent.

"Nothing," the man behind Viktoria said. He restrained Viktoria's left upper arm with his and pulled her away from the bar.

Alex had to think fast. His life was on the line. The first man had firmly grabbed his upper right arm. However, as Alex left his stool with the coffee in his right hand, the man momentarily was thrown off balance. He had to partially release his grip on him. To his side Alex could somewhat see Viktoria being escorted away. Her thug wasn't looking back at him.

As the first man, much larger than Alex, began repositioning his ponderous hand, Alex spun low below his reach and threw the entire cup of scalding-hot coffee into the abductor's face. "Ahhhhhh!" The man roared in agony.

31

Mayo Clinic
Rochester, Minnesota
8:30 a.m.

A man in an olive green jacket, a thick mustache to match his hair, a drunkard's nose and silver-rimmed titanium glasses, parked his car at the Baldwin Building. He had a black vinyl briefcase in his hand. He walked from 4th Avenue S.W., against the one-way traffic to the Mayo Building and the east entrance.

Jittery was not the word. Cops were posted in front of each entrance of the medical center, and at least four undercover FBI operatives were also surveilling the medical center. This was typical for all major medical centers across the United States.

The man in olive could pass for anyone, except that he appeared to be extraordinarily nervous. His picture was taken several times from ultra-long distance atop the Hilton Building using a Nikon N6000 and ISO 6400 film.

He walked into the Mayo Building and made a slow clockwise loop. He checked out the admissions desk, diagnostic and treatment sections for non-hospitalized patients, the cashier's office and administrative offices; and left through the north entrance.

The man left the Mayo Building, walked north on 3rd Avenue

past the Damon Building, deliberated in front of the Eisenberg Building and Rochester Methodist Hospital, and then walked back to his car.

No one saw him drop a 9 and 1/2 by 12 inch manila envelope with pasted-on letters from Life Magazine into the mailbox. The envelope was handled with latex gloves and sealed with faucet water so to not leave a DNA saliva trail.

By 2:30 p.m. the Hospital Administrator had the threatening epistle and the FBI in his office. The terrorist demand stated in crooked, off-center letters:

Pay five million dollars in cash or the fate of your hospitals, medical center and community will be far worse than Ann Arbor and Miami put together. You will be contacted Thursday at noon for further instructions. No police, otherwise.......
YOU'LL ALL DIE!

FBI Headquarters, Washington, D.C.

Director Harlan J. Fiske, one of the few Bush Administration holdovers who was not removed from office by President Climan, had his video monitor on. He was conference calling with Charles J. Stone, Special Terrorist Task Force Director. Stone was in the Minneapolis office. Behind Fiske, he had a projection of the letter, with the paste-up words, and four of his top criminologists at this side. In front of Fiske was an exact laser copy of the ransom demand.

"So what do you think? Is this guy for real?"

"I don't know."

"What about you Charles?" Fiske asked, emphasizing the "char" in Charles. "We need some answers before this maniac strikes again. Is this our man?"

"I agree sir, we do need some answers."

"Well?"

"I don't know. Let me tell you what makes me suspect right off."

"What's that boy?" he said referring to Charles' youth. Charles was a "Wonderkind" at solving mysteries. At twenty-six he unraveled the City Bank Six Million Dollars Bearer Bond heist, that was kept hush-hush from the press. At twenty-seven he was able to piece together two high-profile kidnappings, when everyone else was drawing blanks. "So, talk to me. Why do you think that this guy's not the real deal?"

"Well...first, the amount."

"The amount?" Fiske seemed puzzled.

"To pull off an operation like this...the plutonium must have cost our Doe over a mil, maybe two to three And then to do a deal and ask for only five million...I don't buy it. The economics don't work."

"I'll trust you on the economics, but my gut tells me different."

"Second and more importantly, the quality of his paper...his glue. Real cheap-o stuff. The white adhesive he used is one of the least expensive on the market, probably K-Mart. Also the paper. Not good stock. Maybe an unbleached, recycled eighteen pound grade. Just doesn't fit with someone who would pony up at least two million to buy plutonium."

"Okay," Fiske paused. "What if our perp stole the plutonium and didn't buy it on the black market like you're assuming. Could he be for real then?"

"Yes...I suppose. He would have to be. The key is motive. So far, no one that we believe is credible has taken blame for the sabotages. We have to presume that the motive is money, but more so, we need to presume that it might also be someone who has had some sort of connection with both of the 'nuked hospitals."

"I agree. And what are you doing toward that end."

"Several things. First, we've got our Cray Computers on line with the Mayo Clinic's databases. We've already done that with the University Hospital in Ann Arbor and Jackson Memorial Hospital in Miami. We'll find out if there are any common patients or employees over the last five years."

"What have you found."

"Surprisingly eighty-seven with Ann Arbor and Miami."

"That's an awful high number. Why so large?"

"A lot of Michigan retirees living in Florida in the winter and Michigan in the summer."

"Have you run any of them down?"

"Yes, most of them. But so far, I'm drawing a blank."

"I see."

"However, I feel that by adding this third variable of the Mayo Clinic, we might be able to find something definite."

"I hope so. Anything else?"

"We might get lucky. Who knows? I've got to tell you, whoever is behind this, in my opinion, has some formidable financial resources. The plutonium delivering devices that we've discovered in Miami and Ann Arbor were state-of-the-art."

"I concur."

"So we need to focus on someone who has both the financial resources and motive to pull this off."

"Anything else?"

"We might get lucky."

"Lucky, huh?" Fiske stated, frustrated at the lack of results. Whoever it was that was playing games with him, and Fiske considered *this* personal, was awfully smart. All he had to do is screw up once, and he was done.

"As you know," Stone added, "We've had agents posted around the country; that is, as best as we can, considering manpower limitations, photographing any suspicious characters. We've had four men posted at Mayo, and we have photos from the day our perp dropped off his ransom letter. It was mailed at the Mayo Building. I'm not sure what time, but we might have our Doe's pictures."

"Good work. Is that it?"

"No. We're running down every hotel within a twenty-five mile radius of Rochester to see if we can get a match on any of our photos. So far we have some leads, twenty-two oddballs, between the time the letter was picked up by the carrier, and the previous pickup. I've got leads on three John Does in particular, one that stayed at the Best Price Inn, one at the Colonial Inn and the third at the Starlite. The guy at the Starlite might be our best bet."

"How so?"

"Seems that one of the bell clerks said this average looking white male — dark hair, mustache, light-complexioned, as if he hadn't been out in the sun, 5'8" to 5'10"; was acting real strange the morning our letter was dropped off. Checked in at about 4:30 a.m. He was real tired, as if he had been driving all night. He had a wake-up call at 8:30, left the hotel and then came back and checked out at 11:30. He would have had ample time to make the letter drop. Also, the Doe was sweating up a storm."

"Might be our guy. Chicago?"

"Maybe. Maybe Madison, Milwaukee, Des Moines, Waterloo. Who knows? By the way, when our Doe checked in he paid with cash. The name he used was Michael Smith."

"Pretty original. Dead end?"

"Yes. That's why we especially think that he might be our man. I'll have more for you in three hours."

"Good. Let me remind you Director Stone, how *important* this bust can be for your career. You could end up being the youngest regional director ever, not to mention be in line for a Presidential appointment."

"I'll do my best, sir." Of course Stone knew what Fiske was really saying; and that was, that he better solve this problem or it'll be everyone's ass. And Fiske was right.

"I'll speak to you in three."

"Three."

Stone disconnected the video hookup. He was a crackerjack. He had the investigation wired from the get go. Any possible suspect was checked out, and double checked. Everyone with access, even indirectly to any nuclear installation, anyone or their families who had any major law suit against any of the three hospitals was looked at with a microscopic eye. All hostile foreign governments, Libya, Iran, Iraq, Cuba, etc., who might have something to gain from the panic that had ensued, were scrutinized under the FBI and CIA's jeweler's loop

Stone was checking everything. Terrorist groups, the PLO; and going all the way back to the Red Brigade, Japanese Red Army, Italy Brigade, Puerto Rican FALN, al-Fatah Palestine group, the Shining Path of Peru, France's Direct Action, and all of the identifiable causes supported by Quaddafi.

No stone, no matter how small would be left unturned.

32

A lex had no time to waste. While crouched, with the thug agonizing and momentarily blinded by the scalding coffee, he threw
a kick square into his abductors groin. The man instantly collapsed
to the carpet, as he reflexively grabbed for his jewels.

At the same time the other abductor turned. He partially released his grip on Viktoria. She, as if on cue acted in kind. The second thug lost his equilibrium as he held Viktoria with his left hand
and reached for his gun with his right. Viktoria who was trained in
self-defense spun into the man, and pushed him with both her hands.
With his gun hand reaching into his shorts for the automatic, he lost
his balance and fell backward onto a cocktail table. He knocked
over two chairs.

Alex looked around quickly for a weapon. At the same time he
didn't want to alert the authorities. He found a large ashtray on top
of a table nearest him. Despite his disease, he still had the ability to
respond with an adrenaline rush. He ran to the table and grabbed
the ashtray.

The alert thug lunged toward Alex and tackled him to the ground.

Alex spun onto his back. His fall did not cause him to release his weapon. As the assailant plunged on top of him, Alex crowned him with the five pound paperweight. "Bang!"

A five-inch laceration opened on the thug's forehead and blood spattered onto Alex's chest. The man, whose massive hands were reaching toward Alex's neck frozen in time in a snapshot. Then, he fell to Alex's side just missing him by inches.

"Let's get the hell out of here," Alex yelled as he pushed the bulk's lower extremity out of his way. Alex felt the adrenaline shoot through his body like a bolt of lightning. He felt a rush of euphoria.

"Hurry, follow me," he said, scrambling out of the bar. "This is nuts," he thought, first his body doesn't want to work and now *he's superman.* "What the heck is this radiation shit?" Alex had read that in some rare instances radiation poisoning had paradoxical effects. In one instance he could feel like he was dying, and then in the next he was Superman. Apparently when his adrenal gland was affected it resulted in unexpected or "upon subconscious command" somatic releases of adrenaline.

They shoved their way through the casino, running, colliding and pushing everybody out of their way. They shoved aside a sixty-year old couple, then four college coeds on their first trip to Paradise Island, and lots more.

The thug who was kicked in the groin and whose face was burnt from the scalding coffee got up. He regained his bearings. He wiped the rest of the liquid off his face with his sleeve. The bartender stood frozen. He was determined to mind his own business.

"Quick to the right! The exit!" Alex yanked Viktoria grasping her hand as he dodged more bodies.

The other thug on the floor was out cold. Blood puddled next to his head.

"Where to?" Viktoria asked gasping for breath.

Alex feeling a sense of urgency to escape the hotel ran down brick steps, taking two at a time.

A pair of men, equally formidable, had been waiting outside the hotel just in case trouble arose. The first missed Alex as he ran behind them. But the second spotted Viktoria with her hair flying helter-skelter as she held on tight to Alex's hand.

"They're getting away," the blonde man yelled as he pointed at the runaways.

"Follow me," Alex yelled over his shoulder heading in U-turn, out through a patio restaurant. They jammed their way through the wrought iron glass covered tables, running as fast as they could.

Close behind were the two men who had been waiting outside the hotel. They ran past Paradise Lake through vegetation, in parallel along Paradise Beach Drive beyond a deserted limestone quarry which was covered with ferns and thatch palms.

In front of them lay Club Mediterranee's ivory-covered fence. It was either straight to the white sand beach and a dead end and possibly being caught, or over the barrier surrounding the enclave.

Alex jumped onto a fossilized coral rock and flung himself onto the sticky ivy, his fingers catching the wire mesh underneath. Viktoria followed.

Within seconds they were over the fence, cutting their skin on the prickly ivory branches. Below was a descending hillock covered with Japanese privet and dogrose. Alex fell ten feet to a haunt of calendulas. Viktoria tumbled next to him and almost somersaulted over.

Before them was an open-V riding stable. A slant roof on wooden poles covered the entrance. A bronze statue of a horse and rider about to climb up, Apollo the Archer and Sun God, stood in front of the stable. Inside were twelve white Arabians.

Alex and Viktoria ran through the stalls. They slid on the hay-covered floor. Though they were out of sight, they were easy to track. The startled horses lead the thugs who had just gotten to their feet from their descent down the wall to their victims.

The stalls let out onto a windblown knob, leading down to the ocean.

"Quick," Alex glanced behind him, feeling his calf and thighs burn. One hundred yards ahead and to his right was a second row of tropical trees and a windblock of casvarinas, and then Club Med's changing cabana for the fresh water swimming pool and nude beach. To the left, the hotel lobby, discotheque and restaurants, where pop-off beads were traded and used instead of money.

They ran into the cabana.

"Follow me. I have an idea," Alex puffed out of breath.

They ran into the unisex cabana. The walls were stuccoed white. There were numerous stalls with three-quarter doors. A long changing bench stretched nearly the length of cabana. Large bright-colored terry cloth beach towels were hanging on hooks for the hotel guests.

"Take off your clothes!"

"What?" Viktoria replied panting.

"Take off your clothes now, or we're dead."

A man in his late twenties walked out of a stall. He was naked except for beach tongs.

"My God. This is a nude beach!" Viktoria extolled.

"No shit. Take off your clothes. They'll never find us lying on the sand. We'll blend right in!" Alex's adrenaline rush was running out of gas. He desperately needed a break. A French couple, man and woman in their early twenties, walked out from another stall. They too were naked. She was playfully jostling his genitals.

Alex feverishly stripped off his clothes. Viktoria panicked. She froze.

"I'm a doctor. It's no big deal, remember?"

"I...I..."

"Goddammit, take off your clothes!"

In the background he could hear the horses, and two men yelling in Russian.

Alex pulled off his shirt. He yanked down his shorts and underwear. The cabana was replete with lockers. They were large enough to hang a tennis racket in. Inside there were two hooks.

Alex tossed his shirt at the hook, but missed. It slid to the bottom. Then he turned and helped Viktoria disrobe. She clumsily and slowly pushed her khakis below her knees.

"Take off your panties!"

"No. Not till we get to the beach!" she insisted.

"Oh shit!"

Alex could hear the men coming. They had no time to waste. He grabbed Viktoria's clothes. He threw them into the locker and slammed the door shut. He appropriated two large orange and navy Club Med towels that were folded in four piles on a towel stand.

"Come with me, now!" Sweat was pouring off his brow. Clutching Viktoria's hand Alex tugged her out of the cabana. She was frightened. A short spread of Bahamian grass lay in front of them. It was trimmed to putting-green length. Then beyond was the fine-grain sand.

Without sandals, the sunbeaten archipelago sand instantly burnt their feet. The nude beach was 100 yards wide and sardine-full of naked bodies. Almost all of the flesh was pre-vacation bronzed.

The bottom of Viktoria's feet singed. "It's too hot!"

"Here," Alex pointed. He found a spot thirty feet from tide's edge. He threw down their towels, looking over his head. He could hear the thugs approaching. Viktoria moaned.

Two naked women with their tummy's down were drinking Piña Coladas. They were paging through a French version of Cosmopolitan. They had on wide-brim straw hats and oversized Lolita sunglasses. They glanced at Alex and Viktoria.

Viktoria knelt down and quickly smoothed out the corners. She and Alex plopped their bodies down. She forced the bottom of her feet, big toes groundward, exposing the flats to the sun. Their burning began to cool down.

"Take off your panties!"

"I can't."

"If you don't we're going to get caught. Do it now!" Alex raised his voice. The gal under the brimmed hat, glanced over at them, sipping air from her Piña Colada, the yellow ice getting stuck in her straw.

Viktoria looked up and saw the first of their angry pursuers round the cabana's corner. Glancing at Alex, and now truly afraid for her life, Viktoria kicked off her underwear. She propped herself up on her elbows. She could see the second hound-dog man round the other side of the cabana.

"Put your face down!" he pushed her head onto the towel. She had kicked her panties onto the sand. She didn't have time to retrieve them.

The first man arrived at the beach's edge, then the second and finally the coffee-scalded third, whose was wildly angry. In Russian, the one whose face was vermilion and blistered said "*Get those sons of bitches!* You, Gregov, down that way, check the hotel, you," pointing to the other, "back toward the hotel. We need to stop them before they get away!" The leader's automatic was sizzling in his pocket, ready to be withdrawn.

They were just yards away. Victoria's teeth chattered. She couldn't conceal her fear. Alex, on his belly side next to her, put his arm over her shoulder and buried his head into her neck. He pushed some of her hair over his face, partially obscuring his.

"Listen," he said in a whisper, "Don't move. They'll think we're lovers. Don't say a word!"

She trembled.

The leader, his face and pride stinging, walked onto the sand. He scanned the sun worshipers. A Parisian stood up and cursed the Russian ordering him to get off "his damn" beach. It was for "naturals" only. The thug ignored him.

While on the beach, first the Russian headed back toward the

Paradise Casino. Then he turned around and headed toward the Club Mediterranee Hotel. He stood at water's edge leaving footprints where the sand was firmer. He walked parallel to Alex and Viktoria. He looked down and noticed that something was amiss. Tan panties lay in the sand, not near any towels. He walked to the undies, just four feet from them. Alex could hear his labored breathing. He was out of breath and in blistering pain. The thug bent down and reached forward, kneeling to pick up the panties.

Just feet in front of him, lay the two he hunted.

"Over here," in Russian a voice echoed from near the hotel and down the beach, north of the Paradise Casino.

The leader's instinct momentarily told him different. He scanned the sunbathers, from right to left. He ended on Alex.

The Parisian, who earlier yelled at the thug to leave the beach, stood up in the buff, and prattled in French for the "clothed maniac" to get off the beach.

The leader's glance at Alex was broken. In the background in Russian, "Over here, hurry! I think I've got 'em."

The thug stood, dropped the unclaimed panties, and ran to join his comrades.

33

Viktoria began to cry.

"Shhh. Shhhh. It'll be alright. We'll find your father. Shhhh."

Viktoria cried softly for several minutes. She tried to be strong, but she couldn't help herself.

"Why my father?" she sniffled, collecting her composure.

"I don't know. He discovered the antidote? Maybe whoever was going to do what they did in Ann Arbor and Miami didn't want your father around to help. To save the innocent victims."

She wiped her nose on the towel, "I know that makes sense, but the discs tell a different story. My father failed in his experiments."

"Maybe...*he didn't fail*. Maybe the discs were *deliberately* left for us to read and think he failed."

"But why?"

"Maybe someone *wanted* us to hunt for your father."

"No, Alex. Not us. Whoever it was wanted *you* to hunt for him."

Alex's blood chilled. "This has all been a set-up. There is no doubt in my mind."

"Alex?" Viktoria asked. "Why does someone want you so bad, to go to all this trouble. To kill thousands?"

"I don't know."

"You must. You must have the answer and not realize it. Earlier, my dear, you said that..."

"My dear?" he nervously asked.

"Hush," she put her index and middle right fingers to his lips and pressed lightly. "Earlier you said you thought that the hospital poisonings were related."

"Yes. In a sense." He could taste her skin.

"Expand on that," she said in proper British.

"I mean why, first go to all the trouble and 'nuke' the Miami Hospital, and then almost immediately sabotage the one in Ann Arbor? I don't get it. Someone tries to shoot me, kill me, then zap the hospital. No, I think, had whoever tried to kill me in the first place been successful, then the hospital would have been left alone."

"Aren't you being just a little egomaniacal?"

"No, I'm not. Think about it. If you're going to try to kill me, don't you think that would tip the cops off? Increase the watchful eyes in otherwise sleepy Ann Arbor?"

"Yes."

"If I was going to nuke a hospital, I'd want things as quiet as possible so I could plant my device without notice."

"Yes. So then who would do this and why?"

"I have my ideas. This might sound off the wall, but when I was in New York, right after I heard about my father's heart attack, I was rushing to get a cab. I ran into a man getting out of the taxi. I spilled open his briefcase onto the street. I tried to help him pick up his papers. He got real nervous and pushed me out of the way. He acted like he wanted to kill me."

"Maybe."

"I don't know. I've had no trouble, nothing, until this. That's the only thing I can think of. And it makes sense timewise. So the question is, what was in those papers that I might have seen?"

"Do you remember anything?"

"No."

"Well, it's a start."

"Yeah." He thought for a moment and then changed gears. "At three, I'll get dressed, find my way to the Paradise Grand Hotel and talk to Ahmed. In the meantime, we'll stay here."

"What about me?"

"You wait a half hour longer after I leave, then take a cab and meet me at the hotel."

"That sounds reasonable."

"Alex, who's behind this?"

"I think..."

For the next several hours Alex laid mostly on his stomach, and then reluctantly on his back. He got sunburnt. His post adrenaline buzz had passed and he slept most of the time while on the beach. The brine air cooled his skin as each wave swelled in and then swept out.

His semilucent dreams were violent. He thought about the man and the taxi, about what could have been in those documents. "Hoover," he thought. He remember seeing the word "Hoover."

Viktoria also had been reluctant to roll over on her back. She slept on her stomach for the most part. Then, after a while she too got sunburnt, so she rolled over. She also caught up on her sleep. She was exhausted, afraid and terrorized from the chase. "What," she stirred.

"Nothing," Alex said, "Go back to sleep." Alex pointed to his wrist, where his watch would normally be and said "Time?" to one of his cocoa butter-skinned neighbors.

A girl with ample, tanned breasts looked down at her towel for her watch. She nudged her paramour from last night.

He said, "2:30 mate. By the way."

"What?"

"What was all that yuk-yuk?"

Alex smiled wryly, laying face-up with his eyes closed and said, "They don't want me with his daughter. The guy chasing me. You know how that stuff goes."

"Oh," the Brit answered. He smiled and so did his twenty-year-old girlfriend.

Though Alex could not go back to sleep, he remained supine with his eyes closed. He's the only one who...who would...who could. It's impossible...but...."

At 3:00 p.m. on the nose, Alex opened his eyes and unabashedly stood up. Viktoria's body was lovely. He had not really studied it before. Her skin was bronzing and her breasts were firm and supple. He knelt and tenderly kissed her on the cheek. He wondered why he did that. She was in a light sleep.

"I'll see you at 3:30. Get a cab and meet me at the Paradise

Grand."

Viktoria stirred and turned her hand, shading the afternoon sun with her palm. "Be careful."

"Hey, careful is my middle name."

"Yes." Inappropriately she giggled.

"What's so funny?"

"It might be your middle name, but definitely not your last." She smiled broadly.

"What do you mean?"

It was all she could do to keep from laughing, to break-up the tension. "Do you know what your last name in slang means...in Russian?"

"No."

Viktoria giggled. "I was going to tell you last night," she paused to study him.

"What?" Alex asked impatiently.

"You're Dr. Fertile, Dr. Semen."

"What?"

"Seacourt means semen in Russian."

"Oh. Very funny."

"No, seriously."

"Really?"

"Yes, really."

"Oh. That's...interesting."

"Give me a kiss Dr. Fertile. Please."

Alex looked at her. He knelt and gently kissed her. She touched his lips sensually with the tip of her tongue. He never felt so naked in his whole life. "3:30 and be careful."

Alex stood and returned to the cabana. He put on his rumpled shirt and shorts and left. He walked past the beach on the short Caribbean grass. As he did, he reassessed Viktoria's tanning silhouette. He wondered what it would be like to make love to her.

He walked through the late afternoon inebriated throng. In the distance, fluffy clouds were rising out of the ocean from the southeast. A single-masted forty-five foot sailboat bearing a French flag lay calmly with its mainsail folded in alternative layers onto the yardarm. Skindivers bobbed their heads in and out of the salt water, spraying bands of rain through their snorkels.

Palm trees with their bottom stratum of green leaves turning brown surrounded the hotel's entrance. The orange stucco roof reflected the sun's heat. The brick driveway where Alex waited was the same color as the gable, but hotter.

At first, Alex was reluctant to hail a taxi. He hid anxiously behind a manicured, coned-shaped shrub. Then, after assessing his
surroundings, which he found villain free, he hitched a ride on a
motor scooter from a bar-back. The scooter driver was a gregarious
pitch-black Bahamian. He offered to drive Alex to the Paradise Grand
for free. Alex gave him ten bucks instead.

He arrived sunburnt and revitalized. The hotel was spectacular
and like the Paradise Casino was opulent and impressive. The Paradise Grand had no gambling, and therefore did not have the same
traffic as the Paradise Casino. Nevertheless, it was just as exclusive
a tourist enclave.

Alex thanked his driver. With his ruddy burnt-sore butt he carefully stood and walked through the vestibule and to the bell desk.
The lobby was sumptuous. It had dark mahogany chairs, large overhead brass and glass, late-1920s English chandeliers. Tapestries from
Britain, India, China and Thailand hung on the walls. There was a
blue sculptured Parian marble fountain which was the lobby's centerpiece. In front of the bellboy stand, which had an expansive
counter, was a six-foot tall Santiago figure.

"Can I speak with Ahmed?" Alex asked, looking more touristy
with his alligator red-tanned skin, than before.

The head bellboy pointed to a porter who was standing not far-
off in his proper white jacket. He was just coming on to work.

"Ahmed?" Alex asked approaching the dark-skin Pakistani.

"Yes," he replied with a Neapolitan smile ready to serve.

"Can I speak with you in private?" Alex slipped him a twenty.
Ahmed took the money and told Alex to follow him. They walked
outside, through a side beach entrance across a veranda to an open-
air pavilion with a thatched bale roof. They sat down alone.

"Do you know this man?" Alex asked, showing the bellboy the
photograph of Dr. Siderenko.

"No," Ahmed replied, shaking his head from side-to-side.

"No? That's not what I understand. Your friend Manfred tells
me you do."

"I don't know any Manfred," Ahmed said, looking around. He
obviously knew something, but was reluctant to help.

"Look my friend," Alex said, taking the smaller Ahmed by his
shoulders and shaking him for dear life. "My life depends on it."

Ahmed's brow and palms began to sweat. He squirmed, yet he
refused to answer. Alex shook him again. "Please. I need your help."

"These people are very important. I can't help you."

"Who are these people?" Alex pushed Ahmed free. Ahmed looked at Alex. Alex's sick eyes were sad.

"Who...tell me!"

"All...all I know is that they normally don't come this time of year. I know nothing else. I'm nobody. Leave me alone."

"Look," Alex roared, "My goddamn life depends on it. I've been poisoned. I'm dying. This man in the picture may be the only person who can save my life. I need your help!"

"I'm sorry, but I can't." Ahmed said lowering his head. His eyes and shoulders drooped towards the ground.

"What is it? You need more money? What?"

"I have a family."

Alex threw his hands into the air. Then, he dropped his hands and humbly lowered himself to one knee. In a soft and convincing voice he begged "Ahmed, thousands of people in America, in Miami and Michigan have been poisoned and have died from plutonium radiation."

"I know," Ahmed interrupted.

"Thousands, maybe tens of thousands, like myself are dying. They have been poisoned. This man," Alex said pointing to the photo Ahmed had in his hands, "may be the only one who can save any of us."

"If I tell you, they will kill me."

"Ahmed, I beg you...for all the innocent victims who might die. Please!"

Ahmed stopped shaking. He reached into his pocket where he had placed the twenty and gave it back to Alex.

"It was a limousine. They never come this time of year. That's why I noticed. There were two men on either side of your friend. I remember the old man was scared. It was obvious."

"Are you sure?"

"Look at me. Am I terrified?"

Ahmed was.

"Yes."

"That's how he looked."

"Where did they go? Who were they?"

"If I tell you and they find out, they'll kill me. I'm sure."

"Please, I beg you."

Ahmed paused, letting his conscience be his guide. "They didn't stay long. They were here only one day. The limousine was from..."

It was nearly 3:30 when Alex finished with Ahmed. The early

cotton clouds were turning into afternoon Caribbean storms. The light was a mosaic of intermittent scraps of clear and shade. Alex grasped Ahmed's hand with both of his. He shook it firmly.

"Thank you."

"May Allah be with you," Ahmed prayed.

When Alex released his grip, the single twenty had been replaced by five twenties. They rested in Ahmed's palm. It was enough to help him and his wife and his plethora of children live a momentarily better life.

"No, my friend I can't take your money."

"I'm sorry. You have to."

"May Allah show his blessings."

It was 3:30. Sunburnt and harried Viktoria should be waiting for Alex in a cab. Alex hurried through the hotel lobby, past the entranceway and out onto a heat radiating circular driveway. A white and yellow Chevy and four white Ford cabs were in the first lane waiting for their fares.

A second and then a third row were three and four vehicles long, respectfully. It was there, in the third row, that Alex saw Viktoria waiting. She was facing straight ahead. Her look was stoic.

It was then that Alex felt the gun in his back. The steel barrel bore deep into his rib, just above his kidney.

"Straight ahead and nothing funny."

Alex walked forward. It was over. He was a dead man. Then again he was dead anyway, wasn't he?

The gun's silencer thrust cruelly into his flesh. "Shoot me," Alex challenged as he approached the car. He looked toward Viktoria. The man behind the steering wheel was one of the three that had chased him.

Alex realized that he need not fear anything; for in reality he had little to lose.

The thug with his gun barrel pressed deeply into Alex's back, answered his challenge. He spit off a shot.

34

USA Today, October 1, 1999 Nation in Frenzy Presidential Leadership in Question.

"Washington, D.C. — Critics have attacked President Climan for his inability to take control of the crisis and his Nazi-like marshal law tactics."

New York Times, October 1, 1999 Warrant Served on Radical Group.

"Investigation targets militant factions. Search warrants were served today at American Peoples Party headquarters. Ultra right-wing group suspect among others."

Los Angeles Times, October 1, 1999 CIA Deputy Placed on Administrative Leave.

"Special Prosecutor Appointed William Rodriques, Chief Deputy Director under CIA Chief."

Toronto Star, October 1, 1999 Canada Closes Borders

"U.S., Canada Relations Strained. The United States and Canada, after years of expanding trade and free borders, have closed borders due to plutonium threat."

Moscow
(Kumitet Gosudarstuennoy Bezopsnosti)
"Committee for State Security" — KGB Headquarters
Director Lavrenty P. Yezhov Present

"Comrades, have we made any progress?"

"Yes," Yury Karazhinsky, the associate director, answered. "We have been informed through the GRU (Golavnaye Razvedyvatelnoye Upravlendye or Central Intelligence Office, the KGB's equivalent for Military Intelligence) that the plutonium used in the United States, to sabotage the two hospitals, that killed thousands; was routed through Libya with Maummar Quaddafi's support."

"I thought," a subordinate interrupted," that Quaddafi was out of the business."

"That's correct," Karazhinsky continued, perturbed. "Out of the uranium/plutonium export business as of 1991, but not out of the espionage and transportation business."

"Associate Director Karazhinsky," Chief Director Lavrenty Yezhov said, "That's all well and good, knowing the source of the plutonium, but the germane question is — how much is there and who is behind it? President Cheka is meeting with President Climan in Washington, D.C. tomorrow. We better have answers, or we're likely to lose funding for our joint plutonium/uranium breeder nuclear reactor program. That program is extremely important right now."

"Director, we're doing the best we can."

"Must I remind you gentlemen, our careers and the future of our nation is at stake."

"Director, I have other news...perhaps somewhat unsettling."

"What?"

"Director, we believe that the source of the plutonium, was ..." Karazhinsky paused, ready for the onslaught that he was about to receive, "*our own KGB.*"

"What!" Yezhov yelled, standing up and slamming his palms on the table.

"A renegade KGB agent. General Andrei Tokarev."

"How could this happen?" The director remained standing,

red-faced, the veins bulging out of his neck, "Do you know, do you even know what this could mean to Russia should word leak out!"

"Yes, director. We're doing everything in our power to bring the situation under control."

Karazhinsky's assistant stood. Karazhinsky nodded to him to proceed and pass out the dossiers. They were leather bound and stamped "Ultra Top Secret." On the right side were photographs of Andrei Tokarev and his aide-de-camp Colonel Boriskov Khoklov. On the left, a 28-page stapled document.

"Gentlemen, General Andrei Tokarev left the KGB about four years ago, or that is to say, more accurately started working freelance."

"Freelance?" another associate director asked.

"Yes. In 1991 with the dissolution of the Soviet Union and the far-flung operational cuts that the KGB experienced," heads around the long oval conference table affirmatively nodded in agreement, "some of our senior or more experienced agents were encouraged to retire. Others went on to part-time."

"What about Andrei?"

"He went...to let's just say part-time."

"What does that mean?" Director Yezhov asked.

"We established a loan program, as some of you may know, with our new Democratic allies."

"So you have been lending Andrei out?"

"Yes, in a sense."

"Well, does that mean in a sense 'Yes' or in a sense 'No?'"

"It means, with the approval of President Cheka we lent Andrei to the CIA."

"To the CIA?" Yezhov rumbled, raising his voice again. "I wasn't notified of this."

"Mr. Director, I'm sorry but it was a top-secret mandate form President Cheka to me. No one was supposed to know. Not even you."

"No one?"

"Actually, Mr. Director, I need to tell you there are more."

"More! How many?"

"Twelve."

"Where are they?"

"Since the crisis, they've all been called back."

"All?"

"All, except for Andrei."

"What about Andrei?"

"He and Colonel Boriskov are missing. They're the *wild cards.*"

"Let me get this straight," the Director said boiling over, "The CIA and two of our top agents may be involved in this plutonium crisis?"

"Director, I'm not saying that. What I'm saying is that Andrei's been on loan, and that most recently he has worked for the CIA. That's all I know."

"Mother Hope! Does President Cheka know this?"

"No, not yet, but he will before the day is out."

Freetown, Sierra Leone, West Africa
Coded message from Direction Gnrale
del la Scurit Extrievre (DGSE)
France's overseas covert intelligence agency,
intercepted by MI-6 British Intelligence
and forwarded to "C," the anonymous director

"C, it looks like the KGB is onto something in Nassau."

"What is it?" C asked, annoyed, sipping his evening tea out of a china cup once used by Winston Churchill.

"Sir it looks like...the CIA might be behind the plutonium fiasco."

"The plutonium nonsense?"

"That's right."

"What do you have to substantiate this?"

"Our operative in Freetown, Sierra Leone intercepted a KGB transmission to Moscow. Seems like the shit stinks deep."

"What's the KGB's angle? And what's going on in Nassau?"

"That's what's not clear. Seems that they've taken care of some American loose cannon."

"How's that...?"

Paradise Island, Bahamas

Alex thought he died. His breathing was labored and he had a blinding headache. Pain knife-stabbed deeply below his right shoulder blade, where he was shot at point-blank range by the tranquilizer dart.

"Where am I?" he asked. Alex sat up naked. He was in bed. Sheets covered him from the waist down.

"You have a fever," a voice said.

Alex looked to his right. There was a chair next to a rattan table where a man was sitting. The walls had rattan matting.

"Why am I not dead?"

The thug whose face was scalded folded the Nassau newspaper that he was reading, and with a scowl called for the doctor. A man in the other room placed a call to the hotel lobby, where the Bahamian physician was paged. Within fifteen minutes he arrived at the suite.

"How do you feel?"

"Terrible," Alex pulled himself up in the bed, his head pounding.

"You have a pretty nasty wound in your back. Does it hurt?"

"Yes...and I don't know that?" he replied indignantly as he felt the gauze bandage covering his shoulder blade.

"Let me see it."

"Yeah."

The doctor walked around Alex and leaned over the bed. He pulled down the bandage. There was some stinging. From close range, the dart penetrated into Alex's shoulder blade, ripping the muscles, and drilled into the bone.

"You needed stitches."

"I didn't think he'd shoot me."

"Then don't ask for it next time."

Alex lifted his brow, "Are you in this doc?"

"Nevermind that. I gave you eight deep and twelve superficial sutures. I also gave you a shot of ceflaxan and here are some antibiotics." The doctor finished repositioning the gauze pad. He handed Alex a bottle of red capsules.

"Thanks, doc."

"That'll be all. I'll call you if I need you later," the man with the red face said, still sitting in his chair.

Moments after the physician left and the anteroom door closed, the door opened again. Viktoria accompanied by another man, enter the bedroom. Alex had been out for seven hours. The fast-acting scopolamine had mostly worn off by the time he regained consciousness. The man guarding Alex had not said a word to him. Alex did not speak with him either.

"Why wasn't he dead?" he thought.

"Alex!" Viktoria ran to his side and hugged him. She kissed his forehead, and with her hand brushed back his hair. The man accompanying Viktoria walked over to Alex's side. He stood next to Viktoria. He introduced himself.

"I'm Colonel Gregor Taskonosky, KGB. Dr. Seacourt, I'll cut

right to the chase. We need your help to find Dr. Yevgeni Siderenko."

"What?"

"We need your help to find the professor. We know that you've been looking for him."

"Wait a second. You guys just tried to kill me and now you want my help?"

"Don't ingratiate yourself, Dr. Seacourt. We never tried to kill you, we tried to talk to you."

"You sure have a funny way of communicating."

"Comrade Siderenko has filled us in on what you know and why you're here."

"So what do you want from me?"

"We want you to continue doing what you are doing — hunting for the professor."

"If you have all the pieces, why don't you do it yourself?"

Colonel Taskonosky ushered the scalded-face man out of the room. He told him to close the door behind him. Viktoria and Alex were left alone with the colonel.

"We may have a mole in our organization."

"A mole?"

"Let's just say someone is working both sides of the street."

"Why do you need me...us?"

"My friend, it's a symbiotic relationship. You need Dr. Siderenko..." the Russian said as he began tapping his watch, glancing down at the time, "...*for the antidote*. Let's just say it is a matter of *urgency*. Don't you agree?"

"Yeah, that's true. So..."

"We'll need your assistance in the morning..."

"The morning? If you need my help, then let's get started now."

"Dr. Seacourt, it's 11:00 p.m. The morning's not that far away. In the morning we'll meet with the CIA to brief you on what we have, and how we can help each other."

"The CIA, what does the CIA have to do with the professor?"

"I'll explain everything to you then. In the meantime, you and comrade Siderenko need to spend the night here." They were on the 10th floor of the Paradise Grand Hotel, in a suite. "And don't bother trying to call out or leave. The phones have been turned off and I'll have two men posted outside your room at all times."

"I think..." Alex began to say as Viktoria nodded "no," signaling Alex not to talk.

"Goodnight, Dr. Seacourt," Colonel Taskonosky said. He walked out of the suite, leaving behind two of four agents. One was posted in the anteroom, the other outside the door.

"Are you all right?" she asked. She smothered Alex with a tigress's embrace and then kissed him on the neck, cheek and lips.

"Easy. My back hurts."

"You wimp," Viktoria purred, pushing herself off. She grimaced and pretended to be offended by what he said.

"I don't get it. What the heck's going on?"

"Alex, I think that they want to help us...the KGB."

"What happened?"

"They thought that we were trying to escape. That's why they chased us."

"But Viktoria, is your memory..." Alex was again experiencing the effects of radiation poisoning. He felt groggy. Maybe it was the lingering effects of the scopolamine dart.

"What Alex? Alex, are you all right?" Viktoria steadied him, propped him up in her arms. "Alex, even if we wanted to leave, would you be able to travel?"

"No," he said pensively. "They sure have an interesting way of showing that they weren't going to try and kill us, sticking a gun in my back at the casino, and..."

"Hush, darling. I think they are trying to help. I spoke with Colonel Taskonosky for quite some time. I've heard of his reputation at the Politburo. Word gets around. You need to trust my instincts."

Alex felt disoriented. The room began to spin. Streamers of rainbow colors twirled and danced in the foreground.

"I don't feel well. I need to throw-up."

Alex tried to stand, but was unable to get out of bed. He slumped back down. His brain was cold-cocked.

Viktoria turned off the lights. The Bahamian starlight eased its way into the room through the sheer drapes. The rays soaked the suite in a seraphic mist.

Viktoria walked into the bathroom and turned on one of two vanity lights, the dimmer one over the mirror. She undressed, sliding her shorts below her burnt thighs. Nearly three hours on the nude beach was too much for her. Her buttocks were singed. She explored her naked body. She thought that she was just as attractive as the nymphets on the Club Med beach.

Viktoria had never really viewed her sexuality with any serious thought, since her focus was always politics, law school and her career. She thought that she could lose some weight, and wondered why more European and Asian women don't shave their legs. Viktoria's were shaved, but that was only because she had been to England on numerous governmental trips. She would have been politically incorrect if she didn't dress like a diplomat with a business suit just an inch above her knees and conservative hose.

She found a plastic bottle with lotion. It was also a moisturizer. She rubbed it into her skin, and especially deep into her buttocks, breasts and abdomen; places that hadn't seen sun before. Applying the liquid made her feel her sexuality. She looked through the bathroom door at Alex. He was fast asleep.

She turned off the light and slipped into one of the two hotel terry cloth robes. She walked to the bed and slid under the covers next to him. She studied his silhouette against the night light, and wondered what was going to happen; if her father had really found a cure, if she would be able to help Alex. She stared at his hair falling backward, down his forehead; and watched his mouth perching open, almost microscopically to capture the next breath. His breathing mesmerized her. Before long, she succumbed to his trance and fell deep into sleep.

35

Morning in the Bahamas in late September was tranquil. The summer rainy season had passed and the prevailing winds from the northeast were overcoming the southerlies. The Caribbean pines waved in the eight-knot gusts. A chameleon lizard had worked its way upon the hotel walls and was basking on the verandah, living off the crumbs spilled by careless tourists.

Viktoria nudged Alex. Overnight he had a spiritual and physical revival. He felt a sense of rebirth. His world became crystal sharp and focused. The plutonium poisoning had wrecked havoc with his body, his immune system, his flight-or fight responses, and his psyche. Mentally he felt balanced, but physiologically he could not control some of his auditory and visual sensations. He had acid trips on demand, or so he thought. What an interesting way to go.

The door to the anteroom opened, and in walked two relief KGB agents. Alex had previously seen neither. They brought clothes for him and Viktoria. She was already up and in the shower.

"You have ten minutes," the more substantial one said. He

positioned himself next to the archway between the anteroom and bedroom.

"Do you mind if I get a little privacy?" Alex asked. The taller looked at the other, and acknowledged his request. They walked out, but not before Alex could order some coffee.

He knocked on the shower door. "Mind if I come in?'

"No," she replied.

He felt a little uncomfortable. He stepped into the steamy bathroom. She looked at him. He pointed to the shower, as if asking for permission to join her. Her eyes told him to enter.

He slipped into the shower. Viktoria was washing her long brunette hair. She was running her fingers through it. He watched the lather froth in swirls.

"Alex, you scared me," she said after washing the shampoo out of her hair.

"Sorry."

She touched him softly on his forehead and then ran her fingers down the side of his face to his ear, then along his neck to his shoulder. She gently kissed him on his closed lips. She too felt apprehensive. "Let me wash you."

"Yes," he replied.

She took the bar of soap and washed his brine-prickled skin. She started at his feet and tenderly worked her way up. He stood there and let her baby him. He was returning to his womb. He was going full-cycle.

The droplets of tepid water beat down on her back. She felt sad. Spray fizzed into his face and splashed onto his body in a soothing mist. She could tell that he wanted to make love to her, but he didn't have the energy nor emotional ability to do so.

Viktoria also felt the desire to make love to him, but she was afraid of the radiation poisoning. Telepathically he understood.

"Alex," she softly, melancholically said. "I don't want to see you die."

He stood motionless, his chest to her breasts, the spatter drenching them both. "Neither do I. I won't die. Don't worry about me. I won't."

Viktoria did not believe him. She knew that he had no control over the situation, except for his only hope—to find her father.

They embraced and held each other tightly. They looked deeply into each others eyes. Then there was a knock on the door.

"Hurry. We need to get going."

"Coming," Viktoria yelled through the door. She turned off the water. They dressed, he slowly, and had coffee.

To Alex's surprise the clothes that the KGB agents bought for them fit exactly. He had long pants, a shirt and tie and a light cotton sports coat. She, a manila blouse, short navy skirt and business jacket. They were given new shoes.

"The KGB is thorough," Alex said to Viktoria.

"Yes they are. More than you anticipate."

They followed the two relief agents to the elevator and then downstairs and outside to a garden restaurant. There at a table, set apart from others, were six waiting men. Four appeared very un-American, and two "suits" looked very made-in-U.S.A. They sat in the open air. Palm trees and short olive green shrubs protected them from the island breezes. The two Americans had black coffee. One also had orange juice. Three of the four KGB agents had tea. There were two empty seats next to each other, with their backs to the hotel. The ocean view was limitless.

Alex was introduced in rapid fire to the six. The only name that stuck was that of Colonel Taskonosky, the KGB operative from last night, and Thomas from the CIA Caribbean Covert Division.

"I'll get right to the point, Dr. Seacourt. We want your ass out of the Bahamas and back to the United States, today!" Thomas the Princeton-educated politico snob said.

"Wait a second. I thought this meeting..."

"Dr. Seacourt, what the Russians might have told you last night, and what our position today is, is totally irrelevant." Thomas pointed to the rest, and especially Colonel Taskonosky. Taskonosky acknowledged Thomas.

"Colonel, last night you told me something altogether different, that you needed..."

The colonel interrupted Alex before he could finish, "Dr. Seacourt I'm sorry but the situation has changed."

"Changed?"

"What situation?" Viktoria broke in in sharp-toned angry Russian.

"My father's life is at stake, you son-of-a-bitch. Why the change in plans?"

"I'm sorry, comrade Siderenko," the Colonel replied in Russian. "There has been *a change in venue*. I respect your position at the Politburo. In your short career you've made quite a name for yourself. I promise you I will do everything I can to help you."

"Alex," Viktoria looked at him, who was more surprised then

she, and said in English, "Let's get our ass out of here."

"Not so fast," Thomas said, reaching into his pocket.

Thomas pulled out two airline tickets. He handed them to Alex. Alex did not accept them. "Take them or else I'll have you arrested for obstruction of justice."

"I don't get it. This...is..."

"Take the tickets," Viktoria said, reaching for them and lifting Alex up under the arm.

"Wait a second."

"You're right, Mr. Thomas, maybe you are better suited to find my father," Viktoria said.

"I've arranged for doctors at Georgetown University Medical Center to attend to you once you reach the States. Your parents have been moved to Washington, D.C. You'll see them there."

"Already?" Alex thought, "It's been just two days. They wouldn't have moved...my father was too sick." Then he said, "I see what you mean Mr. Thomas, you're better equipped to handle the situation."

Alex took the tickets from Thomas. He opened them and briefly scanned them. One ticket was to Miami, then a connection to D.C.; the other was to Miami then to London and Moscow.

"I hope you feel better Dr. Seacourt," the Russian colonel told him. Alex walked off. He was befuddled.

"Don't talk until we're well away," Viktoria cautioned.

They walked out of the restaurant, with the two KGB agents shadowing them. They found the first elevator up and took it without the thugs in tow.

"There's something very wrong," Viktoria spoke softly.

"I had a feeling something reeked when the CIA agent told me my parents were transferred to Georgetown University. That's bologna! My father was too sick to be moved anywhere. It was a miracle he survived the trip from Ann Arbor to Detroit."

"Colonel Taskonosky let me know there was something afoul."

"How?"

"I have *no* reputation in Moscow. He damn well knows that. Furthermore, when he spoke to me in Russian he said there's been a change in *venue*. He should have never used the phrase change of *venue*."

"What do you mean?"

"In the old spy days, before the KGB lost much of its power, change of venue, which is a very American term, meant something else in Russian.."

"What's that?"

"Double-cross"

"Double-cross! Are you certain?"

"Yes. Plus the colonel continued to speak to me in Russian. It was rude of me to change languages, especially in a meeting. Protocol would have had the colonel respond to me in English not Russian."

"Why did you speak in Russian in the first place?"

"I was livid. I was insulting the Americans, except they probably didn't even know it.

"Are you positive?"

"One hundred percent. The Colonel was telling me something. He was giving me a message. One of the CIA agents must of spoke Russian, and if not, then certainly the conversation was wired and the CIA would have had it translated."

The elevator opened onto the 10th floor.

"I've gotta tell you something," Alex spoke with a furtive gleam in his eye," I never told you about my meeting with Ahmed."

They walked down the hallway to their suite, slid their room key card into the lock and pushed open the enamel double doors. "Not inside," she warned. Just behind them, as they entered the suite, the two KGB agents were visible as a second set of elevator doors opened.

"We'll wait until the agents come in. I'll tell them that we're going to make love before we leave. They have to let this 'dying man' have his last wish," Alex muffled.

"What do you have in mind?"

"Just follow my lead."

Alex turned on the stereo and took off his shirt, shoes and socks. Predictably, within seconds the KGB agents arrived.

"Dr. Seacourt your plane leaves in one hour. You'll need to come with us."

"Gentlemen," Alex said, whispering, letting the two post Cold War spies in on his secret, "this might be my, you know...last time to make love. If you gentlemen don't mind, this dying man has one final wish."

The agents smirked and looked at each other. Like a pair of college freshman they agreed. "Fifteen minutes. No longer."

Alex began unzipping his pants as he left the anteroom. He walked back into the bedroom. He closed the double doors behind him and turned up the music. A Rolling Stones song, "Jumping Jack

Flash" bellowed. Alex immediately zipped his pants back on, and feverishly dressed. He then ripped the sheets off the bed and began individually rolling them up into bandanna cords.

"What do you think you're doing?" Viktoria whispered below the music, "Do you think that you're going to climb down 10 stories?"

"Yep!"

"Yes? Are you crazy?"

"Of course. Help me."

With dispatch, Viktoria assisted him. They rolled up three sheets from the king-size bed, not enough to rappel more than 15 feet after they were tied together.

"Now what, Mr. Bright Ideas?"

"Follow me."

Viktoria followed Alex out onto the balcony. The verandah overlooked Nassau and the high arching Paradise Bridge between Paradise Island and New Providence.

Alex began tying the sheet in a surgeon's knot to one of the metal struts that came out of the concrete balcony, and was one of four forming the balcony's fence.

"What do you think you're going to..." and then Viktoria looked down one hundred and fifty feet to the ground and sheer rocks below. She knew exactly what Alex had in mind.

"Tell me one thing, before we kill ourselves — what did Ahmed say to you?"

"Not here," he spoke softly. "Ladies first."

36

Thursday, 11:30 a.m.
Rochester Methodist Hospital —
Administrator George Taylor's Office

"Agent Stone here," Special Operations Director Stone answered with undaunted confidence that he was going to get his man.

FBI Director Harlan J. Fiske was all business and in need of a solution. "Shoot, Chuck."

"We've got a positive I.D. That is, our man in the green jacket."

"Go."

"Our Doe definitely stayed at the Starlite Motel. Also, a hospital admissions clerk remembers our man. He was acting jittery. She's fairly positive that it was our man who dropped the letter into the mail box."

"Good job."

"My guess is that he'll be calling via remote, so we might not have a whole lot of time to trace him, but if it can be done, we'll do it."

"Good.... Administrator Taylor?"

"Yes," Taylor replied. He was a gray-haired eminent bureaucrat whose politicking was legend in Rochester and at the state capitol. If anyone wasn't going to scare, it was he.

"I just want to thank you for your assistance. I also want to reassure you that we've thoroughly combed the hospital. I am confident that there is no device anywhere. Nevertheless, I've got a team of fifty agents ferreting-out Methodist...and we'll do so until we either find a device or get our Doe." Stone said.

"Director Fiske, I appreciate your cooperation. We need to do everything in our power to get this son-of-a-bitch. I'm entirely at your disposal."

"Thank you, George...Chuck keep me live on the mobile."

"Done."

At exactly twelve noon, the Administrator's phone rang. Everyone was ready. The voice, which sounded mechanical, said the following without interruption:

> "At exactly 6:00 p.m. today I will have you paged at the University of Wisconsin Student Union in Madison. You need to be there with five million dollars. You will be given instructions. If you come with anyone, the device will be activated and the plutonium released.

> "If you come without the money the device will be acti vated and you can kiss your sorry-ass hospital goodbye. If you call the authorities or are followed or have me arrested, the device will be automatically activated.

> "Only once I have the money, can I deactivate the device. If I am arrested, the device will automatically go off." Then click.

"Got it," one of the agents said, listening into a mechanism that connected directly with their agents at the telephone company. "A direct call from the Friendship Inn, Room 160, in Waterloo, Iowa."

Within twenty minutes, twenty-five special agents, Rochester Swat and ATF backup stormed the hotel room. Inside they found a pocket-size Panasonic tape recorder that had been played into the telephone mouthpiece. The room was ransacked for clues, but none were found.

The hotel clerk, who rented the room, said that he rented it to a drunkard, maybe a wino who said that he was checking in for one of his friends. The hotel was in a seedy part of town, near the stripper district, and was used by hookers and one-hour tricks. Therefore, the derelict's purchase of the room wasn't out of the ordinary.

The bum paid with a fifty dollar bill. The room was $29.95. He put the rest on his account for the telephone. Only one call was made from the hotel room and that was to the hospital.

By 3:45 p.m. they tracked down the down-on-his-luck wino, passed out in a gutter. The feds took him into custody and got the best description out of him that they could. The wino said the following: "The john gave me a hundred and fifty bucks," hiccup, "Did so in twenties, except for the fifty for the hotel room. He," hiccup, "wore...black gloves, a black overcoat, a Detroit Tigers baseball cap, a Led Zeppelin or," hiccup, "...some kind of Hardrock T-shirt and sunglasses. Maybe," hiccup, "AC/DC. His hair was short, or maybe he didn't have all of it, and he smelled like cologne. The kind that I drink sometimes. Maybe," hiccup, "...Mennen. All I know was that I got his money," hiccup, "...out of 'em, and bought some Jack."

The feds took the remaining twenties.

In assistance with the CIA and Langley, the FBI concluded what they had anticipated. The recording was a compilation of different voices, probably from one, or several rented video movies, blended into one tape. They discerned that by the characteristic background VCR electronic hum using their voice analyzing technology.

"So what do you think?" Director Fiske asked Special Operations Director Stone.

"I think that the rendezvous is going to be somewhere between Madison and Waterloo. It's about a two hour drive between here and Madison."

"I agree. Then where?"

"My guess," Stone said, plotting the points on a map he had laid in front of him, "Is East Dubuque, Illinois."

"Good."

"I've got the cops mobilized there. Also, I'll have everything staked out between Des Moines and Madison. We'll catch that prick."

"What about the hospital. Any device yet?"

"None. We're doing the best we can."

"Do you want to close down Mayo Clinic?"

"No, not yet. If this guy's for real, he might detonate the device just to screw with us."

"I agree."

"I think that we can shut him down before he sets off another unit. I'm going to East Dubuque."

"Let's get him. I'm en route."

Within ten minutes, Director Fiske was airborne on his Falcon Jet, cruising at 545 knots/hour. They were going to stop this motherfucker, and Fiske was going to be there to get all the glory.

37

66 Ladies first."

On the first throw Alex tossed the makeshift rope onto the terrace below. The three conjoined king-size sheets hung fifteen feet down, and leaned on the wrought iron railing of the verandah below. The Paradise Grand Hotel had balconies on only the tenth through twelveth floors. Therein lay Alex's plan of escape.

"Afraid of heights?"

"Yes." Viktoria looked down the building's edifice. The heights gave her vertigo.

"Then don't look down. Just climb until your feet hit the railing below, and you'll know your safe."

"All right," she said unconvincingly. Viktoria took a deep breath and went over the top. Slowly, hand-over-hand, she shimmied down the sheets; 12 feet, 10 feet, 9,8,7,6,...seconds later her shoes touched the railing. It seemed like a thousand years.

Had she fallen she would have died instantaneously on the coral and limestone rocks below.

The real peril, however, had just begun. Despite the music's din, and the need for the KGB to respect Alex's last-minute copulatory desires, the KGB agents were getting nervy. Yuri, the bulkier of the two, said, "I think we should check on them. Otherwise, they might miss their flight."

"No. Give them another five minutes, then we will," his companion snickered, "...interrupt them!"

"I don't know. I think we should."

Suddenly, the first of three rivets holding the bedroom balcony's railing gave way. "Snap!" Viktoria screamed as the wrought iron buckled under her weight. A center support, one of the four, broke loose from its footing.

"What's that?" Yuri demanded.

The second rivet snapped in a large pop. Viktoria screamed.

Alex had to think fast, the KGB would be storming through the door any second!

"Crash!" The locked bedroom doors were smashed through, splitting wood from its handles.

Both Russians came booming through the bedroom to the balcony's edge. "Pop!" went the third support; and then the railing's footing gave way and ripped out of the wall. Viktoria had just planted her feet on the terrace, her weight still fully on the makeshift rope, when from above the entire balustrade broke loose, and hurled down past her.

Viktoria screamed. The bed sheets burnt through her hands as the load of stucco and concrete wall attached to the fencing gave the pummeling railing exponential speed downward.

The agents above were frenetic and raged in Russian. "Stop! Stop!" they yelled. As fast as they made their way into the room, and out the balcony's sliding glass door, to the verandahs edge; they bolted out of the suite, to the fire exit's stairs, down one flight and to the room below them.

Quietly and slowly, a quick-witted Alex climbed out from underneath the king-size bed. He hid ensconced by the bed's overhanging dust ruffle.

"I need a weapon, I need a weapon. Think faster than fast Alex. You *only* have seconds before the KGB will get to the room below and realize that you're not there. I've got surprise on my side. Think fast!"

Then it dawned on him, why do anything! Viktoria and he had agreed on a meeting place should they separate. She'll know how to find it. They'll never come back to this room. Nonetheless, Alex slunk out of the hotel suite. He grew nerves of steel.

The Paradise Grand was designed in three prongs radiating from a center. Four elevators made up the central hub. Three hallways emanated from the elevators running at 120 degree angles. Alex's suite was on row A.

Alex traversed row A, passed the elevators and 120° to the right to row C. As he predicted, maid carts, three of them were resting at alternative ends of the hallway. The maids were in rooms cleaning, at least the 1/3 without "Do Not Disturb" signs on them. Alex found a room with its door cracked open and a "Please Clean" placard left on the door handle.

He knocked lightly. There was no answer. He let himself in. On the desk was a red circled note that said "Diving Lessons at 8:00" He knew he was safe. He walked back to the door and flipped over the sign to "Do Not Disturb." He closed and locked the door. He chained it shut.

The first thing he did was call downstairs to the hotel's bell desk. After a few minutes he got Ahmed on the line.

"Ahmed, this is Alex. What do you have for me?"

"I got it. Please, may Allah be with you."

"Tell me!"

"The limousine belonged to the Kodmore Pharmaceutical Company. I'm positive of that. And here's the funny thing. I've been asking around and apparently they came and left the same day."

"What?"

"Yes. I had a friend at the airport do some checking and the Robbins Corporate jet was there and left. Get this—Kodmore Pharmaceuticals is owned by the Robbins Corporation."

"Good job!" Then seriously, "Ahmed, I need one more favor."

Ahmed was hesitant, but acquiesced out of a sense of duty. "What can I do for you?"

Alex explained his situation. And though initially Ahmed protested, eventually he agreed to help.

Below, one floor, but on the same aisle was a hysterically screaming Viktoria. She had fallen to the concrete verandah. She landed on her knees. Inside, the bedroom's occupants were making love: a 6'5" 350 pound former sumo wrestler and his petite 5'2", 110 pound wife.

The sumo wrestler wasn't sure how to react when a strange crying women landed on his balcony , and then the concrete and stucco railing from above tumbling down an instant later. What really got his dander, as he and his wife froze mid-intercourse stroke, was when the two KGB agents stormed into the bedroom, breaking down his doors two minutes later.

To see a naked sumo wrestler interrupted in the middle of intercourse is like seeing a lion who had been starving for two weeks without food, given a fresh tenderloin, and then have his steak ripped from under him. The taste of the meat was still succulent in his mouth. This was enough to cause the sumo to beat the living pulp out of the two marshal art trained KGB agents. Within five minutes both KGB agents were splattered on the floor unconscious. Viktoria had frozen in a crouch on the terrace like a scared bunny rabbit.

"Madam, are you okay?" the extra-large humongous sumo asked, covering himself up with a blanket. There was a knock on the outer doors, the ones that the KGB agents were so kind to crack off their hinges.

Viktoria grinned not quite sure what to say. The 5'2" 110 pound spouse had hidden under the sheets except for her face, as she watched her out-of-control husband thrash the hell out of the two men. "Hi," she said with her hand waving open. Viktoria said "hi" back.

"Who is it?" the sumo said angrily, referring to the knock at the door.

"Laundry," one of the four Pakistani men replied as they wheeled in a canvas laundry bin.

The sumo wasn't quite sure what to think as the hotel employees pushed the cart into the bedroom.

"Quite a mess we have here," one Pakistani said to the other. "Tisk, Tisk."

Viktoria remained huddled still catching her senses.

"Ma'am, we need you to come with us please," the second more heavily accented foreigner requested. "Doctor's orders."

The sumo, who was visibly confused, wasn't sure if he should beat the crap out the hotel laundry attendants, or what.

Viktoria tentatively stood up, stepped over the bleeding KGB agents and looked incredulously at the sumo's wife. "Sorry to disturb you."

"Christ," the sumo said, standing nearly naked. He let Viktoria pass.

The Pakistanis helped Viktoria into the laundry cart and covered her with sheets.

"Have a nice day. If we can be of any further service," one Pakistani said, wheeling out the cart, "just call."

The laundry men pushed the cart fifty feet down the hallway to a set of service elevators just before the hotel's guest elevators. They wheeled her to the basement and from there to a waiting car where she was loaded into the trunk and sped away.

Five kilometers out of the city, the '83 Ford pulled off the main road, down a small knoll and rolled to a stop. The driver got out, opened the trunk and introduced himself.

"I'm Ahmed. At your service."

Viktoria was confounded. She wasn't sure if she should be scared to death from her near fall to her death, resentful that the whale-monster sumo man could have demolished her; or just thankful to a God that she didn't believe in, that she was still alive and breathing.

"Who are you?" Viktoria asked.

"I'm Ahmed and I have been...reluctantly pressed into your service." Viktoria smiled. She was confused. She climbed out of the trunk and brushed off the yuck that stuck to her clothes: lint, a sticky ripped Hershey's chocolate wrapper, and two Gummy Bear cellophanes.

"Where to, and where's Alex?"

"Madam, I'm pleased to announce that the good doctor, though I'll tell you I don't really know how good a doctor he really is, since he got me involved in this mess — is alive and kicking. He wants you to know."

"What happened to him?"

"He hid under your bed and dodged the KGB. They thought that *he* also had ascended your sheet rope."

"Thank you, Ahmed. I was worried about him."

"My young lady," Ahmed said as he watched Viktoria brush off more "kling-ons" from her outfit, "We need to catch a plane."

"A plane? I thought that we weren't going back to Miami?"

"You're not. NOW please get into the front seat and fasten your seat belt."

Viktoria obliged. They sped off, darting past a craggy cliff, a small lagoon, and through jungle-like forests of coppices. A snake slithered over the dark limestone road as the Ford swayed to miss the potential mush. A flock of red and pink flamingos topped a rise.

All of this serpentine driving, with one goal: to double back to Nassau, to just south of Potter's Cay. There, at the basin, on the exact opposite side of Paradise Island, set a highwinged biengine Grumman G73T Mallard Seaplane. The engine farthest from land was running at idle. They had arrived at the Chalk's Sea terminal. In the door stood Alex. He was eagerly waiting. The cab rolled to a stop shooting up a cloud of bleached dust. Viktoria threw open her door.

"Ahmed, how do I thank you?" she asked.

"You don't. Just find your father."

Viktoria ran to Alex. They passionately embraced.

The starboard engine fired up, and the plane pushed-off and bounced into the deep-water channel. It throttled its way north out of Nassau Harbor. They took flight. They were all by themselves except for the pilot, who was wearing noise-muffling headphones.

"Alex!"

"In the flesh."

"How'd you get the plane?"

"I stole it."

"Are you serious?"

"Sort of. I...bribed the pilot to fly us to Freeport."

Alex looked out at the Caribbean and what the Spanish called *"bajamor,"* or "shallow water" islands — the Bahamas. Irregular submarine tableland rose and sank below the North Atlantic's surface. Schools of tuna migrated south, and an occasional swordfish leaped from the water.

"What I was going to tell you and didn't, I'll explain to you now."

"*Dr. Semen,* you amaze me. For a corpse you're pretty resilient."

Viktoria's description was very much correct. Despite his condition, Alex was an enigma. Was it his determination, guts, or sheer luck. His engine kept on humming, purring in high gear despite imminent demise.

"Ahmed saw your father. There is no doubt about it, especially now."

"My God," Viktoria put her hands to her mouth.

"He was brought against his will by two men. He's not sure if he could recognize them again, but he was positive that they arrived at the Paradise Grand Hotel in a Kodmore Pharmaceutical limousine. They stayed for no more than three hours and then left."

"Really?"

"Yes. What stuck out in Ahmed's mind, and why he remembered the limo, was because Bart Robbins, a creepy Howard Hughes like character..."

"Who is Howard Hughes?"

"A dead American reclusive billionaire."

"Oh...I seem to remember him."

"Anyway, this Robbins character comes to Nassau regularly in the Spring, but never in the Fall. That's what made Ahmed suspect, or at least why he even noticed your father. I had Ahmed run a check on the limousine for me, and it went to the airport where the Robbins Corporation has a hanger." Alex paused to catch his breath, "Well here's the best part. The Robbins jet left Nassau airport just after the limousine got there. That's a fact."

"So the plane left, how do you know where it went. And how does that help you?"

"That was the easy part. All jets have to file an IFR or Instrument Rules flight plan. So, I've got this friend in Salt Lake City. He and I have been buddies for a long time. We've gone flying together."

"You're a pilot?"

"Yes. I've flown for a couple years. I'm getting off point."

"Oh."

"Anyway, Kelly is an FAA controller, he has the 118.5 tower frequency in Salt Lake City. I put a call into him, and he punched it up in his computer. Took him a little time, because we didn't have the N-numbers."

"N-numbers?"

"The tail numbers, the numbers that are on the plane's tail, like N43PA."

"I see."

"Well, it turns out the plane was vectored nonstop to Miami and then from there to Belize City, Belize."

"Belize. Isn't that in Central America."

"Sure is."

"But we're heading north."

"We are. That's because this old clunker won't fly to Belize, but it sure the heck will fly us to Freeport, where we can catch a plane to Miami and then Belize."

"Gotcha."

Alex smiled. Seems Viktoria was picking up some American slang.

The flight north was short. Twenty-five minutes after they had taken off, they landed in Freeport, at the Chalks sea terminal. The docking clerk was surprised to see the eighteen-seat aluminum seaplane taxi-up off schedule, and with only two passengers.

"Special fare," the pilot radioed his FBO (Fixed Base of Operations). "Special fares" weren't all that uncommon for Chalks sea terminal. They had run their share of "special fare" gamblers, high-rollers, big shots, and drug lords. And behind the scenes "special fares" were just what the *CIA* encouraged.

With the arrival of the unscheduled flight, an operative who was paid to photograph and report immediately to Freeport CIA headquarters all such "special fares," did just that. Alex and Viktoria had their pictures taken, twenty of them.

By the time they had taken a cab and gotten to Freeport Airport, an agent was waiting for them.

They purchased one-way tickets to Belize City through Mexico City, the quickest flight available. Two hours after they arrived, they boarded the flight to Belize. CIA agent Evan Thomas watched their every move.

"This is T-4," agent Thomas said on his overseas satellite up-link line. A Russian voice with a Czechoslovakian accent answered. The Russian listened patiently to the agent.

"Do you want me to stop the plane? I can finish them off."

"No."

Additional instructions from the Russian were specific. Thomas completed his conversation, knowing that he would be paid well for his *compromised loyalty*.

38

Tampa

Flight 1044 arrived at Tampa International Airport, Florida's third largest city at just before 10:30 a.m. Jack Tandy was told to wait in front of the Delta counter, which he did.

Jack was particularly anxious about carrying so much cash. It's not everyday that the president of a major international corporation such as Kodmore Pharmaceuticals would tote a cool million dollars. It was no problem getting the money, but with all the extra security and paranoia, especially in Florida, his withdrawal of substantial cash from the bank drew attention. He was questioned by Bill DeSoto, the bank's vice president, who was more concerned about a run on the bank's liquid assets by frenzied citizens wanting to flee Florida.

The FDIC bank examiners were called to notify them of the large sum of money withdrawn. Though the amount was not particularly significant for Kodmore's purpose, a nearly billion dollar company, everyone was paranoid. And justifiably so.

At 12 o'clock, Jack Tandy and his oversized Gucci briefcase were paged to the nearest courtesy phone.

The voice, different this time, said, "Do you have the money?"

"Yes."

"There's a tan '75 Plymouth Fury on the fourth floor of the parking garage in the southwest corner with a white roof and a large rip in the vinyl above the passenger's door. You can't miss it. It'll be parked by itself. Under the driver's wheel-well is a Hide-a-Key. Got it?"

"Yes."

"In the glove box there're directions. Follow them carefully and don't be late. Got it?"

"Tan late-model Fury, torn roof, key under the wheel well, fourth floor. I got it."

"Don't take anymore than one hour."

"Yeah."

"Don't be late."

"I won't," an irritated Tandy replied. The voice on the other end disconnected.

Within 15 minutes Jack was on the road. The directions were specific and included a map of the Gulf Coast. He took 275 West, over the Howard Frankland Bridge, through St. Petersburg and then south down the Sunshine Skyway. From there he proceeded down 41 and got off at Venice and then south toward Englewood. "One and two tenths miles on the right, south of the sign that says 'Englewood 5 miles,' will be a sandy coral road with a rusty single-hinged gate. The gate will appear to be locked, but isn't. There will be a 'Private Property' sign, 'Violators Prosecuted.' Drive down to the ocean. There will be a boat waiting."

"Jesus Christ, this guy is so fucking melodramatic," Tandy thought. "One million bucks. And then the company will be all mine...at last. Thirty-two years later; finally all mine, the whole Robbins deal! Kit and caboodle!"

Within an hour, after passing windsurfers in their high wind harnesses, and speedboats cruising the surf, Jack was there.

When he arrived, a forty-two foot Eagle Harbor was waiting for him at a small dock, stern end in. Its twin 6V-92TA Detroit diesels were purring. This off-shore fishing boat, all 36,000 pounds of her, with a 393 nautical mile range, was definitely going somewhere.

Tandy parked his car. A large scraggy man met him. Tandy handed him the keys. Jack was gestured to the boat. The "scuzz" got into the car and sped off.

With his expensive leather satchel in hand, Jack stepped aboard.

The boat's teak deck shined. Tackled massive swordfishing poles protruded from both sides of the vessel. Within seconds of his arrival, the captain released the securing lines and powered the craft out to sea. A mate showed Tandy into the galley. There, sitting at a leather couch, was Boriskov.

"Do you have the money?"

"Yes of course, you moron."

Boriskov scowled. "Throw it on the table," he said, pointing.

In front of him was a mahogany dinette. Tandy slung the briefcase on top, popped the latches and opened it. "See," he said sarcastically, "You guys didn't need to be so goddamn soap-opera. I paid up!"

"Oh, we did," Boriskov said.

It was then that Jack Tandy knew he had just made *the biggest mistake of his life.*

39

36 Hours Left

Plutonium was named after Pluto, God of the underworld. Less than one-millionth of a gram (an invisible particle) is carcinogenic. How many of those, how many grams, what percent of a gram pulsated through Alex's body? How many particles of death pulsated, zapped their deadly alpha radiation? How soon until the effects on the nearby cells showed? When would the liver and bone cancer start; and leukemia rear its ugly head or, was Alex in store for worse?

Sweet mother-brown plutonium.

The Delta flight cruised at 32,000 feet above the Gulf of Mexico en route from Freeport to Mexico City; and then after a 45 minute layover, straight onto Belize City, Belize. The airleg from Freeport to Mexico City was turbulent with ominous storm clouds rising out of the Gulf of Mexico.

As they approached the Yucatan Peninsula, Alex could see the scant outline of tidal marshes, sandy beaches, estuaries, lagoons and mangrove-covered borders. Below were commercial fishing vessels.

Surrounding the boats, hunting and hopeful of morning breakfast were notties, boobies, and seagulls.

The air was stagnant and tawny yellow as they descended into Ciudad De Mexico. The slum districts or Ciudades perdidas ("lost cities") made Alex feel sorry for its inhabitants.

"Alex, what are we going to do when we get to Belize City?"

"I don't know." Actually he had been thinking. So much had happened to him over a short period of time. Why? Why his parents? Who was the man who called at the hospital? It wasn't anyone Alex knew...or was it? *What did the man in the New York taxi have to hide? They were some type of plans that fell out? "Hoover" what?*

"Alex, what are you thinking?" Viktoria asked caringly.

"Thinking about..."

"All right. If you're not going to answer my question," she said a little indignantly, "then let's talk about, why?"

"That's what I was thinking about: Why? I'm sorry. I didn't mean to be preoccupied." He spoke sincerely, "I know that we have to deal with what we're going to do in Belize, but more importantly, I think that if we can find out 'why' whoever is behind this debacle, then we can find out 'who' is behind it."

"Alex, I know that you...you and I have been through a lot, but the whole United States Government, the KGB and CIA are looking into this mess; why do you think that despite everyone in the entire world who is trying to solve this mystery you can?"

"I don't. But I have to try...wait a second."

"Wait, what?"

"What did you say?"

"Say what? I was just explaining to you that if the whole world..."

"No, not that, the KGB...that's it!"

"What's it?"

"Look. Why would the KGB have anything to do with it?"

"I don't know."

"Think about it." Alex pulled out the USA Today from the seat pocket in front of him. He had been reading it earlier. He showed Viktoria the headlines. The paper read:

"Terrorist Groups Blamed"

And the subheading read:

"Shiite Moslems, al-Fatah Palestine Liberation Front Suspect"

"They're looking in the wrong place."

"They're what?"

"Or at least...they want the public to believe that they're look-ing in the right place."

"I don't get you."

"This *isn't the work of a terrorist organization*. This is the work of one man, and only one man."

"I still don't understand."

"The KGB. Why would the KGB be involved?"

"Because..." Viktoria said. "Because...the plutonium came from us! From Russia!"

"Bingo!" Alex planted a kiss on her forehead. "Okay, so this thing is big and someone wants revenge. And so, someone buys plu-tonium from Russia. Right?"

"Right."

"And this someone nukes Jackson Memorial Hospital and then the University of Michigan Hospital."

"Okay."

"See, I think, that logistically the two hospitals are too far apart and involve too much risk, traveling with the plutonium across coun-try, to try to blackmail any hospital or the U.S. government for money. And there hasn't been any real ransom demand yet...."

"That's true."

"Well?"

"But Alex, a number of splinter fanatical groups have been blamed for the massacres."

"Yeah, sure. But none of it's for real. What is real, is that the KGB and the CIA, were *both at Paradise Island, and they both wanted our asses out of there*."

"Yeah."

"Trust me. We're on the right track. I don't know anything about this Robbins guy. But ten will get you twenty, that that's where your father is. *Robbins is the key to all of this!*"

Alex leaned back in his seat. Then out of nowhere he felt nau-sea. His stomach contracted in waves. He was barely able to get the vomit bag to his mouth. He lost his lunch. He stood up on unsteady legs, and slowly walked back to the in-flight bathroom. Another wave of nausea overcame him.

Two hours later, after a short layover in Mexico City, the "Fas-ten Your Seat Belt" light illuminated for a second time. The stew-ardess announced the imminent landing, in English and Spanish.

Alex returned to his seat. He repositioned his chair upright, but was unable to fasten his seat belt. The imps that had previously left him had returned in a fury. He had his good and bad times, which were in cycles of hours. They were also possibly sleep related. His body was fatigued. Pins and needles irregularly pierced his skin in bullets.

Time was running perilously short. Alex needed to find Dr. Siderenko. And haunting Alex, even more so than finding Siderenko, was the question: "Did he have the antidote with him, and would Alex be able to take it in time?"

Already it was too late for the thousands who where afflicted in Miami, and not just those limited to the hospital itself: but also those who may have drank tainted recycled water, or others who may have swum in the ilk off Biscayne Bay, or those whose property may have been watered by the contaminated liquid. Who would know?

The plane touched down in the primitive country of Belize, the only sovereign in Central America whose official language is English. The International Airport bordered Belize City, west of the Caribbean Sea.

When Alex stood up he was weary. The turbulent nausea had subsided. His legs were weak. They felt chickenoid.

"Are you all right?" Viktoria asked.

He attempted to steady himself by leaning his forearm on a passenger seat in front of him. "Yes," was his unconvincing response.

The airport was archetypically Third World Caribbean. The field was coarse and there were no rises. On the ocean side were hangers adjacent to the terminal building. There were no corridors of tarmac, just the asphalt. An old tug, with paint cracking off its side, pushed a deplaning ramp up to the cabin door. It was short of the bulkhead. A trolley with eight connecting carts caterpillared to the jet.

Alex and Viktoria sluggishly cleared customs. The pace was snail torpid. On the other side of the customs gate waited ominous predatory eyes.

"Alex, are we going to find my father?" Viktoria asked hopefully.

"I'm certain," he replied.

They passed through the customs gate. There was no baggage to inspect so they traversed a special line for those with carry-on luggage or less. It was not much different than a quick check-out line at a supermarket, but ultra slow.

"Where to?"

"We need to find out where Bart Robbins lives."

From behind them a deep voice said, "That's exactly where you're going."

The four men each had guns concealed beneath their jackets. They were particularly out of place since it was 82 degrees outside. Each man placed an arm under one armpit. They almost lifted Alex and Viktoria off their feet.

Alex hopelessly looked at Viktoria as they were hauled out of the airport to a waiting limousine. He could see a shiny blue-metal 358 Beretta inside the bulging jacket of the man on the right.

As they were dragged to the limo they passed a Belizean policeman. The cop obviously knew the four kidnappers. Alex watched the officer's face. He knew the cop would do nothing.

They were propelled into a waiting limousine, whose windows were darkly tinted. The four men sat in the back seat with them. They faced each other on separate benches. No one spoke.

"Where are we going?" Alex finally asked.

"You'll find out soon enough," said a man with a handlebar mustache, jet dark hair and face full of scars. He was devoid of emotion.

Alex looked outside through the tinted windows. Two beautiful young women smiled at the black limo. They were dressed in their native white and black skirts. Each had two and then lower down three circumferential lace trim patterns. Their necks and short sleeve blouses were embellished with Mayan markings, and were also white and black.

The limo drove south and west, through Belmopan City, and then east toward the coast and Dangriaga. The Mayan Mountains swallowed them up. They drove past two river valleys with cascading streams and the thousand-foot Hidden Valley falls that plunged over granite out-croppings into the forest. Closer to the ocean again, they passed huge palm and tubroos trees. As they were approaching Placenia, a coastal city at the southern tip of the Belize Barrier Reef, there was the shell of a dead armadillo on the road. The driver uncaringly ran over it.

Past Placencia, and just before Punta Gorda and the Nim Li Punit Mayan ruins, they turned off onto a secluded road that had just years earlier been cut into the jungle. A sign, in both English and Spanish was embossed on a white on red inverted triangle, and was mounted on the center of an electronically controlled gate. The entrance was set back from the main road, so not to attract attention. The limo slowed only momentarily to turn toward the ocean and the Robbins complex. With a touch of a coded remote, they crept through the gateway onto the grounds.

Video cameras were hidden within the trees, one at the cut-off from the road south to Punta Gorda, another at both sides of the property entrance, and a fourth facing up the road, toward the mansion. The Robbins compound was a forty-eight mile square preserve, six miles by eight miles. Two rivers which merged in a fork before they reached the Caribbean Sea served as the vortex of the Robbins property.

Six hundred yards within the compound, the road became paved again. It was lined with black orchids, palm trees and banana plants. The property was courtesy of a Bart Robbins one million dollars gratuity to the Minister of Tourism and the Environments, the Honorable Young Rauel. Since ownership of land by foreigners was forbidden in Belize, special concessions needed to be made by the Supreme Court. The cash in hundred-dollar bills went to the Honorable Rauel. It was spread on many platters.

In addition, Robbins was required to expand the airport at Big Creek just west of Placencia. He lengthened the asphalt runway to seven thousand feet, for both the national benefit and to handle the Robbins fleet of various jets.

The airport, except for flights from Tropic Air, an intracountry turboprop carrier, which fed San Pedro and the Ambergris Caye resorts, an island north of Belize City and just south of the Yucatan; was off limits to private traffic except for the Robbins caravan.

At the entrance to the complex, as they approached the clinic which was built *just* for Helen Robbins, sat a bust. It was Helen's proud, young face. Her hair was austere and pushed back. Her lips and cheekbones abundant. No smile was evident.

Below the marble statue were the words *"Dedicated to the Memory of Helen Monica Robbins and to the Unborn Child, Who One Day Would Have Ruled the World. God's Vengeance is Our Strength."*

Beneath was a meticulously carved bolt of lightning.

The clinic, which they passed prior to arriving at the Robbins mansion, was as modern as any in the United States. The facade new, with double-paned bulletproof windows, was built of pressed red brick and blue Argentinean tile.

The massive Robbins mansion was 20,000 square feet. It was built by the best artisans from around the world in early 1980 with Brazilian rainforest mahogany, Honduras pine and Eucalyptus, Pentelic Greek marble from Attica, Mediterranean tile from the Tigris-Euphrates Valley and stained glass from Vatican City.

As they pulled up before the massive exterior, the driver lowered the limo's passenger windows. Four men, one cloaked in a black fedora with a swarthy scarf around his face, awaited. One of the men was frail. He could hardly stand. His forehead was broad, disproportionally larger than the rest of his face. His hair was burnt brown, with streaks of gray emerging from over his large Rus ears. He had a small mole that sprouted two hairs which flourished from the same plug. It was untrimmed. It was hard to imagine that this was the same man in Viktoria's picture.

"Father," Viktoria cried as the limousine stopped. "Father, it's me Viktoria. It's me father."

"Vik...toria." he said in thick Russian, moving away from the two men, unrestrained. Before the vehicle could come to a stop, Viktoria pushed her way out from between the two thugs and ran to her father. She embraced him.

"Oh father, father. I've missed you so. I've been so desperately worried. Father..." He acted confused, not sure of who he was dealing with. "Father, it's me Viktoria."

He patted her auburn hair, running his hands down her locks and then onto her shoulder and back. He explored her cautiously.

"Everything will be all right. Everything is all right," he replied in Russian. He knew that he was being listened to. "Viktoria?"

"Yes, it's me father, Viktoria."

Alex stepped out of the limo. He watched the emotional embrace and then he followed the man in front of him.

The thug who sat to Alex's right, reached into his pocket and withdrew a CO_2 loaded air-injection gun. The cassette contained a vial of 10 milligrams of Versed, a short-acting general anesthetic. The predator stepped out of the limousine. As Alex was standing, assessing the situation, before he could say a word, the gun's nozzle touched the back of his neck. A pulse of air-driven chemical entered his bloodstream...once again.

"My God!"

Alex never knew what hit him as he tumbled to the ground. He tried to get up, to balance with one knee, but couldn't. Then the darkness came.

40

The dungeon smelled like death. The air was rancid. The floor was medieval, with cold brick and straw matting. The sorrel thatch was blackened with mildew and decay. Insects, termites, and spiders scurried between the rotted footing. Cockroaches had made their temporary home under Alex's aching neck. He could feel one, then a second scamper across his close-eyed face, as he struggled for consciousness.

"How much time? How much time left?" He endeavored to sit up, brushing the roaches off his face. He used the sodden wall behind him for support.

He breathed through his nostrils. He could feel the blood coming once again. The copper forewarned him that his time was short. He could feel the gun's sting in his upper back muscles and neck. "Goddamn them," he muttered.

Overhead, he could hear a voice...two voices from the stairs above. A New York peep slot opened. Two snake eyes gleamed in.

"He's up."

The slot clanged shut. Alex propped himself and looked at his watch. It was 7:49 p.m. Bahamas time. "24 hours left. I've been out for three hours. No time."

He stood up. He began to slowly pace. He had a headache that could crack a walnut. His previously shaky, tenuous hands had steadied. But his vision had changed. No longer were objects sharp. They were now blurry, and nearly double. A line of grout between bricks appeared smudged into two. Colors were tentative. Reds turned to grays and the straw was obscured into a mesh of cobweb strands.

He did not hear anyone approach, yet they were there. The heavy oak door flung open.

"Ta...", Andrei proclaimed, "So, as the cliché goes, we meet again."

Andrei was accompanied by two behemoths who stood a safe distance behind him. His chin was rugged with a Kirk Douglas cleft. His hair was slicked back, and his eyes and nose made a discerning sharp triangle. He was middle-aged, strong and over his right eye he wore a black-leather patch.

"Dr. Seacourt, do you know who I am?"

"No," Alex replied as he coughed phlegm-coated blood into his hand.

"Do you remember New York?" Andrei was irritated that Alex did not remember.

"No."

"The taxi?" he asked.

Alex's thoughts were slow in coming.

And then slowly, with deliberate extraction, a memory that should have been crystal clear began to take shape. It was not the Versed that was injected into him that caused the delay, but the plutonium; the "God of Pluto," that was wreaking havoc.

Then it came back. Andrei was the man that he had knocked over in his haste to catch a cab to the Waldorf-Astoria and back to Detroit when he had just heard about his father's heart attack. Alex remembered the briefcase he rammed open and the legal papers that flew everywhere.

He remembered his black slacks and alligator cowboy boots and his eye-patch that he didn't notice the first time.

"I ran into you... leaving a cab?"

"Ah, not bad."

"And I knocked open your briefcase and spilled your papers into the street. I..."

"Come on, don't be shy now Dr. Seacourt."

"I helped you with some architectural plans that had fallen into a puddle?"

"That's it! Good boy."

"I don't understand?"

"Doctor, understanding is irrelevant, action is paramount."

"What ... do you mean?"

"You didn't see them did you?" Andrei asked curiously.

"See what?"

"Well, let's just say that your accident of fate, your trying to help me is why we're here right now."

"I still don't..."

"The plans my friend, which fell into the water, those precious architectural renderings that my contact from the city clandestinely retrieved from the Department of Interior... it cost him, my friend, the same fate that I'm about to indulge you in." Andrei laughed.

"What did I do to you?"

"Nothing. It's not what you did, but what you..."

"Might know?" Alex asked as he tired to recall what the plans were about. He vaguely remembered the word "*Hoover.*" But Hoover what? "So this is why you tried to kill me?"

"Exactly," Andrei said as he threw the first pulverizing kick that landed square into Alex's jaw. Alex's bone cracked.

Blood began flowing from Alex's friable gums as he fell to the ground. He tumbled onto the brick-and-straw floor. Andrei threw a second boot that landed deep into his abdomen. The force of the penetrating blow rooted into Alex's spinal cord. He could feel the undulations of nausea begin again. But this time, pain served to awaken him. He turned his head toward Andrei.

More out of muse than vengeance, Andrei threw another kick to Alex's face. This one landed on his right cheek.

The blows thwacked into his abdomen, chest and into the face. Blood spurted from Alex's mouth in rivulets.

And in answer to Alex's thought, Andrei responded "Surprised?" Andrei asked as he leveled another sissy kick into Alex's chest. The thumping momentarily stopped. Alex had a chance to catch his breath.

"Yes," Alex answered, working his way back to the wall, struggling to sit up again. Alex no longer had fear. He would not, could not be afraid. Kill me now or later. What difference does it make?

"You saw something you weren't suppose to see, my good doctor. So I had to kill you." Alex glared at Andrei. Andrei continued, "Actually that's where I got the idea to nuke the hospital in Ann Arbor. Funny...," he paused to amuse himself by kicking Alex in the ribs.

Andrei scoffed. He trudged through the straw back to the heavy door. He shook his head disdainfully, *"Cést la vie."*

"You bastard!"

"Ha," Andrei evilly chuckled, "You don't even have a clue what I have in store for you. Do you?"

"You're sick! Thousands of people have died, or will because of you! You scum!"

That infuriated Andrei. He ran at Alex and kicked him just below his right eye. A large laceration opened in Alex's cheek. Blood flowed freely down the side of his face to join the stream that already emerged from his mouth.

"Ann Arbor," Andrei puffed, "was a bonus. You were a bonus. The fact of the matter is, that this whole fucking thing is far from over."

"Fuck you!"

"Your pathetic piece-of-shit country hasn't even seen, or hasn't any idea of the terror that I am about to wreak on them. President Climan will beg for mercy."

Andrei laid one last wallop into Alex's gut. It was a kick so strong that it caused Alex to stop breathing momentarily. He faded into darkness. In the distance, he could hear Andrei tell one of his assistants to prepare him for the "snuff film."

Four hours later the fumes from an ammonia smelling salt was placed under his nose. The piercing vapors creeped into his consciousness, causing him to startle into the present.

Alex tried to shake his head. He couldn't. It was being held by Boriskov, the powerful Sino-Eurasian ex-KGB colonel. Boriskov lumbered easily on the balls of his feet, three hundred pounds of muscle, as he balanced with perfection and pulled Alex by the strands of his hair.

Dried copper flakings were caked on Alex's face, his mouth and chin. The gaping two-inch laceration below his eye had stopped bleeding except for a small percolation that again started with Boriskov's marionette tug.

In an ash-gray suit, a somber silk dinner tie and leaden shirt, stood Andrei. Andrei wore a mischievous boyish look. "Are you prepared to meet your maker?"

Alex was hazy, but defiantly answered, "I'm always ready to meet my maker." He coughed blood, and the wound below his eye opened, "Are you?"

"Ha!" Andrei howled, flashing a primitive double-action revolver. "Dr. Seacourt do you know anything about guns?"

"No. Why?"

"Dr. Seacourt, or should I say Alex. Which do you prefer?"

"Whatever."

"You know," Andrei said. A third man walked behind him. He wore army-green pants and a T-shirt with the sleeves rolled up and sweat permeating through the front. He set up a Sony Super-8 video camera on a light-weight aluminum tripod.

"I've been a gun buff most of my life. Sometimes I think that I've been cheated in life, by not being born earlier."

"Earlier?"

"Yes," Andrei glanced at the assistant spreading the tripod legs, and screwing the video camera onto the tripod's rectangular platform," I'd give my right arm to have been born just around the time of the Civil War. To have fought at Gettysburg, to have killed, crippled and mutilated there."

"You're crazy."

"Did you know that the first successful six-gun, very much like what I have in my right hand, was patented by Samuel Colt in 1835. It was a .44-caliber cap-fired percussion piece. It became the principle sidearm during the Civil War."

"You're a lunatic."

"Early weapons were *single-action*. Did you know that?"

"No. Who cares if a gun is single-fucking-action or double?"

"Oh...Oh...my precious doctor, don't get testy," Andrei retorted, brushing the weapon against Alex's face, "A *single-action* gun is very much like this one, except that the shootist is required to cock the hammer prior to each shot. The action of cocking the hammer causes the weapon's cylinder to rotate to the next bullet. In double-action guns this is done automatically."

Andrei slowly pushed the weapon's muzzle into the bridge of Alex's nose. He bore down hard. Alex could see into the cylinders. The shiny bullet tips peered out at him.

"Poof, cylinder automatically advances."

"No, I didn't know that," Alex rebelliously said.

Boriskov pulled his grip tighter on Alex's hair. He yanked Alex's body upright. Andrei walked to the video camera and tripod.

"Smile for the camera sweetheart," Boriskov whispered as the operator focused the lens on Alex's face.

"Did you also know that bullets don't fly in a straight path?"

"Who cares."

"I do!"

"Where's Dr. Siderenko?"

With his free hand, Boriskov slapped Alex across the non-bleeding cheek. "Quiet, while the man is talking," he said.

"Now, where was I.... Bullets don't fly straight. Did you know that most people think that a bullet flies downward in an arch with gravity?"

"So." Alex spit as he felt the persisting sting of the blow.

"They fly in parabolas."

"No shit."

Boriskov again struck Alex. Andrei wanted Alex's undivided attention. Boriskov put his fingers to his lips and went "shhhhhh" into Alex's ear.

"While guns are theoretically aimed along a direct line-of-sight, or an imaginary line running through aligned sights to the target, bullets actually fly in a shallow curve or parabola, called trajectory. Correction of one's aim, therefore, is required for scoring on a target outside point-blank range."

"That's great."

"Well, Dr. Seacourt, in part that's why we're here today."

"Tell me."

"To test the laws of physics."

"Physics?"

"You see, in my hand is a .44 Remington Magnum. Unlike all other guns, this weapon is one of the few examples of a pistol whose bullets barely rises over a one hundred yard shooting distance."

"That's really special," Alex rejoined sarcastically.

Boriskov cleared his throat in a sign again for Alex to shut-up. "You see if I had, for example, a .444 Marlin and shot it over a 100 yard distance, the bullet would actually rise 2.1 inches before it began to fall. If I had a 7mm Mauser it'll rise 2.5 inches, a .308 Winchester 2.3 inch rise, etc. Those are rifles I just mentioned, but the same applies for hand guns, and even more so." Andrei flashed Alex his .44 Remington Magnum, "This gun, your *death instrument*, has a shell; and I bet you didn't know that the bullet has your name on it. It weights 240 grains, or just more than a half an ounce. It travels at 1,350 feet per second and produces muzzle energy of 971 foot-lbs. Bet you didn't know that either."

"No. I didn't."

"So, what we have here is a little experiment in physics. What I'm going to do is this..." by now the man who set up the camera had wheeled in another device. The mechanism was a vice-like grip that was mounted on a cart with three black-plastic swivel wheels.

The vice had been custom molded so that the gun that Andrei was brandishing would fit exactly into its claws.

The man left again and then shortly returned with a second camera. This one was a high-speed Nikon that shot frames a thousand frames per second. Finally, after setting up the second camera, the assistant left and returned with what appeared to be a bodyboard or back brace. The bodyboard was half-size, and had straps in positions around the torso and upper arms to secure the victims. On the board's rear were two latches, male components that protruded from the apparatus. The top of the board had a cervical neck collar similar to ones that paramedics use to immobilize car accident victim's. Alex got the picture.

On the wall were several female latches that matched the backboard's male latches. They were at different heights, in order to take into account for a variance in height among victims.

"How tall are you?" the man asked matter-of-factly. He sized up Alex.

"Tall enough."

"Fair, fair," Andrei growled as he estimated Alex's height and placed the board flush with the wall into two female latches. "Stand him up."

Boriskov and the other assistant lifted Alex by the armpits and dragged him to the wall-mounted bodyboard. Alex could see that the cervical collar had old blood on it.

"Do you know how many of these I have?" Andrei asked.

"No. How many?"

"77. I have 77 trajectory films."

"Yeah," the assistant laughed, "snuff films."

"That's very humanitarian of you."

"You're number 78."

Boriskov and the short-sleeved assistant placed Alex into the restraint. Andrei stepped back to study Alex in his bondage. Alex was set-up slightly shorter than Andrei wanted. Andrei needed to stretch Alex's neck to its maximum without strangling him. His feet were already barely dusting the thatched floor.

"A little higher," Andrei ordered. The two men repositioned Alex. Andrei again studied his victim, like an artist would an unfinished oil painting. Then he began the meticulous job of correctly positioning the cameras and his gun.

"You know," Andrei said as he made some last minute adjustments and then walked to the perpendicular camera that would film the bullet's trajectory, "I thought about giving you a Colombian necktie."

"What's that?" Alex spit, as the brace forced inordinate pressure onto his throat.

"I have twelve of those videos. I thought I could use another one to add to my collection. But," he sighed, "too messy. Anyway, Bart would get all bent out of shape. I don't know... Oh...to answer your question..." Andrei made final adjustments to the perpendicular camera. He looked into its viewfinder and then checked its leveling device. "It's what the Colombians do if you rip them off in a drug deal." Andrei snarled moving his right index finger across his neck as if to slice his own throat. "To make an example of you. Slit your carotid arteries. Blood goes everywhere as the carotids pulsate. Plop. Plop. Plop. Has an interesting fluid dynamics."

Andrei walked back to the video camera that was set up in front of Alex and was focused directly on his face. He turned on the camera and began to film. "Blood, it's thick and sexy. Spurts out of your neck," he motioned with his hands, making broad gestures, painting a picture of the macabre, "pump, pump, pump." He spread his fingers to exaggerate the flowing nectar of life, spurting out of his victim's neck.

Alex could feel his stomach squirm at the thought of it. "One question."

"What's that?" Andrei asked, still toying with the focus.

"Why the hospitals?"

"You haven't figured that out by now? Tisk, tisk Dr. Seacourt."

"No I haven't. Tell me. Why?"

"I suppose.... Why not. Well, first things first, as they say. Jackson Memorial Hospital in Miami, that was for revenge, for Bart Robbins' revenge."

"Revenge?"

"Yes, and there are more to come."

"More?"

"Let's just say you're going to miss the *piéce de résistance*."

"What's that?"

"Now, now doctor let's stay focused. Did you wonder how we knew that you were at the airport? Oops. There I am getting ahead of myself."

"Yes," Alex squirmed.

"It was for Bart Robbins' *unborn son's and sister's death*," he said, referring to the hospital.

"What?"

"You know, I used to think that I was unconventional. All those years with the KGB, the Ricin darts in umbrella tips. Did you know that stuff is twice as deadly as cobra venom?'

"No, I didn't."

"Made form castor-oil plants. Used it four times. Run into someone at a rail station — a slight nudge into the meaty part of the calf; the needle penetrating through the pant leg. A CO_2 cartridge would cause the poison to inject immediately into the bloodstream. The victim never knew what happened. By the time he turned to check his leg to see what hit him, I was gone. Disappeared in the crowd."

"What about the hospitals?"

"Robbins' sister and Robbins' unborn child died at Jackson. This is all about revenge."

"What about the child's mother? Did she..."

"Silly boy — the *child's mother is the sister.*"

"Alex thought hard...and then he realized. Robbins had *impregnated his own sister.*

"Ann Arbor was a bonus."

"Bonus?"

"Yes. I wanted you. For my own purposes, which we discussed earlier. I sent an agent after you. He tracked you to Ann Arbor. That was the easy part, running down your cab, where it took you and then the message you received from your mother at the Waldorf-Astoria."

He tried to snuff you at the hospital, but you eluded him. Then I thought, why not play a little game with you, and at the same time give Bart Robbins-baby, a little more bang for his buck. So I nuked the U of M hospital instead of another one that we planned to zap."

"You're deranged."

"No, I prefer to think of myself as an inventive creative artist."

"You need help pal."

Andrei scowled. "Come on old boy, this is my profession. My job. Just like yours is being a doctor. This is what I do for a living, what I do best."

"That's great."

"I'm glad you approve. Look, old buddy, my plan was to have some fun with you. Give Robbins more '*bang*' for his buck. I had my agent plant the device in the hospital, to release the plutonium after you left for the evening. Unfortunately, the timer failed, and the mechanism began doing its thing earlier than I anticipated. That's why you got nuked. My design was to zap your family, your parents, and then...well of course the rest of the hospital."

"You're demented."

"I guess I should take that as a compliment...huh?"

"Screw you!"

"So my man followed you to the Wayne State Medical School Library, and then from there to the airport. That's where I got the idea...to plant a seed for you. To lead you to me, so I could have you live on film. Candid Camera. So I sent Boriskov after you in Moscow."

"What seed was that?"

"The word *Pan* on Dr. Siderenko's blackboard. I knew that you would be smart enough to follow the trail to Paradise Island, and then from there here. Plus, I needed the girl, and you offered me a vehicle to abduct her from under the KGB's watchful nose. Doesn't take a fucking genius."

"Yeah, no genius."

"So now I've got this unexpected bonus. You're dying of radiation poisoning, and there isn't a damn thing that you can do about it."

"Who tipped you off in Paradise Island, that I was on my way here."

"You have to figure that out for yourself. Now it's down to business my friend. Time for Hollywood, U.S.A."

Alex's blood chilled. He could feel his heart beat. He struggled to free himself. The straps were too tight. They had held those more powerful than him.

"Turn on the other camera," Andrei ordered. The T-shirted man followed the command. With both cameras rolling, Andrei was ready. "Tell me what you're thinking," Andrei respectfully, almost kindly asked "Tell me your inner thoughts." Andrei looked through the viewfinder at Alex's face. His vivid outline filled the entire visual field.

"Screw you! I hope you pay! Fry your ass in *Hell!*"

Andrei gently placed his finger into the .44 Remington Magnum's grip and in a mothering manner said, "Say good-bye." Without further ado, and carefully studying Alex's face, he *squeezed the trigger until...*

41

East Dubuque, Illinois

Within hours the feds, who flew in from Rochester on two National Guard Huey UH-1 choppers, had established a makeshift base of operations in the East Dubuque Sheriff's Office on 330 1/2 North Bench Street. As fast as the fax and copy machine papers could fly, a sketch artist's rough depiction of the suspect was distributed to the law enforcement authorities within a twenty-five mile radius.

At six o'clock, another call was placed to the University of Wisconsin switch-board, and routed to the Student Union. Overhead, the Rochester Hospital Administrator George Taylor was paged. The call was traced and recorded.

The message was:

"At exactly 6:25 a.m. Amtrak passenger train headed for Denver will be leaving the Columbus, Wisconsin Station. Go to the sixth passenger car, to compartment A-23. You will be given more instructions. If anyone follows you, any helicopters, any person, anyone is alerted; I will detonate the device."

The phone went silent.

Taylor headed to the Amtrak Station. Because of the nature of the University of Wisconsin switchboard, and the fact that the caller ingeniously first called the University of Wisconsin Hospital Medical Center, and from there had the call transferred to the University of Wisconsin switchboard, the call was impossible to trace.

Stone arrived at the sheriff's office just as his men were about to tell him the bad news.

"What do ya got?"

The agitated FBI agents who wanted to get "this scum" were reticent to say. Nevertheless, agent Whitaker who had Coke-bottle glasses and a stringy face said, "He got us."

"What?" Stone demanded.

"Our perp routed his call through the University Hospital. It's a dead-end."

"Goddammit!" Stone threw a dossier he was carrying on top of the sheriff's desk. Loose papers flew to the floor. Stone realized that he had lost his composure needlessly. He bent over and picked up the NCIC reports. "Sorry, gentlemen. We just need to get this prick before he kills anyone else. What about the message?"

Whitaker replied, "Sounds like the same deal. Tape recorder compilation. Not the perp's real voice."

"We'll just have to play it out."

"Director Stone," Whitaker asked somewhat nervously, "Have you found the device?"

Stone looked at Whitaker with the eyes of a little boy who lost his homework, due at the next school bell, "Not yet. But we will."

In Dubuque, Iowa, on the other side of the Mississippi River, Rod Cheevers a police corporal was filling in for one of his men, whose child had been hurt in an accident. It had been awhile since Cheevers had done patrol. His department was short-staffed and he liked the idea of getting out for a while and driving the squad car. It was a change in routine.

At three minutes after six he drove past the Chevron on Kennedy at Dodge. It was then that he saw a fidgety man in a green army jacket remove a tape recorder from the mouthpiece of a pay telephone, place it into a black duffel bag and fumble with his keys to get it into his car.

Normally, Cheevers wouldn't think twice about something like that, but everyone was on edge with this "hospital shit." And then...wasn't there something about a tape recorder, that he heard coming over the wire?

Cheevers made a mental note of the vehicle, a blue '92 Buick Skylark, Iowa plates. It was too far to see the license plate from where he was.

Cheevers was held up at a traffic light while the suspect was on the kitty-corner. The caller left the open-faced pay phone at the service station office. He pulled out and headed for downtown Dubuque.

The light changed and the still curious Cheevers followed. He was between seven and four cars behind, but was able to follow the Buick Skylark down Dodge to Bluff Street and then eventually to Central Avenue and 16th Street to Koestler, Reely and McCoy a stock brokerage firm. He knew now where he had seen the car and the man, he was Arthur Koestler.

Koestler had been involved in a stock market bankruptcy swindle about two years back. Koestler was never indicted, but came as close as he could. His deal involved two Saudi Arabian sheiks, Najd Faysal and Alid Zaydi, who turned out to be phony. The investors lost millions, and Koestler and his firm lost millions also, including its credibility.

Koestler resurfaced beat-up and bruised. He was going through bankruptcy proceedings. He was on the verge of losing it all. And if Cheevers remembered correctly, that meant his real estate holdings, which included his downtown buildings, a thousand-acre Holstein dairy farm, a summer house in Boca Raton, Florida and more.

Cheevers cut a corner past Koestler, Reely and McCoy and in a U-turn headed down Central back to his route. He got on his radio.

"Horace," he said, referring to the dispatcher Josie Horace who was anything but all woman. "Cheevers here. Got the coffee brewing babe?"

"Yeah, Cheeve."

"I'm not use to this patrol shit." He turned another corner and headed up Dodge Street.

"Have you heard, corporal?"

"Corporal? What's this corporal shit."

"Sorry Cheeve. Have you heard, the feds think that the plutonium guy might be in our vicinity."

"No shit?"

"Yeah. He's been running a wild-goose chase with the FBI. The feds are on the other side of the river. They think he'll show up in Illinois or something."

"Good. I hope they catch that son-of-a-bitch bastard baby killer."

"Yeah. Well, I just wanted you to know. The chief wants you to come back and pick up a fax photo of the suspect. We've got an APB out on him."

"Sure," Cheevers clicked off. He hit his red and blues, flipped his patrol car around and headed downtown to the station. "So what's the guy look like?"

"Oh, I don't know. Wearing an army jacket maybe. Green. Average height and weight. Wirey."

Cheevers wheels started working. "Anything else?"

"I don't think so. Just an average Joe."

"I'll be there in just a few minutes. If you got any ideas, let me know."

"There is one more thing."

"What's that?" Cheevers asked as he blasted past traffic forcing cars onto the shoulder out of his way.

"The feds think that he's using a tape recorded message to place his calls."

Within ten minutes the neighborhood surrounding the offices of Koestler, Reely and McCoy was cordoned off. No immediate attempt was made to enter the building until FBI Director Stone arrived. Exactly two minutes after the cops had shutdown the block, an unaware Koestler stepped out of the rear entrance of his 1930's rococo building and got into his blue Buick Skylark. He was wearing a very uncharacteristic green army jacket, and had with him three large suitcases and one carry-on bag. He was obviously going on a trip somewhere.

Koestler drove down the alleyway, and cut onto Central Avenue, when the first of three cop cars squealed in front of him, grinding to a stop.

Koestler threw his vehicle into reverse. He jammed his Buick down the alley, smashing into garbage cans. Trash, mostly shredded paper and bagged financial newspapers flew everywhere.

Looking over his shoulder Arthur slammed into an abutment protruding from a brown-brick building. Masonry and mortar flew in shards as his car screeched to a halt.

Behind him two other cop cars charged down the alleyway. Koestler was bruised and shaken by the sudden stop. Nonetheless, he scurried out of his vehicle climbing out of his car window and ran with a briefcase in his hand.

The officers in front of him, had already left their black-and-whites. They assumed the "firing" position as they hid behind the fronts and backs of their cop cars.

"Stop!"

"Stop or we'll shoot!" a different cop yelled. This one was trigger-happy. His index finger was itching.

From the rear, a different batch of cops slammed to a stop smashing into Koestler's Buick. They tore out of their vehicles.

"Stop or we'll shot!"

There was no way that Koestler was going to stop. He had only one way to go. And that was not to jail. Like an alley cat Koestler leaped up onto an overhanging fire escape ladder. It slid down with his weight. Koestler scrambled up toward the roof.

The trigger-happy cop again yelled, "Halt!" However, that was only after he had made up his mind to shoot. This was exactly what he did.

The country was scared to death, in a trance over the plutonium terrorism. The killings needed to end. The trigger-happy officer's reaction expressed the nation's mandate. A hailstorm of bullets followed. Koestler's body lit up like a Christmas tree. He convulsed and seized as he was hit time after time. He fell fifteen feet to the concrete and his death. On the ground next to him lay his toppled briefcase. It had broken open, exposing Koestler's handheld Panasonic tape recorder, his plans and an airline ticket to Brazil. His poorly coded diary was deciphered by the feds in two hours. It had detailed his plan. The location of the plutonium device was not mentioned.

What Koestler had planned was the following:

He had Mayo Clinic Administrator George Taylor arrive at Amtrak 320 East to Denver. There he would board and go to sleeping compartment A-23, where Koestler had a confederate put directions underneath the bed's mattress.

Taylor was to take his two legal-file briefcases full of money, each one-foot wide by one-and-one-half feet high and long; and fill two large black Nike duffel bags. Each briefcase was packed with duct taped garbage bag squares. Looking at the silver-taped bags, nobody would have any idea that they were full of stacked one hundred dollar bills.

As Koestler saw it, his only risk was the Soldier of Fortune mercenary. Koestler thought that if his guy tried to steal his money the mercenary would just get his ass caught, and Koestler would strike another hospital.

Taylor was to carry the duffel bags to the far forward right seating compartment and to place them in the last overhead storage compartment. Then, Taylor was to return to his sleeping compartment for the duration of the trip.

At a certain time, the confederate would unload the Nike bags and pack the money into one large Northface camping knapsack. He would then repack the Nike bags with sheets and throw them out of the train 10 miles before the Mississippi River.

When Amtrak 320 was over the Mississippi River the confederate was to throw out the waterproof knapsack. Koestler would be waiting below in a speedboat.

The confederate had never met Koestler. He was hired through a newspaper ad in "Soldier of Fortune" Magazine. He was told that he was assisting the CIA in a covert operation. He was paid ten thousand dollars up front, and was to get fifteen thousand at the end. He had no idea that the Nike bags contained money.

Koestler checked the confederate's references. The mercenary had experience in Rhodesia, Desert Storm and Panama. He was reputed to be extremely reliable.

The press went berserk.

All the networks, in an orchestration of orgasmic frenzy, proclaimed that the most fiendish human scum that had ever set foot on this planet had gotten his due. He was worse than Hitler and more evil than Ida Amin. He had been brought to justice.

After a painstaking and incredibly thorough search no bomb was ever found. The "Plutonium Bomber" as he was dubbed, had been stopped while in the process of attempting to collect a five million dollar ransom in a bizarre ending to an even more bizarre story.

Yet questions remained unanswered: Where did the bomber get his plutonium? Was there ever a device at the Mayo Clinic? Were the first two water-activated units the only ones that existed? and more specifically why?

42

The Robbins Complex

The early-1800s post-colonial chestnut-stained oak table was set for five. The William the IV piece sat fourteen.

The room was a canopy of several influences, but mostly West Indian. On the wall was a neomodern Haberle oil painting "Torn in Transit" which depicted an oil painting shipped through the mail. In several versions of the subject, the wrapping was broken open to reveal a broadly handled landscape with seemingly individual touch.

There were other mismatches in the room: An 18th century Spanish painting by Miguel Cabera that overlooked the dinning room. There were trumpeting archangels which rested on a sideboard, and Thai bronzes on crystal and Roman sculpted stones from Palazzo and Pallazzeto Venezia. An antiquated Chinese tapestry was on an opposite wall. It depicted Genghis Khan's capture of Peking in 1215.

Andrei and Boriskov were sitting at the table drinking '67 Laffitte-Rothschild when Viktoria and her father were brought in. Andrei was wearing what he had on when he had taken care of business with Dr. Alex Seacourt. He looked more Italian than anything else. That was part of his mystique — the ability to be a chameleon. First he was Czech, then Russian and now Italian.

Prior to dinner, Viktoria and her father had been taken to one of many master bedrooms. Viktoria was given an alluring black dress to wear. All the while, her captors kept a watchful eye on her and especially her interaction with her father. While she changed, she sat on the end of a large brass bed. She spoke softly to her father, almost whispering into his ear.

"What have you done to him, " she asked Andrei as Andrei began to nibble on a small scoop of lime sorbet.

"He's a victim of his own work."

"What?" she said, clinging to her father's hand.

"It's what he did to himself."

Viktoria sniffled. One of several attendants, of Creole and Mestizos descent, brought Viktoria and Dr. Siderenko lime sorbets. They were served in antique silver half-goblets. A servant poured a petit glass of white wine, and then retired to eight feet behind them.

Viktoria lifted a linen napkin to her cheeks, smudged the tears off and asked, "What...happened."

"I took your father. My KGB sources led me to believe that the professor had a breakthrough with his formula. That he was able to reverse the effects of radiation poisoning. Your father had proceeded beyond the uranium experiments and into the realm of plutonium."

"What happened?"

Andrei slurped more of his sorbet with his miniature spoon. "Working with plutonium has certain inherent risks. I, or should I say, we, needed your father as insurance to those risks."

"Insurance?"

"Just in case something went wrong. To cover all our bases."

Viktoria looked over at her father, who appeared nearly catatonic. He was in a state of semichronic stupor. "You wanted the antidote to sell it as ransom!" she said.

Andrei took another sip of his white wine. He swished the '67 Rothschild in his mouth, enjoying its bouquet and texture before he swallowed it. He smiled.

"My problem is this. Your father had worked out three alternative formulas. The experiments in Siberia, which you obviously are aware of by reading the discs..."

"You're the one who planted the discs in my father's apartment. The KGB didn't leave them."

"That's correct." Andrei took another sip of his wine and then continued. "The Siberian prisoner experiments were by and large unsuccessful. However, through failure your father may have discovered an alternative formula that worked. The problem was, he wasn't willing to risk more lives. When I found him, he was like this. You see...before I could abduct him, he decided to take his own formula. To try it on himself first. Over time he has gotten progressively worse."

"I don't believe you. You did this to him deliberately." She grasped tighter onto her father's hand.

"My assistant, Boriskov, is an expert of information extraction. As best as I could narrow it down, the formula would be safe to use with only a slight alteration. Your father made the mistake of taking one of the three alternative antidotes. It resulted in his own demise."

"My God."

"Our dilemma is, we're having a difficult time deciphering your father's handwriting. We need you to help us."

"But you tried to kill me?"

"Never you, only Seacourt."

"Why him?"

"Other reasons. Why... are you interested in him?"

"Alex is dying. He's been poisoned."

"I know. If you can help us, you may be able to help your father, though I think it's too late. But certainly you might be able to help your friend Alex."

She nodded.

"I have chemists that you can work with. All I want you to do is the best you can."

"The best I can?"

"Let me put it this way...the best you can means success, otherwise..." he looked at the professor, and then said with a beaming smile, "otherwise you too will be *forced* to take the wrong formula."

Though the table was set for five, four of them ate. They had mussels, escargot and heart-of-palm salads. For the entre they were served filet mignon and they had bananas flambeaux for dessert. The meal was better than any French restaurant.

"Where is Mr. Robbins?" Andrei asked.

"He should be down shortly," Boriskov replied. In reality, Robbins was eating his dinner in a nook, not far from the dinning room. On video monitor he watched and analyzed every word that was said. After the four had finished eating and cups of Jamaican coffee were served, Robbins made his deliberately histrionic entrance.

Bart's inadvertent imitation of The Phantom of The Opera was unnerving. He wore his symbolic all black outfit, swarthy fedora and inky-dark silk scarf. He hid under the hat with its felt brim angled out and downward. The low crown was creased lengthwise with exactness.

Bart subconsciously believed that he deserved every bit of pain and torture that he got in life. To Robbins the abomination, each day was an anguish-filled crucifixion.

Two bodyguards followed into the room

"Viktoria, I'll be brief," he said sitting down. She looked at him with disgust. "Coffee please," he commanded one of his valets.

Outside the complex, through the picture windows, Viktoria noticed several heavily armed sentries marching back and forth. The guard doubled once Robbins entered the room.

"I need you to solve our problem. Tonight!"

"Tonight? I'm no scientist."

"Tonight."

"I'm not even sure I can read my father's handwriting."

"We know that," Andrei interrupted. "It's your father, if you want to see him alive in the morning...that is, then I'm counting on you to interpret his scribble."

Robbins spoke furtively, to one of his thugs. The man left the room. He returned shortly with four chemists, all of whom where in long white lab coats.

"You have at your disposal four of the best technicians in the world. With your assistance, they should be able to crack your father's cipher. It's *extremely* important."

Viktoria knew she had no choice but to help. Besides, Alex's life was in jeopardy, and maybe she would be able to save him. Maybe she could come up with the antidote.

"Why are you doing this?" she asked.

"Doing what?"

"Doing this. All these people that have been killed."

"You see my point now; why it is so important to make the antidote work. Perhaps the victims might have a chance?"

"I don't get it."

"You're not supposed to," Robbins traded glances with Andrei.

"Why do this at all, why kill and make so many people suffer, potentially tens of thousands, and then want to save them?"

"And more," Robbins replied with certainty.

"Why, why do this?" Viktoria rose to her feet yelling, "You monster!"

No one should call a monster a monster, especially someone as powerful as Bart Robbins. Robbins leaped to his feet and ripped off his hat, flinging it to the floor. He tore off his scarf, his black jacket and ripped off his shirt. "Why?" he howled, spewing his hatred for all man in a spitting vitriol, "Look at me, and imagine the pain I've had to endure for two years! When I was thirteen I was blown-up in a car bomb—70% of my body was burned! Everyday I was in agony. Everyday my skin was peeled off me so that new skin could grow. *But it didn't!*

"Instead I *became this abomination!* And then...and then..."spittle drooled down his chin, "And then in the same hospital my sister and my unborn child *died*!.... It was *a sign from GOD. I AM HIS AVENGER. PEOPLE EVERYWHERE WILL FEAR AND SUFFER, AS I DID—AND DIE AS MY SISTER AND CHILD DID. REVENGE IS MY DESTINY!"*

Before Viktoria and the professor stood a demon, the likes of which she had never seen nor imagined. His skin was hideous and his face was distorted from the pyrotechnic ravages.

"See who I really am!" he proclaimed jackaling, *"See what society did to me! Now it's time for everyone to pay!"*

Robbins knew that he might eventually be caught. Getting *even with society* had its consequences. But at least he would have the opportunity to purge his anger, to settle his score before his house of cards came tumbling down.

Robbins' eel skin escarpment, with webs of melted tissue fibers, tangled in confusion with porcine grafts; appeared alive. His naked skin was dripping candle wax; oozing off his bone and sinew, foaming in microbubbles off his face, ready too burst in a torrent of self-repulsion.

"Find the solution," Robbins bellowed, *"or find your death!"*

Robbins signaled his two behemoths to take Viktoria away, to follow his crackerjack chemists to solve the mystery...before it was too late for everyone!

Or was it already too late?

43

22 Hours Left - Time Was Slipping Away

" *Haaaaaaaaaa!"* Andrei roared like thunder as he squeezed the trigger on the .44 Remington Magnum. *Alex remembered that when he came to.* The chamber was empty. Bullets were in the other five. Andrei made sure that he saw them, studied them, when Andrei pressed the pistol to his forehead. Andrei made sure Alex *knew* that he was going to murder him in *cold blood.*

"Bang!" but no bullet. "Bang!" to photograph not Alex's execution, but the terror on a man's face who knows that he is going to die. "Bang!" to record for posterity Alex's visage of dread. "Bang!" for the late night cocktails to impress other sick creatures. "Bang! You're dead!"

Andrei had left the room two hours earlier, after scaring Alex nearly to his grave. He wondered if there were others. There must have been.

Alex knew that Andrei was not done with him. Andrei was just toying with him, playing with his prey, clawing his supplicant before his bacchanalia. Andrei was screwing with him until he decided to consume his morsel: slowly, and in agonizing bites — but not until he was good and ready. And then...

The dungeon door launched open. The rusty hinges creaked. A groggy old man was thrown into the cell with Alex. Alex immediately recognized Dr. Siderenko. Siderenko fell to his knees and then rolled onto his back. His face was troubled. His features looked like a man who had been in pain, who had been tortured.

Alex had been released from the bodyboard and had been lying on the straw. He propped himself up against the wall and slid his legs and buttock toward the brick. He hobbled over to Siderenko. The professor was disoriented. One of the two guards who brought the professor into the cell hit Alex in the gut. Alex tumbled to the ground. He was breathless, spewing blood.

The guards slammed shut the door.

Alex got up on all fours and crawled over to Dr. Siderenko.

"Are you all right?"

"*Dve Tisyachy.*"

"Are you okay?"

"*Dve Tisyachy.*"

"I don't understand."

"*Dve Tisyachy.*"

"Please. Please," Alex begged, "I'm a doctor let me help you."

The professor babbled unintelligible phrases in Russian, over and over again; different words — but most of all repeating the phase "*Dve Tisyachy.*"

"Please, speak English. Do you speak English? Let me help you."

He continued to mumble. He did not respond to Alex.

Above, the overhead light, a hypnotic 30-watt bulb, shined dimly through a wire mesh cover. Screws holding the dome in place gave Alex an idea.

With difficulty, he worked his way to his feet. He removed his belt from his pants. The belt stubbornly slipped out through the loops. As he removed it he could see a crystal snow-hallow appear around the light source. Hallucinogenically the corona grew.

"Click," a switch flipped outside his prison. The overhead corridor light beamed. Alex wasn't sure what time it was. All he knew was that he needed to work on the wall.

He made his way to the wall latches. He ran his fingers along the wall. He felt the indentations, and irregularities in the cinder block, the thick paint on top, and the grooves where the mortar was laid. He took the hook at the end of his belt and began digging into the latch. When he was up on the wall, he heard a creaking sound. Eight inches, maybe six if he was lucky, the set was buried into the wall. It had begun to give way when he was hanging on the bodyboard.

Slowly, Alex scratched around the eyelet into the latch with the point of his belt. He was careful not to bend or break the metal belt tip. Cautiously, he dug, wiggled, and whittled away the metal latch from the wall.

Another wave of nausea overcame him. In the darkness the room danced with imaginary specters. It consumed all his energy to remain standing, to work upright against the wall.

Alex had come here to find Professor Siderenko, to get the antidote — and here he was. And all that the Professor could speak was incoherent babbling Russian. He was unable to communicate with Alex, and Alex with him.

"I need the antidote," Alex thought, "Why didn't I check his pockets? I need to check his pockets. Maybe it's there." He continued to dig at the wall. Instinctively, he knew that he had to do this first. "But I didn't check his pockets. I need..."

Alex had come all this way. To Moscow, then Nassau and now somewhere in Belizean hell. So ironic. So close, but no cigar.

44

66 Fools!" Robbins bellowed as he stormed into the electronics room where Andrei and Boriskov were watching the monitors. The room was lit by two imposing verandah sliding-glass doors, each ten feet tall by fifteen feet wide. The doors dwarfed the room. Outside, the ocean swells brusquely rolled in.

The monitors had each of the different networks droning: ABC, NBC, CBS, FOX, WARNER, UPN, BBC, CBC, CNBC and most importantly CNN. CNN was blaring on the huge central monitor's screen.

"Arthur Koestler, the mastermind behind the plutonium sabotages in Miami and Ann Arbor was killed today in a bloody shootout in Dubuque, Iowa, en route to collecting a five million dollar ransom....Koestler had threatened nuclear contamination of Mayo Clinic's Methodist Hospital....After an extensive search of the hospital no device was found. It is believed that there are no other nuclear devices and that the extent of the contamination has been limited to only Miami and Ann Arbor...."

"*Idiots!* We have a device in Methodist Hospital and they didn't even find it. Goddamn fools!" Robbins thundered through the electronics room.

"All the better for our plan. Don't you think?" Andrei passively stated trying to calm Robbins. Andrei wasn't sure if Robbins was enraged that the American public thought that there was no longer a nuclear threat; or that the authorities had incorrectly placed blame on Arthur Koestler, who was obviously a copycat.

"Fools. Goddamn fools!"

Then, Andrei and Boriskov were summoned by one of Robbins' men. They both left the room. Robbins, with a crazed unpredictable look, slowly calmed down. He sat at the center of the "U" sofa and watched the news reports.

The insipid CNN broadcaster Rock Evers droned on, always enthused to report a major scoop. "The world 'might' be safe again," he narrated, "but new precautions need to be taken to prevent an episode as diabolical as this from happening again."

Fifteen minutes later, Andrei and Boriskov returned. Boriskov held a snake keeper's canvas sack.

"Everything is ready for the remaining targets."

"Good," Robbins replied, turning from the news and muting the sound. "I want to activate the device at the Mayo Clinic first, just to show those dumb bastards."

"It's undetectable with the plastic polymer coating. The polymer is impervious to alpha-radiation emission, and thus the plutonium is undiscoverable with Geiger counters or scintillation detectors, no matter where we plant the devices. They're toast."

"Excellent.... Where's the unit?"

Boriskov smiled and Andrei began laughing. "Right under their noses. You know that the fed's murder of Koestler was a good thing; it took some heat off us temporarily, so that we can proceed properly with your plan."

"So where's the device?"

Andrei beamed and then walked over and whispered into Robbins' ear. Robbins chagrined, "*Idiots!*"

"Of course," Andrei said, patting himself on his back.

"What about the girl?"

"I'll keep her working on the antidote...interpreting her father's notes."

"Good."

"Also...I have other plans for her," Andrei said, intimating a man-to-man carnal knowledge. "Matters I need to take care of privately."

"Go. Take care of your business." Robbins waived Andrei off. "Just as long as I have a solution."

"Don't worry. It's taken care of. Oh, by the way," Andrei gestured Boriskov. "Here's a little bonus."

Boriskov threw the canvas snake charmers sack onto the squat 8-foot by 8-foot table that made up the room's centerpiece. It perched between the three couches that faced the monitors.

Robbins bent down and unlashed the bag, rolling out its contents onto the mahogany table. Out tumbled Jack Tandy's severed head, eyes bulging, skin blanched, the neck muscles and dangling vessels bloodless.

"What's the meaning of this? What have you fucking done! Do you know who this is?"

"This is the man responsible for your family's murder."

Bart froze. In an instant the thought of that fiery afternoon vividly flashed into his mind. He remembered playing as a child. And then that day coming back from London and driving in the family limo from the airport when.... He could still see the flames, feel himself being blown out of the limousine, flying through the air; napthene sticking to his skin and burning in arcs of white-hot pain. He felt himself being hurled into the photinia bushes. He was dazed and unable to put out the fire. And then a paramedic covered him with his yellow rubber jacket.

Then, he was on his way to the hospital. He could smell his skin, the burnt flesh that had dripped like beeswax from a candle.

He could vividly see the two years he spent at Jackson Memorial Hospital, preserved and *pickled as a freak*. He saw each day pass in a montage of mercurial pictures exploding in his brain.

"How? Why?" He asked. Robbins needed to know.

"Your father," Andrei said with compassion, "was a genius. He built the Robbins Company into a giant from nothing. Many people were jealous. When your father was first assassinated and your family annihilated, the authorities thought that it was either the work of Brazilian terrorists who were incensed with the Robbins Company strip mining of the Amazon; or someone at rival Hartax Pharmaceutical Company, that was about to release Duomet, Kodmore's competition for Pepsafe as an antiulcer drug."

"How do you know this?" Robbins asked angrily.

"I do my research before I work for *any* employer."

Viktoria, who had just walked into the room, could not keep

her eyes off the bodiless pate.

"So why Tandy?"

"You tell me."

"He was one of my most trusted men. Number two in the company."

"Maybe jealousy. Maybe he wanted Robbins Company and Kodmore Pharmaceuticals for his own. Tandy believed that it was he that made Robbins the company that it was — yet your father owned everything."

Bart slowly walked around the inlaid table. He looked down at the head with venom and disdain.

"How did you find out?"

"It was one of my ex-KGB agents. He did the job freelance. When I had you checked out, the information worked its way back to me. Since you are now my employer, my loyalty is to you. And thus, I took it into my own hands to settle the score...as I would presume you would do for me."

Robbins continued to circle the table like a vulture preparing to pounce. "I would," he said mesmerized.

"I know."

"When?" Robbins asked monosyllabically.

"When is not important. What is, is that your family has revenge."

Bart stopped walking. He stood motionless for nearly a minute and then he began yelling. *"Never, not until our plan has been completed. Never! My sister and child are dead! Never until I say so! It is over when I say it is over!"*

Robbins took the head by its dried scalp and slung it at the sliding-glass door window, aiming at the sand and surf outside. The head tumbled against the paneglass leaving its mark on the door, but not shattering it.

"Tandy thought that by eliminating your father, he would take control of the company. No one would ever blame him. Fingers would be pointed at Hartax and Amazonian rebels, as they were.... I'm sorry."

Robbins ran from the room wailing.

"Let's go," Andrei ordered. "Have a driver take the girl, the planes waiting and make sure that the lab is ready in Vegas when we arrive at McCarren. And I want our men working on the antidote while we're in flight."

"It's done," Boriskov replied. "I think we've just about cracked it anyway."

"Good. And one more thing, once the scientists come up with the antidote...you know what to do."

"Of course..."

"Remember, time is of the essence."

Andrei had Viktoria taken to the airport to one of Robbins' auxiliary jets, a Challenger 600, that was ready for their three thousand mile flight. Andrei and Boriskov would catch up shortly.

What Andrei did not tell Bart Robbins was that the ex-KGB agent that murdered his father, mother, brothers and sisters...*was him*. It was Andrei, the double agent, the freelance operative, who had been hired by Jack Tandy twenty-three years earlier to assassinate Billy Robbins.

Jack Tandy had lied to Andrei. Tandy told Andrei that Robbins had gone to London on business, without his family; that Robbins would be coming home alone. Andrei planted the plastique device under the Robbins limousine, on the rear tie rod. He used C-4 and napthene to ensure that if Billy Robbins survived the explosion, which he was sure he wouldn't, Robbins would be burned to death by the napthene.

Andrei didn't kill children. At least not at that point in his career. Jack Tandy had tricked him into murdering Robbins' entire family. If Andrei had known, he would have murdered Robbins a different way. There were so many.

That experience had jaundiced Andrei. After the Robbins car bombing Andrei never felt the same. That was the reason he started collecting "faces of fear," "faces of death"; videotaping his victim's demise. The car bombing made Andrei into every bit of a monster that he never thought that he could be. He was no longer the ultra-cool professional KGB killer. Now he had to, at least subconsciously, live out the role. He had to play the part.

Like Bart Robbins — they were both tied, linked by an invisible strand, a destiny that had to one day come full circle. And now...with Tandy's demise, it had. Andrei had copiloted his destiny. He had made himself whole again.

And for the finale...*he had a second agenda, a secret one*. In a nutshell — he was going to make himself one of the richest men in the world.

45

16 Hours Left

Alex was determined to change his luck.

His gray matter was no longer functioning as it should. Synaptic signals were miscuing. Visions, thoughts of proper reality, were distorted into flashes of green half-truths. "His pocket," Alex thought. "Did I check his pocket?" Alex had worked feverishly for hours. Despite the diminution of his strength, he had all but completed his task.

"I need to check Siderenko's pockets. Don't forget." He reminded himself with resolute purpose.

His finger's were raw, working his belt buckle and the metal prong that fed into the belt's holes, at the other end. The darkness turned into scintillations while he worked. Black became color and the murk metamorphosed into a phosphorescent hue of abstraction.

In the distance, Alex could hear footsteps coming down the corridor. Despite his condition and the pain and disorientation from the plutonium poisoning, he feverishly toiled to finish the job. Closer came the footsteps and the droning voices. He quickly pulled out the set screw, which held the female latch into the wall. The screw in and of itself was probably useless —but it could be used as a weapon! That was what Alex was counting on.

A key entered the door lock.

"Think! Think! There is something else I have to do," he said to himself, returning to the floor on all fours hoping that his captors did not see his handiwork. "God. What do I have to do?"

Alex pressed his hands to his face, trying to force out the thought. "What? What?" He mumbled, almost chanting in desperation. "Hummmmm."

The men, four of them, pushed open the dungeon door. He was on his hands and knees. Blood drooled out of his mouth. He looked up and did not recognize any of them. The light cast its rays in a triangle, illuminating Siderenko, who was prone and unconscious. It spared Alex its glance. Two of the men reached down and lifted up Siderenko. He was a sack of potatoes.

Alex glanced at the wall where he had been working. He saw flecks of paint, tainted with crimson that had fallen but stuck to the cinder block below. He hoped that his captors would not see his handy work.

As the henchmen lifted Siderenko up by the professor's arms and began dragging him out the door, Alex could see a bulge in the professor's pocket. A bulge that could represent a vial.

The two other men hoisted Alex under the arms, and likewise dragged him out of the room. Momentarily, one of the men stopped and glimpsed at the wall. He noticed a change in contour. His eyes had not adjusted from the bright light in the hallway to that of the chamber.

"Come on Joe. We gotta job to do," the other said, attempting to get Joe's attention, so that they could carry-out Alex. Joe was looking at the wall. He knew that something was wrong. He needed to let his eyes accommodate.

"Come on man! Let's get our ass moving."

"Yeah. Sure," Joe replied, presuming that what he had seen was probably the result of Andrei's handiwork from earlier. Joe had seen a lot worse — guts and blood on the wall. That stuff was no big deal.

The professional soldiers, men in the employ of Andrei, carried Alex down a long hall and then out from beneath the Robbins mansion into the bright sunlight and onto a lush grass rise. One hundred yards farther was the water.

White rock steps led downward from the rear of the complex onto a chalky sandy beach. Not far from the beach was a boat dock, where two vessels lay in wait: a fifty-two foot cigarette and a one hundred forty-eight foot yacht. An ashen road wound on the other side of the docks and in a semicircle around the Robbins complex and clinic, merging into a small terrace between the main house and the clinic. The drive was used to bring supplies to the clinic and the main house from the vessels.

The dock jetted two hundred and eighty yards into the Caribbean Sea. Beneath, the ocean floor was deeply dredged and could berth a small freighter's draft.

The men dragged Alex to the dock. The winds blew in from the southwest at six knots. His legs, his shoes touching, were drummed over the planks until he arrived at a waiting group of sailors. Bart Robbins was standing before them.

"So, if it isn't the wild card that's been mucking up the works," Robbins said, glaring down at Alex.

"Who...who are you?" Alex asked.

"Me," Robbins replied, stepping over Alex, examining his prize. *"I'm God."*

Alex was not all that disoriented to not appreciate the situation that he was in, and who he was dealing with. "Are you Robbins?" he struggled.

"I am," Bart answered inspecting his carcass.

"Why?"

"Why?"

Alex looked at Robbins out of the corner of his vision. The sun pierced into Alex's eyes. "Why?"

"Well..." Bart began pacing. "You know...that you've caused my friend here some grief?"

Alex turned his head and saw Andrei. Andrei glared down at him.

"I don't know. At first, for revenge — for my child and my sister. But then more so to teach society a lesson. They made me like this you know, evil, reproachful." Bart circled Alex stepping over his sprawled feet. "I can't tolerate what this world has come to. The doctors ripping-off everyone. You know, they're nothing more than stuck-up greedy pigs. And then, the pharmaceutical companies profiteering on others' misfortunes.

"Then there's the hospitals, *they're Satan's place.* They need to be squashed, snuffed-out like pesky bugs. Put to sleep permanently. It's my job. *I was chosen as the patron saint.* Think of me as Johnny Appleseed, planting the embryo for future generations."

The thought sickened Alex. All he wanted to do was to reach

into his pocket and remove his makeshift weapon. He wanted to drive the eight-inch set screw through Robbins' depraved heart. But there were too many of them.

"Is the jet fueled?" Andrei asked a uniformed man that appeared to be the pilot as he stepped away from Alex.

"Be ready in 10 minutes."

"And the girl?"

"She's already on board."

"Excellent. And she has the professor's notes?"

"Yes."

"Make sure she's working on it! I want a solution by the time we get to..." Then Andrei faced Alex, realizing that he had said too much. He stood next to Robbins and scrutinized him.

"Gotta go friend. It's been fun." Andrei started to leave, then turned and hesitated and said over his shoulder in a vinegary voice "Oh...by the way, have something to drink yet?"

"No."

"Just wondering. Enjoy the fishing, friend."

Boriskov was standing behind Robbins and Andrei. Alex had not previously noticed him. Boriskov smiled. Andrei followed Robbins off the dock. Boriskov took up the rears. As he trailed, he walked out of his way to deliver a punishing kick to Alex's gut. The blow caused Alex to retch in deep pain.

"Happy trails," he said. Boriskov and Andrei left for the airport. Bart Robbins stayed behind where he had business to attend to. Everything was coordinated.

The four thugs who had taken Alex and Dr. Siderenko out of their dungeon loaded them onto the Princess Star's aft fishing platform. The Princess Star was a Norwegian registry one hundred and forty-eight foot yacht with a twenty-nine foot beam. It had three 3500 hp MTU engines with KaMeWa waterjets and cruised at thirty-two to fifty-four knots. Above, they were partially covered by a sunbathing deck. Below, Alex could hear the engines fire-up. The diesels hummed. The men came on board, except for one who disappeared for ten minutes. He returned with two blocks of frozen chum.

Two mates and a captain yelled the "all clear." The mates unlashed one forward, two mid and one aft line, and pushed the lumbering yacht out onto the cerulean blue water.

Three of the thugs went into the aft living room. They poured themselves drinks. They had a Chivas on the rocks, a "man's drink." The remaining thug sat upright in a director's seat in the open salt air, keeping Alex and Dr. Siderenko company.

Alex wanted to stand. He feebly thought that at best he could impale the man, but his strength had abandoned him. Then he thought, "what did Andrei mean 'Did you have something to drink?'"

"You ever go fishing?" the thug asked. Alex looked up. He could feel the boat bounce as it picked up speed leaving the Robbins dominion, north of Punta Gorda. They were headed into the Caribbean Sea. Alex knew this was a bad sign. "No, not recently."

Alex forced himself up, in a sitting position. The buzz of the engines beneath him grew to a scream as the yacht began to plane. It was deafening. Instinctively the thug withdrew his 9mm Glock and pointed it at Alex. "Mind if I sit?" Alex asked.

"No."

Alex shimmied up farther, and tried to force himself into one of the six director's chairs. He, however, only had the energy to lean up against the port wall. Underneath him, the grooved teak deck bit into his skin.

"Where are you taking us?" Alex asked.

The thug smiled. "To Davy Jones's locker."

Alex knew it was over unless he did something now. If only the man with the gun would look away, let down his guard. But he didn't.

Inside, the music wailed and the gangsters howled and laughed as they consumed drink after drink. They were boffooning about Alex and the professor's demise.

Once, a steward came back to check on their bodyguard, to see if he wanted anything to eat. The man abstained. The slight steward ignored the two captives.

After forty-five minutes the yacht cut power. The stern sank into the Gulf deplaning the vessel and the Princess Star slowed considerably. Alex could smell the chum. The odors had leaked through the cooler as it melted.

Three of the four men returned to the aft deck, snickering. Two of them with their fourth cocktail in their hands.

"Let's go fishing. What do ya say?" The first said to Alex.

"Yeah, good idea," the second replied.

"Fuck the fishing, let's go chumming!" The fat one said looking down at Alex. "Here give me a hand," he said to two of the gangsters.

The three men picked up Siderenko and threw him overboard. The boat was rocking back and forth, despite its immense size.

Alex believed he was going to die. He wasn't sure if he should've felt terror, or acceptance. He still had the screw. There was no way that by himself he could fight off these behemoths.

He could hear the men laughing. In the ocean, between swells as he drifted off the starboard side, he caught Siderenko's mumblings. Again and again he heard the words *"dve tisyachy, dve tisyachy."* Fortunately for the professor the thick salt water kept him afloat, lest he drown in his semiconscious state.

"Over we go," the one with the gun ordered. Before Alex could react, the others followed the thug's command. Alex was sea bound. Even his decision to use his weapon was too late, his reaction timing blurred in misperception.

His body shuttered as he struck the salt water hard, stinging his wounds.

"Chop up the chum and throw it overboard," the man with the gun ordered. One of the thugs took an ice pick that he brought out of the galley and began smashing the blocks into shredded pieces of frozen fish guts and blood. He scooped up the remnants and threw them into the sea in snow cone slush sprinkles. Soon the water turned a faint red.

"Let's blow this pop stand."

"Na. The boss said that we need to wait around."

"Bullshit," the biggest of the four replied, swirling his Chivas between his gums and then down his fat gullet. "These fucks won't survive the half hour. Let's boogie."

"Man, the boss said stay..."

"Fuck you. Fuck the boss. He doesn't have to know any different. The sharks 'll get em, they always do. Sides, who the fuck is going to swim thirty-five miles back to shore. It ain't happenin. Let's blow. I'm gettin' seasick."

"I ain't takin' responsibility," said the armed man.

"It's my ass, and I say, adios. So, adios!"

The leader picked up the deck phone and called the bridge. He gave the captain an order. The MTU's fired-up. In a stream of turbulent jet spray, leaving an enormous wake behind them, the Princess Star was gone.

Alex floated up and down, in crest and trough. The sun fiercely beat down on his face, salt water washing onto his lacerations. He dog paddled over to Dr. Siderenko. He eventually reached the professor. Soon, the first of the predators showed up.

Darting barracudas with their pointy razor-sharp needle teeth, then squid, dorado, tarpin, needlefish, amberjack. But no sharks.

"Professor, professor," he shook the doctor.

Siderenko was unpredictably agitated. Again he repeated the words, *"dve tisyachy, dve tisyachy."*

"Professor. Can I help you?"

And again, *"dve tisyachy, dve tisyachy."*

Alex placed his arm under the professor's. He kicked deeply into the brine to help prop up Siderenko so that he wouldn't drown. As he did, Alex felt the screw jab into his weary thigh. "Jesus, I didn't check the professor's pocket." He swam around Siderenko, the waves pushing against him. Salt water splashed into his face. The saline blurred his vision. He felt the professor's left pocket — nothing. Then he explored the right and jackpot! A vial!

Alex dug his hand deep into Siderenko's trousers and withdrew a small, amber vial. It had markings in Russian. He strained to see the words. Already he began to formulate a scenario. He would drag the professor under his wing. Maybe they could swim ten miles in a day. In the worst event, they could make land in three days. He would take the formula; but what was it Andrei said, "Did you have something to drink?" Was this a trick...was the vial poison? He had no choice but to risk it. Yet, in the back of his mind a voice told him that this was all wrong...and then...the first of the dorsal fins appeared!

46

The first of the *blue (Prionace) sharks* arrived.
"Mother-of-God!"

Alex grabbed on tight to Dr. Siderenko. Siderenko was babbling unintelligibly. Alex buoyed the professor under his arm and steadied the old man with a firm embrace. The waves tumbled, making it difficult to maneuver the vial and twist off the cap.

The antidote was a milky liquid, cold-cream white. Carefully, while bouncing over the swells, Alex attempted to unscrew the vial. The plastic top was frozen shut. He yanked at it and then it gave way. *That was when he felt his first bump.*

He wasn't sure, but something underneath a large, rubbery snout nudged against his thigh. He curled up his legs into a sphere, cannon-ball style.

Alex knew that the only chance that they had was to stay perfectly still. Sharks, he learned while attending medical school at the University of Miami, are extremely unpredictable. They usually prey on small sharks, fish, squid, octopus, shellfish and some species on trash. Larger sharks, such as the voracious white or "man-eater" attack seals, sea turtles, large fish and occasionally people. Normally sharks feed while attacking in schools.

"Jesus", he thought, quickly scanning the horizon for other fins. There were none.

Siderenko began to mumble again. Alex needed to shut him up. Alex knew that he had to open the vial, and if they were to survive he had to quiet the professor, now!

Alex took his right hand and precariously tucked the unopened vial under his chin. He then reached around Siderenko, in almost a bear hug, and covered the professor's mouth.

"Haaaaaa."

"Shut your damn mouth," Alex ordered as he quickly scanned for additional fin movement. None broke the surface. They floated for ten minutes in the rough Caribbean Sea. The container remained secure, at least momentarily, under Alex's chin. Siderenko had stopped muttering.

Alex scrutinized the horizon. Nothing. Waves surged line after line in curls and lifts. No blades coursed through the surface.

Then...*BANG!* Alex's thigh was rammed. He and Siderenko were pushed thirty yards in a spray of sea water, ripping the two of them apart. Siderenko, who until now had been nearly catatonic, awoke in a craze of screams. Blood spurted everywhere; the water, previously a Napoleon blue, turned river red!

Alex dropped the vial, his only chance for survival, and swam feverishly over to Siderenko. The professor was being pulled like a cork in and out of the water. Alex reached into his pocket and withdrew the 8 inch set screw and dived to Siderenko's rescue.

Eight feet in front of the professor, and only two feet below the surface, Alex could see the slippery, thrashing body of the shark his teeth shearing and sawing away at Siderenko's legs.

Alex worked his way up the monsters body. He reached "ride'em bronco" onto the dorsal fin, and violently stabbed the set screw again and again into what Alex though was the sharks head. With each lunge, he withdrew the screw in a tearing motion, as he tried to rip away as much of the tissue as he could.

Thick streams of blood began to flow into the water, but this time it was not Siderenko's.

Something collided with Alex's legs, slamming against him. He was not the target but a second shark was aimed at the professor.

He had done what he could. He swam as fast as possible away from the ferocious attack. The ordeal nearly exhausted him. A third shark arrived, then a fourth, fifth, sixth and seventh. Alex had lost his weapon, leaving it imbedded in the carnivore's carcass. The sharks were in a frenzy. He could see, as a wave carried him down into a valley, Siderenko make his last appearance above the surface. Water and sanguine were mixed in an orgy of gore.

"Gotta get away, gotta get away..." Alex swam as far away as he could. Then, after a grueling swim that seemed like forever, in exhaustion he passed out, motionless in Neptune's Kingdom.

One hundred and sixty-five feet from him, the blue sharks were in a feeding frenzy.

However, in the excitement they had attacked the eighteen-foot blue that Alex had ravaged by opening a gaping, bleeding dorsal wound. The fight was fierce. In the end, the monster succumbed as did the professor.

When the sharks were through, they disappeared as quickly as they arrived, into nowhere.

Two hours later Alex was dragged aboard a trawler. Its metal hull plates were rusty and its superstructure was barnacle encrusted. It was a mysterious relic.

Alex would have been rescued sooner had the reconnaissance satellite more accurately pinpointed his and Dr. Siderenko's dump-off spot.

His clothes were ripped, his pants torn and waterlogged, and his shirt in shreds. He was taken to the infirmary. The room was microscopic with two uncomfortable beds, an operating table, and stainless shelves with latched glass doors.

"*Vam khorosho?*"

Alex did not respond.

"*Vam kharosho?*" He slid a smelling salt under his nose. The ammonia drifted deep into Alex's sinuses.

"*Kak vas zavút?*"

Alex twisted his head. The nightmare at last was momentarily over. As he began leaving darkness for light, he could still see Siderenko's screaming visage, and the sharks ripping away the professor's life. Reflexively he curled up his feet.

"Vam khorosho?"

Alex turned his head and looked up at the Russian doctor. A benign smile was on his salty, bearded sailor's face. "Whaaa..."

"Are you all right?" this time he asked in English. Alex was dizzy. He could sense that he had been given an injection into his upper arm, the muscle sore from the deep plunging needle. His wounds had been cleaned and his nasal bleeding stopped with silver nitrate sticks.

Alex pushed back his saline sticky hair. "Where am I?" he asked, as he still sensed the shark rip away at Siderenko. It was a horrible feeling.

"The fishing trawler 'Tretiakov.'"

"I mean where am I?" Alex asked again.

"Fifty kilometers east of the Yucatan."

Alex sat up. He was still dizzy. He felt better. Whatever the injection was that he was given, it brought him back to the planet earth.

"What was in the shot?"

"Amphetamine, B-12, thiamin and prochlorperazine."

"The vial..." Alex realized that he lost trying to save Professor Siderenko. "The vial."

"What vial?"

"I need to go back. I need to go... to the airport."

"Where?"

"Belize."

In another room the conversation was clandestinely monitored and recorded. Simultaneously, the discourse was bounced off a satellite and fed into KGB headquarters in Moscow.

"What's at the airport?"

"I need to go. They were taking her somewhere?"

"Taking who?"

"Viktoria Siderenko, the professor's daughter. They've taken her. We need to go back now."

The doctor listened with concern as Alex told him about the sharks and his kidnapping. When Alex finished, the doctor handed him a bottle of pills. They were 10mg dextroamphetamine, ten of them. "Here, take this," the doctor said and then walked to an intercom mounted deep into the bulkhead wall and pushed a black button. He spoke in Russian and then returned. "The first mate is on his way down to speak with you. We'll take you back to Belize."

Alex could feel the ship change direction beneath him, his body swaying with the vessel's change in course. "You need to stop them. Before they kill more people. You need to contact the authorities now!"

"Stop who?"

"Robbins."

"Robbins who?"

"Bart Robbins."

Alex went on to tell the whole story. He told the doctor what he had already gleaned: that Bart Robbins was behind the plutonium sabotages, that there may *be more*, many more than anyone realized. Alex told of the complex, the Robbins mansion, the clinic, the Princess Star and Professor Siderenko.

"I've got to find the girl. They've kidnapped her. She's the only who can help me. She has the professor's formula. They've got her working on it. She knows I'm dying."

"What formula?"

"A formula to stop the radiation poisoning. I'm running out of time."

"How many men? Do you remember how many men?" the doctor asked.

"I don't know."

"Were they armed?"

Alex knew that the questions were being asked by someone who was more than just a physician. It didn't matter. "You need to contact the authorities. They need to be stopped."

Every word of what Alex said was analyzed by a computer voice modulator for truthfulness. The computer confirmed that he was not lying. Within two-and-one-half hours the troller lay one mile east of the Belize Barrier Reef, off the coast of San Pedro.

"I have just one question for you." Alex asked the doctor.

"What's that?"

"What does *dve tisyachy* mean?"

"It means *2,000 pounds*. Why?"

"The professor. He was saying that in the water. Over and over again."

Alex was given a change of clothes: a generic gray sweatshirt and pants, a fresh T-shirt, clean boxers, and slip-on deck shoes, a one-size-fits-all. Fortunately for him, he still had his passport and wallet which survived, but were badly waterlogged. He was taken by a twenty foot neoprene and wood dingy, with dual 350 horsepower turbine engines, to Belize City. When Alex arrived, the afternoon was coming to a close.

Simultaneously, forces had been deployed by both air and sea. They left from Pinar del Rio, Cuba, the Russian base-of-operations in the Caribbean, and were headed for the Robbins Complex.

The crack Russian troops, the best of the best, the rakish Spetznaz and the naval Aval Spetznaz arrived in quietude, with their silenced AK's, RPG-18 anti-armor weapons, RP46 light machine guns, percussion grenades and tear gas projectiles.

Alex had only 11 hours left!
The shot of amphetamine sulfate that he had received was wearing off.

47

Though President Climan had used the opportunity of Arthur Koestler's demise to let the nation lay at ease for a while; it soon became clear to him, the FBI, ATF, CIA, NSA and the whole professional law enforcement world that Koestler was a copycat bomber. Still, there was no credible ransom demand, no clear motive.

First on "Larry King Live" the question was breached when Larry King interviewed Special Director Stone and FBI Director Fiske on split screen.

"Gentlemen, I'm having problems with the assumption that Arthur Koestler, the lone Dubuque, Iowa stockbroker, would have the financial resources and skill to single-handedly pull off the plutonium sabotages."

Stone was the one who was supposed to take the heat on this. "Larry, let me first thank you for the opportunity to come here tonight and discuss the situation candidly with the nation. To answer your question, we certainly are not closing the door to the possibility that other individuals may have operated in concert with Arthur

Koestler. However, as of now, every indication is that Koestler acted alone."

"Director Fiske let me pose this question. It has been privately stated by members of your staff, that they do not believe that Koestler could have been in Miami to place the first device. How do you respond to that?"

"There are always inconsistencies in the early stages of any investigation. And certainly we do have to admit that we're having trouble placing Koestler in Miami."

"Director Stone, there has also been criticism that Arthur Koestler, if he acted alone, did not have the financial resources to pull off this calamity. For example, it has been estimated that it would have cost Koestler in excess of a million dollars to buy the plutonium. Every indication is that Koestler was broke. Where would he have gotten the money and the plutonium?"

"That's very true Larry. Every indication is that Koestler was financially strapped. As I said, we're in the early stages of the investigation. That's why we believe that Koestler may have been acting as a front for another organization."

"So what is it Director Stone? Was Koestler a front for another organization or did he act alone?"

"I'm sorry Larry, if I wasn't clear. What I meant to say is that we are investigating the possibility of Koestler acting as a front for another organization."

"Then let me ask, has an organization been identified as of yet."

"No."

"So the idea that Koestler was really a copycat bomber—not the real man or group that you're after, is the most likely scenario."

"That's a likely scenario Larry," Director Fiske answered as forthright as possible. "But let me assure the American people that there is no evidence that any other device exists in any hospital anywhere. We've found *no device* at the Mayo Clinic, and as of now we are fairly satisfied that Koestler was our man. Larry, let me clearly state that we are continuing to investigate with all the resources available to the Federal Bureau of Investigation. I just want to assure the American people that there is no further nuclear threat."

Next it was "Meet the Press" that assailed Koestler as the possible perpetrator. Tim Russert questioned Vice President Monte Oliver on the premise that the entire scheme could have been pulled off by someone of Koestler's resources.

"Isn't it true Mr. Vice President, that there has been no evidence whatsoever that Arthur Koestler had the know-how or knowledge to construct a device as sophisticated as the ones found in both Miami and Ann Arbor?"

"That's correct Tim. And let me remind you, that there are still many unanswered questions. The President is doing everything in his power to come up with those answers. There is a distinct possibility that Koestler was not working alone. We are also looking into the premise that Koestler may have been a 'copycat.'"

"So, Mr. Vice President, one can say categorically, that even if we have found the right man in Mr. Koestler, the nation may not be any better off? That there may be other nuclear devices?"

"I'm not saying that, Tim. You know that the point that I'm trying to get across," Vice President Oliver was getting irritated, "is that we have done everything in our power to ensure that no future episodes, such as those that occurred in Miami and Ann Arbor will happen again. I can say, *categorically*, that every hospital in the United States had been extensively probed by federal, state and local authorities; and that there are no more devices."

"Can you guarantee this to the American people?"

"Yes," the vice president lied.

And on "Face the Nation," Bob Schiffer and the United Nations Secretary General Juan Alberto Rivera.

"Mr. Secretary General, what is the United Nations doing to prevent this sort of macabre atrocity in the future."

"Mr. Schiffer, the United Nations Security Council is meeting as we speak to establish a new set of international guidelines and safeguards that will prevent any future dissemination of nuclear materials, specifically plutonium and uranium. We are developing protocols and strict enforceable controls and international regulations."

"What does that mean?"

"What it means is that in the future all nuclear materials will multilaterally be accounted for. The United Nations believes that the plutonium that caused the incidents in Miami and Ann Arbor may have been the result of the repartitioning of the previous Communist Bloc and the lack of adequate nuclear safeguards once the new nations were formed."

"Mr. Secretary, are you specifically talking about the dismemberment of the Soviet Union into the CIS, Commonwealth of Independent States?"

"No, I'm not. What I am specifically saying is that as a result of changes in borders, there has been a concomitant lax in security and controls of nuclear materials, both warhead and nuclear energy generating."

"Mr. Secretary, in the recent incident involving the stockbroker Arthur Koestler, the FBI stated that Mr. Koestler was more than likely the sole individual behind the incidents in Miami and Ann Arbor: Do you believe that Mr. Koestler was personally responsible, or that there were others and Koestler was just part of a larger conspiracy?"

"Mr. Schiffer my role is not to comment on the integrity of the FBI's investigation. I will, however, say that there are many in the Security Council who have grave concerns as to whether or not Mr. Koestler was actually *even involved* in either the Miami or Ann Arbor nuclear sabotages."

"Mr. Secretary, it certainly is true that Mr. Koestler attempted to blackmail the Mayo Clinic for five million dollars. So why do you say that..."

"No, I'm not..."

"Let me rephrase my question. Why do you say that the Security Council doubts Koestler's role in Miami and Ann Arbor?"

"The Security Council's intelligence reports, which of course you know are made up of the best intelligence agencies in the world, feels that as the "New York Times" and "Washington Post" have already suggested that Koestler was an exploitist 'copycat.'"

"So, the Security Council feels that Koestler is not the plutonium saboteur. And if he is not, then who is, or what group is responsible?"

"What the Security Council is saying is that it has grave doubts that Arthur Koestler is the individual responsible; and that more than likely, as I presume your government already believes, that the origin of your cancer is a yet to be identified terrorist organization that has something to gain from their actions...."

That was the country's sentiments. Though Koestler gave the nation a short-term fix, the public and media saw right through the FBI's proffer. Koestler was obviously not the plutonium psychopath.

Once again America was loosing its temporary false sense of ease. A malaise and paranoia was setting in. But deeper this time.

48

The Russian assault M-24 Hind-D helicopters, similar to the Apaches, but with bigger caliber everything and greater maneuverability; came thundering twelve feet over the ocean's surface, their rotor blades deceptively quiet. The heavily armored gunships with four-barrel 20 mm nose turret cannons, four pods each with thirty-two 57 mm rockets and four anti-tank Swatter missiles on the stub wings; stormed onto the Robbins complex. The Hind clandestinely deployed its teams of Spetznaz.

At the same time, high-powered, notch-transom, pad-keeled hull specially modified Fountains, the types used for drug smuggling, offshore racing and covert operations, stormed onto the beach after sprinting from Pinar del Rio, Cuba at ninety knots an hour. Each flying boat, whose stern only barely skimmed the water as it shot straight to Punta Gorda, carried nine crack Aval Spetznaz frogmen.

Hell had seen no fury like the Russians scorned!

The sandy beaches of the Robbins complex ran with blood. Bart Robbins and his entourage, despite all the money and top-notch mercenaries and paramilitaries, were no match for the superior trained, and incomparably armed Russian forces.

Camouflaged to blend into the jungle foliage, their faces were painted chameleon green. The troops surrounded the Robbins complex and using silencers immediately took out the unsuspecting mercenary guards. With the electronic sentinel wires cut and the perimeter surveillance cameras disabled, the assault team, with grappling hooks and heavy lines, entered the Robbins mansion on the third floor.

The fighting was fierce. Robbins' men, most of them with previous experience in Rhodesia, South Africa, Chad, Colombia, and Bosnia-Herzegovina, put up a stiff resistance. Pockets of defense throughout the complex made penetration and progress slow. Skirmishes were often room-to-room.

In the end, the Hind-D's blew the mansion's front wall out to complete the full-scale assault. Robbins' men suffered forty-eight causalities by the time the Spetznaz finally made their way down to the vaulted control room in the second sub-basement.

Bart Robbins and twenty of his heavily armed paramilitary warriors lay in wait for the Russians in the bomb shelter.

Bart sat in front of his satellite control panel pondering his fate. Above him, thirty-two television screens were seated into a concrete wall. His eyes were glued to the tubes. The video monitors displayed the futile firefight. One-by-one, with the penetration of the Russians, the screens went dark.

"What are we going to do?" Oswall, the former South African general and head of security, asked Robbins.

"Nothing. We're going to die."

Oswall was prepared for his death. As opposed to many others, the specter of demise never bothered him ; but rather he embraced the Grim Reaper. "We do have an option."

"Option?" Bart turned to ask Oswall who was standing behind him.

"Yes."

Outside, the commandos were attempting to penetrate the twelve-inch steel-doored chamber, which in turn was encased by an additional six inches of solid lead. Their efforts were futile. The shelter that Robbins had built for his base of operations was designed to withstand a nuclear strike.

The breathing air was recycled using a similar hydrogen and oxygen system as in the Space Shuttle. There were enough provisions for ninety days. And if need be, they could stay one hundred and twenty.

Robbins' swiveled his chair and spun to his second panel of video monitors. He activated the console. He lifted up a switch cover and inserted a round seven pronged peg-key and turned it one full revolution to the right. The key, one of two, hung by a platinum dog tag chain around Bart's neck. After the electronics were activated he allowed the key to hang freely, but this time outside of his turtleneck.

Above each Sony black-and-white video console were the names of different cities: San Francisco, L.A., Denver, Boston, Chicago, New Orleans, Dallas, Seattle, Cleveland, St. Louis, New York, Pittsburgh, Salt Lake City, Albuquerque, Phoenix, Portland, Indianapolis, Buffalo. In total, there were 18 major metropolitan areas. Each corresponded with a prominent university teaching hospital. Ironically, thirteen of the eighteen hospitals had already been thoroughly searched by the feds for additional devices. The water systems and physical facilities were carefully scoured. Nothing was found.

However, in each of the major metropolitan hospitals, in wait lay a live nuclear device — quiet, deadly and undetectable.

Each device was installed in the hospital's Heating, Ventilation and Air Conditioning System, deep into the ingress air ducts, a place not searched. Andrei had changed the delivery nexus since he knew that the feds would be looking for devices in the hospitals' water systems. Each mechanism had its own self-contained water supply, three gallons of distilled water, which was more than sufficient to do the job. Upon a signal from a satellite that orbited 22,300 miles above the earth, the mechanisms would activate.

The devices, except for their antennae, were undetectable. Each atom of plutonium was coated by the water soluble plastic polymer. The plutonium's alpha waves were shielded, and Geiger and scintillation counter impermeable.

All it took was a press of the button, and all eighteen mechanisms would go to work. Slowly, in a fine mist, the plastic encased plutonium would be released into the air. As the plutonium came into contact with the water, the plastic would instantly dissolve, and the plutonium mutate into plutonium dioxide. The vapors would be propelled though every duct and orifice of the hospital.

"The alternative," Oswall said, "is that we parlay our trump card, the devices that we have on line now. You fire-off one, let our assailants know that we mean business, and we set the other seventeen to go off by timer in sixty minutes, lest our foes not let us make our get-away."

Robbins pondered the advice that General Oswall gave him. He thought that it was sound.

Kumitet Gosudarstuennoy Bezopsnosti
(KGB)Headquarters Moscow

"Comrade Kosnosomol, this is Field Operations Commander Zvuk."

"Over, Commander Zvuk." The line went straight to Moscow.

"We've taken the Robbins complex. Forty-eight opposition casualties, eight friendly, and twelve opposition and nine friendly wounded."

"What about the devices? Have you been able to neutralize the complex."

"Negative. We've been stopped by an underground bunker. My explosive experts are currently working on it. I anticipate another forty-five minutes until penetration."

"I've got bad news."

"What's that?"

"There's been electronic activity within the last five minutes from the Robbins complex. Our Mikoyan-Gurevich infrared satellite picked up a hot spot. We think Robbins has remote capabilities and he's going to activate his mechanisms."

"How many and where?"

"We can't tell."

"Should we blow the place to smithereens?"

"If you have to, that's affirmative."

"I got a feeling we're going to need some assistance on this."

"What do you anticipate?"

"AA-22 Advanced Atoll missiles."

"Can do."

"One second." A munitions expert entered the room. He had a brief conversation with Commander Zvuk, who then got back on the line. "Problems."

"What's that?"

"Look's like we're dealing with at least twelve inches of case-harden steel and maybe six to eight more inches of lead."

"What does that mean?"

"Well, there's a problem with that."

"What's that?"

"It's going to take more time to penetrate than I initially anticipated."

"What's your solution?"

Commander Zvuk paused. "We'll need to find the antenna. Robbins can't be broadcasting through his bunker. He must have laid cable and has a remote broadcast point. I'd anticipate it can be as far away as eighty kilometers. We'll just have to find it."

"We can handle that on our end...but remember...time is our enemy."

"Affirmative." Zvuk closed the communication.

Thirty-five thousand, nine hundred kilometers above the earth, the Mikoyan-Gurevich satellite was busy locating the remote antenna. The satellite digitized images from the Robbins complex.

An aid entered the room at the Robbins' mansion, a large ornate den with nineteenth century oil paintings and rococo furniture, where Zvuk was coordinating his assault on Robbins' bunker.

"With nitro and plastique. I anticipate sixty minutes, maybe ninety tops for penetration."

"That may be too long."

In ten minutes Commander Zvuk received a call back.

"Got it."

"Where?"

"Fifteen kilometers west in the Mayan Mountains, north of Nim Li Punit.... How long will it take you to knock it out?"

"I'll have it vaporized in ten minutes."

"Might not be soon enough."

"I'll do the best I can."

Within five minutes, three Mig-23 Floggers Gs that were based out of Pinar del Rio, Cuba, which had been flying reconnaissance off the coast over Punta Gorda and Placencia, screamed like a bat-out-of-hell down onto their target.

Robbins' Bunker

"Get me the President," Robbins ordered Oswall, who was able to intercept a direct scrambled line to the pentagon and Chief of Staff William Ready. Within seven minutes, a startled President Bill Climan was on the telephone with Bart Robbins, CEO of one of the world's largest corporations, Robbins Inc. a.k.a. *Murder Incorporated*.

"Mr. President," the psychotic Howard Hughes-like character said in a mesmerizing voice, "It is I, Bart Robbins, not Arthur Koestler, not the Palestine Liberation Front, not the Libyan New Left Militia, nor any other organization that is behind the plutonium murders."

"What are you taking about Bart? And how did you get on this line?"

"Have your troops withdraw immediately. I have devices planted throughout your country: eighteen of them. If you don't withdraw your men at once, I'll unleash all of them now!"

"Robbins, I really don't..."

"And just to show you that I'm serious, I'm going to nuke Cook County Hospital!" In a rage, Robbins slammed down the phone. He took his second dog tag key and entered it into a secondary portal. As with the pervious seven-notched circular key, Robbins spun it 360 degrees clockwise. Eighteen buttons lit-up, glowing above name tags that represented each individual hospital.

With a twitch, demented Bart Robbins pushed the Chicago button!

49

Alex knew that Viktoria was his only hope. Ahead of him was a task that he did not know if he could handle. But did he have a choice? It pained him to think that he was already too late to help his mother and father. Time had run out for them. It had been more than six days.

In his pocket Alex had his waterlogged passport and wallet. His money had turned a parching green. Credit cards, several business cards and his pilot's license were ruined. Was life supposed to be like this? Was he supposed to have suffered so much? The losses were immense. But what about the others? The thousands that had lost their lives, their families and more due to the plutonium?

Was it too late for him? Did he still have a chance? He had lost the vial at sea, trying to save the professor. But was the vial a trick? Why would Andrei have asked him on the dock if he had "anything to drink?" Also, Alex had overheard Andrei say something about Viktoria working on the professor's notes. Viktoria must have the antidote. Plus, it was Alex's obligation to save her. But where had Andrei and Boriskov taken her?

Alex remembered hearing them say something. What was it? "Fuel up the plane." They would be taking the jet, the Robbins jet...where? And more importantly why? Why would they leave Bart Robbins when they did? Did Andrei the ex-KGB general have another agenda? And what about the 2000 pounds, why was the professor incessantly babbling the words "two thousand pounds?"

Alex trudged slowly up the virgin white-coral beach. Belize City was a third world city. The housing and office, factory and storage buildings were from the days of the British Commonwealth, when Belize was part of the Great Empire of King George and known as British Honduras.

Alex hitched a ride to the airport. Edward, a fisherman on his way home, picked him up. Edward had been up since 2:00 a.m. laying and resetting his lobster traps. He had done well. It was slightly after 10:00 a.m. and time to go to bed when he saw Alex and stopped.

"Where to?" Edward graciously offered after Alex caught up with him. Alex looked like death warmed-over.

"Airport." Alex could feel the blood beginning to run from the cauterized spots in his nose. The silver nitrate was not holding its glue.

"Nice day." Edward said, squaring off a corner as he turned right onto Mary Street, en route to the airport. Alex did not reply.

"Wife and young'uns are going to have green turtle soup for dinner. Caught it myself yesterday. Not supposed to catch the turtles anymore, but..." he noticed that Alex wasn't paying attention. "Mister, ever had turtle soup?"

"No," Alex said, staring straight ahead. Inside he felt wired and bitterly fatigued. The green '63 Ford Fairlane stumbled across the fist of two speed bumps as they neared the airport. "I'm sorry. I've been preoccupied."

"Turtle soup. Tastes like chicken, the white meat. It's really good. A little rubbery. But mother tenderizes it first with a wooden mallet. She beats the toughness out of it. Then she cooks it in a big fat pot for six hours. Makes a broth, with tomatoes, chives, onions..."

Alex stopped listening. "There had to be a second agenda," he thought..."Tenderize the meat with the mallet before you cook it real good in a big pot..." There's been no real ransom demand... Tenderize the meat. *Work 'em over real good before you go in for the kill. Nuke a few hospitals before you go in for the real big kill!*"

They pulled up in front of the airport terminal, along side several sun-charcoaled cabbies, each trying to hustle the next tourist.

This thing wasn't over. Alex knew it. *He could feel it in his gut!*

273

There was something else on the platter: another agenda!

The first thing that Alex did was find the airport manager. With a few dollars spent in the right place, one hundred to be exact, Alex discovered that one of the Robbins' jets had left four hours earlier for Vegas. It had two pilots, a team of scientists, lab and technical equipment, and two men and an unwilling guest — a woman. It was a Challenger 600 and registered to American First Insurance Company, one of Robbins' many tentacles.

"About 5'7" tall, dark hair, maybe auburn," Mr. Bates, the black-as-coal manager said, "She could have worn that scowl on her face from here to China. I wouldn't forget who she was!"

The next flight to Las Vegas was Delta 414 at 11:30 a.m. Alex was lucky, there were still seats. He purchased his ticket with his warped credit card and sat down in one of the moody blue contoured concourse seats with fake leather. A corner where the material had been torn-off had understuffing poking through. He sat almost motionless, his sense confused, fighting between excitation and fatigue, stimulation and lethargy.

Around him, others were reading. A *Newsweek* had the headline "Our Nuclear Death." The *USA Today* had "Death Toll up to 7,980."

At ten minutes after eleven the intercom chimed for the boarding of American Airlines 2104. Alex trudged into line. He cleared customs with the inertia of a slug. He needed to take one of the pills in his pocket. The vial had ten, he thought. Maybe they would help. The shot of amphetamine he received on board the trawler Tretiakov was only a short-term fix.

He had the aisle seat. Next to him sat an obese woman who wore a tent-sized pale-green frock and smelled of cheap perfume. By the time the flight took off Alex was again feeling the effects of his radiation poisoning. His stomach was tied in knots. His nausea pulsated trough and furrow. He saw himself floating with Dr. Siderenko, bobbing like a cork; waiting for the sharks to come. And then he saw the first blue dorsal fin. Alex reached into his pocket. His vision had begun to double. The blurredness was slingshot repetitive with streaks and floaters appearing before his eyes.

Alex probed almost surrealistically deep into his pocket. The pocket was as fathomless as the Grand Canyon. He felt the vial and pulled it out of his sweats. "Was that what he was wearing, sweats?"

He cupped the plastic cylinder in his hand.

The amphetamine was powerful, however, slow acting. And because of Alex's radiation poisoning, it didn't last long. Maybe two hours, maybe four. That was it.

Alex twisted the plastic cap. The nasty groves bit into his fingers. Inside he could see the pills, or were they capsules. Eight? He poured them into his palm. Like a shower they rained down onto his hand. All of them except for two, bounced off his palm, oily with poison sweat. The free ones tumbed down onto his seat and into the crack behind him.

He tried to dig out the pills that had become buried into the crack. He was incapable. The whole world around him was in slow motion, thick like cottage cheese. The pills were lost forever.

It was all that he could do to take one capsule. The effort required to bring the pill to his mouth was monumental, nearly impossible. His hand stuck halfway in mid-effort; and then when he finally got it into his mouth, he couldn't make it close.

The last conscious thing that Alex remembered was the capsule sticking to his throat, trying to ease down into his stomach. He remembered the lump and the pill's synthetic taste coming back up. He passed out with his eyes wide-open, thirty-two thousand feet above the Gulf of Mexico. The noise in his ears was a barrage, the "buzza-buzza" of the high pitched jet stream air slipping around the American 777's fuselage.

50

Russian President Cheka sat in the opulent Lenin command center. The ceiling was vaulted, the furnishings antique and they were hand-crafted from fine Russian black hardwood. On his desk sat a computer terminal, a reminder that this was modern-day Russia. Across from him, on the other side of the boardroom conference escritoire, were Lavrenty P. Yezhov, Director of the KGB, Arkody Travkin, Chief of Staff of all Russian Armed Forces, Georgy Ilich Secretary of State, Valentin Ulanova, Special Minister of Joint Russian-American Nuclear Energy Development, and Russian Attorney General Aleksey Mussorgsky.

President Cheka picked up the red "hot line" telephone and placed a call to President Bill Climan.

President Climan was sitting in his office in his large burgundy leather armchair. It was the one that John F. Kennedy sat in when he and Castro were playing chess with the world, and Kennedy decided to blockade Cuba.

At 11:57 a.m. Eastern Time the telephone rang.

"Bill, this is Nikolay. How's the world for you?" Cheka was

like a cat: brilliant, articulate, a consummate politician, who next to Yelstin and Breshnev, was one of the most powerful and shrewd leaders to come out of the East.

"Jesus Christ Nikolay it's nice to hear a friendly voice. What a goddamn day...what can I do for you?"

"It's what I can do for you Bill. I can solve your headaches."

"Headaches?" Climan had just hung up with Bart Robbins. He knew what headaches were. And, in reaction to Robbins' he had just minutes ago ordered Secretary of Defense Bill Justice to deploy troops to Belize.

"Bart Robbins."

"That son-of-a-bitch. He just was on the goddamn line, direct to my office. He..."

"He's how do you say in English, 'bagel?'"

"Bagel?"

"No, no...I'm sorry. Toast!"

"Okay. What can I do for you Nikolay?" Climan became suspect.

"Mr. President," Nikolay was going in for the kill. No holds barred, no corner cutting. "I can make you look like a worldwide hero. But I need your help."

Still the politician, and ever wanting to get re-elected to a *second term* and go down in history as a revered President, Climan hoisted his antennae. "What can I do for you Nikolay?"

"Approximately 15 minutes ago my elite Spetznaz and Aval Spetznaz raided the expatriated American industrialist Bart Robbins' compound in Belize, on the Caribbean Sea. Bart Robbins, head of the billion dollar Robbins conglomerate is the person responsible for your problems in Miami and Ann Arbor...."

"Yes."

"There are eighteen other devices that have been planted in hospitals throughout your country. Our men have already disarmed the satellite system that was controlling those weapons of destruction."

"Thank you, Nikolay."

"My reconnaissance suggests that you could have your Marines on the Robbins compound within forty-five minutes and take full credit for the sortie."

"That would be great Nikolay."

"My troops can hold point until your Marines arrive. Then they can disappear into the oceans from where they came, and no one would be the wiser."

"Good idea."

"Mr. President you would be a *hero*."

"I like that."

"I suggest you call in the media. Your Marines take full credit. A good time to make a military muscle show of things. And if I may say so, provide you with an excellent opportunity to improve your popularity ratings. Don't you have elections coming up?"

"Of course."

"In fact, you might even win the Nobel Prize because of your efforts to make this world a safer place." Cheka was pushing all the buttons he could. President Climan knew what Cheka was doing.

"What can I do for you in return, to show my appreciation Nikolay?"

"Simple. You obviously have received tremendous political pressure to shut down our joint breeder reactor program. This would have horrific economic implications for Russia."

"I have. I also understand that the economic implications would be more than devastating."

"That's correct."

"How do you propose that *I not shut down our joint nuclear program* in light of what's happened here in the United States?"

"I propose the following: That not only do you allow Russia and the United States to move forward with our joint breeder reactor program, but together we also make this world a safer place to live. And isn't that what everyone wants?"

"Of course Nikolay. But Nikolay, I've had incredible pressure to abandon the breeder program." Climan knew he would get even worse heat if he didn't jettison the Russian/American joint breeder reactor effort.

"You don't throw away a whole bushel of apples if there's just one bad seed, do you?"

"No, you don't Nikolay."

President Cheka went on to explain a comprehensive plan that, *together* in a worldwide press conference, he and President Climan would unveil. The plan would entail a detailed new safeguard program and an International United Nations Oversight Committee with *police powers* and its own full-time on-site compliance officers. The new committee would actually become a seventh arm of the United Nations.

Cheka's plan was brazen, gutsy and ambitious. A lot of countries would definitely not like the United Nations sticking its regulatory nose into their national affairs; but with a military arm to enforce compliance, what happened in Miami and Ann Arbor could never happen again.

President Climan was impressed. He would come out a hero. Cheka would get his breeder reactor money machines, and the people of the world would live in a safer place.

"Bill I'm counting on you to help us out here. We need the *economic push*."

"Nikolay you've saved my ass on this one."

"One more thing Bill."

"What's that?"

"You have a dirty CIA agent or agents working with Robbins."

"Shit!"

"Your agent Evan Thomas out of Freeport is one. I'll fill you in later, but I think you ought to know. Let me give you Press Secretary Volsky. We'll handle first things first."

Press Secretary Rostislav Volsky got on the hot line via speaker phone. "President Climan, this is Press Secretary Volsky. I've already put together a proposal for a joint press conference with both President Cheka and yourself. I've taken the liberty to fax you my packet in anticipation that we'll have this Belize situation resolved to your satisfaction."

"Fine, fine. I'll have Press Secretary Gaddis on top of it immediately."

"President Climan, I would anticipate President Cheka's arrival in Washington within twelve hours..."

"Bill," Cheka got back on the line. "Secretary Volsky is fairly eager to move forward with this joint news conference. Don't you think it's a good idea?"

"It's handled Nikolay."

"Good. Dasvidán´ye."

"Dasvidán´ye."

At the exact instant that Robbins pushed the button to release the deadly plutonium in Cook County Hospital, the entire complement of AA-2-2 Advanced Atoll missiles fired from the three Mig-23 Flogger Gs. They slammed into the hidden antenna tower deep within the dense jungle, sending a cannonading percussion shock wave through Belize, the Yucatan and most importantly the Robbins complex.

Forty-five minutes later, the commandos led by Major General Zvuk, Field Operations Commander, penetrated the Robbins bunker in a bloody firestorm. The firefight was intense and casualties on both sides high. In the end, Bart Robbins and his mercenaries succumbed.

When the smoke cleared, Major General Zvuk, Field Operations Commander noticed that each of the eighteen buttons had been pushed on the control panel, and all eighteen devices detonated: except for the fact...that only at the *very last second* the communication antenna was disabled.

Above the gun-riddled console and TV monitors were shelves that held coded files which allowed the elite team to supply the United States with the necessary information to locate and dismantle each device.

There was no sign of Bart Robbins anywhere, though a charred body that might have been Robbins was identified.

Forty-five minutes after the Spetznaz and Aval Spetznaz had secured the compound, the first of the United States Marines arrived. As quickly and with stealth equal to that of their advent, the Russians disappeared.

CNN was the first on the scene, no more than a quarter hour after the Marines landed, and correspondent Glen Levy was given exclusive coverage of the Marine's successful capture and disarmament of the Robbins complex, which eventually lead to Glen's first Pulitzer Prize.

In Belize, the press swooped down on the Robbins complex like a pack of ravenous hyenas. The official word was that Bart Robbins was killed in the skirmish, his body burnt beyond recognition; though some doubted the veracity of this claim

Within minutes after the announcement of the Robbins fiasco, Robbins stock plunged 15% of its value on the New York Stock Exchange, and all future trading was suspended pending further notification by the SEC.

Robbins' properties in Coral Gables, Florida, Long Island and Santa Barbara were raided by massive multiagency federal and state task forces.

The country, which had been thrown into a state of national hysteria, could finally breathe a sigh of relief. Immediately, with President Climan's announcement, mothers again allowed their children to play outside, and fathers who before didn't permit their families to drink tap water, did.

There was frenzied celebration in the streets in the offices and in the bars. By noon, businesses, banks, schools and even the post office suspended the normal work day. Everyone was celebrating. Life in America had turned 180°, from a place of suspicion and mistrust, into a home full of glee and commemoration.

Already Russian President Cheka was en route to Washington, D.C. aboard his Ilyushin 11-96M transport. Cheka was preparing his speech with People's Press Secretary Volsky. Whatever it took, to not lose the thirty-five joint breeder reactor program with the United States. Billions of dollars in saved energy costs, and equally potential revenues were at stake. Russia would be able to sell her excess power to Western Europe, Greece, Turkey, and its CIS sister countries. The excess could amount to as much as sixty-five percent.

That was the real agenda. Economics. What the *new Russia* needed was in infusion of American and Western European cash.

51

Twenty minutes prior to landing, as the widebody jet descended like a rocket, with flaps lowered 1/4 way, Alex awoke from his trance. The flight attendant was alarmed. If it wasn't for the plump lady next to him, physically closing his eyes, the stewardess might of thought that he was dead. Alex did not move, however, his shallow breathing was barely evident.

"Sir, are you all right?"

As if instantly snapped out of a voodoo trance he replied, "Yes. Yes. Fine. Can...I have a Coke?" he knee-jerked.

"Sir, we're landing in twenty minutes."

"Can I have a Coke? I need something to drink," he asked again.

Instead of arguing, Alex's personage frightened her so much that she acquiesced, otherwise she was afraid that he might die on her. Within a very few minutes she returned with a clear-plastic glass, lots of ice cubes and fizzing pop.

"Sir," she said handing Alex a napkin. "You need to see a doctor."

"Oh?" he asked as he carefully took a sip.

"Were you affected by the radiation?"

"Radiation?"

"At the hospital, in Miami?"

"No."

"The reason I'm asking is, and I don't mean to be rude, but I had another passenger who was. That is, sick like you. Are you sick?"

The woman next to Alex got nervous, and though there was nowhere to move in her seat, she did her best to slink away from him.

"No, I'm not sick. I feel fine."

"Are you sure?"

"Yeah.... jet lag."

Alex's profusely sweaty back had stuck to his sweat top. His buttocks was numb and had fallen into a pins-and-needles sleep. Blood had pooled in his breached muscles, and his skin had turned purple and black-and-blue.

"Will there be anything else?" she asked less apprehensively.

"How long until we're in Miami?"

"Miami?"

"No, I'm sorry, Las Vegas," he was losing it again.

"Fifteen minutes. We're descending for landing."

"Do I have time to go to the bathroom?"

"Yes." She wasn't going to deny him, her pilgrim who scared the crew, and some of the other passengers. The captain didn't want to make anyone nervous about Alex, especially with the radiation poisonings. They didn't want anyone to panic on their plane.

The stewardess knew just by the statistics, that they coming out of Miami before they closed the airport, and now out of Fort Lauderdale to Belize then Vegas; they had to be carrying infected people. The news reports said that she should be safe. "Radiation poisoning was like AIDS. That one really couldn't get it from someone else, unless they were badly contaminated. And if the victim was that sick they wouldn't be able to walk. They'd probably be dead."

3:45 p.m. Eastern Time
Washington, D.C.
The White House

The President of the United States, Bill Climan went on nation-wide TV. Every television and radio stations' programs were interrupted for Climan's announcement.

President Climan was dressed in a raven-green suit. His shirt was white and his tie a slate burgundy. He looked tired. He had been emotionally drained by the nation's deaths, that ultimately he felt was his responsibility .

Perhaps, indirectly, Harry Truman had to deal with similar ghosts: the specters of people who have been murdered as the result of radiation poisoning. The walking dead and the disfigured, their blood on his hands.

Climan was a proud and ethical man. He held himself solely responsible for what had happened in both Miami and Ann Arbor. Though intellectually he realized that the deaths, the mutations, and the future generations chromosomal aberrations were not his fault; they *were his responsibility*. He had done everything in his power to bring the crisis to an end. Now, despite his best efforts, the exigent situation had been brought to a close by Russia.

Much of this was his fault. *A rogue CIA agent or agents.* Are his efforts in the future going to be sufficient to prevent any further nuclear abominations and catastrophes?

All President Climan could do as the leader of his great nation was his best. And that was what he had done.

"My fellow Americans, ladies and gentlemen of the press. I come before you this afternoon in these grave times with good news. I am here today to tell all Americans that once again it will be safe to sleep at night."

Climan was teary-eyed.

"Over the last week, the crisis that has faced our nation has been one of such unprecedented magnitude, threatening the safety of our citizens, that I have devoted all national resources to bring an end to this nuclear peril.

"This afternoon at 2:50 p.m. Eastern Time, the United States Marines invaded a remote paramilitary complex in Belize, Central America. The complex was controlled by an industrialist, Bart Robbins. At the Robbins complex, the Marines discovered an electronics network that controlled the two devices that were placed at Jackson Memorial Hospital in Miami and the University of Michigan Hospital in Ann Arbor, Michigan. In addition, another eighteen devices have been identified that are currently in hospitals throughout the United States.

"These eighteen devices, each containing fifty pounds of plutonium, have all been disabled. Agents from the FBI, ATF, NSA and

Nuclear Regulatory Commission are in the process of removing those mechanisms.

"In addition, the Marines have discovered a satellite system that activates each device. The satellite has been permanently disabled.

"There is no future danger to *any person*, and I emphasize *any person*, in the United States.

"The threat to our country and the peoples of the world has been extinguished, *period*.

"This morning, before the press conference, I saw a broadcast where Pope John Paul II had tens of thousands praying in St. Petersburg Square for the safety and welfare of our people and our nation. Those prayers have been answered. But even more so, the events of the last several days have brought a new understanding of our vulnerability to any terroristic maniac's desires. This can no longer happen. People, any people of our planet, can and will never again be placed in such a position.

"As each person in Miami and Ann Arbor have suffered, I have suffered," President Climan's welling eyes began to drip tears. "I have great empathy for each victim and their loved ones. As much as they have been traumatized, I also have been injured. The world will no longer tolerate such acts of inhumanity."

Climan dramatically paused. He glanced over his shoulder at Major General Powell Nash, United States Marine Corps. He then looked back at the press corps. "General Nash will brief you on this afternoon's operations."

President Climan was visibly shaken. He gestured to General Nash to take the podium. Then, Climan left the press room.

The national media was moved like they had never been. They went berserk. Questions came flying at General Nash like artillery shells sailing in from all directions. Everyone wanted to know why. As best as Major General Nash could do, since Robbins' motives were still nebulous, Nash gave concise and honest answers: That is, all but the *KGB's presence* and the fact that it was the KGB that really ran the operation and prevented the loss of potentially millions of lives. But that was politics.

Back in the ready room, President Climan was extremely unsettled. The thought of all the dead and maimed, grieved and depressed him. But more than that, President Climan was a master who knew how to let his emotions flow. What he did, was exactly what he wanted to do: leave the press hanging, waiting, foaming at the mouth for more. "What did Climan mean by never again?"

Like heroin addiction, the press *needed more*. And the President knew how to work them like a carney. This was part one of his installment plan.

52

8 Hours Left

Alex was barely alive—and in his unusual clothes he stood out like a sore thumb.

Word had already reached Las Vegas. The nation was again secure from the threat of nuclear holocaust. The previous Soviet nuclear arsenal, that in a bizarre turn of events had leaked into the West, and ignited fears of a new type of nuclear horror, was over.

Officially the plutonium was pegged as coming from Libya, or Iran, even possibly Iraq; but in reality it had come out of central Kaliningrad, an enclave on the Baltic, from a Russian nuclear laboratory. The "how" of the "how and why" the plutonium leaked into the United States, would never be known.

Nuclear terror "for sale" would not be heard of again. After the politicians had their way, legislation would be enacted requiring the mandatory death sentence for any person caught buying or selling as little as five one-hundreths of a gram of plutonium. The days of the world's open market for weapons grade plutonium would evaporate.

As President Climan had put it: "We've crossed a threshold

into an ugly 'Brave New World.'" Countries such as North Korea and Pakistan, that prior to the crisis had been independent nuclear powers with plutonium of their own, would now join the World Nuclear Alliance.

"Pits," or fist-size spheres of plutonium which came from the dismantling of 2,071 warheads, and were the elemental core of the nuclear weapons, had their storage security increased three-fold. New methods for accounting of the over one hundred metric tons of plutonium taken out of warheads, and the additional one hundred and ten tons produced at the nuclear power industries, would be instituted.

The governments of the world would need to make a show of force to restore any eroded public confidence, and let their electorates know that they could be trusted.

Alex was on fire. His right heel, which before did not trouble him, felt like it was going to crack in two. He trudged through the terminal, nearly dragging his right foot. Before he reached customs, he stopped, rolled down his sock and looked at the ball. Blood had seeped through his skin.

People hurried past him on their way to customs. He was baggageless. All around him placards advertising for Circus-Circus, the MGM, and Caesars Palace, were glaring back at him. Nearly naked women, wearing garrulous clown make-up smiled uncannily.

Alex did not know it yet, but the world outside had turned into a Mardi Gras. The crisis was over, the threat of annihilation had passed. The whole of humanity that had been glued to their television sets were now free to live their lives unthreatened. The fear which had engulfed the nation like a whirlwind, blowing away hopes and tranquillity, had dissipated with celerity.

The moving walkway Alex stood on en route to customs lumbered with certainty. Friendly expressions, Cheshire Cat toothy grins winked back at him.

"Huma, huma, huma," the walkway plodded.

Before it came to an end, there was a break where Alex traversed concrete, and then again returned to his impelling pathway.

At the end, he came to the customs desk. There sat the extra cautious feds with their computers.

"Do you have anything to declare?" the pug female in her blue jacket asked. She had a gun strapped to her side in a holster, covered by a leather flap. Everyone, it seemed, was now wearing guns.

"No."

"Do you have any luggage?"

"No."

"Were you traveling on business or pleasure?" she asked, scanning through his passport. She noticed the amazing amount of miles and places that he logged over the last several days: Moscow, Miami, Nassau, Mexico City, Belize, and now Las Vegas. Was Alex smuggling drugs? or worse, nuclear weapons? Everyone was suspect. The customs agents were paranoid.

Behind the desk the agent scrolled her screen. She was already suspicious since Alex had no baggage. She then projected a secondary, then a tertiary screen. A flashing message appeared on the cathode ray tube. Alex could not see what it said, but the luminescent image reflected off a glass barrier perpendicular to the agent. In the center were big, bold words that blinked bright red. She looked up at Alex, very suspect, forearm and hand sliding down to her holster.

"One moment please."

She signaled for two other armed agents to join her. They also read the screen and then looked at Alex with suspicion.

"Could you please come with me," the senior agent politely asked.

"Sure, why not?" Alex replied sarcastically. He followed the emissary to several seats behind the customs counter. He wasn't exactly arrested, but then on the other hand, he wasn't exactly free to go.

Alex waited for twenty minutes. His patience was at wit's end. He nervously twiddled his thumbs, watching the electronic clock above him spin off the minutes. His fingers were turning numb, pricking sensations began to crystallize on his nose and around his mouth. Was Viktoria going to be able to help?

Despite taking the amphetamine pill, he could feel its effects waning already. He wished he had the whole bottle. Why didn't he try to get the pills under his seat? He forgot to. But at least he had one left.

He was perched in a government chair, one of four connected together in series. A knee-high table, with magazines—*Cosmopolitan, Newsweek, People, Better Homes and Gardens, Ebony, Field and Stream* were before him. He fanned through the periodicals, none of them current, none expressing the nation's fury.

He rubbed his eyes. He pressed his fingers on his lids. It made him see glistening psychedelic images of his impending death.

A man finally arrived. He had a boyish grin, thick eyebrows and a full crop of impenetrable hair. He was dressed conservatively, his clothes spelled government. The manchild was in a position of authority. He gave Alex the once over. Then without direct eye contact he matter-of-factly said, "You can go." As adroitly as he arrived, the obtrusive official disappeared.

"What was that all about?"

Alex stood, pulled up his khaki green pants, cracked his neck, and left.

He walked into the main airport terminal. Above him were two advertisement placards. One was in large fluorescent lettering and was a promotional for The Mirage Hotel. There were two split pictures. On the right, the hotel — its monolith structure, tropical waterfalls with a live volcano and feather palm trees in the foreground, alluring the traveler. The other, Siegfried and Roy, two mystical New-Age magicians. Roy was standing atop a four-foot high 1980s disco ball. It had small glass mirrored squares that reflected light in laser beam perfect angles. On top was a white Siberian tiger. Roy was straddling the tiger. He was dressed in a blue sequined tuxedo, his face was beaming with a show biz smile and his hands apart, wide-open in a display of wizardry "magic."

The other advertising placard, the same four-foot by eight-foot size, had a black-and-white photograph of the Hoover Dam and the Colorado River. Behind it was Lake Mead. It was full to nearly the brim, its shores only barely expressing a chalky white outline, which had once been under water.

Seven hundred and twenty-six feet below, two sets of generator plants paralleled the water egress. The chiseled granite rock walls stood impressive and intimidating.

"Gotta get going. Time's running slim," Alex thought. He didn't realize the importance of two omens he just saw.

He picked up his pace, bumping and whacking into people, until he finally descended into the Taxi terminal.

"Signature," the cabby knew where Alex needed to go, to the Fix Base of Operations, which was at the opposite end of McCarrin International Airport. Alex, a pilot, had done his training in Internal Medicine in Las Vegas at Southern Nevada Memorial Hospital. He was familiar with the airport. There was no reason to waste time. He knew where the Robbins jet would have gone: to the corporate terminal.

"Four bucks," the taxi driver said. Alex paid him ten and forgot about the difference. "Was Viktoria all right?" They were on his turf now. Alex knew Vegas like the back of his hand.

"A Challenger 600, is one here?" he asked the countergirl, certain of her answer. She was tall, nearly six feet, and had a full face and a genial disposition.

"Do you know the tail number? They're three."

"I don't." Alex didn't look like he belonged. "Look, I'm Dr. Seacourt. I've flown in here before. Four three Pappa Alpha, you have me on file in your computer. I'm sure," he said referring to Signature's computer database that was used for gas, oil and maintenance records and billing.

"So," she said with peculiarity.

"Look I need to know if you have a Challenger here from Belize. This is real important."

"Just one second," she said. She slowly logged onto her computer and began searching through the daily entries.

"Could you please hurry."

She seemed to find what he wanted, but said, "Wait till the lineman comes in, I'll have you speak with him first."

Alex was frustrated and he didn't want to get angry at her. So he went to the bathroom. For the first time in the bright fluorescent light he really took a hard look at himself. "Jesus Christ, no wonder she didn't want to help me." His eyes were sunken. The whites were pierced with fiery, throbbing blood vessels. His face was gaunt. He had a healing laceration on his cheek. The hair on his head was matted, and there was crusted blood coming out of both of his nostril, and his right ear.

He washed his face, splashing cold water onto his dulled mug. With a paper towel he scrubbed his visage as clean as he could get. He pushed back the dried blood. He looked frightful. He looked like those dying nuclear people on TV. That's what the countergirl was afraid of and why she didn't want to help him. "Maybe she thought she would die if she touched him." He didn't blame her.

Chuck the lineman and a mechanic were in the lobby when Alex returned.

"I apologize for my appearance. I didn't realize I was so scary looking."

Chuck smiled. He felt empathy for Alex. "You looking for a Challenger 600?"

"Yes."

"Why?"

"Friends of mine. I need to link up with them. It's real important."

"Rock star?"

"Who?"

"You."

"No." Did Alex really look that bad? "I'm looking for friends. They flew in a Challenger registered to American First United Insurance."

"They're here."

"Do you know how long ago they got in?"

"Early morning."

"Did they register with you? Do you know which hotel they're at?"

"No," the counter girl said as she read the AV-fuel, oil and maintenance record on the computer screen.

"Is there anyone who might know where they went?"

Chuck scrutinized Alex trying to decide if he should give him the information.

"I'd really appreciate your help. Please." Alex was nearly pathetic.

Chuck's assistant Cecil spoke up. "One of our line guys called a limo for 'em. There was a bunch of them. Some came with equipment. They looked like engineers or something. A van picked them up. But the other three took a limo."

"A private van, or airport."

"Private."

"How many of them were there."

"Lots."

"Do you know where they went?"

"No, but I'll call the limo driver at home for you, see if he knows where."

Cecil walked into a windowed office and made one call. He spoke for a few minutes, hung up the telephone and thumbed through a circular Rolodex card file. He passed over the index card he wanted, returned to it, and then made a second call. This one lasted longer, maybe ten minutes, until with a lost look he returned the phone to it's cradle. He came back to the lobby.

"They chartered a limo. Something about going to a casino. Could be anywhere."

"With whom?"

"Triple-A."

"Does anyone know where they went?"

"Don't. They paid cash in advance for 48 hours."

"Any idea?"

"None."

"Are they on radio?"

"Sometimes. But not this trip. I asked pal...sorry, they could be anywhere."

"Shit. Thanks."

Alex's time was almost gone. He was as good as dead if he didn't do something. It was getting dark outside. It was nearly 7:00 p.m. They could be anyplace. One hundred hotels, forty or fifty major, and they don't even have to be in Vegas, though most likely they were. They could just the hell as well be in Laughlin, or could be cruising the town. What was the point? And what about the scientists and the equipment? There had to be more to this!

53

4 Hours to Go

Alex felt like he had malaria or sleeping sickness. He was unable to force the plague out of his stomach.

He had been on the telephone. He called every hotel that he could think of. He worked every possible lead. No luck. "Are you kidding?" the valet or bellboy would say. "There are 100 limos a day that come through this place. Fuck you!" And most would hang-up. Alex had been on the telephone trying to make something click for nearly an hour. Basically, he was wasting his time. It was a balancing act, though. Could he make more happen working the phones, or out on the street?

At first he thought that the telephones were the way to go. But he was finding out that he was being hung-up on while he was waiting to speak to someone, or that he waited for a valet or bellboy to get back to him after he had been put on hold for nearly fifteen minutes. What if the limo was there? but the person on the other end just really didn't try to find it, or was the guy just saying that the limousine wasn't there when he really didn't look in the first place.

"Gotta find a cab."

Alex left Signature half dead. He stood outside on a concrete abutment and looked at the parking lot. The world was on fire and hypnotic — and he was going to miss it. A taxi, one of three pulled up; the others were posturing, waiting for a charter junket out of L.A.

"Help ya?" Mick's face was ruby and his eyes were bright and full of vigor. He had red hair and was as Irish as a shamrock.

"Yeah," Alex said, sliding into the back seat of the lemon yellow Chevy Impala. The cab had already seen its day and its odometer had been disconnected on more than one occasion.

"Where to?" Mick looked into his rearview mirror. Then he turned his head around. He slung his ape arm along the edge of the front seat. "You need to see a doctor, pal. You sick with radiation poisoning?"

"No."

"Pal, if there's any..."

"Look, I've got a problem. Maybe you can help me." Alex looked into his wallet, thinking that maybe some money would motivate Mick. The curled, shrunken billfold with its brine coating was almost empty. "Only fifty-eight dollars."

"What's that?"

"I said I have only fifty-eight dollars. Here's my problem." Alex could feel another wave of queasiness rolling up into his stomach. "My friend's been kidnapped. I need to find her. She's in a Triple-A limo somewhere."

"Man why don't you call the cops and save your dough?"

"I can't do that. Besides, it'll be too late." Alex didn't trust the cops, let alone anyone right now, especially considering the double-cross in Nassau.

"Too late for what? Buddy, if you don't mind, you really look terrible. Are you sure ya aren't sick?"

"Sure..."

"I mean...if you are, I'm not going to hold it against you or anything. The news says you can't get sick from anyone, unless you share body fluids...like AIDS."

"Look..." Alex demurred, "I need help finding a girl. Can you help me?"

"Yeah. Go ahead," Mick sincerely answered, "What can I do?" Mick was an honest guy. He was always willing to lend a helping hand. He was the kind of guy who would give you the shirt off his back if you needed it.

"Here's the story. My friend was kidnapped by some very bad

people. But I don't think anyone would think that she was kidnapped if they saw her. She's with two men, and cooperating because she thinks if she doesn't they'll kill her father. They've leased a limo for forty-eight hours. I've called Triple-A and they have no idea where it is. They weren't too helpful. I've already called a bunch of hotels, spoke with some valets and bellboys, but no luck."

"They won't help, not unless you grease their palms."

"I've found that out. Anyway, I've only got a matter of hours left before it's too late."

"Too late for what?"

"Look." Alex paused. He had no choice but to tell the truth. "I lied to you. I'm..."

"Pal, you needn't explain. I figured it out for myself. You look like total crap."

"Yeah, don't I."

"I've got an idea," Mick replied as he began driving. He explained his plan. Alex agreed and Mick went to work.

Mick radioed dispatch and told them that he had a VIP who missed his private jet. A real "mooch" willing to blow some big cash if he could get some help. The "mooch" needs to find his friends. They took off in a Triple-A limo from the Signature Terminal.

In the meantime, Alex and Mick headed for Caesars.

The spider web of tentacles from Yellow Cab to Checker, to Desert, to ABC Union, to ACE Cab, to Henderson Taxi and A-Vegas Western Cab, spread like wildfire from dispatcher to driver and then one driver to the next; everyone wanting to help out the "mooch," the big money player.

Crawling north down the Strip they barely made it past Bally's when they got the word.

"The limo's at the Metz. Tony Tucca's driving," the radio buzzed from Lucky, Checker Cab driver No. 2314.

"Thanks pal," Mick machine gunned over the radio.

"Don't forget to hit me later."

"Not a problem."

They made a U-turn and plowed through the quagmire. They cut off a Cadillac DeVille and nearly sideswiped another. Within ten minutes they were at the Metz, a trendy, high flash New York-style disco. It was a place where stars were seen, models in miniskirts gyrated to trendy tunes, and men wore their best Armanis.

They pulled up between a row of cars in the strip center next to the club. Conspicuously there was no Triple-A limo. Mick spun a loop around the parking lot, behind the sixteen thousand-square-foot discotheque. Nothing. He took a rear gravel road and drove around onto the Strip. He cut illegally across onto the sidewalk, scaring the bejesus out of three little-old lady tourists, and back into the parking lot, the way they came. No limousine.

"Sorry pal, the limo's not here."

"Could it have been here, dropped them off, and come back later."

"Possible"

"You think?" Alex was always the optimist, not willing to lose hope. "How accurate is your information?"

"As best it gets."

"Then let's go in"

They parked in a line, in back of the other cabs and limos. Mick turned the "Off Duty" light on. It didn't matter what day or time it was today, it was New Year's Eve all over again. Mick had juice at the Metz, so they went right in despite the line. The Metz was a riot of bodies, music pounding, bodies grinding, lights flashing, the venue out-of-control.

"I'm looking for a brunette, maybe five-seven, shoulder-length chestnut hair, with two men, one bald, semi-oriental eyes. Big guy, you can't miss him. The other wearing an eye patch."

"Got ya."

"These are bad dudes, so be careful."

"Not a problem."

"We'll split up. You take the balcony and work your way down, I'll start at the back bar, and work my way up front. We'll meet at the main bar."

"Done deal."

Before Alex started his hunt he went up to the main bar and got a glass of water. He took his remaining amphetamine pill. Then he worked his way through the throng. He probed through hysterical bodies groggy with booze and drugs. As out of place, and as much as his clothing made him stand out, nobody paid any attention.

Alex thought that he spotted one of them, a broad-shouldered man, but he was mistaken.

Then suddenly, a bolt of lightning struck deep into his chest. At first he thought he was shot. He fell to his knees in agony. Then a second struck, whizzing its cutting edge deep into his stomach. He needed to catch his breath as his eyes bulged in uncontrollable pain.

After a few seconds a third bolt jarred into his brain, rifling any thoughts that he may have had. Alex barely worked his way to a booth. Despite the fact that a party of people were howling and hooting, shooting down kamikazes, he threw himself against a cushion.

Mick meticulously searched the balcony, the side and front bars. If there was a girl to ferret-out, he would do it. Alex's description, though feeble, was enough to get Mick going. Mick threaded through the masses. He didn't find her. Then he went to their meeting place — the main bar, and waited for Alex. Alex didn't show up. After fifteen minutes Mick began his hunt for Alex. Mick was worried that Alex was a lot sicker than he had said.

After ten minutes of searching for him around the main bar, and then back to the front desk, where they paid ten bucks to enter OZ, Mick headed into the thick of things.

In the distant echoes of his mind Alex knew that he was shot. He couldn't talk, the world was flashes of photo-studio light. He could feel his essence slip away. Still he had to ask himself, why? Why take Viktoria with them to the casino? For protection? A hostage? Did she know something? Or better yet, did she know something and not know that she knew it?

And why did Andrei and Boriskov go to all the trouble of coming to Vegas? *What was their agenda?* And why to date was there no demand for ransom? That never made sense. What did Siderenko mean? Why was he babbling *"dve tisyachy, dve tisyachy?* And what about the scientists?"

What difference did it make now? *He was shot three times and he was going to die.*

54

The Mirage Hotel: A live volcano explodes in natural gas eruptions every fifteen minutes, spewing smoke and orange-red fire one hundred feet into the air. White tiger habitats, a south sea oasis, a dolphin haunt and a twenty thousand-gallon aquarium with sharks, rays and angelfish. That was where they were.

"Let me make this clear as day," Andrei ordered with the benevolence of Mephistopheles, "You fuck with me and your father dies. Do we understand one another?"

"Yes."

"One word, one peep, and he dies."

"I understand." She was terrified. Andrei was an example of all of which was once noble and right with her world, of mother Russia, that had gone bad.

Boriskov tightly grabbed her upper arm, enough so that the color in it had blanched out. Their Triple-A limo driver Tony Tucca dropped them at the hotel, and then blew until 1:00 a.m.

This place was the one spot that Andrei wanted to see before he was *either going to change the face of the world, rearrange Southern California's architecture* — or get his due. His scientists had finished their work on the plane, thanks to Viktoria's help. Now it was time for him to enjoy her.

"Alex, Alex," Mick firmly shook him. Alex 's head flogged like a lowrider Mexican Jesus. "Alex are you all right?"

Alex slowly turned toward Mick and looked around. They were in the back seat of Mick's taxi.

"Where...where am I?"

"Man, you passed out."

"What time is it," Alex asked as he looked for his watch that was not there. He then peered up at Mick. Alex felt his scalp: no wounds, no knives, no blood. "What happened? How long have I been here?"

"Nearly two hours."

"Two hours?"

"Man, you disappeared."

"I did? I was shot?"

"No, nothing. I found you catatonic, passed out in a booth. I carried you out of the joint."

Alex knew that it was the plutonium. It wasn't doing what the textbooks said. It was doing worse. He was losing control. Did he regain consciousness because of the last pill that he took. He remembered that its effects were delayed.

"I have news."

"What news?" Alex felt his body for bullet and knife wounds. There were none.

"I found your friends."

"Where?"

"Here."

"Where's here?"

"The Mirage," Mick pointed. One of Mick's taxi driver friends had let them double park. They were in the rear of a long line of twenty cabs. "I know where they are. I saw them inside. Do you want me to call the cops?"

Alex tried to get his bearings. His brain was different. He was disoriented. He was half in dream state, only partially anchored in reality. "Where...where are they?"

"At the Siegfried and Roy show. I saw them go in. It's your friend all right. You can't miss the one with the eye patch."

"How long ago?"

"Fifteen minutes. Pal, if you didn't come out of it in the next couple, I was going to call the cops myself; and an ambulance for you."

"Thanks. I can handle it from...here."

"Are you nuts?"

"Mick...I'm fine. Thanks...for everything."

"Pal, I've come this far. And I'm telling you right now we're going to finish this together, whatever it is."

On the radio, Alex could hear faintly "the crisis is over...eighteen locations, in Los Angeles, Chicago, St. Louis...over nine hundred pounds...Authorities have estimated that *a total of one thousand pounds of plutonium was used in Robbins' scheme...*"

"Let me help you." Mick lifted Alex out of the cab from under his enfeebled arms. In contradiction, Alex's legs were again nimble. His lower body was ready to play a set of tennis doubles. He felt screwy. The dextroamphetamine made him feel wiry. He didn't like it.

Alex looked over his shoulder at the city. The neon lights stuck him with the intensity of burning headlights. Behind him, the artificial volcano was aflame. The ground rumbled with its ersatz geyser. In the distance, he could just barely make out the red rock mountains.

"Let's go in," Alex said surrealistically as he left his body in astro projection. Mick steadied Alex's gate and they fused with the crush of people. Through the myriad of bizarre, absurd and disconnected bodies was the Mirage Hotel Siegfried and Roy Showroom. Mick had no juice there.

Two ushers stood at the door blocking the entrance. The spectacle was already one hour into its performance. Siegfried and Roy, the worlds greatest illusionists, were performing their multimedia extravaganza six nights a week for seventy-five dollars a pop. On stage, over makeuped showgirls in their nothing outfits pranced, half of them topless. Their G-strings were sequined in purple, red and silver; and their black dance shoes were staple 3" pumps.

"Are you sure they're in there?" Alex asked Mick as they approached.

"Positive. The one with an eye patch paid the concierge. They're sitting in V.I.P. seats. Front row."

Alex was on fire. He had a mission in mind. *He had only two hours left.*

Would it have been easier to ask the ushers if he could just have gone in and looked for them? Should he have? Nevermind. He was a mess. He was disheveled. He resembled a bum, not a doctor. Knowing that the ushers would turn down his plea to enter the show and look for Viktoria, to save her — he walked right in.

Mick tried to run cover.

The theater was dark. The spotlight was on the magician's assistant, a girl who had been cut in two. There was one large box that was sawed into two smaller ones. The box on the left had wiggling feet. The other had the girl moving her hands and arms; and she did this as the two smaller boxes were separated. Alex knew how it was done—the box with the feet were mechanical.

"Click, clack...click, clack" He was mesmerized, frozen midway down the steps in the blackened showroom. Alex needed to remind himself why he was there, he needed to find the girl.

He scanned the theater. Tiny footlights spilled into the aisles, faintly illuminating the steps. Alex's eyes slowly accommodated. Tops of heads became backs of heads, and then images; faces become real. He walked past a railing closer to the front. He squinted. Then he found them. He spotted the bald head with stagelight bouncing off its shaved dome.

There was Viktoria. She had to know that he would come for her.

"Come with us," two men suddenly tugged Alex from both sides, then a third, fourth and fifth. "No derelicts allowed."

As fast as he arrived, as quickly as his time was running out, Alex was yanked out of the theater. There was an explosion of pyrotechnics ending the illusion that he had been watching, and the two-boxed girl disappeared from both boxes.

"I need to get...I."

They threw Alex and Mick out of the casino and onto the sidewalk. One of the gorillas waited for them to leave the Mirage property. Mick tried to explain that a girl was kidnapped. But the security guard didn't give Mick's plea any stock.

"I need to...she may have the antidote." Alex begged.

It was useless. Mick carried Alex back to the car. Mick started up his taxi. Mick wasn't even worried that these "bums" might ban him from the hotel. He drove off.

"Please help me. Please," Alex pled to Mick.

55

The bouncer/security guard raised his fist in disapprobation as Mick melted into the flood of vehicles. They left the Mirage, going anywhere but forward. Traffic was snarled. Thousands of people were celebrating on the Strip. Despite their prompt send off, the cab was only able to make turtle's-pace progress.

Mick turned on the radio. He pushed buttons for music. All he could find was news chatter: "Motive's murky... Predawn raid on the Robbins Complex... Previous incidents foreshadowed by Bart Robbins' loss of sibling... *A total of 1,000 pounds*...Governmental leaders to meet at U.N... Conference to be televised worldwide... Officials fear copycat... Hospitals remain on alert."

Something was wrong, deadly wrong. Something started to click in Alex's brain, but he didn't know what. "I need to get the girl."

"This is not over," Mick said as he carefully watched his rearview mirror, waiting for an opportunity. The security guard stood amongst the multitude for ten minutes. By the time the cab had driven down the quarter-mile exit drive to the Strip's entrance, he left.

When the green-jacketed man disappeared, Mick made his move.

In the thick of deadlock, Mick forced his cab onto the curb. He triple parked beside two limousines at the point where they came together in a chain. He was blocking their exit.

"This is it pal."

"What's it?"

"This is it, D-Day."

Alex looked hard into Mick's coal eyes. He knew that there was no reason compelling Mick to help him, except for the fact that Mick was a good guy.

"Follow me."

Alex was more able now. Inside a light switch was clicking on and off. One minute he was good, another he was bad. He stood. He was beat-up but gamey. He was ready, thanks to *Russian speed*.

Mick played point guard, and blocked the bodies out of their way. They headed to the street. Once on the strip, they made a one eighty and entered a parallel double one-way automated walkway into the hotel.

The people mover was illuminated in burnished silver and fluorescent caisson lighting. It buzzed quickly into the Mirage Hotel. As they entered the hotel they came upon the white tiger habitat. Behind a glass prison the giant Asian cats ranged on artificial rockscapes. They had a bathing pool. A fountain shot jets of water that splashed into an ambling steam which re-entered the natatorium.

Three adults and one cub looked at the gawking tourists. The cats, swishing their enormous tails, were more interested in the people, than the tourist in the tigers.

"There must be a stage door, a side entrance."

"Of course, there had to be," Alex said, as he was regaining his momentum.

They entered the casino. It was swarming with people. They made their way to the showroom. Just before the ticket counter were two double doors. They were closed, and probably led backstage. Alex remembered that there were three exit doors in the theater. He remembered the glimmer of light that thinly irradiated from behind the plastic exit signs. The showroom had three levels that sloped downward to the stage. He hoped there would be three doors down the hall. He would be able to find Viktoria.

Suddenly, two green-jacket security guards appeared out of nowhere. They were both part of the goon squad that threw them out earlier. They positioned themselves in front of the backstage double doors.

"Crap," Mick said. "We can't get past those two bums. That's it."

"Let me think."

They walked to a row of five dollar progressive poker machines. The overhead jackpot was up to $33,549.98. Alex sat down and Mick took off to see if he could find a way past the sentries. He returned in five minutes. There was none. During that time, Alex pondered. His mind was now sharp. He studied the milieu. He had an idea.

"Help! Help!," a woman with a butch haircut, tacky bodysuit and a large quart cup full of silver dollars, ready to play her *next jackpot*, screamed.

"We need a doctor," a man yelled.

"Hurry," a third ran to the seizing victim.

"Help!"

A man had fallen to the unpadded carpeted floor in a fit of epilepsy. His legs and arms were flailing. His head was shaking in an earthquake tremor.

Forcing their way through the crowd, the security guards that were positioned in front of the backstage doors ran to the victim's aid.

In a rage of contempt it took them only moments to realize that the convulsive man was Mick — Mick the cab driver that they had just escorted out of the casino. By then, Alex had already made his way back through the stage doors.

"Who the fuck do you think you are?"

"Help me! Help me!"

"Fuck you!"

"Goddammit," the bigger of the two said, as he brought Mick to his feet. The gamblers loudly protested. They didn't realize Mick's ruse.

"You can't do that."

"Leave that poor guy alone!"

"Call an ambulance!"

"How dare you!"

The problem was that Alex did not quite close one of the push-bar doors all the way shut. The bigger security guard looked over to the backstage doors. Though he had not seen Alex enter, he was sure that Alex had gone in.

The security guard pressed a radio-controlled mike that ran from a transmitter under his jacket to his left green lapel. "We've got an intruder in the show! Repeat, an intruder in the show!"

There were not three doors as Alex anticipated, but only two. They were at the far end of the hall on the right, and both within rather close proximity of each other. At the end of the hallway was another set of double push bar doors. They lead to "who knows where."

"Which door?" Alex thought. He didn't have much time. Nimbly, he tried the first. Locked. This had to be the one that went into the showroom. It probably had trifurcating halls: one hall that split into three, each leading to one of three exit doors.

The second door was too far down to open into the showroom. Nevertheless, Alex tried it. He was correct. The door opened to hanging ropes, sandbags, a catwalk, and numerous painted, fabricated-on-plywood show scenes. The backdrops were mounted into stage tracts while others were on wheels. He knew that this was the wrong place. He retreated back into the hallway. He was hopeful that somehow he would be able to pry open the egress door.

As Alex was nearly to the first door, ready to give it his best pseudo-karate kick, three immense green-jacketed security guards came storming through the casino doorway. They headed straight for him!

Alex knew he was in deep. He spun around, on the ball of his foot farthest from the green jackets, and headed in a dash back to the second door.

He had a good ten-second lead on them. Behind him as he slammed shut the backstage door, Alex could hear the men yelling, "You, stop!"

He quickly looked for something to jam the door shut. The door had no internal locking device. A cart full of dirty towels and costumes sat several feet past the entrance. Alex ran over and pushed it in front of the door and then he threw down some chairs, to at least temporarily block the green coats' passage.

The Siegfried and Roy Show was in full swing. The pre-recorded orchestra blared out strings and brass, and then a drum roll as the audience followed with an "Ooooh," and then an applause.

Alex needed to decide which way he was going to cut. If he went right toward the stage his exit would be blocked by gaffers and showgirls waiting to go on. If he went to his left it would lead him to props: a twenty-five foot high smoke breathing dragon, a motorcycle and a human shooting cannon, and then to the other side of the stage.

"Crash!" The green-coated security guards charged through the doorway, two of them tumbling over the temporary obstacle.

No time to decide. Several set riggers who were waiting on cue at the stage's edge turned around. They impotently observed Alex's intrusion.

Alex didn't go left or right as initially he anticipated his choices; but to his extreme left and into the costume room. He swiftly hid behind a row of Roman pagan costumes with headdresses, ducking under a shelf.

Moments later, one of the three security guards arrived in the costume room. He began rapidly asking, but not too loud, if anyone had seen an intruder. Alex was out of sight, but within feet of the green coat. "No," a dancer answered.

"His goose was cooked," Alex thought.

"No one's here. Get the fuck out!" a bossy Julie Newmar type said. The green jacket scanned the surroundings, made at the best a cursory hunt and then left.

Next Alex heard the voices of men. Obviously, the changing room was coed. He worked his way into a corner. Twelve performers came in. They quickly disrobed. They removed their Roman warrior outfits and hung them up on a different set of wooden hangers, and then changed into the pagan outfits. Each of them placed wreaths on their heads. Alex had hid behind a Moroccan carpet that was rolled up into a three-foot diameter spiral. The discarded prop stood on its ten-foot tall end.

In wooden cubby storage spaces was the armor that each performer wore including helmets, chest, forearm, and leg protectors. The cubby holes were labeled with masking tape and the name of each performer was written in black marker.

By crackled radio, the two green coats that had subdued good-hearted Mick, were called backstage immediately. That was where the real crisis was.

"Goddammit, let me go!" Mick implored. The gaggle around him were hostile to the security men's *insensitivity*.

"Can't you see that this man's had a seizure, for Christ's sake!" A well-healed Mirage regular said indignantly, "I'm a lawyer, and if you want a son-of-a-bitch piranha to sue their ass, I'm your man."

"Sorry sir, but this man's a..."

"Get the fuck off him!"

Before anything else could develop, the security guard responded to the radio call. The green coats abandoned Mick and made a bee-line for the stage doors.

Alex had to get to Viktoria. This was his only chance. Quickly he ad-libbed. He changed into one of the Roman Warrior outfits. He placed the helmet that he could barely hold up on top of his head. The armor was heavy and cumbersome. Despite this, he made his way to the stage. He was now part of the show.

On stage, spotlights blared into his eyes. He scanned the audience. "There!" Dead center in the front row were the three of them — Viktoria, and on right and left, Andrei and Boriskov.

Alex's advantage was surprise. He developed his plan as the security guards arrived at both sides of the stage curtains. Others came and blocked all three side exit doors, which Alex correctly anticipated bifurcated in reverse and emptied into the first of the two hall doors.

It was ironic that he wasn't recognized. They were looking for a man in green.

On stage the show was nearing its finale. Eleven white tigers were on a series of risers. Siegfried and Roy were performing with a flaming hoop. They had the largest of the white tigers jump through the blazing obstacle, and then repeat the feat in reverse. The audience showered the performers with applause. From above, a four-foot diameter disco-days-sphere descended. Its exterior was highly polished one-inch square mirrors. As the sphere was lowered, spotlights flashed spectacularly onto the reflective surfaces and laser-sharp beams of light ricocheted in all directions.

Though Alex was invisible to everyone, *he was not to the tigers,* who sensed that there was something wrong. Maybe it was his smell, his glands secreting sweat that was vitiatingly abnormal.

The sphere was suspended in midair with two invisible high tension aerial wires, and was controlled by gaffers on an overhead catwalk. It appeared as if the globe had descended on its own, controlled by the magician's incantations.

Roy, the dark haired illusionist who had been teamed with Siegfried for the last twenty years, summoned the ball to stage level. With his hands apart, spellbinding the audience, he ordered the ferocious tiger on top. Then he jumped on board and straddled the beast as Siegfried commanded the globe to rise to the heavens.

Carefully, the gaffers followed the magicians incantations and mechanically raised the reflective sphere to ten feet above the stage. Next, in a spectacular gesture, Siegfried commanded the sphere to spin along its axis, rotating Roy and the tiger three hundred and sixty degrees.

From the crossbeams the gaffers rotated the wires mechanically in a slow circular motion, each wire hung at the far ends of a metal girder, the center point the axis of rotation.

As the music reached crescendo, all eyes were glued to the tiger and Roy revolving — from front, to side, to back and then returning to front. It was then Alex made his break.

Alex walked on stage, over an artificial rock and water rise, heading straight toward Viktoria. In his right hand he had an eight foot gladiator spear, in the other, a shield.

Not a sole in the audience realized that he was not part of the performance.

The tigers knew different. They went berserk. The first of five started growling ominously. And though Siegfried was supposed to be controlling the illusion, he needed to turn and face his cats. They were uncharacteristically agitated. And that could spell disaster. Then Seigfried saw the Roman soldier who was very much *not part of the spectacle*, walking across the stage, straight toward what he thought was him.

Alex headed, with no retreat toward Viktoria. Fire spit out of Siegfried's eyes. Siegfried saw the intruder as a threat, disrupting his animals; some idiot wanna-be trying to make his mark. Three other cats on the ersatz rocks began growling. One started pacing and another pawing with its razor-sharp claws.

As Roy finished the first of three revolutions, the gaffers above recognized the disturbance and terminated the illusion, afraid of an attack. But the gaffers made a crucial mistake. Instead of slowing the mirrored sphere gradually, they stopped it abruptly.

The tiger on top was thrown off. Roy nearly fell, but caught his balance on one of the two guide wires, giving away the illusion.

"Predator," the beautiful rare white tiger, landed on all fours. He was undaunted by the fall, and now even more so agitated with Alex.

In a leap, that seemed histrionically orchestrated, the beast sprang onto Alex. The crowd applauded, thinking that the cat's routine was part of the show, choreographed in perfect timing to the music. *But this was no act!*

Alex was thrown to the stage floor, the tiger lunged its fangs into his face. However, with the speed and agility that the beast landed on him, Alex raised his shield, and blocked the white tiger's attack.

Immediately, Siegfried rushed to Alex's side. Siegfried grabbed "Predator" by the scruff of his neck and ripped him off Alex's shield. The crowd again applauded. They rose out of their seats in standing ovation. The music continued in sync to the madness.

Next, two additional tigers sprang down from above, heading straight toward Alex. Roy jumped off the sphere and admonishingly thwarted the cats' attack.

Alex, the wind only knocked out of him, rose to his feet. A third time the crowd applauded in standing ovation. Without a moment to spare he jumped into the audience and grabbed Viktoria by the arm, hauling her off. She was shocked and confused. Surprise had overtaken Andrei and Boriskov, who were also mesmerized, thinking that Alex was part of the show.

Then, Andrei recognized Alex. "Stop them!" he stood up and yelled, "Stop them!"

Viktoria had no choice. If she went with the man, Andrei would have her father killed. Mid-aisle she stopped. The lights brightly went on throughout the showroom. A green coat sortie descended toward Alex.

"It's me, Alex." he said, pulling up his awkward helmet, enough so that Viktoria could see his face.

Suddenly Alex was yanked from behind, by first one, then two green coats. "Viktoria, it's me, Alex."

"Oh my God, it is!"

A third then fourth green coat security guard surrounded Alex, and then more on all sides. The audience was on its feet, everyone was now watching Alex . "I brought it. I've got it," she said, as she slid something into his pocket. But before she could do or say more, or stop the security guards, they hauled him off.

In the distance he could hear her say, "*President Hoover,* my father. It's too late...*all of Southern...*" Boriskov's stern hand clasped tightly over her mouth, pulling her away in another direction. Andrei followed.

"Remember what I told you. You try to get away, you try anything and I'll kill your father!" Andrei vehemently warned. Viktoria did not know that he was dead already.

"Yes, yes, I promise," she muttered underneath Boriskov's brutal palm.

On stage the white tigers were growling and snarling. They were still agitated. Siegfried and Roy huddled them together to calm them down. Slowly, the tigers regained their composure as their sense of territorialism was reconfirmed. Their routine was restored.

Siegfried and Roy finished the show after the disturbance was quelled. Two handlers joined the illusionists with a bucket of raw chopped meat, to bribe the tigers into submission. This was the same meat that the magicians palmed and the audience never saw; that they gave to the beasts for a reward of a job well done. The payola worked.

Andrei, Boriskov and Viktoria exited one of the three stage doors; the one on the right middle, with thirty audience members who decided that they had had enough.

Despite the minor inconvenience, Andrei knew that soon the world would be his oyster. He had gotten the formula—he'd have his due. Despite this trivial interruption, things had gone just as he planned.

The struggle and the beating that Alex endured from the security guards caused him to experience an *endorphin release*. It was much like a jogger would experience after a ten-mile run. Except in Alex's case, the endorphin release didn't cause an athlete's high, but rather induced him into hallucinations. His reality became a phantasm. Objectivity was distorted by all five of his senses.

56

One hour to go

A lex was handcuffed. He was disoriented. His breathing became labored. As the endorphin release peaked, so did the aftereffects.

He was placed in a security room. Two green jacket guards stood before him. They watched intently with their Beretta 92 9mms in shoulder holsters, which they kept secured under their uniforms. They were constantly paranoid of a stickup. One had recently occurred at the Stardust with three insiders taking down nearly a million dollars during a casino cashier's shift change.

The security guards had nailed this degenerate scum, and the Las Vegas police were on their way. Alex sat in his underwear. His clothes, found backstage shortly after his apprehension, were on the tabletop before him, along with his wallet, passport, fifty-eight dollars and no change. Underneath his billfold were some sheets of paper, and next to that a vial with a stringy-thin yellow liquid. The amber plastic container was three-quarters full. It was different than the one that was in Siderenko's pocket.

"Who is this fucking crackpot?"

"Frankly, I don't know and I don't give a shit," the second guard said.

"How did the rest of the show go? Did he fuck-it-up?"

"No."

"Good."

"No harm, no foul. Huh?"

"Yeah. Boy, Roy was pissed."

"No shit?"

"Yeah. But, fuck him! Fag motherfucker, if he can't take a joke."

"Yeah, fuck him."

Alex waggled his head, and then slumped it.

"Anyone get hurt?"

"Beats me."

"I'll radio and see."

Alex lifted his head. With humility he asked in a disconnected voice, "I need the vial. Can I...have it...please?" His words were toothpaste thick.

The larger of the two security guards ignored him. The other cavalierly said, "Fuck you! You piece-of-shit."

"Please?" Alex feebly asked. He wasn't sure if he was dead or alive, or if he was existing in the twilight zone between the two.

"Yeah, you fuck," the other said. He walked to the table and opened up the two papers that where folded into fourths under Alex's wallet.

"What's this, commie plans?" the large security guard asked, grabbing Alex by his matted hair. The green coat pulled his head back and pointed to the document that the other security guard was holding open. He displayed it to him. It had Russian handwriting.

"Was this why Viktoria was still alive. Did she know, did she have something that the others wanted?" Alex's mired mind deduced. "Did Andrei get as much out of the professor as he could? But Andrei and Boriskov were both Russian, they could read the professors notes...or could they? Were they coded? Maybe they thought Viktoria could decipher them? Maybe the professor wouldn't cooperate and decode his scribe? Maybe that's why she was still alive, for insurance!"

"Yeah it's Russian...and I know...all about the plutonium sabotages!" Alex gambled. What was he saying?

The hairs on the back of both the security guards' necks stood up.

"He's one of them," the larger one said to the other. "The police will fuck you, you fucking commie pig!" and then he railed a punch into Alex's gut.

"I need...the antidote. That's the..."

"Ahhh!" He let loose another heavy slug into Alex's stomach.

The smaller security guard picked up the vial, and held it up to the fluorescent light. "Wouldn't it be a pity if it spilled," he said faking to pour it out onto the counter.

"Please, I need it...or I'll die!" Alex begged with sincerity, holding his head up as high as he could, looking at his phantasmagoria captors.

"Fuck you," the larger security guard said. "We'll wait till the cops get here." He punched Alex square in the jaw. Alex's lip puffed up.

"Fuck you Russkie. You can't have shit till the cops get here," the other one said. He slammed the vial onto the counter, out of Alex's shackled reach.

"Let's get out of here. This guy stinks."

The two guards double-checked Alex's handcuffs. They were secure. The larger one took out a second pair and shackled his legs to one of the chair's legs. They left.

The seat was bolted to the floor. Obviously, the Mirage had other troublemakers grace this room. Alex struggled, but no matter how hard he tried, he wasn't able to get the antidote. And even if he made it, he rationalized in desperation, *nineteen out of twenty of those who took it died.* What difference did it make? Then again, he could be the 20th, couldn't he?

Nearly an hour passed. The sight of the vial before him was maddening. He was helpless.

Finally two plainclothes cops entered the room, followed by the security guards. Each of the men were dressed in nondescript suits, had short hair, were clean shaven and wore dull ties. They could be sniffed out from twenty miles away as undercover Las Vegas Police detectives.

"This him?" the first cop asked in an ultra businesslike manner.

"Yes," the large security guard replied.

"And all his stuff?"

"Yes."

"Are you sure?"

"Fucking sure."

"Good. Uncuff him, we'll use our own. And get his ass dressed."

The second gumshoe gathered up Alex's possessions. He put them in an evidence bag. The security guards uncuffed Alex. By now Alex was nearly catatonic. They dressed him in his clothing. Alex was mumbling something, trying to ask the police for help, but the words weren't coming out.

"Is that everything?"

"It is," the larger green coat replied.

"Good, lets blow Nick."

"Do you need any help?" the shorter security guard asked.

"No." With Alex's hands cuffed behind his back, the two cops dragged him out of the office.

Ten minutes later, because traffic on Las Vegas Boulevard was in gridlock due to the victory celebration, *the real police arrived.*

57

There is no time left.

The two nondescript plainclothes men dragged Alex out of the casino. They left through a fire exit between two buildings. They walked past trash dumpsters that were flush to the structure on the right and concealed behind fences. They left the Mirage property through a rear service entrance gate.

They got into a tan nondescript car. They drove onto Industrial Road, the street that ran parallel and west of the Strip behind the Mirage. It was virtually deserted.

Industrial Road had commercial laundries, small light manu-facturers, an uninteresting salvage yard, an industrial plumbing sup-ply company, and a cowboy bar, the Palladium. Next to the Palla-dium was a perpendicular strip mall of warehouse and wholesale shops, a glass and white concrete office building and then the I-15 underpass.

The "cops" drove south down the dimly lit street and pulled in between an office building and the industrial strip shops. They hid in the shadows, away from street view. They were halfway between Caesar's Palace and the Mirage

Alex was as good as dead.

One of the two cops got out of the car. He fumbled his hand deep into his pocket and found the handcuff key. He widely open the back door. The other cop opened his jacket. Alex could see a long-bladed knife tucked into a leather sheath. The scabbard slid two-thirds the way down into the cop's pants.

The first cop sat down into the back seat. Alex looked at him. The man seemed familiar. The cop slid the key into the handcuffs and undid them. Then, in paradox, he roughly grabbed Alex's head, and yanked it back exposing naked flesh.

Alex was unable to put up a struggle.

The cop reached into his jacket and pulled out the eight-inch knife. Alex looked at the blade as it glimmered back at him, catching the last moments of his life. He could feel his exposed bulging carotid artery pulsate in fear. He could do nothing about it.

The man, whose face became even more familiar to Alex, lifted the knife and held it straight up and vertical to Alex's face. The cold steel only separated them by inches. The man worked the blade with his hand, rotating it in 90° twists.

Then he sliced off a lock of Alex's hair that the other cop had been holding.

The man took Alex's brown locks and placed them in his upper jacket pocket. The first cop slid the long-bladed knife back into its sheath. The cop then removed the vial from the evidence bag. He twisted off its top, revealing the life-giving elixir. The man in the rear forced Alex's head back and neck forward again. They poured the contents of the vial down his throat.

Confused, Alex looked at the cop in the front seat. The man was not a cop after all. Alex knew he had recognized him. He was Ilya, *Ilya the taxi driver from Moscow.*

"You're...Ilya..."

"Yes, my friend."

"Why?"

"No time for why. It's very important, did professor Siderenko say anything to you?"

"Viktoria. Viktoria. Will...she be all right?"

"Later. We need to know right now about the professor. Did he say anything?"

"Yes...Something."

"Do you remember?"

"Yes. I think...*dve tishaho?*"

Ilya thought, "Could it have been *dve tisyachy?*"

"Yes that's it...I think."

"*Kharasho.*"

"He was muttering it...over and over again. Why?"

"Later, my friend."

"They told me on the boat...it meant...*two thousand pounds.*"

"I know."

The stringy-thin yellow nectar coursed its way down Alex's throat, burning each inch that it descended.

Alex wearily looked through the periphery of his narrowed visual field at the bright Vegas lights. The colors — the flashing marquees in their reds, yellows, come-gamble-with-me blues — were Andy Warhol freakish. Unreal.

"Bright Lights, Big City."

Then he slipped into nothingness.

58

Somewhere

❝ Something I have to do, otherwise *thirty million people will die.*
What is it? My parents dead. I'm dead." Something she said to
him at the Mirage. Something that he didn't even remember hearing, but in reality he heard and was unable to process.

Babies, pre-infants still attached to their fetal umbilical cords,
black thread sewed through their lips, the needle hanging loose with
only two more stitches to do. Now the suckling evolving into me.
Gods of flesh, thunder and desire, who have all eternity to cause
their suffering — make me suffer, hurl me down the vortex of no
return and hell.

Feeling like he was going to die. Like Santana's Black Magic
Woman, like his head was going to blow-up; full of noxious marsh
gas imploding into him.

"Ticktock. I'm dead. Ticktock *thirty million people are dead.*
Ticktock you're screwed."

In the background the TV drone. *He had come full circle,* memories began to ferment into reality. His hands wanted to connect with his brain. His legs responded in genuflection. He was remembering now. This is where his story began.

"Ticktock *President Hoover is dead*. Ticktock, *everyone is dead. No one lives.*

Thoughts came in bombardments. Laser bursts of realities reassimilated in Dr. Alex Seacourt's brain. The world black for so long, dark and full of tenuous spider webs coalesced into shape. He was remembering the whole story. Now things...were starting to make sense, come into focus.

"Ticktock."

In the background the TV was blaring. An instructional gaming video was on. Larry Minetti, the actor from the Magnum PI TV series; and a blond-haired woman, maybe the one from the show were talking. They were giving gaming instructions.

"Blackjack is relatively simple to play. The goal is for the player to get 21, or as close to 21 as possible, but not over. Players are dealt cards face-up from a shoe..."

"Viktoria," Alex thought, "*People, lots of people are going to die.* But what was it. She said something to me, *something...he has to do.*" His mind was still obfuscated, but getting stronger.

In the background, "Blackjack, or twenty one with an ace and any card valued at ten pays one-and-one-half of the original bet..."

Alex was sitting in front of a mirror, his hands pressed hard to his face. His clothes, a green something, reeked of sweat, defecant and urine. He looked into the mirror. His face reverberated—his dark eyebrows changing, growing larger and smaller with each pulsation of blood.

At the borders were bright colors, a rainbow of sensation V-ing in at his face.

"Gotta do something. *Dominoes. President Hoover.* Where am I? I need to focus. Where am I? Ticktock."

His elbows lay resting They were sore and impatient. His middle digits had been touching each other at 180° angles.

Alex spread his fingers and ran them through his oil-slickened hair.

"Hard numbers," the video continued to drone, "are special ways of hitting each point and getting large payoffs. For example, a hard six is a three and three, a hard four is a two and two..."

"How'd I get here? Where am I? How long?" Alex gazed awkwardly at his reflection. He was still not a whole person, but partially a hallucination.

"What happened?" He remembered a white tiger, no tigers. Then images zapped electrically into his brain. The sharks, the set screw, blood pouring into the ocean, the fishermen, the hospitals, Moscow, Viktoria, the Robbins jet, Andrei's eye-patch, Dr. Siderenko drowning, his parents, Ann Arbor...and more. He screamed at the memories and clamped his hands over his ears. "Ahhhhhh!"

Schizoid he rose to his feet, still screaming at the top of his lungs. "*Ahhhhhh!*" Suddenly as fast as the images came, they stopped. He threw himself onto the bed. He closed his eyes and looked through them above at the ceiling. In the distance the television continued its inane buzz. "Roulette, is one of the most popular games of chance that dates back to the French Renaissance Period and Louis the XIV."

Alex's arms and legs shook. And then it was over. He sat up, and oriented himself to the television set. He was breathless. He scanned the room, the telephone, the menus, the show advertisement. He was at Caesars Palace.

He stood, his legs not yet seaworthy, but responsive and effective. He found the TV remote and cautiously changed the channel to CNN News.

To his side, and on the back of the room's door was a full length mirror. In his pants, and down his leg was a puddle of brown and yellow scat. He was disgusted. He stripped off his clothes, kicked them into a pile, and ran into the bathroom. He turned on the shower water, as hot as he could tolerate, and plunged in.

Salt, dried sweat, excrement rinsed down the drain in an abhorrent pool. Alex stood in the shower, on tip-toe, in a corner, letting the fluids and filth shift down the drain. Finally the tile floor was clear, waste and residual gone, and Alex moved to the center of the stall.

He stood in the shower, nearly hyperventilating, for almost twenty minutes. The steamy water reddened his skin, until he could take no more. And before he emerged, he had washed himself three times, scrubbing the nightmares away.

When he stepped out he took a large bath towel and cleared the fog off the mirror. Small droplets still remained.

"Authorities believed that a total of *one thousand pounds of plutonium* has been accounted for, including the two devices that were used at Jackson Memorial and the University of Michigan Hospitals. There is no further threat..." in the background the television set chattered.

Alex stared into the mirror, his eyes once again focusing sharp. A horrifying chill ran through his body. Professor Siderenko was babbling over and over, "*dve tisyachy*," or "*two thousand pounds.*" And then it came to him. He remembered what he couldn't remember, what Viktoria was saying to him: *12:00 on Sunday, President Hoover.*

"But Viktoria didn't mean *President Hoover*, she meant goddamn *HOOVER DAM*! Andrei *was going to blow up goddamn Hoover Dam and kill thirty million people*. Andrei the ex-KGB assassin *had another one thousand pounds of plutonium*. Nobody knew about it except for Alex!

"That's it. That's why there was no ransom demand from Bart Robbins. Andrei had his own agenda. Andrei wanted everyone to think that it was safe. Andrei wanted Bart Robbins to get caught. Then he was going to nuke Southern California. He's going to blow up the fucking dam.

Or better yet, *maybe* Andrei blackmailed someone, maybe Andrei already got his money and it was kept quiet. And maybe he was going to nuke the dam anyway — for economic reasons.

And though Alex didn't know it, that was exactly what Andrei had done. Andrei had secretly blackmailed Russian President Cheka. He blackmailed Cheka for one hundred and fifty million dollars in uncut South African diamonds, lest he ruin America's victory celebration and take the remaining one thousand pounds of plutonium and nuke New York, or L.A. or wherever.

President Cheka knew Andrei was crazy enough to do something like that, so he paid up. One hundred and fifty million dollars in South African diamonds. If he didn't, Cheka would lose his breeder reactor program, the Russian economy would be in ruin, and millions of people would die. President Climan would lose face and détente and economic cooperation would come to an end. Cheka had no choice but to pay.

Andrei, however, after he got his diamonds figured that he could double or triple his money. By nuking Hoover Dam and Southern California the world financial markets would go into a tailspin. The value of the American Dollar would plummet, and hard commodities would increase in value. *Andrei's diamonds could be worth double or triple their original price.* In addition, Andrei should be able to make another hundred million for the antidote that he now controlled. Once he nuked the Southwest United States he would sell the Americans the cure to their newly acquired radiation poisoning — one hundred million would be a cheap price to pay. It was simple.

Boom! Everyone is dead. All of Las Vegas, Southern California, L.A., Phoenix not to mention the fallout. *Boom!* and then Andrei's one hundred and fifty million dollars in diamonds is worth three or four hundred million. Perfect! *Boom!* His formula would be priceless. He'd be one of the richest men in *the world.*

In the background the television continued to play, "President Climan and Russian President Nikolay Cheka jointly announced that new United Nations controls were being implemented to prevent nuclear terrorism..." And later, "At *noon today*, both leaders will be addressing the world from the United Nations..."

"*He's going to blow up Hoover Dam at the exactly noon.*" Alex said. "Jesus Christ! This guy's a lunatic!"

Alex ran, still soaking wet, into the bedroom. The digital clock read 10:51. What day was it?

Quickly he lifted up the telephone receiver and dialed "O."

"Caesars Palace. Have a lucky day."

"What day is it?" he frantically asked.

"Sunday. Will you be checking out today sir?"

"Sunday, Sunday!"

"Yes. Can I help you?"

Alex slammed down the receiver. He had been unconscious for *more than two-and-a half days*. He could call the police. But they would never believe him or think that he was a wacko! He didn't have enough time. *Only one hour.* And besides, they might not know who or what they are looking for. Andrei could be disguised, he could be anyone.

Alex rapidly assessed his room. There was no suitcase. He scoured the dresser drawers. Nada. Than he ran to the closet. Nothing, only a white courtesy terry cloth robe.

Alex threw on the robe and ran out of the room. He was on the eighth floor, and though he knew that he had to do something, he couldn't run through the casino with wet hair and only a bathrobe.

To the right was a room with it's door slightly ajar. Alex could just barely see three suitcases at the door's edge waiting for the bell-boy. He scanned the hallway. A couple walked toward the elevators. They wouldn't see him.

Alex darted into the room and swung the door closed behind him. He chained it shut. He rummaged through the first suitcase: women's clothing. Then, breaking the lock he ripped open the second: men's clothes. He pulled out a neatly-folded pair of pants. Not his size. The waist was too small and the legs too short.

Alex threw back on his robe and sped out of the room. He left the suitcases gaping open. He traversed the hallway, distancing himself from the elevators, then he found another similar room. This one had four suitcases and one hanging bag. Inside the hanging bag Alex hit pay dirt.

Chestnut tan Dockers and a too-often-washed faded yellow Polo shirt. It's collar was curled. There was no belt. Alex threw on the outfit. It was slightly bigger than his size. Swiftly he frisked the bag. He found two pair of shoes; one a dress polished black, the other blue Sperry boat shoes, with almost new laces. "Bingo!" He was in business and ready to roll!

Alex ran out of the room just as a bellboy was about to knock. Alex pushed him aside. He glanced briefly over his shoulder as he ran down the hall. He yelled behind, "Take the bags. I 'll meet you at the valet."

The bellboy walked into the room and the scene of Alex's ran-sacked cyclone.

59

Alex tore down the hallway in his ill fitting clothing in a burst of renewed energy. He ran to the elevator and then onto the lift. His fingers did not want to wait for the elevator to settle to the casino floor. They tapped in a frenzy against the copper wall mirror.

"Why did Viktoria have a vial? Who were the men who saved me? Why was I rescued?" He looked down at a watch a man was wearing. Nearly eleven. Hoover Dam was forty-five minutes away. No money. Gotta get there. No time.

On the 8th floor, unknown to Alex, a maid had been positioned in the hallway. She was secretly watching Alex. She saw him slide into the four suitcase and one hanging bag room, and then steal the clothes he was wearing. She radioed into a concealed microphone sewn into her lapel.

Alex shoved his way through the weary gamblers, many still up from last night. On the right were six sets of one hundred dollar blackjack tables. On the left — roulette, and two crap games. Alex mowed over a woman who looked like Dolly Parton with garrulous make-up, but taller.

Past slot machines, and others slowly making their way out of the casino, Alex shoved through the bodies, through two sets of double sliding entrance/exit doors and onto the valet and taxi four row marble steps. The bright sunlight rocked his world. A marble water fountain with fifteen foot high oval water jets shot to the skies, and a clog of cars, limo's and taxis lay before him. There were at least forty people in line waiting for a cab to the airport.

Desperately, Alex looked around. He tried to figure out a plan, what he was going to do? He ran his hands into his new pants pockets, hoping that he would luck-out and find some money. He did not.

"No time! None!"

Alex saw two limos pull up, and then three rented cars — a Cadillac, a blue something and a Lincoln. The Lincoln was first in line on the cobblestone drive.

The valet reached into the glove box while the car was still running and popped the trunk. The driver and passenger side windows were rolled down to cool the car and let air circulate inside. A bellboy wheeled a framed metal cart with four suitcases, two carry-on bags and a long blue-and-silver sequined evening gown covered in a dry cleaner's clear plastic.

"Be careful, you don't damage it," a persnickety woman ordered.

"Yes ma'am," the bellboy replied.

Her husband cowered as she began to make a scene. "And don't fold it, just lay it down flat on the clothes. That dress is a Bob Macki original, cost me $12,000."

Alex ran in front of the car, hopped into the driver's seat and slammed the door. He peeled out of the car park with the burgundy trunk open. At the end of the two hundred-foot driveway, traffic had ground to a halt. At least five cars were stuck, waiting to merge into traffic as Alex plowed toward them.

Behind him, the bellboy fortunately still had the gown in his hand.

On Caesars Palace's roof two men were perched with binoculars. They were looking down at the valet. One man spoke into the radio, "I think we've got him."

Alex nervously looked into his rearview mirror. Time, like grains in an hourglass, had nearly run out. Behind him, eight men, all big and burly stormed toward his "borrowed" car. Any second they would be upon him. The cars in front of him were not moving.

There was only one thing that he could do. He threw the Lincoln into reverse. Four of the men were Caesars valets. They fearlessly lunged onto the sedan.

Alex gunned it. He traveled at a terrifying fifty-five miles an hour for less than one hundred yards, then he slammed on his brakes. Three of the gutsy souls flew off the Lincoln. At the same time the trunk slammed shut.

Then, Alex hot-wheeled it into the underground parking garage. He descended down, to a one-way dead end. More men quickly pursued him.

He slammed on his brakes skidding the car sideways. He bashed into three parked cars, including a white Rolls Silver Shadow and a concrete wall. By now the police had been called. Alex would be trapped in the underground garage with no way out. "Gotta get out of this place. Gotta go before its too late. Gotta do it now!"

Alex again threw the car into reverse and headed back to the garage entrance. It had been swiftly blocked by two Caesars limos. More angry men headed toward him.

On the passenger's side the remaining security guard hero had worked his way into the car. Only his feet were extending outside the vehicle.

Alex slammed the Lincoln up the garage, to the second floor. A bevy of running guards were in rabid chase.

The hero in the car was thrown off balance, by the quick turns. He was lunged into the back seat and then onto the floor.

"Stop!" the strapping valet ordered as Alex was nonetheless approaching the end of his road. "Goddammit!"

Alex had come to the top of the parking structure and there was no way out. He slammed on his brakes as the hero took grip on him. The valet flew headfirst into the windshield. He was knocked out cold. Alex was thrown into the steering wheel, but he was all right.

Alex felt for the valet's pulse and quickly looked at his pupils. They were stable and not dilated. He'd be okay

Alex scanned the digital car clock. Time was evaporating. It was nearly too late. He flew the door open. He was ad-libbing, not quite sure what it was that he was going to do next. "Think on your feet like a cat Alex, think!"

Nearly upon him, and no more than seventy yards away were an army of men. In the distance he could hear sirens, police sirens!

"He had to improvise. Another car, the keys are always kept in them—no way out, the exit blocked? What to do?"

Alex began running, his legs were able to work now, the cure changed his life. He headed toward concrete exit stairs, farthest from the hunt. But as he got close, other men appeared out of the stairwell. They were heading straight toward him. These were more able-bodied security guards. And they were raging.

That's when he saw it, his only chance. A one-in-a-million-shot; a primo restored 1963 full-dress red, gold and enameled Harley Hog. The keys were resting upright in the center ignition port, just below the mint Corvette-style speedometer. "Bingo!"

Alex ran to the bike. He lifted the heavy 1200 cc off its stand, and began pushing the bike in a downhill run. He headed in the direction that he came from, straight toward the vigilantes. He tried the kick starter. Nothing!

Already the first man from the stairwell was upon him, trying to stop the motorcycle. Fortunately, however, he was also out of breath from his sprint. Alex turned the key, which he forgot to engage, and again hit the kick starter. Nothing!

"Get the fuck off, you prick!" the man puffed.

Alex kicked the man. He caught his deterrer in the face, knocking him to the ground.

Alex, rolled the motorcycle faster, straight to his pursuers—40 yards, 30 yards, 20 yards...the men were slowing to set up a second blockade. Alex again jumped on the kick starter. The bike sputtered, but nothing.

Then he realized that he had forgotten to turn on the gas. Fifteen yards and rolling at ten miles an hour. Alex flicked the gas cock forward. With no time to try and again kickstart the bike, he threw it into gear.

"Vrooom!" The engine fired up immediately.

Alex shot the Harley around in a quick U-turn. Blue smoke burned out of its exhaust pipes.

Only one way out, and he had to go for it!

"They've got him cornered in the garage," one of the two men on the roof reported, asking his superiors for instructions. The other was looking through his binoculars. Suddenly, out of nowhere, the primo Harley Hog flew out of the second floor parking structure at forty-five miles an hour. The motorcycle shot thirty-five feet in the air and traveled nearly one hundred and fifty feet from the structure onto the Palm Springs manicured lawn. "Vroooom!"

"Jesus Christ! our boy just went flying out of the goddamn garage!"

"Go, Alex, Go!" the other rooted.

Alex blasted onto the lawn. He was scared breathless. His chest was thrown into the crossbar, badly bruising it, and then in counterreaction he was pumped back onto the tricycle seat.

The cops had arrived. In front of him was a wall of Roman sculptured pines, each thirty-five feet tall. Alex hit his brakes. Again there was no apparent place to go. Behind him, four Las Vegas PD cars squealed to a halt.

A cop barreled parallel to Alex on the driveway. He slammed to a stop. His partner jumped out of the passenger seat, and with his pistol drawn yelled, "Halt!"

Alex spun around, digging a groove into the manicured lawn, and gunned the Harley. He charged full-speed ahead back to the valet and the quagmire of cars, people and panic. When he reached the exact spot where he stole the Lincoln, he found himself surrounded by three cop cars and eighteen security guards all with their guns drawn at point blank range. The gamblers were yelling. The situation was pure panic.

"Stop or we'll shoot!" one cop yelled, and another barked, "Stop!"

There was only on thing that Alex could do, and that was to go straight toward the valet box. He rammed over the stand which had a pile of a hundred keys on it. He barreled toward the moving one-way catwalk. One hundred people were on it heading toward the hotel. Shots spit off, two of them narrowly missing Alex, zinging past his head, like Cochise's arrows.

The catwalk was a one-way feeder into the casino from the corner of Bally's, The Barbary Coast and what previously was the Dunes Hotel. It began at the corner of Flamingo and Las Vegas Boulevard (the Strip), and ran to just short of the valet stand and the main entrance for Caesars Palace. Mostly enclosed by clear Lucite polymer jet plastic, except at the very beginning and very end, the moving walkway ran uninterrupted to the casino.

This was Alex's egress. He flew fullblast into the one-way throng of people. Bodies went flying in all directions, dodging the maniac biker. The tunnel filled with noxious exhaust fumes, and several bullets were aimed on their mark, but *none* were shot due to fear of hitting the tourists.

"We have a crisis," the man said from on top the hotel. He listened into his earpiece as he was given orders.

Alex shot out of the walkway at the far end. He slammed into a statue of a Roman warrior mounted on a steed. He was unable to slowdown in time. He was thrown off the bike. The Harley skid on its side. Alex tumbled onto the concrete and into the road, scraping skin off his right forearm, and buttock; but not enough to stop his ambulation. *The game was on!*

Police cars screamed onto the scene from both the Strip and Flamingo, heading straight for him.

Dazed, but not confused and still mobile, Alex got to his feet and ran through traffic. He shot across the street and toward the Flamingo Hilton.

Cop cars in hot pursuit were trapped in snarling traffic, mostly gawkers anticipating a bank robbery, or some kind of casino stick-up. Though eager to ogle, they were too chicken to move their cars.

Once at the front entrance of the Flamingo Hilton, a winded but ready Alex had his choice of vehicles he could steal: a Mercedes 600 SL, a BMW 850 CSI, a Porsche 911 Turbo Carerra and...MORE! Alex went for the Porsche.

The candy apple red pocket-rocket idled as the California attorney and his paralegal mistress, twenty years his junior, were tipping the valet. The attorney was twelve grand richer and on his way back to Bel Air.

No dice today. The Porsche Carerra, with its convertible top down, was a simple hop, skip and a jump for Alex to fly into. And he did!

The race was on.

Alex vrooomed the sports car into second gear by accident, grinding the Tipronic gearshift, and bulldozed past a new Ford Taurus station wagon, grazing the Taurus's side panel and smashing in his own right fender.

Alex popped into the northbound strip and cannoned his rocket, from zero to 60 in 5.3 seconds.

Playing dodge'em cars with the cars and running through red lights, Alex eluded the cops.

Problems! His progress was spotted. Live at 5 News Chopper had caught up with Alex's car, after they intercepted the incident on their police scanner.

"This is Ross Keeler live on News Chopper 5. Below we have an incredible saga unfolding..."

"Great stuff!' the news director enthusiastically fed into Ross's receiver earpiece, "Stay on him." Both the pilot, cameraman and Ross Keeler got the message loud and clear.

Ross was a seasoned pro who was sick of his traffic beat. He deserved better. This could be his big break. He kept on reporting, while at the same time listening to his boss' tyrannical directions. They stuck to Alex.

"This is just amazing stuff Ross. Do the police anticipate an apprehension before anyone is seriously hurt?" Dick Morris the news anchor reported on a split screen back at Channel 5 News headquarters. Channel 5 was in the middle of its one hour 11:00 a.m. Sunday local news report when Ross picked up the perpetrator.

"So far, there are no reports of any serious injuries...one moment." The camera zoomed in on Alex's stolen Porsche as it headed toward the Sahara Hotel. The police had made a barricade of their own, lining vehicles on both sides of the road. Cops were out on the concrete with their pump action shot guns primed and ready to fire. This was going to be great stuff.

Alex screamed upon the Sahara barricade faster than he realized. He slammed on his anti-lock brakes, skidding one hundred feet. He did a full one-eighty. A barrage of bullets rang out of the 12 gauge shotguns. Several of them pierced the Porsche's engine compartment and smoke began to plume out of the vehicle's rear.

Alex gunned the Porsche. The car squealed off...but then suddenly it died...just three hundred yards from the authorities!

"Son-of-a...!"

From all directions the police were converging onto the red sled.

"What to do? What to do?" He jumped out of the sports car and bolted in the only direction he could go, east into the Sunday packed Wet 'n Wild Waterpark.

Hoover Dam

One hundred thirty-five feet deep, Andrei was making final preparations on the nuclear mechanism that contained *one thousand pounds of plutonium coated in plastic polymer pellets.* The concept was incredibly simple.

The device was two watertight containers, each with five hundred pounds of plutonium polymer. Between the barrels was a satellite-controlled detonation relay with five pounds of C-4. With the remote, Andrei could detonate the device from anywhere in the world. The polymers would dissolve and the plutonium spontaneously bond with the water molecules, forming plutonium dioxide. With the vast amount of plutonium instantly converting into plutonium dioxide, a tremendous amount of energy would be released. This event, in combination with the C-4 explosion, would be enough to trigger a nuclear catastrophe. The plutonium would convulse in an atomic blast.

President Cheka had ponyed-up with one hundred and fifty million dollars in uncut South African diamonds. In exchange, Andrei was going to return the remaining stolen plutonium. Nobody knew about Andrei's deal except for President Cheka and the KGB. That's why the KGB was desperate to stop Andrei.

The diamonds were deposited on Saturday into a Swiss bank drop box. Andrei had already had them transported to another destination.

Unknown to Cheka, Andrei was going to detonate his plutonium. His plan was simple—blow up all of Southern California, and the diamond market would go crazy. His one hundred and fifty million dollars in diamonds would be worth two or three times that price.

Furthermore, Andrei held the key to any of the survivors longevity — the antidote. The nexus was worth another hundred million dollars in ransom. Andrei had already gotten enough antidote out of his scientists for his blackmail needs, and had eliminated them Saturday evening in the course of doing business.

President Cheka had known of Andrei from his reputation with the KGB as a top ranking "spy's spy." Cheka knew that Andrei meant business. And Cheka was also smart enough to know that Andrei might double-cross him after he got his bounty.

Andrei had planned for the bomb to go off no matter what at noon. He had a helicopter waiting for him nearby. Detonation would be done by him, using his remote arming device.

60

Wet 'n Wild, a water park built in the late 1980's, had water slides and twisty tubes that convoluted in crazy sometimes serpentine, seemingly impossible directions. Wave pools produced artificial surf three feet high, large enough to body surf on; precipitous water slides with terrifying drop-offs, and six-story high superslides with nearly straight down vertical free falls — sleds to toboggan down cascading tracked water routes — hot dogs, Pepsi, beer concessions, sandy beaches and surf had found their way to the middle of urban bustle.

The place was always lively, but Sunday was the busiest day of the week.

Alex, ran into the park and hopped a fence as shots zinged out at him. The sun worshippers screamed, pulling their towels in front of themselves to protect their Coppertoned oily bodies from the bullets.

"Stop!" three plainclothesmen and two cops in a patrol car ordered from behind the gates, as the authorities rapidly encircled the park. Police cars converged in from all directions, closing off all possible exits. From above the Las Vegas Police helicopter had arrived with one pilot and a spotter. There was no marksman, at least not yet. The "copper chopper" gave the ground troops moment-by-moment directions.

"The sight below is unbelievable," Keeler reported. He was going nuts. Keeler had found Nirvana — the exclusive story, that chance at the Pulitzer that he so richly deserved. "The suspect is on foot, perilously running into the crowd, endangering life and limb..."

Alex ran through a group of waiting people who were in front of a concession stand. He shoved several of them and knocked over some of their drinks. Close by were twelve cops converging from different entrances with the guidance of the police chopper.

Alex dodged under the pilings of a crazy-looped closed-tube water slide. He climbed a fence, plunging into a small puddle where water had leaked out of one of the tube's gelcoat seams.

Forty yards behind him were the cops, in heated chase.

"Where to go!" Alex was frantic. He prayed that he could make it to the other side of the water park, and hopefully steal a car from the parking lot. But no luck. As he arrived at the lot, it was full of cops. Above the police chopper was stirring up ground dirt in a swirl of debris. The police from behind were closing in, and now a new batch were heading straight at him from in front.

Alex made a 90° cut, and headed back into the park's bowels.

He flashed a look at a clock on the concession stand while zigging and zagging, through yet another pack of people. Most of the "parkers" were frozen catatonic as the chase proceeded.

Alex sideslipped the entrance to the Wave Pool, and then dodged under the ropes to a second larger serpentine slide. This snarl of tubes was not completely enclosed and ended in a fifteen-foot waterfall drop into a deep pool.

"Stop," yelled another officer over a bullhorn, this one coming from straight in front of him.

Alex had only one escape: *And that was straight up!*

"Are you getting all this," the director howled, ecstatic at this "once-in-a-lifetime" live action footage.

"Absolutely," the cameraman yelled back, as excited as anyone at the outrageous getaway chase.

"I want you to pull in as tight as possible on the guy. Let's get some shots *no one else has ever done. Think Pulitzer baby! Think Pulitzer!*"

The cameramen, reporter and helicopter pilot were all in agreement with the "Chief's" orders. The cameraman gave the aviator the thumbs-up signal, and then flashed his hands in a tight gesture to signal to the pilot to bring the chopper in closer.

The Bomb Bay superslide tower had a pair of twin slides, ninety feet and six stories high. It was the scariest thing since Godzilla. That was where Alex headed. Nowhere else to go, but straight up. Running full blast, he hopped the turnstile. He pushed through another frozen line of people, many of them ducking, and headed up the flight of stairs that lead to the sky.

Behind him, an entire team of police.

There was no time left. Minutes were evaporating into seconds, and seconds into nothingness. There were only 15 minutes left. "What to do...what?" His heart pumped at a million miles an hour.

The Channel 5 Live Eye Chopper closed-in on the tower, a dangerous thirty feet away. Ross Keeler was strapped-in and hung out onto the skid. His mouth foamed in frenzied words.

One level below Alex, was a bevy of officers in blazing pursuit. Their guns were drawn and ready for action. Now they could get a clean shot.

The tower, a swirl of seven spiral turns to the top, had broad safety rails. Immediately above and slightly south was the perturbed police chopper, perturbed over the Live-Eye's interdiction. The News 5 chopper was closer into the superslide than the cops, hogging for a close-up shot.

"Pull in tighter," the direct ordered.

The top of the structure was open. There, watching the action, were twelve sliders and two attendants, one of whom stood at each slide. They manned their positions next to the slides, ready to help each victim slider take their plunge.

Out of breath, Alex arrived on top. He ran to the edge of the slide, nearly falling off the platform, 90 feet straight down. Below, at the end of the vertical plunge was a team of cops waiting for his arrival. He glanced at an overhead clock — seventeen minutes left. "No time! No time!"

He looked above. The helicopter was blowing his hair fiercely, the camera zooming in on him. They were only thirty feet above.

The first of many officers arrived.

"Give it up. Hands to the sky, scum."

"They're going to blow up Hoover Dam!"

"What's this," the reporter said, as the cameraman aimed the sky mike down toward Alex.

"Hands above your head. Now!" another cop yelled with the sight of his Smith and Wesson automatic trained on Alex's forehead.

"We've only a few minutes, Goddammit! They're going to nuke Hoover Dam."

"Down to the deck, motherfucker!"

"Bring the chopper closer," the reporter ordered, momentarily closing off his mike; and then reported back to his director, "Apparently the suspect is saying that Hoover Dam is going to be blown-up." The reporter looked at his watch. It was a quarter to twelve.

The first of two officers lunged toward Alex. Alex dodged and the cop stumbled headfirst into a restraining bar. The second came after him, grabbing him, and the two locked in a bear hug. They struggled only momentarily until Alex kicked the cop's footing out from under him. Alex threw him into the water stream. The officer tumbled down the waterslide head and back first. He slid six stories, scared to death, but was no worse for wear.

"Give it up, or we'll shoot." Another new arrival said, and this one meant business.

On one of the restraining rail walls, behind where several scared-witless slide-surfers and the two attendants were cowering, was a Wet 'n Wild life preserver. It was tied to 30 feet of striped rope. The nonfunctional "beach" festoon was loosely attached with staples.

Alex ran to the wall, and with little effort he ripped the life preserver and rope from its attachments. The cops weren't going to shoot, they were afraid to hit the bystanders. Nevertheless, they quickly closed in.

Alex stepped over the railing and precipitously held onto the wooden fence.

"Give it up."

The Live-Eye helicopter dipped to only fifteen feet from the tower.

With a single gutsy, one shot only accurate throw, Alex hurled the life preserver. In James Bond-style it caught the front helicopter skid and locked into the eyelet. It was like running thread through a needle. Alex leaped from the tower as he grasped onto the rope for dear life.

"Jesus Christ," the reporter howled, "This is fantastic! What do we do now?" he yelled into his mike, to his director.

"You want a story don't you? Pull the bastard up. And don't stop shooting, whatever you do, don't stop shooting! This is unbelievable, great stuff!"

The cameraman and reporter reached down onto the skid. The cameraman braced the reporter, and then Ross Keeler heroically crawled onto its edge and secured the rope. They began pulling Alex up.

The officers had their guns trained on the chopper. They momentarily held-off their artillery fire.

The cameraman made certain that he had positioned the camera, vice-locking it into place, so that the entire world could see "that the news team were heroes."

With twelve minutes left, the fearless helicopter crew had Alex on board. They were only feet away from the platform.

"What's this about the Hoover Dam being blown up?" the reporter asked frenetically, making sure that his cameraman had a tight shot on his face. Ross, in his best acting mode, looked as concerned as possible.

"In minutes they're going to blow up the dam with a nuclear device! Take me there now!"

"A...Um...," Ross lost his composure. He wasn't sure if this crackpot was for real, or what.

"Look at your watch," Alex grabbed Ross' forearm, "We only have eleven minutes left!" The cameraman shot down on Ross' watch.

"Take him to the **GODDAMN DAM, NOW!**" the director yelled.

The pilot hearing the command responded immediately.

The helicopter made a quick looping turn, and blasted in a beeline to Lake Mead.

The police chopper followed in chase.

With the camera closely fixed to Alex's face, despite Ross's consternation that he wasn't in the shot, Alex told his compelling story. It scared the living daylights out of everyone. *If they didn't get there in time, thirty million people would die. **One thousand pounds of plutonium was enough to blow up the "whole fucking universe!"***

One hundred and thirty feet below the surface, Andrei was making final preparations. He had tightly packed the C-4 into place and he carefully secured both red and yellow, positive and negative wires, into the plastique. He double-checked the connection to the underwater detonation device. Perfect. Soon, he would be one of the richest and most feared men in the world.

61

From the air, Hoover Dam appeared toy-like. It was a chunk of concrete slid in a wedge between two granite rocks.

For millions of years the Colorado River had left its mark on the land, cutting great chasms along its fourteen hundred mile course from the Colorado Rocky Mountains to the Gulf of California.

Behind the monolith and its four million four hundred thousand cubic yards of concrete was Lake Mead.

The dam, which was crucial in regulating the Colorado River—would be vaporized in a matter of minutes.

As they approached from above, the four spillway turrets appeared as double push buttons connected by a thread. Two popped out of each lakeshore side into the water. The forty-foot-wide upper structure bowed backwards in a reverse arch, pushing the water to the lake's sides.

Below was a precipitous drop. Stone had been blasted out. At the base, water spilled into a narrow gorge in a tuft of white water turbulence. The road, a ribbon beneath them, curved semilunate with traffic. Cars were parked at each end, toward the Colorado River side. The ants were admiring the 7th Engineering Wonder of the Modern World.

The news chopper descended with alacrity, as the entire nation began picking up the "Live-Eye" feed. Damn if Ross Keeler wasn't going to get his Pulitzer after all.

The story that Alex revealed, in the short flight, though harrowing and so completely bizarre, was at best a tall tale told by a mad man. Yet, would anyone have ever even imagined that an entire hospital, let alone two, would be sabotaged with radioactive plutonium? No one would have even believed you if you would have told them that story a week ago.

Alex had no idea where Andrei had planted the bomb. Was he in a boat near the dam? Did he plant it inside the dam itself? Was it below the dam in the Colorado River?

Several pleasure boats were at the dams reverse arch, floating as close to the fluorescent orange buoys as allowed.

"Buzz the boats," Alex ordered. The chopper following Alex's command, the entire crew mesmerized by his heroics hit the lake's deck.

Below was a Magnum, a Riva, a Carver, and two Bayliners. All were relatively small, and replete with the obvious sun worshipers and fishermen.

They overflew the top of the dam close to the rim. They scraped the tops of cars. Wind from the rotator blades wreaked havoc below.

Nothing! Vehicle after vehicle, people out on their Sunday drives, doing the Hoover Dam tour. Others were on their way back to Phoenix, turtling over the dam, driving slow enough to take in the scenery.

"Wait a second," Alex said in a moment of revelation. "What's that below."

"Nothing...a utility vehicle doing routine maintenance I suppose," Keeler replied, still live, each second of their ordeal being recorded for posterity.

"*On Sunday!*" Alex exclaimed, "*On Sunday! Let me down now!*"

The chopper swooped down and landed onto the archway. Automobiles screeched to a halt. Alex barreled out.

"Up! Up! I want you to shoot all of this from the air. Now!" The director ordered into the crew's headsets.

In a scene made for an Arnold Schwartzenegger action/adventure movie, the helicopter ascended to sixty feet above the public works crane. The yellow city vehicle had its crane proboscis extending over the Lake Mead side of the dam, and from the snout hung a steel cable, dropping downward, submerging into the lake. Over the concrete railing was suspended a nylon utility ladder that dangled down into the water. The crane was secured by four steel mounts protruding from each corner, propping the huge vehicle slightly off the concrete.

Fluorescent two-foot-high orange cones surrounded the crane, diverting Sunday traffic around it.

Above, the police helicopter plummeted down. Had the Las Vegas P.D. had time to get a sniper on board, it would have been curtains for Alex, but that was not the case.

"Give it up!" the megaphoned voice yelled from the Hughes 500 gold and tan helicopter as it jockeyed for airspace with the "Live-Eye" News 5 chopper. "Give it up! Hands to the sky, now!"

Alex ignored the enjoiner, as he ran to the crane's cab. The cab was empty. There were no signs of Andrei. The controls to the derrick were confusing. Levers for hoisting and for moving the cranes extendible rail forward, or into retraction. There was a placard explaining the use of the controls.

Alex leaped out of the crane's cab and ran to the diesel's cab — the nerve center which drove the crane on the highway.

Again from above the police chopper warned, "Give it up or we'll shoot!"

Alex ignored the command and climbed up into the operations center. Nothing. Keys were in the ignition, the radio was off. Behind him was a storage area and what appeared to be a sleeping compartment. He reached in back of the driver's seat, past a mess of old papers, rumpled empty 7-11 Big Gulp cups and opened the cubby door.

There was Viktoria, bound and gagged.

Viktoria was semiconscious. Alex gently shook her. There was no response. Then again. This time she stirred. Her eyes opened, slowly, fully. She looked up at Alex, who began untying the ropes, and peeled back the duct tape that covered her mouth.

The "Live Eye" chopper lowered its hover pattern, to even with the dam's rim on the Colorado River side. The cameraman dramatically zoomed in for a shot. He angled through the open diesel's door, onto Alex pulling Viktoria out of the sleeper compartment.

"Are you all right?" he asked almost in tears as he held Viktoria close to his chest.

"Dr. Fertile?" she smiled.

"Yes, it's me."

"I knew that you would come Alex. I knew that you would come for the antidote. That's why I had it."

"You saved my life."

"My father? My father?"

But Alex didn't need to answer, his eyes told the story.

"Oh..." Viktoria looked down at the cab's sheet-metal floor. Tears began to flow freely. "I knew that they would kill him. I knew that he was lying."

"Andrei?"

"Yes," she lamented softly, still looking downward, crying and then sniffling. She lifted her head up toward Alex. "He's going to blow up the dam. He's gotten 150 million dollars in diamonds from President Cheka. And he's going to do it anyway. He's going to blow up everyone."

"Oh my God. Where is he?"

Two foreboding things occurred while Alex was rescuing Viktoria. First, from Las Vegas, a late model car arrived at the entrance of the dam. Unable to get through, with the police helicopter and the "Live Eye" chopper hovering dangerously close, and because traffic ground to a halt — the Vegas car diverted back the way it came, then it cut-off the road and drove under the dam's two million kilowatt high-tension power lines at a spot that was one hundred fifty feet above the superstructure.

At the same time, Andrei emerged from the depths of Lake Mead with his wet suit and scuba gear on, and weight belt tightened around his stomach. With fins in one hand, he climbed up the nylon ladder.

As Andrei arrived at the dam's rim he saw the police helicopter hovering over the diesel cab, and heard the chopper ordering, "Come out with your hands up." Without hesitation he headed for the cab. On his way he dropped his fins and scuba gear to the concrete. From his weight belt he removed a twelve-inch crescent wrench.

"He's placing a nuclear device, 1000 pounds of plutonium into one of the dam's water intake pipes."

"Why didn't he kill you?"

"Because, my father didn't perfect the formula. Or at least he didn't in part."

"What does that mean?" Alex asked worriedly.

"What it means is…" she hesitated, "is that it works, but only temporarily. But Andrei doesn't know that. He thinks that I decoded my father's notes on the flight from Belize. He thinks he has the correct formula."

"What do you mean *only temporarily*?"

"I mean that the formula works for only a week or so. You get rid of all the poison, the plutonium. You urinate and defecate it out of your body, but…"

"But, what?"

"The formula produces a toxin, a byproduct to the antidote. Those discs that we found didn't tell the entire story. Yes, nineteen out of twenty of the Siberian prisoner's who took the antidote died, but none from plutonium poisoning. *They all died from a by-product of the antidote. Everyone of them died after two weeks.*"

"Jesus," Alex mumbled.

"That's what my father was working on. That's why Andrei kept me alive. To make sure my father finished his work."

"But…Andrei killed your father."

"Yes," she sniffled again.

"I'm sorry."

"My father was working on something, though. He wrote it in code. They wanted me to translate it, I did it in part. They made the antidote on the plane and here in a lab. That's what I smuggled to you at the Mirage. I slipped a copy of the notes and a vial into your pocket. Did you get it?"

"Get what? I…don't know."

"Papers. Two sheets. My father wrote down three alternative formulas. One should have worked. However, he didn't want to risk anymore deaths so he tried it on himself. You saw the results. I decoded another, that's what Andrei's men made up and what I had in the vial for you."

"Yes."

"Andrei wanted to keep me alive for insurance, just in case the new formula didn't work. He still needs me."

"It's okay, Viktoria. Everything will be all right."

"I got you the best formula I could. I don't know if it will help."

"Don't worry," he replied.

"Look out!" Viktoria yelled. A crescent wrench sailed through the air toward Alex's face. Viktoria pushed him out of the way. The wrench hit her on the head. Blood gushed from the wound.

62

Out of instinct Alex threw a sidekick from his crouching position in the cab. Alex was not an amateur in fighting and had limited training in the martial arts in college. But that was years ago and when he was young.

His foot landed squarely on Andrei's chest. The blow propelled Andrei out of the diesel onto the street. Above the police helicopter blared at Alex, but this time with the spotter's limited range Smith and Wesson .38 special handgun aimed at Alex. "Stop or we'll shoot."

The cops assumed that the diver was an innocent bystander that was valiantly trying to save the day.

Alex spun around to assist Viktoria. Blood was pumping out of her head. She was knocked out cold.

Andrei arose from the concrete. He was damaged but was no worse for wear. Above, the police chopper was hovering ominously close. Again the cop's voice echoed, "Stop or we'll shoot."

Andrei made his way back to the cab. He yanked Alex out by

his feet. Alex fell face first onto the cement. Only his forearms buffeted his contact.

Andrei kicked his right foot into Alex's groin. Alex let out a ringing yell.

"You getting all this? Don't stop shooting, no matter what, don't stop!" the director roared into his headset. The "Live Eye" chopper hovered to the east of the dam. They were still at road level, in front of the Colorado River, maneuvering for a better position.

And again from above, the police chopper positioned over the two pugilists, with its final admonishment. "This is our last warning. Give it up!"

Alex was writhing in pain. Andrei picked him up with scuba gear gloved hands, balanced him on his two feet, and then laid a walloping punch into his chin. The blow sent Alex nearly across the street.

One maniac driver, late for a Sunday meeting back in Scottsdale, Arizona, attempted to sneak past the lunacy. He inched across the road, then in a burst sprinted towards the other end. He swerved as Alex appeared out of nowhere, stumbling to his feet. The driver slammed on his brakes, stopping the vehicle dead in its tracks.

Alex rose in agony, and then Andrei, in a feat of almost superhuman strength, lifted Alex up and throw him onto the car, a '96 Lexus. Alex's head smashed into the windshield. He cracked the glass. Blood pulsed from his scalp.

But the blow seemed to revive Alex. Maybe it was the antidote he took, that acted like speed and gave him needed stamina and renewed strength.

Andrei jumped onto the vehicle, thinking that Alex was an easy mark; but instead, Alex threw his own right cross nailing Andrei in his temple. Andrei flew onto the road.

"Unbelievable, great stuff! Don't lose 'em! Get every possible shot. Unbelievable!" the director was rabid and was losing his voice from all his ranting.

Andrei was slightly disoriented as he made his way to his feet. Alex took advantage of Andrei's wooziness. He popped off the hood and nailed him in the jaw. Andrei tumbled backwards onto the concrete.

Alex wanted to fight, but he feared the bomb was going to blow any second and with all of them on the dam. He reached down perniciously and lifted Andrei up by his wet suit. "Where's the bomb you son-of-a-bitch?" Andrei was groggy. He did not answer. "Where's the goddamn bomb?"

Andrei smirked a Cheshire cat grin and at the same time nailed Alex in the breadbasket with the best blow he had ever delivered to *any victim in his entire career.*

"Ahhhhhh!"

Alex hit the road, his back wounded and the tissue underneath swollen. Andrei saw this as an opportunity to finish him off once and for all. He ran to the driver's door, and threw out the protesting man, propelling him to the sidewalk.

Andrei gunned the metal gray Lexus straight at Alex, as Alex regained his footing.

"Boom," Alex's body ricocheted off the front fender, deeply bruising his left thigh, jostling him onto the concrete.

Alex spun around and used his arms to successfully brace his impact. Through the rearview mirror, and then over his shoulder Andrei saw the lack of his success. He cannoned the car in reverse, aiming dead square for Alex. With only seconds to respond, Alex rolled out of the way. The Lexus smashed into the crane, slamming the trunk in an accordion crunch.

Again, Andrei rifled the car forward. This time with better aim, straight at Alex. He slammed the Lexus into the concrete wall, impelling the car partially over the Grand Canyon edge, front wheels spinning in mid-air. Andrei thumped into the steering wheel. The airbag exploded into his face.

This was the opportunity Alex was looking for. Alex threw open the driver's door, and heaved Andrei out.

A brawl ensued, with each pugilist giving the other their best shots. Two blows to Andrei's face, returned by another two from the villain. In the long run, however, Andrei the trained killer, was much tougher than Alex.

Alex got the licking of his life. In sadistic pleasure, with the two helicopters hovering above, Andrei beat the living daylights out of him. He nailed Alex numerous times in the jaw. Alex fell to the ground; and over and over again, Andrei pummelled him. Alex was ready to go down for the final count.

Finally with blood coming from his nose, mouth and right ear; Andrei in one powerful blow threw Alex onto the restraining rail. Seven hundred and twenty-six feet below was the rock, concrete and swallow water demise of the Colorado River spillway.

Andrei strangled him with his powerful hands, squeezing the life out of his body. Alex tried to stop him. He attempted to kick and feebly punch Andrei, however, Andrei blocked his blows and laughed. *"I am your demise!"* he snarled, releasing Alex's neck from his death vice. Alex fish-gasped for air.

He wheezed for oxygen. Andrei picked Alex up by his shirt. His grip ripped part of the fabric, while the remaining material was still sturdy enough to maneuver him.

"The dam?" Alex labored for air, "You're going to blow it up, aren't you?"

"Yes."

"Now?"

"Maybe. Do you see this?" Andrei asked Alex holding the triggering device before Alex's eyes.

"Yes."

"I can activate the bomb from anywhere in the world. And if, for some reason that I don't walk away from here," looking up at the police helicopter, "then I push this other button, the red one...and in one hundred twenty seconds boom! goes everything."

Andrei lifted Alex higher, and then threw two shots to Alex's jaw. A cracking sound emanated after the second one. Alex tumbled to the cement, nearly unconscious. Andrei bent over and again picked Alex up. Andrei slapped Alex's face several times, bringing Alex back to the living.

Precariously Andrei hurled him upward and threw him halfway over the rail. Alex's body was microseconds away from falling seven hundred and twenty-six feet down into the spillway.

With Alex's head nearly a foot below his feet, bobbing toward his death, Andrei said "It's time to die Dr. Seacourt. Once and for all."

Then suddenly a razor-edge shot rang out. Blood welled out of Andrei's wet suit in the exact spot of his heart. Andrei's mouth filled with crimson. Above them, in the car that earlier detoured onto a cut-off mound looking down onto the dam, were two men: one had binoculars and the other a marksman's bolt action rifle with a telescopic sight. The man with the rifle had let loose the round that ended Andrei's life. Ilya, the Russian taxi cab driver. Ilya, the fake cop, the real KGB agent and crack marksman, saved Alex's life. The KGB had been watching and following Alex at Caesars Palace — the maid, the men on the hotel roof, more people than he was aware of.

Andrei released Alex. Alex's body slipped over the edge. Only at the last second did Alex catch his right foot under the guardrail, bracing his fall as his back slammed into the Colorado River side of the dam. His knees were his life-saving pivot point around the barreled rail.

Hanging upside down, Alex forced his bruised and pounded stomach muscles to work. He barely did a sit-up, to come over the bar; and then fell onto his face, his extremities still tangled in the restraining rail.

Andrei stumbled to his feet at the rails edge. His face was dazed and surprised. He never expected to be shot. Then with his dying breath he looked down at Alex.

"I," he coughed frothy blood, "am still your demise." *Andrei pushed the red button* and stumbled over the restraining rail plummeting to his second death below. As Andrei fell, a scream echoed into the river basin.

Shakily, Alex stood. "*Oh my God! one hundred twenty seconds.*"

63

“ This is completely unbelievable Dick," Ross Keeler reported in a tumult to the news anchor, "I've never seen anything like this." And like the dogs that the news crew were, the "Live Eye" chopper descended into the river basin to get a picture of the rag-doll dead body. Andrei lay smashed on top of the generating station. He missed the water and rocks by only inches. Blood pooled onto the building's surface in an ever-increasing copper silver dollar.

Noon
United Nations General Assembly, New York

The General Assembly was full to capacity with every nation in attendance including representatives from the Security Council, the Economic and Social Council, the Trusteeship Council, the International Court of Justice and the Secretariat.

Introductions were given in the five official languages of the United Nations (English, French, Spanish, Russian and Chinese) and then President Climan and President Cheka ascended to the podium to give their mutual address.

Climan spoke first.

"My fellow world citizens,   America has undergone and survived its most trying time. The crisis in Miami and Ann Arbor was worse than Hiroshima, more devastating than Nagasaki. Thousands of people have already died, and many thousands more will perish. Atomic contamination, in their generation and future generations, will cause illness, cancers, blindness and genetic mutation.

"This tragedy has lead the American people, and the people of the world, to a day of reckoning," President Climan said gesturing to President Cheka, who nodded his head in affirmation.

"Never again will the circumstance be made available to any terrorist group, any organization, or any individual. Never again will any one person, or any country be in a position to exploit the nuclear insanity that has recently overwhelmed my nation. Never again will the horror that has driven a stake of fear deep into my countrymen's hearts be allowed to endure."

Cheka next dramatically spoke:

"Our nations have come together, the United States and Russia, to offer a solution, a proposal before the General Assembly, which will make our world safe. What we tender today will allow every human being to live in a safe world, a world without the fear that any of us may be secretly poisoned."

Alex shakily stood. He needed to stop the bomb now or *thirty million people will die*. He ran to the crane. He looked around quickly. The device had to be in the water.

In the nearby distance from Las Vegas and Kingman, Arizona a river of flashing red and blue bubble gum lights converged from both sides of the dam.

"He had scuba gear on. The bomb had to be in the water, but where?" Alex ran to the other side of the crane. He noticed the boom and the steel cable that descended into the murk. On the Lake Mead side of the dam lay Andrei's scuba gear, a mask and snorkel and double oxygen tanks. Just past the ditched gear was what appeared to be a ladder that extended over the concrete and rail wall. "This had to be it!"

Alex grabbed the mask, threw it over his head, and with his other arm he reached into the scuba harness and slung the gear over his shoulder. Then, without securing the harness, nor the mask over his face, he flung himself over the rail, down thirty-five feet into

Lake Mead.

The water separated in a billowing splash as the gear tried to rip off his shoulder. Momentarily Alex lost the mask, but quickly he found it again.

He put his other arm into the harness, and then descended into the depths.

He did not have a weight belt, and his plunge was incredibly difficult; his body, due to its own buoyancy wanted to return to the surface. Alex pulled his way down the cable, purging his ears twice, then a third time. Hand over swollen hand, he sprinted down the steel guide wire. 20 feet, 30, 40, 50, 60, "How far down is this thing?" The pressure was intense and tortured his injured body. 70, 80, 90, 100, 10, 120, 130 and then finally at 140 feet the cable abruptly ended at an ingress pipe for one of the four giant water intake towers. There in the gloom, the cable latched into place onto a mesh grill. Alex could barely see. The water was icy cold, and his arms and legs were frozen.

Alex swam into the tube, through the shadows toward bubbles.

Boriskov was making final preparations. Boriskov was unaware of the fact that Andrei had armed the bomb and that it was going to blow any second.

Alex swam in a jet pushing Boriskov away, reaching toward the device. Two black-ribbed one hundred and five gallon oil drums were lashed together by a series of fiber strapping belts, and then cranked tight. Between them, wedged into the "V" that the two drums made, was the C-4 plastique and a sophisticated triggering device. An underwater antenna and two wires, one yellow and the other red, leading from the electric package to the explosive, sat on top of the arming device.

Alex kicked his finless feet toward the C-4, almost in reach of the mechanism, when Boriskov grabbed him from behind. Boriskov ripped his mask off his face and threw him wildly against the water ingress tunnel.

Thrown to the side, Alex's maskless vision was blurred. He could faintly see the bomb before him, and the lunging figure with a knife in his hand.

Alex grabbed Boriskov's knife hand with both of his hands. The two of them spun in the deep, like piranha fish caught in a fight over the same carrion, flipping over and over in a feeding frenzy.

Boriskov ripped loose Alex's scuba tanks. In a fit, Alex trying not to lose his oxygen, kneed Boriskov in the underarm, causing the Russian to drop his knife.

Alex broke free and swam toward the device.

"Only seconds left." 10, 9, 8, 7,..."Gotta do something!"

Just then, Boriskov recovered the knife that fell to the tunnels ribbed floor. He flew up at Alex. From behind he cut Alex's airline. Bubbles in a fury burst upwards, while at the same time blinding Boriskov's attack.

Without air, and deep down, 140 below the surface feet, Alex swam desperately onto the mechanism. 6, 5, 4, 3, 2, 1....

The only thing he could do was...

12:05 p.m.
United Nations General Assembly, New York

President Climan was speaking:

"President Cheka, the Security Council, and I have developed a plan that once and for all will prevent the kind of terror and tragedy that has befallen my country.

"The plan, which we are here today to jointly present, pivots around the formation of a seventh principal organ of the United Nations: The Nuclear Proliferation and Security Council.

"This unprecedented arm of the United Nations will replace the Atomic Energy and the Disarmament Commissions, whose previous roles were the control of the atomic energy, weapons and their weaponry of mass destruction.

"This new body, The Nuclear Proliferation and Security Council will not only deal with the question of armaments and the control of nuclear proliferation, but also the worldwide control of atomic energy, the mining of atomic ores, their creation, storage and destruction."

President Cheka spoke:

"The new commission will have the power, through its own world police force, to act if any nation refuses to comply with the new standards in the matters of atomic energy control. The Nuclear Proliferation and Security Police will act *immediately* if there is any threat to the strict regulations and rules that the Council will adopt...and if there is any threat to world safety and the breach of that security, the Security Police will respond with uncompromisable force."

Alex grabbed the yellow wire and jerked it free.

Click! A stream of electricity pulsated through the water, shocking both Alex and Boriskov. The C-4 did not detonate.

Without oxygen and deep below the surface, Alex was stunned by the automatic discharge. He had only moments left, and he was now facing death from anoxia. Boriskov grabbed Alex by the leg, as Alex attempted to make his way to the surface.

He pushed Alex onto the intake tube's floor. Boriskov was trying to drown Alex, burying him below the surface without air. Alex struggled to no avail, the bigger man was too powerful for him.

And then, out of the corner of his eye, he saw what appeared to be a shiny reflection, with a dark handle. Alex strained to reach...

He grabbed the knife by the handle and swung it, stabbing Boriskov in the shoulder. Boriskov fell in agony to Alex's side.

Up, up and away Alex went, kicking as fast as he could, pushing the scuba tanks off of him. Faster and faster he ascended, seeing above only faintly the glimmering blue light of day. Without the tanks, he shot bullet-swift to the surface.

Then everything went black.

64

The "Live-Eye" news chopper, that floated above Hoover Dam was in hysterics. Sixty police cars had arrived at the bomb scene. Nevada and Arizona Highway Patrol, Sheriff's Officers from Boulder City, Henderson, Las Vegas, everywhere! The police helicopter circled overhead. By this point the cops were so extremely irritated at the "Live Eye" Chopper they were ready to press charges for obstruction of justice.

Not willing to miss a scoop and the story of the century, Ross Keeler had the second chance of a lifetime: to be an honest-to-goodness hero.

Alex had surfaced. He was motionless, face down in Lake Mead, when Ross in a fit of his reporting frenzy realized that Alex needed help.

In a move that was sure to win him at least an Emmy, or an anchorman's slot at a prominent metropolitan news station, Ross ditched his microphone and headphones. He dove into the lake, from thirty feet above, and saved Alex's life.

"What a shot! What a shot!" the director went berserk. He

was foaming at his sycophantic mouth. "This is incredible. The best stuff ever! Fantastic! Fantastic! Unbelievable!" And it was.

Ross performed mouth-to-mouth resuscitation on Alex, while in the distance a National Park Service eighteen-foot cutty craft approached, ripping through the water.

From above, on top of Hoover Dam and its shores, all guns were trained on Alex. Ilya, in his nondescript car, with his equally chameleon partner, inched his way off the mound, down the knoll from where they sat and saved Alex's life. They headed back to Las Vegas.

Alex's lungs filled with the wry air that reporter Ross Keeler labored into them. Though eventually Alex started breathing on his own, he never regained consciousness. He had gotten the bends. He had ascended one hundred forty feet to the surface, too fast. Nitrogen bubbles had precipitated into his tissues and caused nitrogen narcosis.

The Park Service boat finally arrived, and within a few minutes a Life Flight Chopper from Desert Springs Hospital hovered over the cutty craft.

Alex's convulsing body was taken by stretcher to the helicopter, and with an escort of three irate Sheriff Deputies and Keeler himself, the Life Flight made a straight shot to Edward's Air Force Base, to the nearest decompression chamber.

The B0105 Life Flight Helicopter jetted at 150 knots, faster than the police chopper or the "Live Eye" bird. On board, the doctor worked feverishly. Alex had developed an irregular heart beat and had gone into a Wolf-Parkinson-White rhythm, then atrial fibrillation. The flight surgeon administered IV digoxin and dexamethasone, and then three times electrically "zapped" him.

Ross sat holding Alex's hand, wondering what would have unfolded, had Alex not gotten to the dam when he did.

It wasn't until an hour later, that he learned what would have been the worst possible scenario.

The underwater naval divers secured the nuclear device by 1:10 p.m. They found that it contained one thousand pounds of plutonium, enough to nuke almost all of the Southwestern United States, or if not nuke it, the fallout would kill twenty to thirty million innocent people.

A behemoth of authorities had ensnared Hoover Dam and the body of water below it. Lake Mead was closed on an emergency basis, as well as I-93 over the dam as far west as Boulder City, and as far southeast as forty miles north of Kingman, Arizona.

Despite the massive manhunt that followed, there was no trace of Boriskov. He had magically disappeared.

65

The effects of the bends can be devastating, even fatal. It is the formation of gas bubbles in the body as the result of rapid transition from a high-pressure environment to a lower. Bubbles forming in the brain, spinal cord, or peripheral nerves can cause paralysis and convulsions, difficulties with muscle coordination, and sensory abnormalities, speech defects, and personality changes.

Treatment from decompression sickness usually can be achieved only by recompression in a hyperbaric chamber followed by gradual decompression. Permanent tissue damage, however, may still remain after decompression.

"How is he," she asked the doctor.

"Real bad."

"What does that mean?"

"Alex has a pneumothorax or a 'burst lung,' and trapping of gas into the tissues of the chest. We're not sure, but we also think that the nitrogen gas extended into his pericardium, or the sac around his heart, and up into his neck."

"What's his prognosis?"

"That's not all. I need to tell you that there's also the possibility of arterial gas emboli into the brain. We've taken him down to six atmosphere abs and are very slowly recompressing him to make sure we get out all the cerebral bubbles."

"Oh."

"We're doing everything in our power to save him."

"*Spaeba*. Thank you." Viktoria's eyes grew tears.

Dr. Piotr Jaroszewicz, a patriarchal polish immigrant Jew with half-semicircular spectacles, a scraggly red-brown and gray beard that was eight days past trimming, a long greyhound face and a full lower lip, was the best in his field. He was brought in from UCLA Medical Center by the military. The equipment that he had to work with at Edward's Air Force Base was the most advanced hyperbaric decompression chamber, equal to the facilities at San Diego Naval Base and Miramar.

"I've got a question for you," the doctor asked, very concerned.

"Yes," Viktoria snuffled.

"Has Alex taken any medication recently?"

"Why do you ask?"

"We're having some problems with him."

"What are those?"

"Well, his body isn't responding as we would normally expect to the decompression treatment."

"How so?"

"Normally, the saturated nitrogen comes out of the body's fatty tissue in a much more rapid manner. In Alex's case, however, we're getting a much slower rate of nitrogen reabsorption from the tissues, back into the blood stream; at a rate of one-tenth the usual expulsion."

"Doctor...he did."

"What kind of medication?"

"My father's antidote. Also he was exposed to plutonium in Michigan."

"Yes we know about Michigan," one of Dr. Jaroszewicz assistants who was hovering over Dr. Kingman's shoulder, said. "We've checked that out, and there is no sign of any plutonium in him"

"What was the antidote you gave him?" Dr. Jarosewicz asked. But before she could answer, a military attach who was also flanking Jaroszewicz whispered into the doctor's ear. He asked him to step aside for a private conversation.

The physician and the Air Force Military Intelligence General walked into a soundproof anteroom. They looked into the decompression chamber behind two six-inch Plexiglas windows at Alex. Alex was naked except for a thin gown covering his chest and abdomen. IVs ran into his forearm from two poles. One a bottle of antibiotic, another 0.9% sodium chloride solution.

From underneath the gown a Foley catheter tube extended, and a green fluorescent urine flowed from Alex's penis to a translucent plastic bag hanging from his bed. He had telemetry units monitoring his heart rate and EEG (brain) patterns. The readings remained regular. In the meantime, he lingered in a coma and was unresponsive.

Inside the decompression chamber a nurse in a spacesuit was checking Alex's vitals. She withdrew blood from a venous line attached to the surface of his hand, and exchanged urine bags for a clean one. They would be measured and analyzed.

"What the hell is this stuff." The nurse had never seen florescent-green urine. The doctors had said that Alex must have taken something, and that whatever it was, it was doing some pretty bizarre stuff to his body.

National Center for Disease Control and Prevention
Atlanta, Georgia

Dr. Eric Freelander's office was one of the most meticulous, well-organized bastions of intellectual retreat that had ever befallen any director of the NCDCP. Dr. Freelander, an avid jogger and chess player, who at the precocious age of 13 was the State of New York Junior's Champion, had a thirst for knowledge that was unquenchable. He matriculated medical school at 21 and graduated from dual residencies in pathology and infectious disease by the time he was 28. He was a phenomenon.

Dr. Freelander had never seen results like those that were now laying on his desk. He stood up from his computer terminal, pushed the remains of his balding hair from his brow, and looked out his office window.

"Dr. Freelander," Donna his sassy brunette secretary said over the intercom, "I've got Dr. Kingman on the line."

"Thank you." Eric said as he sat in his leather Cromwell chair, and pushed the speaker button, while at the same time hitting the space key on his computer to revive the screen that had momentarily disappeared.

"Eric, Piotr Jaroszewicz here. What's the prognosis?"

"We've solved it."

"Solved it?"

"The problem with the antidote."

"Go on."

"Serendipity. Or maybe I should clarify — your Boy Scout Dr. Alex Seacourt did."

"What are you talking about Eric? That antidote is no good. Sure it gets the damn plutonium out of the victim's system, but the byproduct ends up killing the victim in two weeks. Deader than a doornail. And that goes for even the new formula that Viktoria Siderenko interpreted from her father's notes."

"Did you ever wonder what was coming out of your Dr. Seacourt's urine?"

"Yes, of course," Jaroszewicz was offended. "That's why I sent you the urine for analysis."

"We took that urine, plus a sample of Seacourt's hair and Professor Siderenko's notes. We figured the thing out."

"The formula?"

"Yes...we made it work, but only because of Seacourt. And you know...better than that, everyone who has been nuked already, that's still alive, that the radiation hasn't devastated too bad, can still be saved."

"My Lord." There was silence on the line for several moments until Eric broke in.

"The bastard got the bends, forcing nitrogen into every cell of his body. *With the decompression that he is undergoing right now, not only is the nitrogen coming out, but also the byproduct of the antidote, the deadly toxin!*"

" That's what the green fluorescent urine is!"

"Yep. I've placed a call to the President to tell him the news."

"But one question: does everyone with radiation poisoning have to be decompressed?"

"No, we've got other methods. Now that we know about the nitrogen binding with the antidote's byproduct in the tissues, we can twist the antidote's structure and chemically combine it with a polyvalent trimolecular nitrogen polymer to make it work."

"Congratulations."

"Thanks. The antidote, by the way, is the reason the decompression process is taking so long; why your boy isn't responding in a normal manner."

"Huh."

"Yeah, huh. Isn't it funny? Just like penicillin. Discovered by accident. Serendipity. If Seacourt didn't go down one hundred forty feet into Lake Mead after the bomb and then get the bends, *one hundred thousand people would have never had a chance at survival.*"

One Week Later

It wasn't until nearly seven days from the time that Alex blacked-out and was rushed to the decompression chamber that he finally regained consciousness.

By then, the decompression process had been completed and Alex was moved to U.C.L.A. Medical Center. Viktoria was at his side when he awoke to the ringing of his bedside telephone. Alex turned his head to answer. As he looked up, Viktoria picked up the receiver.

"Yes it is.... Yes I'll be.... Thank you." She hung up.

"Who was that?" Alex asked, his voice rusty.

"Oh my." Viktoria looked down at him with a beaming smile.

"Oh my. Not a 'good to see ya;' or a 'thanks for saving the world?'"

"Yes. Good to see you. Thanks for saving the world." She reached over and hugged him. She kissed his forehead, his eyelids, his neck, ears, and mouth. "Good to see you. I love you, Dr. Alex Seacourt. I love you."

"I love you... too" he said.

"Where am I?"

Viktoria replied as she simultaneously pushed the nurse button. The room was a floral shop of flowers sent in from well-wishers from all over the country, including President Cheka and President Climan. Next to Viktoria sat a CIA and FBI operative for Alex's debriefing. Viktoria excused them and they left momentarily. "Los Angeles, at U.C.L.A. Medical Center."

"What happened? How long have I been here?"

"Two days."

"Two days?"

"I mean yes and no. You've been at Edwards Air Force Base, in their decompression chamber for five."

"Man, do I have a headache."

" I wouldn't expect anything less."

"What about the others? The formula? Did the bomb go off?"

"No. You saved them."

"I did? No, I didn't. It was your father's formula."

"Yes and no. The formula worked, but the byproduct was worse. It killed everyone. That is...until you got the bends. The nitrogen narcosis forced the toxin out of the cells and made my father's formula safe to use."

Alex pushed his way up against the head of his hospital bed, propping himself up.

"How 'bout some food?" Then Alex wore an apprehensive frown, remembering "And my parents?"

"That was them on the telephone. Your mother is being discharged tomorrow, and your father in another week."

"My father?"

"Yes, they'll both be all right."

"How? I don't understand.... My God."

Alex reached over to the tabletop next to his bed to pour himself some water. Instead, Viktoria stopped him. She insisted, and lifted the plastic pitcher for him. She splashed water into a disposable hospital cup, sprinkling droplets onto the counter. She handed Alex the water, and with his weakened paw he slowly drank. The liquid soothed his parched mouth.

"You have to promise me one thing, my love."

"What's that?" he looked at Viktoria.

"Take me to Vegas."

"To Vegas?"

"I always wanted to go there, but on my terms. Promise me."

"I promise, just no white tiger show."

"Deal." Viktoria beamed. Alex grew a boyish grin. She said wryly, "Okay Dr. Fertile."

Alex gleamed at Viktoria and then reached his hand out to her, pulling her by the wrist closer to his face. They locked in a tender embrace.

After several minutes, and their body chemistries boiling over, Viktoria tenderly pushed Alex back, "Now behave."

It was then that Alex saw the laceration that was sutured on top of her scalp.

"Bend over."

"I hoped that you wouldn't see them. They're coming out tomorrow."

"What happened?"

"Don't you remember?"

"No, not really."

"I was hit on the head with Andrei's wrench."

"I vaguely remember."

"What about Boriskov? What happened to him?"

"The authorities never found him."

"Who shot Andrei?"

"I think we need to talk about something."

"Why, who shot Andrei?"

Viktoria said no more. She placed a telephone call. Then minutes later two KGB agents who had been patiently waiting in the hospital lobby came up. The first one was Ilya. The other man Alex did not recognize. He was lanky, fair-skinned and had brown hair.

"Do you remember Ilya," she asked. Alex nodded no. Ilya bent over and gave Alex a "comrade kiss" on both cheeks.

"I was your cab driver. I saved your ass at the Mirage, and gave you the antidote."

Slowly the memories returned.

"Dr. Seacourt, if it was not for you," Ilya continued, "Mother Russia would have been in grave peril right now."

"I don't understand."

"Do you mind if I have a seat?" he asked, and pulled up a chair next to Alex. "Normally this is where I would begin smoking, but these damn American environmental laws."

"Smoke. I don't care."

"No, but thank you. My country is greatly in your debt Dr. Seacourt. Let me give you a little history lesson if you don't mind."

"Go ahead."

"Approximately six months ago, right after President Cheka came to power, the United States and Russia formed an alliance where the two countries would enter into a joint breeder reactor program. The United States had the technology and the expertise to build the breeder reactors, which previously had ground to a halt after the near meltdown of the Enrico Fermi I breeder in Michigan in 1966.

"To make a long story short, in 1977 President Carter declared an American moratorium on the operation of breeder reactors. Just getting the United States to come to the table in a joint effort was a bit of a miracle."

"So 'who' and 'why' did the crisis in Miami and Ann Arbor affect the Russian government?"

"Basically, the United States had the experience with a new way to safely use liquid sodium."

"Liquid sodium?"

"Breeders need liquid sodium rather than heavy water to cool the reactors. Liquid sodium, however, is extremely dangerous and ignites spontaneously when exposed to air. On the other hand, breeder reactors, which are fueled by a combination of plutonium and uranium, are extremely efficient to run. Plus, they 'breed' plutonium in the process generating electricity. Breeders are fueled with plutonium and uranium 238. In the end, a breeder creates more plutonium than it consumes."

"So what was the problem?"

"The problem was that someone had stolen, or should we say that we suspected a team of renegade KGB agents had stolen some of Russia's stored plutonium, and were poised to sell it on the black market. If this came out, this could have put an end to the U.S./Russian deal."

"And the sabotage?"

"We never anticipated it. We had been on Andrei's trail for a number of years. Who would have thought? Governments buy plutonium to make bombs, not renegade psychopathic industrialists to sabotage hospitals.

"When the crisis occurred in Miami and then in Ann Arbor, we knew that it had to somehow involve Andrei. If we didn't shut this thing down before the Americans did it would have killed our deal, and the development of thirty-five breeder reactors that were to go on line in the next five years. The project was worth billions to Russia, and would have supplied invaluable jobs and money in a time of economic crisis. It would have given President Cheka a vote of confidence. Thus, you see why it was so important to at all costs stop Andrei and as we later found out, Bart Robbins."

Alex said nothing. He could hear the electronic clock's second hand buzz past the twelve.

"I have something to confess," Viktoria said hesitantly, "My name...is not really Viktoria Siderenko."

"*What?*"

"My name is Galina Pavlova and I'm...a KGB agent."

"A KGB agent?" Alex uttered under his breath in shock.

"Yes, Dr. Siderenko does have a daughter, but I'm not her."

"You're not?"

"No. It was a plan for us to infiltrate Andrei's organization. We anticipated that whoever kidnapped Dr. Siderenko had planted the discs in Siderenko's apartment for you to find — to put you on his trail, to find the antidote and to find Siderenko. Though Andrei was cagey, we bet that he didn't have any recent photos of Siderenko's daughter. We decided to roll the dice and I'd be her surrogate. It was a risk we had to take."

"And I suppose the kissing and touching we did, and the 'I love you' just now was all made up?"

"No, that was real."

"And the escape, the KGB agents chasing us?"

"That was staged. However, we never expected that some rogue CIA agents would be involved with General Andrei and Boriskov. That completely threw us for a loop. Apparently, Robbins had the CIA under contract doing freelance work and supplying his organization with information."

"Oh, that's great. I always love being thrown into the drink with the sharks."

"Sorry, but it was our men who saved you. Our KGB fishing trawler. You were always under surveillance by satellite. We knew where you were every minute."

Alex turned his head away.

"Alex, I meant it when I said that I wanted to go to Vegas with you. I really do." Viktoria took her hand and cupped Alex's face. "I love you."

Alex was appalled, outraged by what had gone on.

"Get out! Everyone get out of my room now!"

"Alex," Ilya offered, "I know that you're insulted, but if we didn't do what we did, you would have never led us to the antidote, and eventually to saving the lives of hundreds of thousands. We didn't know about Paradise Island, you discovered that clue on the professor's blackboard. Alex, you're the hero, not us. How do you say, what's the phrase. You can take a cow to the water but you can't make it drink."

"No, horse you asshole, not cow!"

"Well, whatever it is," Ilya said perturbed. "It was you who drank the antidote, and it was you who saved everyone's life by getting the bends, not us."

Alex knew that Ilya was using psychology on him.

"Frankly Dr. Seacourt, we all owe you a debt of gratitude; myself, personally, and Russia."

Before Alex could lambaste Ilya anymore, Viktoria interrupted. "To answer your question, it was Ilya who shot Andrei and saved your life."

Alex paused, restraining the rage. And then, suddenly...he just let it go. "What the fuck, Viktoria or Galina, or whatever your name is. What the fuck."

Alex had too much going wrong with his life and with his parents' tragedy. The only important thing is that his parents were alive, that the world would be safe. Andrei the assassin was dead. "What the hay."

"I'm sorry I had to deceive you."

"Maybe it's time that we leave," Ilya said to the other man who remained quiet. He just stood stiffly. "Dr. Seacourt, the nation of Russia and the Commonwealth of Independent States is in your debt."

The two men left. Some pieces of the puzzle had fallen into place. Viktoria slid into bed with Alex and nuzzled up to him. She placed her neck under his and blew kisses into his nape. Alex couldn't refuse.

"I kissed you and touched you because I wanted to. I wasn't ordered, and if I was, and I didn't want to, then I wouldn't."

"They can order you..."

"That's not what I meant. What I meant was...that I did it because I fell for you. You have courage and integrity. Those are traits that aren't very often seen."

"Thanks," Alex said. The buttering-up was working. "By the way, my name really isn't Alex."

"What?" Viktoria asked, immediately sitting. "Alex is your name. I know...it?"

Alex didn't say a word. He just wanted to let the seed he planted take hold.

Galina slugged him in the chest.

66

Caesars Palace, Las Vegas

The casino was rocking and rolling. Electricity was rife. Alex was dressed in his black Armani suit, white shirt, and Italian silk tie. His watch, a black and gold Cartier matched his raiment.

She was a goddess, a vision of radiance. Her evening gown was a testimonial to her beauty. She wore a sassy black wide-brimmed hat. Her dress, radiant and equally black, was strapped, and plunged deep on her back. In front, she flaunted her ample cleavage.

Caesars cocktail waitresses in their Roman togas made sure there was plenty of pliable booze for the victims.

Alex and Galina walked through the casino holding hands. On the right were the dice pits. Thousands of dollars were being wagered in a single throw. Men were in Hugo Boss, Armani and Zanetti suits. Women dressed in glitzy sequin, Valentino and Donna Karan dresses.

On the left, high-stakes blackjack games, with a pit full of one hundred, two hundred and five hundred minimum bet 21 action. They stopped and watched behind a one hundred dollar table, with five of the six spots full. The players were intent on winning. The house odds nonetheless had a different plan.

"Wanta play?" Alex looked down at the empty spot, giving Galina the nod. It was hard for him to think of her by that name...Galina.

"I don't care. Whatever you want."

"Look, if you don't mind, I'm going to call you Viktoria. Galina is too confusing."

"Call me what you will...just as long as you call me." She pulled Alex tight to her and meowed into his ear.

The blackjack shoe went from bad to worse. Alex watched for a few more minutes and decided to try his luck elsewhere.

They walked past the last of the one hunded dollar games and came to roulette. The white marble ball bounced out of the black six, backwards into the red twenty-three and then spit across the diameter of the wheel, skipping crosswise four numbers. It bounced onto the metal fins and came to the rest in green double zero. No one was a winner.

Alex laid a twenty-five dollar chip down on the red. The croupier exchanged his green chip for five yellow roulette chips. Alex let all of them remain on red. The dealer spun the wheel, and in reverse direction he shot the marble into play. The ball made revolution after revolution, almost hypnotically until it finally bounced into the wheel's spokes.

Suddenly, Alex felt an unnerving feeling come over him, a *deja vu*. The sensation was overwhelming. His legs turned into mush and he nearly lost his balance as a wave of galvanizing current passed through his body traveling downward from head to toe. The room got small and his vision went tunnel. In tin-can distance he could hear the yelping high-rollers screaming for their numbers.

And then he saw it, black dominoes with white dots. Trance-like as the marble was about to fall into its spot, Alex left the roulette table. There were the black ivory dominoes with white dots, the other part of what he had to do. *"President Hoover and black dominoes with white dots."*

"There is something I have to...something else."

Alex's head was spinning. Aimlessly he walked over to the Pai Gow table. There, before him were the exact dominoes that he saw in his hallucination.

"That's it, it was...a vision. Something I must, have to..." A petite full-mouthed female oriental dealer with mirthful pretty eyes, collected the dominoes after the game's play ended. She then mixed them face down, their raven jet sides reflecting the overhead light.

Around and around, back and forth in a narcotic blend, she wove the dominoes, merging them into a coalescence of color.

Viktoria walked over and grasped Alex by the upper arm. She had the winnings from the red sixteen.

"Are you okay?" she asked.

"Shhhh." He watched the pile of black marble stir on top of the green felt, as the dealer mixed the dominoes. He then closed his eyes, and the vision became crystal clear.

With eyes shut, he could see all around the casino. Color was intensified and the room was noiseless. Ubiquitously action was happening. Players shooting craps, requesting another card or whooping for a ten; but in quietude. As he turned his head, he passed a spot in the casino that had an audible buzz. And as he moved his head away, the buzz faded and disappeared.

Alex returned his face to the direction where the noise came from. It intensified the most as he stared at a drape hanging from the casino wall. Next to a corner it separated the Keno pit from the rest of the casino. It was only twenty feet away. As he focused in on the noise, the room which not until then had he noticed, changed from black-and-white to color, all except for the drape.

He stared harder, intently; his eyes burning into the drone.

Then, from behind the gray and white curtain emerged Boriskov with a .32-caliber Ruger Mark II pistol in his hand, and a silencer on its end. In slow motion he took aim at Viktoria, raising the gun to sight his target.

Viktoria began tugging Alex's upper arm, "Alex, Alex, are you all right?"

Alex opened his eyes to see that he was in fact staring at...the drape was now in color — scarlet, maroon and gold. And from behind the curtain, with the exception of the people walking in front of his line of fire, *was Boriskov with a pistol in his hand.*

"Watch out!" Alex yelled, pushing Viktoria down to the ground as two shots spit out of Boriskov's weapon. Both hit Viktoria, one in the forehead, the other in the heart.

They fell to the ground in a thump. People began to scream. Alex threw himself over his love, "Noooooo!"

"Alex, Alex wake up. You're having a nightmare."

"What?" he struggled, rolling over onto Viktoria's naked body, as he flailed his arms and legs.

"Wake up you're having a nightmare."

"What?" Alex replied again, this time forcing himself awake.

He looked around, rubbing his eyes. He and Viktoria were in Las Vegas, in a hotel room at Caesars Palace. They were sleeping in their king-size bed with a mirror overhead on the ceiling. They had arrived last night, and had been up all night, gambling and boozing. They had fallen asleep making love, at four in the morning. The heavy blanched drapes covered the windows and they had no idea that it was light out, already 10:00 a.m.

On the TV in the background was the instructional gambling program, the one that the casino puts on to teach its guests how to play the different games, so that they can lose more.

Larry Minetti was with a blond-haired woman, maybe that one that costarred with him on Magnum P.I. He was explaining how to play the different casino games, and in particular *Pai Gow*.

The same black marble dominoes with the white dots were on the screen that Alex saw in his dream, and in his "vision," as he awoke earlier after taking the antidote.

President Hoover was real. The Hoover Dam was real. The black marble dominoes, with the white dots were an illusion.

"Come back to bed," Viktoria said.

They made love, passionately. Alex set his nightmare and the fears that burnt his realm aside. "Come, Dr. Fertile," she giggled and play-bit his earlobe.

Robert Charles Davis

THE FINAL CHAPTER

New Zealand is situated in the South Pacific more than one thousand miles southeast of Australia, its nearest neighbor. The country is comprised of two main islands — the North and South Islands — and a number of small islands, atolls and archipelagos, some of them hundreds of miles from the main group.

Flung in icy seas are the Auckland, Campbell, Antipodes and Chatham Islands which are among the world's loneliest places. Scientists and meteorologists are the only regular visitors to most of them.

One group, the Chathams, has a resident population of about seven hundred eighty and lies eight hundred kilometers east of Christchurch. The Chathams have three main islands in the group, and are inched just inside the international dateline.

The Chathams geographically are similar to the Falkland Islands in the South Atlantic. The weather is wild and ambiguous. The local economy, like that of its self-governing British colony counterpart, is supported on sheepfarming and fishing.

Thirty-nine kilometers south, in the barren, gelid Pacific sits a one hundred square mile island that twelve years ago was purchased by the Holmadale Trust, which is held by the Waitangi Holding Company Ltd., which in turn is controlled by another ten shell companies, each a successor to the former, and each located in a different country of origin: Poland, The Isle of Man, Iran, Portugal, Morocco, Oman, Zambia, Northern Island, Moldova and Suriname.

The island, Bora Two, lays in rugged isolation. There, surf crashes violently onto its desolate beaches, and unsettling winds and heavy rains are the norm. Its denizen are few with the exception of the seemly albatross and a scurrilous long-haired rat.

Harsh life is the rule and not the exception. Volcanic black rock and scattered bush and ferns irregularly dot lonely escarpments. A solitary lifeless mountain lay at the northwest corner of this realm. Its six hundred forty three foot summit had been carved by the hundred-year squalls into a macabre tombstone.

This was Bart Robbins' new home. He had exiled himself here and despite his limited links to the modern world through clandestine satellite transmissions, this stark purgatory was going to be where he would die.

Bart the genius, Bart the crazed and maniacal madman had planned for every eventuality. He had bought Bora from the Morioris, the indigenous Chathams, through a layer of agents long before he had become a quarried fox. Now he was a victim of his own treachery who was going to perish in the abysmal nowhere land, a wanted man.

"Why?" he asked as he looked into the mirror. "God, all I wanted was a child, one child — *a normal me.*" He stared deeply into the gargoyle scars that made him who he was. "It wasn't my fault! Please God, all I wanted was a child. A man-child. An unscathed me."

Bart cried.

What he had prayed for, what he had wanted in his twisted way, was the perfect offspring that he *could not be.* He wanted a beautiful boy, part from his seed, and half from his sisters. He in the child would be reborn. He in his baby would anew taste the nectar of life.

"It was not my fault God...I had no choice but to become what *you made me.* Why did you do this to me, why?" He looked to the heavens for answers. Tears flowed down his disfigured face.

He remembered the car bombing thirty-two years earlier. He was there at Jackson Memorial Hospital, his sarcophagus, and he felt the Christmas tree of spider-web tubes that came out of him. He remembered the twenty-seven operations that he had—all of them,

and the painful whirlpool baths and sterile dressings with silver nitrate; and how much it hellfire stung each time the dressings were
applied.

He tasted the skin grafts from cadaver donors and xenografts,
and creaked his Frankenstein-like bolts and screws in erector-set fashion that were jerry-rigged along with metal devices to hold his bones
in place.

He remembered Caracas and the International Hotel that sat
upon a rocky grass knoll and overlooked the city. He remembered
the Harvard trained MBA Colombian national who was tied to the
Santos-Castillo cartel, and how it was there, that afternoon he made
his *final* decision.

He had no choice to do what he did. He was compelled to. God
had given him a last chance for redemption, a second go around at
life. This rebirth was through the artificial insemination of his sister.

He was going to have a boy-child. He would live again.

When Helen died at Jackson Memorial Hospital, the *same place*
where he was *tortured* for two years... he had no alternative. "Don't
you see God, I had to do what I did. I had to."

He sat, tapping his thin crush black-leather gloves on the rose-
burgundy marble table. He stared at the original oil rendering of a
Scottish castle. Then he was at his mansion in Belize. He stood before the marble bust he had sculptured of Helen. He read the words
he had inscribed beneath it:

*"Dedicated to the Memory of Helen Monica Robbins and to
the Unborn Child, Who One Day Would Have Ruled the World.
God's Vengeance is Our Strength."*

He remembered his twenty thousand square foot mansion that
was built from hand by the best artisans from around the world. It
was his royal palace.

Then there was his day of reckoning .

It was...the invasion of the Punta Gorda complex by the Russian assault helicopters and the teams of Spetznaz and Aval Spetznaz,
and his desperate last-minute activation of all 18 HVAC plutonium
devices. Bart realized that his bunker with the twelve-inch steel and
six-inch lead wall doors was going to be penetrated, but he was
prepared.

He had employed as one of his bodyguards a physical height
and weight clone. He knew that if his plan for revenge was foiled,
that he may need his body double's services.

Hidden within the ten thousand-square-foot bunker, behind a supply laden ceiling with high metal shelving, was a false wall. Behind the facade was a shelter within a shelter. This safe-within-a-safe had enough food and self-contained air supply to last ten days. It also had a secret exit that led out onto the Robbins compound two miles to the north near where the two rivers merged in a fork before reaching the Caribbean Sea. He had to dig through a three-foot layer of soil...which in itself made for a perfect cover for his sanctuary exit.

Also hidden below ground and easily excavatable with the assistance of hydraulic lifts and a complex trolley system, was a one-of-a-kind Bombardier eighteen-foot X1230 K LCAC (Landing Craft Air Cushion). This ACV (Air Cushion Vehicle) skimmed inches above land or sea at 92 miles an hour.

At the height of the firefight, once the Spetznaz and Aval Spetznaz penetrated his bunker, Bart was prepared for Judgment Day. He torched his height and weight physical clone with an incendiary device. "Here catch," he said as he disappeared into his inner tomb.

Bart, in anticipation of this worst scenario, had his sacrificial lamb's dental records switched with his in the clinic files. In addition, architectural master plans were deliberately left in an easy to plunder fireproof safe in the CMS complex office. The renderings *did not show the clandestine shelter within the bunker.*

Ten days after the firestorm, propitiously at midnight and with the diligence of physical effort, Bart Robbins escaped from his compound. He left completely undetected.

Despite the Russians' suspicions that Bart had not perished and that he used a body double, and despite the fact that their Mikoyan-Gurevich satellite meticulously digitized dollar-bill size reconnaissance images from thirty-five thousand nine hundred kilometers in a three hundred mile radius; they were unable to find him.

Using connections that he had in the Yucatan and Panama, Bart Robbins secretly worked his way to Bora Two.

Then on Doomsday Sunday, like the rest of the world, Bart discovered Andrei's plans. It was shortly thereafter that Bart was able to make satellite contact with Boriskov and unearth the crux of the double-cross.

Boriskov, unlike Andrei, was loyal to his employer. Andrei had led Boriskov to believe that the blackmail scheme was Bart's plan all along. He did not question it. Once Bart realized what had occurred, Robbins arranged for Andrei to collect the one hundred and fifty million dollars in uncut South African diamonds that had ironically been deposited by President Cheka into one of the Swiss banks that Bart controlled, and then transported to another destination. Boriskov, after minimal furtive efforts and a trip to Tunisia, got his one-third cut.

The room that Bart Robbins lived in like the rest of Bart's life, was perpetually dark. The lights were dimmed low and the drapes were permanently closed. It was "his reality." The only one he cared for.

He still wore his one uniform; Italian-tailored black slacks, the Swiss black socks, shoes and sports jacket. His hand-sewn raven silk shirt buttoned to its last eyelet, and then underneath an onyx turtleneck.

Malleable thin black-leather gloves weaved from the skins of fetal calves or something else covered his hands. Only the smallest amount of flesh was exposed to the world.

"I have one more job for you Boriskov."

"What's that?" he asked over the scrambled satellite line.

"It pays ten million."

"That's a lot of money."

"And it's an easy job."

"What?"

"Seacourt. I want you to take care of Dr. Alex Seacourt. I owe him a thank you card."

"I'll do that one for free."

Unbeknownst to Robbins, despite his elaborate machinations to conceal his flight, he overlooked one exacting detail: his coded communication with Boriskov was on a channel that as of three days ago was no longer secure. His conversation was intercepted by the KGB at its Malta telecommunications relay ground station. Within eight hours the KGB's southern-hemisphere Sojuzkarkta-Vitali satellite pinpointed Bora Two.

President Cheka was notified by KGB Chief Directorate Lavrenty P. Yezhov at 4:45 a.m., Moscow time. In posthaste tirade Cheka ordered yet one more mission for the crack Spetznaz and Aval Spetznaz. This one would lead to the total annihilation of a hundred-square-mile island.

Las Vegas

The front desk clerks were busy as usual, all nine of them, stand-

375

ing behind their pulpits, with their multiscreen computers. They were ready for their guests, eager to check them in and out of the hotel as efficiently as possible. The entire focus of their job was to get the "new ones" onto the gambling floor as soon as possible.

The lines were average, nothing particularly long about them, and no one unusual in them, either arriving or departing.

Behind the nine clerks was a desk supervisor, who scribbled some notes from her computer screen, onto a tablet of paper. The husky woman, with auburn cinnamon hair, and a pretty English face; took a final drag on her cigarette, and then put it out.

She ripped the 2 x 3" sheet off the Caesars tab, slid it into a pocket in her skirt and excused herself for a few moments. Her assistant would cover for her. Ten minutes later she was standing underneath Cleopatra's Barge, a ship that was constructed onto an artificial pond inside the casino. The replica of the vessel that Cleopatra herself might have sailed on, was used as a bandstand and dance floor for casino parties and the never-ending guests to get soused on.

The barge was painted in Egyptian gold, turquoise, royal blue and red. The tip of the barge had an edifice of a topless women carved into wood, wearing her royal cloisonné jewelry, which was silver inlaid with turquoise around her neck, and a lapis lazuli and colored-glass headdress with an aphrodisiac serpent emerging above the bridge of her nose.

Underneath Marilynn waited impatiently.

"Don't turn around," a man said from behind. His shoulder was still sore from the knife wound, that he sutured himself. Startled, Marilynn did not.

"Do you have it?"

She nodded.

From the rear a man's hand reached menacingly around her, his palm large and threatening. He opened it up, just enough for her to see two one hundred dollar bills. Cautiously, Marilynn exchanged her slip with the information on the ripped Caesars note sheet for his Benjamin Franklins.

"Did you tell anyone about this?"

"No."

"Spend it in good health."

The DMSO-coated upper surface of the second hundred dollar bill stuck to her skin immediately. Within the DMSO, a universal solvent, was the Ricin poison. Ricin made from the castor-oil plant was three times more deadly than cobra's venom.

By the time Marilynn arrived back at her post as front desk supervisor, the first signs of her fatal condition manifested itself. Her heart began to palpitate and her breathing became labored. Within five minutes she was dead.

The man who had taken the paper was always careful and took extreme precautions. He wore a toupee, a hat, and a thick beard. However, one of the disadvantages that Boriskov had, despite his best disguise techniques, was his overwhelming size. Nevertheless, he took no unneeded chances.

Boriskov opened the paper and read the name and room number.

"Dr. Alex Seacourt Room 723."